The Envelope

No good ever comes from procrastination, my mom always told me. But now I know differently. If I hadn't procrastinated that history paper, my life would never have changed. It was procrastination, combined with a little bad luck. If the printer hadn't run out of paper, I never would have found it. So maybe that was actually good luck. I don't know. But my new life began the moment I found the purple envelope hidden under a precarious stack of books on my dad's desk.

The moment I saw it, I did a kind of cartoon double-take. The envelope just lay there innocently, beckoning me with my name, Mia, scrawled on the front in my great-grandmother's familiar, unsteady script. My hand felt like it was moving in slow motion as I reached out to it.

"Looking for something?" my dad drawled from behind me.

My hand froze on the envelope. I had almost forgotten why I had been frantically rooting through my dad's private desk.

"What?" I mumbled, trying to stall for time.

"You're going through my desk," he growled, more irritated than I'd anticipated. "I'm sure you must have a very good reason." Sarcasm. Not a good sign.

"Um, Dad, I need some more computer paper. Just one piece, actually. I was sure you would have at least one piece floating around here somewhere." I was starting to babble. I hope he didn't notice my hand surreptitiously snagging the envelope as I turned around.

"I have to turn in my history paper this morning. If it's late, he'll dock me 50% off." I made my large brown eyes look as innocent and pleading as possible.

My dad sighed; he never could resist me when I pulled my puppy dog eyes.

"I'm out of paper. Check your mom's desk. Third drawer on the left side."

"Thanks." I slid past him and kissed him lightly on the cheek as I stuffed the envelope into my jacket pocket.

He looked at me slightly suspiciously, and then glanced at the clock.

"You *are* running late, aren't you?"

One look at the clock snapped me back to reality like a rubber band.

"Crap," I muttered under my breath. I didn't even have time to change my clothes from yesterday. This stupid paper had kept me up all night.

"Dad, please, can you drive me to school? I know you don't teach this morning." I wasn't sure the eyes would work a second time. "I'm too late to catch a ride with Jace. Please?"

My dad rolled his eyes. "Fine, but you better step on it. I have a meeting this morning with the dean."

"Thank you so much." I mugged enthusiastically, feeling giddy and wired on zero hours of sleep. I started shoving my mom's paper into the printer and pressed the Okay To Print button. My bibliography slid out slowly as I bounced up and down on the balls of my feet.

"And Mia," Dad added, "stay out of my desk. If you mess with my order, I'll never find anything again."

"Uh, sure, Dad," I agreed. My eyebrows rose as I perused his desk.

He caught the glance and scowled, eyebrows forming an all-too-familiar V. "Hey, it's cleaner than your room."

"I didn't say a word, Dad," I said hurriedly. I grabbed my bibliography sheet and ran for my book bag. I'd staple the stupid thing together in class. "I'll meet you in the car in two minutes." I tossed my bag over my shoulder as I tore out the door.

THE CAR WAS warm. Too warm. The warmth and gentle motion were like a lullaby to my brain. To revive myself, I snapped down the mirror, trying to gauge the humiliation I was likely to face at school. I rubbed at old mascara that had crept under my lashes. The dark circles made my already huge eyes seem even bigger. My forehead creased as I remembered Ben in my art class calling me a perfect anime character. Well, my face at least. I tried to artfully arrange my short spiky hair, but like always, it had ideas of its own. Whatever. I was just grateful it was Friday and I could come home and crash. Not like I had a date or anything.

I closed the mirror and let my head rest on the back of the seat. I liked my dad's car. It was comfortable, and the leather seats still smelled good, even though it was several years old.

My dad's voice startled me. "Don't your feet freeze in those things?"

"Nope," I murmured sleepily as I wiggled my toes in the warmth blowing from the heater. I hated shoes and socks and even though I got in trouble constantly with dress code violations, I couldn't stand wearing anything but flip-flops.

"*Humpf.*" For a college professor, my dad used a lot of made-up words. I glanced over at him with half-shut eyes. He looked ridiculously large in this tiny sports car. He stood a bit over six feet four and intimidated the heck out of most people when they first met him. His gruff manner was just a convenient way to hide an unlikely shy personality. His students at the university were usually terrified of him at the start of a semester and walking all over him by the end. My mom used to give him assertiveness lessons, but realized early on he was a hopeless case.

"Are those new earrings? Your design or Sarah's?" Wow. Dad was obviously trying to be extra nice this morning. He almost never noticed what I was wearing. I must look really thrashed if my dad was trying to cheer me up.

"These are new ones from Sarah," I admitted. Sarah was my best friend Jace's mom. She was like my second mom. I spent most of my childhood at her house playing, eating, and learning to make jewelry. "I haven't had any time lately for creative fun, Dad. School is slowly sucking everything out of me. Pretty soon I'll be an empty shell. Then you can hang me on the wall like a piece of modern art."

"Has anyone told you how weird you are?" my dad laughed.

"You're the first today," I said wryly.

"Don't your students all look like zombies, too?" I asked, to change the subject. "It's midterms, isn't it?"

"Don't remind me," my dad groaned.

"You need to get your TAs to do more. Mom has hers working like slaves."

"Of course she does," my dad chuckled. "They're all terrified of her."

The image of my petite, five-foot-two mother glaring her insolent, junior high school students into meek submissiveness made me start giggling. My giggles came a little too easily. I could tell I was too punch-drunk for school. The day was destined to be awful. I leaned back again and put my hands into the pockets of my well-worn leather jacket.

My hand touched the envelope I had hastily stashed in my pocket. Well, now. I had almost forgotten that little discovery. But it would have to wait for lunch. I didn't have time for any emotional grenades right now. High school was dangerous enough. The car slid to a stop by the curb and I braced myself mentally to face the day.

"Have a good one," my dad offered tentatively. I knew he had hated his high school years as much as I hated mine.

"Not a chance," I grimaced back. "But thanks anyway. I appreciate the ride, though."

I closed the door and stalked off. The final bell rang. I was late.

I SLUNK INTO the classroom as quietly as possible. Everyone was handing in their history papers.

"You're tardy, Miss Stone," Mr. Clemmons frowned. "I assume you have your paper ready."

"Yes, I do. I just need to staple it together." I looked at the other papers as I walked up to the teacher's desk. It looked like most of them had professional-looking report covers.

I slammed the stapler a little harder than necessary and set my paper on top of the pile. A flash of worry crossed my face, and then I shrugged. As my mom always noted, the fancier the report on the outside, the emptier the substance on the inside. I knew my paper was good, even if I had written it all in one night. If Clemmons penalized me for not buying a lame cover, well, I was just too tired to care. It was done. And now I wanted to go to sleep.

I was hoping for a long, boring video so I could put my head down on my desk. Unfortunately, we started a new chapter and I had to force my hand to take nit-picky notes on WWII reconstruction. The minutes felt like hours.

I looked over at Jace. He grinned back. He started miming huge yawns at me. I gave him a dirty look and then, of course, started yawning for real. My mouth felt like it was going to crack open, and I couldn't seem to stop.

"You are gonna pay," I mouthed to Jace. All he gave me was an innocent, "Who, me?" I wished, not for the first time, that my best friend wasn't a boy.

The class was finally over. As I packed up my book bag slowly and clumsily, Jace strolled past with smirk, saying, "Meet you out front for lunch." I considered sticking my foot out to trip him, but my brain was too groggy, and he had already gone by before I could take action.

My next class was Art. Always my favorite class, but never more so than today when Ms. Richards dimmed the lights immediately for a long slideshow on Picasso. I lay my head on my desk with a contented sigh.

I awoke with a start, worried I'd been snoring. Nobody was staring at me rudely, so I'd probably kept quiet. The clock showed a few minutes left before the bell. I carefully removed the mysterious letter from my pocket and turned it over in my hands. I could feel it was lumpy and I had an idea what might be inside. Looking at my nan's writing on the front made my stomach clench. I wanted to open it. I felt a sudden, urgent need to know what was inside. I slid a trembling finger under an edge that was peeling up slightly on the back. Suddenly a bell jarred me from my task. Lunch.

Resigned, I stuffed the envelope back into my pocket and headed out of the classroom to find Jace. Not that he'd be hard to find. He was about half a head taller than most of the boys here. And his dark hair stuck up as crazily as mine. I think he actually used more gel than I did.

I spotted him just outside the cafeteria and managed to give him a flat before he saw me.

"Oh, that's very mature," Jace said as he punched me in the arm.

"Hey, you so deserved it after giving me a yawn attack this morning." I punched him back and quickly gave him another flat.

"Are you two breaking up?" a sickly sweet voice asked from behind us.

"Shut up, Randi," Jace and I both spat at the same moment. Neither of us could deal with Miranda Wilks on a good day, and today was not a good day. We still called her Randi, as we did when we were kids and our parents forced us to play together. She hated that nickname. Miranda lived around the corner from us. We usually tried our best to forget that fact.

Miranda's eyes narrowed at the nickname and she flicked her long blonde hair over her shoulder. "You know, Mia, I thought that outfit was unflattering when you wore it yesterday. I can't imagine why you would wear it again. The *next day*, even. You must realize how it emphasizes your hips." Behind her, Miranda's friends smirked with laughter.

I felt my face flush. Miranda always could hit my buttons. I'd been a chubby kid and she never let me forget it. It burned me that I could never think of a good comeback until she walked away.

"I think you look great," said Jace, taking my arm. "Hey, did you hear that Mr. Barlow is giving a pop quiz in English? I heard that if you went over the last half of *King Lear*, it would be cake. Did you bring your copy of Shakespeare? I think I left mine at home." Jace said all this casually while we were walking away, and then he turned and winked at me. I choked back a grin and began to moan. "Oh man, I didn't even read *King Lear* last night. I was too busy with my history paper. It's going to take all of lunch to go over that play."

We got to a couple of wooden benches and sat down. I peeked back at Miranda. She and her friends were frantically pulling out their Shakespeare books and flipping pages. I saw one of them had a copy of the Cliff Notes.

Jace and I looked at each other and burst out laughing.

"Nice one," I gasped when I could catch my breath. "She's going to be royally ticked off, you know."

"Who cares?" Jace shrugged. "She totally deserves it."

"Of course, she'll take it out on me," I sighed.

"Don't let her get to you." Jace popped the lid off his soda. "Relax. Life's too short to worry about people like her."

"Yeah, that's so easy for a guy to say. You have no idea what it's like to be a girl," I muttered, getting out an apple. I bit into it fiercely.

"You're even moodier than usual today. You definitely need a nap."

I glowered at him and put my hand in my pocket, looking for a napkin. Again, my mood did a 180-degree flip.

"I forgot—I have something you've got to see," I said excitedly. I pulled out the envelope and held it up.

"What is it?" Jace looked closer. "Wait a minute. Is that from your Nan Stone?"

"Uh-huh." I kept staring at the writing.

"But Mia, isn't she, well, dead?" Jace sounded apologetic. He knew how much I loved my nan. He'd even come and spent a week with me at her house one summer.

"She is," I nodded sadly, shoulders drooping a bit.

"Where did you get the envelope?" Jace persisted. "Have you opened it?"

"I found it buried under a bunch of stuff on my dad's desk. I haven't had a chance to open it yet. One part of me is dying to open it. The other half is totally freaked. I'm afraid I'm gonna start bawling in the middle of school," I admitted.

"Want me to open it?" Jace offered.

"Okay," I conceded. "But be careful. Something besides paper is inside. It's kind of lumpy."

Jace felt the envelope warily before tearing open one side. He tipped the contents into his hand.

A long silver chain made with large oval links pooled into the palm of his hand. The unusual pendant lay still, winking up at us in the sunlight. Jace held it up for a closer look.

"Is that a four-leaf clover charm?" he wondered. "It is. Is it a real clover, do you know?" He looked over at me.

I was mesmerized by the necklace Jace dangled in front of my face. I recognized it immediately, of course. My nan had worn it for most of the time I had known her. I don't remember when it first appeared, but once she had it, she never took it off. She would wear it to the lake with her swimming suit, or even to church or a fancy party, when a strand of pearls seemed more appropriate. My mom gave her several elegant necklaces for presents, but they stayed tucked away in drawers, forgotten. I used to ask her if it was lucky, and she would smile this secret, melancholy smile and whisper, "No, definitely not lucky. But very precious."

I was snapped back to the present with another thought. She had a matching ring and bracelet, too. "Is there anything else in the envelope?"

"Here, hold this." Jace draped the necklace over my reaching hand. "I'll look." I held the pendant closer to my eye level. The tiny clover was embedded in some kind of enamel or crystal. A silver bezel surrounded it, and three tiny gemstone charms clung to delicate silver loops along the bottom. An incredibly beautiful and sophisticated piece of jewelry art.

Jace unfolded a slip of pretty stationary paper.

"Listen to this," he began.

Dear Mia,

I miss you so much. This place leaves much to be desired. I miss my own home more than I can stand, but I realize now that I may never be able to go home.

I need to talk to you, Mia. I know that if I send you this necklace, you will come quickly. You know how important it is to me. Keep it safe. Never take it off. Never give it to anyone. I will explain everything when you come. I probably should have explained it all to you before now. But I was always hoping against hope that I wouldn't have to. Please come soon. I can tell that my time is running

short. Call me when your dad gives you this note. I know
he will bring you back whenever you ask. He's a good
grandson and a good father.
> *I love you very much,*
> *Nan*

While Jace read, I reached up and tried to fasten the necklace around my neck. I fumbled with the clasp, my trembling fingers bungling the simple task. After he finished the note, I tried again, finally securing it as Jace looked at me with a worried glance. He's wondering what to do if I lose it, I thought. I tried to put on a brave face, but the strain couldn't be hidden from someone who knew me as well as Jace.

I cleared my throat, testing my voice. "No bracelet or ring?" I picked up the torn envelope feeling it, looking at the writing on the front again.

"No," Jace said softly. "Are you okay?"

"Why did my dad hide this from me?" I crumpled the envelope in my hand as I tried to reign in my emotions. Anger was starting to win over misery and frustration.

"Maybe he just lost track of it," Jace suggested. "Even *I* know what his desk looks like."

"That's not a good enough excuse," I said severely.

"So, what are you going to do? Are you going to ask your dad about it?" Jace furrowed his brow, thinking. "Do you even know what your nan was talking about?"

"I have no idea," I whispered. "Now it's too late. I'll never hear her voice again. I'll never know what she needed to tell me." Tears pricked my eyes and I lay my head against the back of the bench. Jace looked down and concentrated on his pizza.

Don't think about it, I told myself. Don't think about her. No matter how sensible those wise words seemed, my traitorous heart wouldn't listen. My eyes closed and the images came.

I COULD SMELL the wet pine needles. They were the bane of my summers as a child. They covered every inch of my nan's backyard, falling by the bucketful and covering my toys in a sticky, prickly mess. I remember trying to maneuver the huge porch push broom up onto the trampoline. I about gave my nan a heart attack when I lost my balance and fell on my head. The next day she bought me a tiny yellow broom of my own. She laughed as I viciously swiped at every needle and pine cone and spider that landed on my precious trampoline. Then, tossing the broom aside, I jumped until my legs ached. Exhausted, I sprawled on the bouncy bed, gazing at the huge evergreens towering fifty feet over me, listening to the windy words they whispered to me.

I flipped onto my stomach, looked over, and saw my friend Eileen laughing, pulling her little sister Hazel toward the trampoline. Behind them I saw a teenage boy standing with his arms folded—their brother. What was his name? He looked torn. I could see he thought he was too old to jump, and yet I think he really wanted to hop on with his sisters. I saw Nan smiling, urging him to climb up, but reminding him to be careful of all the little girls.

He made up his mind and dashed forward just as a cloud passed over the sun. A chill ran over me and my arms began to goose bump. I turned onto my back as large raindrops splashed onto my surprised face.

"Let's go in!" I yelled against the sudden wind and rain. No one was there. The backyard was empty. But it didn't feel empty. I had the sensation someone was watching me. I clambered to my feet, turning and staggering on the unsteady, slippery trampoline. Still I saw no one. My feeling of unease became panic. I felt exposed, vulnerable to some kind of unfamiliar presence. I tried to climb down the side of the trampoline. My shorts caught on a coiled spring. I tugged and tore at the fabric, frantic to get away.

A heavy hand grabbed my shoulder and shook me.

I woke up with a gasp, a scream dying on my parted lips.

"Hey, calm down." It was Jace's voice. "Mia, you fell asleep. You must have been having a nightmare."

I took several deep breaths and tried to shake off the fear and panic.

"Come on," Jace insisted, pulling me to my feet. "We're going to be late for class."

I grabbed my book bag, chucked my half-eaten apple into a garbage can, and trudged behind him toward the school.

"No more scary movies for you, young lady," Jace mocked. He was trying to annoy me and take my mind off more serious matters, I could tell. "Your mom is right. You can't handle it."

"I can, too," I countered automatically, still half in the dream world. I kept peeking over my shoulder, not sure that the alien presence was quite gone.

Jace and I argued all the way to English, eventually agreeing to see the current horror flick Saturday, so I could prove I wasn't a wimp.

The day dragged on. Finally, after dealing with nasty looks from Miranda in English, and embarrassing head jerks and twitches in Government as I kept dozing off, I escaped. I ran to Jace's car and stood fingering my new necklace until he dashed up, looking flustered and excited. He tossed his keys at my face as he made a quick U-turn. I ducked, and they smacked the window and tumbled to the asphalt.

"Are you trying to gouge my eye out?" I shouted at his back. "My instincts are on vacation today. Remember?" I bent over and picked up the keys.

"Car's yours today," Jace yelled over his shoulder. "Michelle is giving me a ride home after I'm done shooting hoops." He grinned a sloppy smile and I gave the most enthusiastic thumbs up I could manage. He was already gone. I shouldn't have bothered.

Sighing, I got in the car and sped home as fast as I dared.

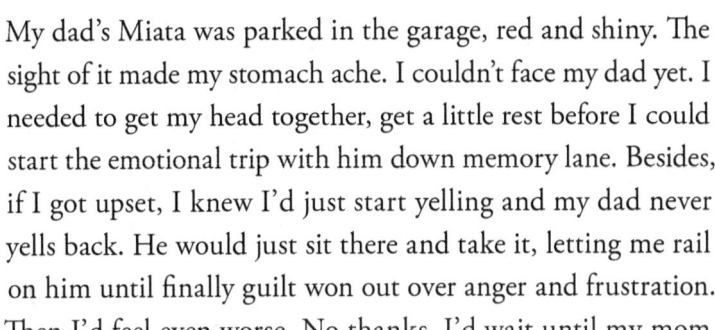

Haunted

My dad's Miata was parked in the garage, red and shiny. The sight of it made my stomach ache. I couldn't face my dad yet. I needed to get my head together, get a little rest before I could start the emotional trip with him down memory lane. Besides, if I got upset, I knew I'd just start yelling and my dad never yells back. He would just sit there and take it, letting me rail on him until finally guilt won out over anger and frustration. Then I'd feel even worse. No thanks. I'd wait until my mom got home. She'd fight back.

I parked the car outside Jace's house and knocked while walking inside.

"Sarah, you home?" I made my way through the hallway back into the warm, red kitchen. Sarah was sitting on a stool next to the stove. She looked as tired as I felt.

"Hi Mia," she smiled. "Did Jace ditch you?"

"Yup. But I don't care. I didn't really want to watch him play basketball. I'm a total zombie today." I came over to stand behind Sarah, peeking over her shoulder to see what she was stirring. "Besides, he's all excited to ride home with Michelle."

"That boy. He grows six inches and all of a sudden he's a girl magnet." Sarah looked like she didn't mind all that much. It wasn't that long ago that Jace was all flustered and tongue-tied every time a girl walked by. I used to think it was hilarious, but Sarah was the kind of mom that worried about everything.

Sarah looked pointedly at me. Uh-oh. I knew what was coming.

"So, when are you going to get excited about a boy?"

"Sarah," I assured for the millionth time, "when I find a boy worth liking, I'll let you meet him."

"You have to kiss a lot of toads, you know," Sarah began.

"Hey, there will be no talk of kissing!" I reached for my new necklace and held it up. "Look at this," I said by way of distraction. "What do you think? It used to belong to my Nan Stone."

"Wow," Sarah whistled, appraising the charm with a practiced eye, "That is exceptional craftsmanship. I wish my projects turned out that beautifully." I shook my head in disbelief. Sarah made amazing pieces of jewelry art. She'd even had some of her designs published in national beading magazines. I was lucky she was a good teacher, too. She used her influence to get me a part-time job at the bead store where she gave classes every now and then.

"Is this a new inheritance? Early birthday present?" Sarah gave me a quick, curious look, and then went back to studying the charm.

"Well, it's rather complicated," I confessed. "Do you have a few minutes?"

"I've got to stir this sauce for probably twenty minutes. Talk about tedious. I could use a good story to make the time go faster."

Sarah knew a lot about my nan already. I'd talked her ear off for years about the summers I used to spend in Washington. So I jumped right into the circumstances of finding the necklace and the details of the note. I still had the note in my pocket and handed it to her so she could read it herself.

Talking about it started my stomach churning again. I could feel the blood rushing to my face. My forehead and eyes began to ache, like I had a sinus infection. I started to massage my eyebrows with my fingertips. I leaned over and lay my burning cheek against the cool, smooth granite countertop. I closed my eyes.

"You look exhausted." Sarah reached over with her free hand and rubbed my neck. "You are as tense as a coiled wire. Take a couple of deep breaths."

"Look, Mia, I don't know the significance of this note, either. But I do know that you need some rest before you talk to your parents about it. You've already worked yourself into quite a state. How about a nice little nap here before you go home and start an intense inquisition?"

"You're right," I agreed. "I was up all night writing that stupid history report."

"Just lie right there on the couch. I'll turn on some background music. While you sleep, I'm going to ponder on that letter." Sarah clicked a couple buttons and Sinead O'Conner's voice floated softly around the room. I pulled an afghan over me and curled up on my side. The haunting voice and lyrics soothed my disturbed mind and throbbing head. I slipped into an uneasy sleep.

I was tearing down the hall, passing what seemed like miles of lockers. I was looking for my history class. I couldn't remember which classroom to go in. I passed room 492. Something's wrong with the numbering system, I thought wildly.

All of a sudden, a door flew open. I swerved inside.

"I brought it. It's done," I announced triumphantly. The room burst into whistles and applause. I looked down. "*Crap!*" I was in my pajamas. My face grew hot, but my feet felt frozen to the floor. I was unable to move. "Nice boxers," someone shouted. They had little clowns all over them. I hated clowns.

I held up my report in self-defense, but it had changed into a paper airplane. Humiliated again, I threw the evidence out the window. The paper airplane morphed into a seagull and flew away, squawking into the sunset. I turned again to face my audience. The room was silent and empty. The lights flickered and dimmed. I could feel someone behind me now. Someone who had been watching all these tortuously embarrassing moments. I looked over my shoulder. The room was still empty. I had a déjà vu feeling. This had happened before.

"Who are you?" I yelled into the stifling air. "What do you want?"

No answer. I ran to the door, fingers clawing at the doorknob, trying to turn it. It resisted every effort. I peered behind me again. I felt so helpless standing there in my pajamas. I was trapped. Claustrophobic waves began to engulf me, making my head swim.

"I know you're there. I can feel you looking at me." I felt my eyes sting with panicky, useless tears.

No answer again, but the presence seemed to grow less malevolent. It seemed to become curious, questioning. Yet I didn't feel any safer.

"Where are you?" I tried to scream, my voice cracked. "Why can't I see you?"

I heard a soft voice, right next to my left ear, whisper my name doubtfully. "Mia?"

"Stop stalking me," I whispered, more terrified than ever. "Leave me alone!"

I struggled to wake up, fighting against sleep like a rip tide. The dream kept trying to engulf me, sucking me back into its murky depths. I was disoriented, and it took a minute to find a clock. I'd slept about an hour. Sarah had left the room. Something in the oven smelled delicious and my stomach growled loudly. I got up reluctantly. I needed to go home.

I slunk in through the garage door, sneaking like a thief into my own house. I slipped down the stairs into the basement without being detected. I quietly closed my door, relieved to be in my own room. The bad dream still clung to me like a bad smell. I turned on my iPod and sat down at my desk. Papers, books, and notes littered the desk and the floor beneath. I pushed most of it onto the floor to clear a spot. Then I reached up to my shelf above the desk and pulled down a small scrapbook.

I flipped it open to a random page. I saw my five-year-old face laughing back at me. My long, strawberry-blonde hair looked even lighter and more unruly than usual. My skin was a golden brown and several freckles splattered across my nose. My swimsuit strap was slipping off my shoulder, and I was pointing a big red shovel at my lopsided sandcastle.

The next page showed my nan holding my hand as we walked down the sunny dock. People were fishing off one end, and kids were swimming in the lake all around.

I must have taken the next photo. The center was completely off. Nan was sitting back on the sand, gazing off into the distance. Her face looked youthful, despite the creases of age. Her expression was peaceful, satisfied. I noticed that she didn't have her necklace on.

I skipped ahead, scanning each page briefly. There it was: the first photo with my nan and her necklace. I must have been nine or so. Where did she get it? I couldn't remember. My nan looked older and more melancholy in these final pictures, the peaceful look faded into worry lines and deepening wrinkles. Was that only the ravages of age finally catching up? I thought it seemed like more than that.

I stood up and stretched my back and surveyed my messy room. The loft bed was unmade. Clothes were strewn along the closet floor. My bulletin board was on its third layer. I saw my running shoes sticking out from behind my large floor mirror. I suddenly knew what I wanted to do.

I flung on some comfortable clothes and put on the only pair of shoes I ever wear. I ran upstairs for a quick energy snack.

Mom stood in the kitchen, a bottle of water in her hand. "Hey, Mia. Give me two minutes and I'll join you."

Not exactly the getaway I had planned.

"Mom, I need to think, not talk," I hedged.

"That's okay. I could use some time to just zone, too," Mom said. "My day was quite stressful."

"Fine," I gave in. "I'll be outside warming up." I put in my earphones and opened the door.

We ran our usual three-mile loop. It started with a brutal uphill on pavement. My mom kicked my butt, like she always does. But then we got to the trail. My feet flew to the rhythm of my music. My head felt clearer than it had all day long. I returned glowing and sweating and high on adrenaline.

"Feel better?" my mom asked, as we stretched out our legs using the retaining wall in front of the house.

"Much," I admitted.

"After you shower, let's talk. You have that 'I need to get something off my chest' kind of look." She raised her eyebrows at me as if daring me to disagree.

"Alright, over dinner," I agreed, and went to clean up.

Confrontations

Delicious smells came wafting down the vents into my room, causing me to speed up faster than I had originally planned. I showered in record time, ran some gel through my hair, and dressed in a pair of old sweats. Then I took a deep breath and braced myself for the fireworks waiting for me upstairs.

Dad had made dinner while Mom and I ran. Lucky for us, he's pretty good in the kitchen. He was hesitant to try new recipes, but his few tried-and-trues were tasty and satisfying.

I was starting my second helping of chicken stir-fry when Mom finally popped the question.

"So, Mia, what's bothering you?"

In answer, I reached up and unfastened Nan's necklace and lay it the center of the table, along with the crumpled purple envelope. My parents gazed in surprise at the evidence, and then flicked each other guilty looks.

"I found the envelope when I was scavenging for paper this morning," I accused, trying to keep my voice level.

My dad picked up the necklace and sighed. "You think we were keeping this from you on purpose?" His voice sounded sad. "That was never our intent."

"So, what then," I asked cautiously, "you just forgot about it?" I pushed my plate away, my hunger evaporating. In fact, the food in my stomach started to feel like a lead weight.

Dad was silent for several minutes, his fingers absentmindedly touching the clover charm, his green eyes far away. I glanced at my mom. She gave me a 'be patient' gesture and I bit my lip.

"Nan was in the rehab center after her first stroke when she gave me this envelope," Dad began at last. "I brought it home planning to give it to you. She wanted to see you right away. I wonder if she had some kind of premonition. I told her I was going to bring you back that weekend." Dad rubbed his eyes. "Then, that night the hospital called. She had her second stroke and everything went downhill from there."

My dad raised his eyes to mine. His troubled eyes conveyed the truth of his words. I knew this was painful for him to relive. After all, Nan had raised him after his parents died in an auto accident when he was only ten.

His voice sounded anguished as he said, "I thought her letter would be too much for you. You were only twelve and you loved her so much. I planned to give it to you later, when your grief had settled down, when you would be emotionally able to handle it. But the timing never seemed right." He shrugged his shoulders.

"Then you conveniently forgot about it by burying it in that desk of yours," Mom added.

"Out of sight, out of mind," Dad agreed. "I'm not saying it was right, Mia," Dad said quickly, noticing my scowl. "It's just what ended up happening."

I took her note out of my pocket and asked them to read it. Heads huddled together, they scanned her note with interest. They looked at each other quizzically when they'd finished.

Their expressions gave me an answer I didn't want. "You don't know what she's talking about either, do you?"

They shook their heads simultaneously.

"Do you at least know where she got this necklace? Her note sounded so urgent. I can't help but wonder what she needed to tell me. Whatever it was, I'm now five years too late to do anything, though." My voice sounded bitter.

"Well," my dad looked a bit abashed, "I always thought she had a secret admirer that she was too shy to tell me about. Grandpa had died quite a few years before. I thought someone might show up at the hospital, or at least to the funeral, but no one did. I wish I had asked her about it."

"Don't worry, I asked her," Mom admitted.

"That figures," Dad smiled. "You're never afraid to ask anyone anything."

"She said it was from her sister," Mom replied. "I thought you knew that."

"What?" Dad looked like someone had knocked the air out of him. "Her twin sister Anna?"

"Who?" I piped up. "Nan had a twin sister? How come I didn't know that?"

Dad looked shaken. "Anna disappeared when she was sixteen. Nan had an old scrapbook about Anna with photos, newspaper articles of the search, and a program from the funeral, among other things."

I was shocked. "So what happened to her?" I whispered.

"I only saw the scrapbook once by accident when I was maybe fifteen. When I asked Nan about Anna, she just clammed up and refused to tell me anything. I became quite curious, but she hid her scrapbook and I never found it again. I'd have studied it more closely if I'd known that was going to be my only look," he said ruefully. "I think the newspaper article said Anna's body was never found. The funeral was probably just to give the family a sense of closure."

I turned to my mom. "But Nan told you her necklace was given to her from Anna?"

Mom nodded.

"I was going through my photo album today and I don't have any pictures of her wearing this necklace until I'm about nine. After that, she's wearing the necklace in every photo. What made her start wearing it sixty-something years later?"

"I have no idea," Dad scratched at the stubble covering his chin. "This is quite a mystery, Mia. I doubt we'll ever be able to solve it."

Mom stared intently at me, noting the determination stealing over my expression.

"We'll help you, if possible," she said, more gently than I expected. "We just don't want you to obsess, or get your hopes up. You have other things you should be concentrating on right now," she added pointedly.

I rolled my eyes. "*School,*" I snorted, like the word was a disease.

"Your grades are pretty good, but we both know you could do better if you really applied yourself. Plus you have the SAT coming up."

I kept silent, not pleased with the direction the conversation was taking. Higher education was not an option to my parents, it was a requirement. I, however, was not convinced that college was for me. Ignoring the last comment, I picked up the necklace and began putting it back on. "It's mine now," I declared. "I'm not taking it off again."

Dad nodded, letting the rest of the conversation slide, probably happy I hadn't started yelling and fighting with Mom.

Mom gave me a resigned look, realizing that now was not the time for further discussion of my continuing education.

"I'm so tired, I'm about to pass out," I said, closing the subject for good. I picked up my plate and headed for the kitchen. "I'm going to bed early, okay?" I turned back. "Oh yeah, I have to be at work tomorrow at ten. Which car should I drive?"

"How about I give you a lift?" Dad offered, trying to look casual.

Not my first choice, I thought gloomily, but I tactfully agreed. "That's fine. I'll bet Jace will give me a ride home. We're going to a movie tomorrow night. See you in the morning."

Not for the first time, I wished I had my own set of wheels. However, with only a part-time retail job, even paying for my own gas and insurance was a joke, not to mention the cost of the actual car. Having two parents in the education field meant we weren't exactly rolling in money. At least they were always generous with their cars in the evening and on the weekend, and Jace always let me use his car if I got in a jam.

I rinsed my plate and stuck it in the dishwasher. The stairs seemed extra steep as I stumbled down them to my room. I went through the automatic motions of washing my facing and brushing my teeth. I barely made it up the ladder to my loft bed before collapsing into an exhausted sleep.

I stood in my nan's backyard, soggy pine needles and pinecones strewn across the yard. The air was heavy and damp, and remnants of a recent fog lingered in the trees. Under the evergreens, I spied little houses made from rocks, tiny twigs, and flowers. Hazel, Eileen, and I spent hours making those miniature towns during the summer, each house meticulously designed and executed.

I sat on the wooden porch bench, swinging my legs contentedly, even as the rain started sprinkling down. My hair became soaked and stuck to my skull like a mop, allowing trails of water to run into my eyes, ears, and mouth. I closed my eyes and mouth against the invasion.

I jerked violently when a loud, cracking sound hit my ears. Lightning had split one of our evergreens in two; half of it began falling backward, taking out the backyard fence. The other half, blazing with fire, shot toward me and the house. Terrified, I fled to the side yard that led to the front of the house. I stumbled over an old stump and flew forward onto my palms, scraping them as I scrambled to my feet, slipping on wet bark and pine needles. I reached the front yard in time to see the old shingle roof burst into flames.

I stood in the street, mesmerized with horror, as Nan's house blazed like a huge bonfire. The flames licked at it evilly, devouring the house I loved. I wept freely, shivering and soaking wet, yet burning with anger and loss at the same time.

Someone stood beside me. I felt an arm go around me. I heard my name, a whisper of sympathy. I turned blindly to the source of comfort. But I found myself alone in my despair.

I awoke to bright sunlight gleaming through my blinds directly into my eyes. I rolled over, relieved I had been dreaming. My alarm started to beep annoyingly on my shelf. I swatted at it distractedly.

I lay back on my pillow, the dream still fresh in my mind. Someone was haunting my dreams. The feeling was overwhelming. But the presence had changed since that first dream at school. At first, all I felt was anger, rage, and confusion directed at me. Now it was like the ghost or whatever it was, recognized me, knew my name, and wanted to help me. But how in the world was that possible?

Wait a minute, what was I thinking? I was starting to think crazy thoughts. I rolled up to sit on the side of my bed, trying to clear my head. It had to be my overactive imagination stuck in some kind of rut. No one could actually get inside a person's head or into their dreams. That sounded like a bizarre science fiction film. Still, I wished I could make the feeling go away. It was really starting to bug me. And I kept dreaming about Nan. My emotions were all mixed up, like they'd been stuffed in a blender and set to whip.

Get it together, I scolded myself as I stepped into the shower. I set the water as hot as I could stand, trying to wash the last lingering bits of my dream down the drain. After I got dressed, I grabbed a quick bowl of cereal and a glass of juice. My dad appeared as I was finishing up.

"Ready?" he asked.

"Just let me brush my teeth," I said, swallowing the last of the orange juice.

My dad was waiting in the car listening to one of our favorite CDs. I slid into the low-slung seat with my bag on my lap, picking up the chorus of Social Distortion's fabulous remake of "Ring of Fire."

"Are you going to show everyone at the store your new necklace?" Dad inquired when the song ended.

"They are going to be blown away. No one there has ever made anything so cool. I wish I knew who made it." I slid the charm back and forth on the chain.

"Maybe we could go back to Nan's house over Thanksgiving break," Dad suggested tentatively. "I left things pretty much alone since she passed away, you know. I just couldn't face going through all her stuff." Dad glanced sideways at me. "But if you wanted to help me, maybe you could find some clues."

"Are you serious, Dad?" I could hardly believe his offer. "I would love to go back there."

"It might be harder than you think to see the house without her in it," Dad warned. "But I'm game, if you are," he smiled. "Your mom's been after me for years to get it done."

We had arrived at the bead store. "No problem, Dad. I really do want to go. I'll make sure I can get the time off work. Thanks for the advance notice."

I closed the car door, feeling a tingle of anticipation at the thought of what we might discover at Nan's house.

I stopped short at the sign on the front door. I had forgotten it was the big annual sale weekend. *Ugh.* The store was bound to be clogged with bargain hunters. Oh well, at least the time would go by quickly.

By the time Jace came to pick me up, I felt like I had been chained to the register for days. My back was aching and my fingers twitched. I collapsed into the front seat in relief.

"Thanks. I'm beat."

"You look better than you did yesterday," Jace teased.

"Thanks a lot." I poked him as he started to back up. "So how was the ride home with Michelle?" I teased back. "She's pretty cute, and surprisingly nice. I give you my permission to like her."

"Permission?" Jace rolled his eyes. "You know you aren't actually my sister, and I am a whole two months older than you. I should be the one giving *my* permission."

"Find me the right guy, first," I challenged. "Of course, I'm sure you wouldn't approve of anyone I might like. Besides," I grimaced, "I always seem to like the ones who don't know I exist."

"That's conveniently safe, isn't it?" Jace raised an eyebrow at me.

"Hey, I'm not that picky," I defended myself. "This school is just too limited. Just wait 'til we're out of high school."

"And no blind dates with you and Michelle. Got it?" I added quickly. "Why are we going to a movie when you could be with Michelle, anyhow? Are we meeting her there?" I looked at Jace suspiciously. "You aren't going to ditch me at the movies, are you?"

"Relax, she's out of town this weekend. We aren't even serious yet anyway. I just kind of like her." Jace looked serious.

"Don't worry. I'm sure she likes you, too," I soothed. "Can we stop by my house first? I really want to change before we go. Are we getting something to eat on the way?"

"The movie starts at seven. We don't have time to stop. My mom made you a sandwich to eat on the way. We can eat after the movie."

"You look fine," Jace said as I began frowning.

"I'm going to be cold," I grumbled.

"No you aren't. I got your leather coat on the way."

I looked surprised. "Thanks."

"Didn't that coat used to be your dad's?"

"Yup, he was a rebellious teen. Can you believe it?" I laughed at the thought. "He wasn't very happy when I stole his coat. He seems to have some fond memories attached to it. Not that he'll tell me any of them. Something about a Social Distortion concert."

"*Ewww*, I don't even want to know," Jace grimaced. "There are many things I don't want to know about my parents. Of course, it might be good for blackmailing purposes," Jace added thoughtfully.

"I agree with that." I began rummaging around for my sandwich behind the seat. I pulled it out. "Turkey and avocado. Your mom is the best." I had been so busy at work, I'd skipped lunch. I finished just as we pulled into the parking lot.

"Now I won't have to eat any of your disgusting popcorn." I had gotten sick after eating a huge amount of buttered popcorn once, and now I only ate it if I was starving.

"Keep your weird opinions to yourself," Jace said.

We bought our tickets and sat down near the front just as the previews started. I was a little nervous, truth be told. I do like scary movies when I'm watching them, but they tend to disagree with me afterward. And with the bizarre dreams I'd been having, well, I was sure tonight's dreams would be memorable.

Things turned out better than I had hoped. The movie was scary, but also extremely campy, which took the edge off. I relaxed and enjoyed jumping and screaming. I actually managed to get a great scream out of Jace when I grabbed his arm suddenly. His ego bruised, he gave me a dirty look.

The night was turning out not so bad after all.

So of course, I was knocked for a loop when Miranda appeared.

We were hanging out in the lobby, talking to one of Jace's friends after the show when I heard a familiar, snotty voice.

"Nice outfit. Shopping at Bargains R Us again?" Miranda was hanging on her date, looking well-dressed and satisfied. Her voice told me she was still mad about yesterday.

"Have fun studying?" Jace inquired sweetly.

Miranda's eyes narrowed. "You two are so childish." She pouted like a runway model and tossed back her shiny hair.

I hardly noticed her. My gaze had been snatched by her date. He raised his eyes to me and I felt a shiver run through me. Miranda's rudeness seemed miles away. In fact, I was hardly aware of where I was. I didn't know her date's name, and yet he seemed oddly familiar. His long, brown hair was tied back in a ponytail. His eyes shone a very pale blue against his dark skin. He was good-looking, of course. Miranda wouldn't have given him the time of day otherwise. I tried to remember if I had I met him before.

I suddenly realized I was staring; my eyes felt dry. Had I forgotten to blink, I wondered. I tore my eyes away, feeling awkward and embarrassed. He looked rather amused. Yikes, I thought. What was I doing? I turned to talk to Jace's friend, trying to ignore the situation behind me. With eye contact broken, I could hear the conversation again.

"So, Griff, you just move here and you're already going out with Randi," Jace was saying. "She's the top of the food chain around here, you know. What I was wondering was," he drew out his question, "did you ask her, or did she ask you?"

"None of your business," Miranda retorted quickly, making the answer obvious.

My smug smile as I turned sent Miranda into attack mode. She walked purposely toward me, running her eyes up and down my outfit.

"What is up with the way you dress? That beat-up old jacket is just hanging off you. And what is this?" She reached out and grabbed my necklace before I could react. "A four-leaf clover," she laughed meanly. "Maybe that will help get you a boyfriend, but I doubt it. Can something scrounged up from a bin at the Salvation Army actually be lucky?"

"Keep your hands off it," I seethed through gritted teeth.

I reflexively yanked myself backward and the clasp snapped painfully at the back of my neck. The broken necklace dangled from Miranda's fingers. "I knew it was a piece of junk." She sneered and let the necklace drop onto the grimy theater floor.

I grabbed her elbow and spun her around as she tried to flounce away.

My hand was shaking, I was so angry.

"Don't you ever touch me or any of my stuff again! Or you will be very, very sorry."

Miranda tried to act nonchalant, but her eyes revealed she was startled. "Are you threatening me?"

"Look," I said fiercely. "You have been picking on me since elementary school, and I am sick of it! You are the most selfish, shallow, petty person I've ever met. Stay away from me and Jace or you will *regret* it."

I picked up my necklace and stormed out of the theater. I needed fresh air. I couldn't believe I had just told off Randi. I mean, I fought with my mom all the time, but this was completely different. I was never that aggressive with anyone my own age. I knew I had better get out of there fast before my adrenaline died and I lost my nerve.

I was sitting on the edge of the empty fountain, fiddling with the broken clasp, when Jace found me.

"I didn't know you had it in you," he grinned.

"She broke Nan's necklace." I held up the evidence. "She totally crossed the line."

"I've been wishing you would tell her off for years. I didn't think you ever would."

"Why does she always pick on me?" I felt my anger receding. Frustrated tears threatened, but I blinked them back furiously. There was no way I would let Miranda make me cry in public. She wasn't going to have the last laugh.

"Isn't it obvious?" Jace said. "She's jealous of you. Always has been."

"You are so full of it, Jace." I kicked him in the ankle.

"Ow!" Jace yelped. "It's true. You don't think you're pretty, but I could name a dozen guys who think you are. Miranda knows it, too. So she tries to make you look bad because of what you wear, or how you style your hair."

I shook my head. This must be a dream. I knew I wasn't gorgeous like Randi and I never would be. Hey, I have a mirror. I know what I look like. I glared up at Jace. He was going way over the top trying to make me feel better. That, in and of itself, was odd. Things were getting way too weird. I figured that strange, ghostly presence was going to show up any minute. I started looking over my shoulder in anticipation.

"I know you don't believe me," Jace sounded a bit exasperated, "but Randi freaked out when she saw Griff looking at you. She thinks she's so hot, nabbing the new kid in school. I doubt he'll be going out with her again." He paused and gave me significant look. "I saw him smiling after you smacked down Randi."

I ran a hand through my hair, trying to sort out my tangled thoughts. I gave up.

"Let's just go." I stood up. "I want to get out of here before someone comes out and sees me."

"Okay," Jace gave in. "Still want to get something to eat?"

"Not in public. Does your mom have any more avocados?" I asked. "I could go for another of those sandwiches."

Jace wrinkled his nose.

"How about a drive-thru on the way back?" I compromised. "I could use a chocolate shake right about now."

"Yeah, I could deal with that," Jace agreed. "Let's go to Dairy Queen."

The Power of Dreams

The kitchen counter was covered in wire, beads, and tools. Sarah looked up at us in surprise, pliers frozen in one hand and silver wire grasped in the other.

"You guys are home early." She studied us quickly. "Everything okay?"

Jace scooted some wire out of the way and dropped a bag of fast food in the cleared spot. He glanced over at me and, realizing I wasn't going to open my mouth first, said, "Mia finally let Randi have it." He couldn't contain his grin. "In public, too."

Sarah looked at me with eyebrows raised high.

I sat heavily on a stool. "I couldn't help it. She made me so mad. I just let it all out. I'm actually embarrassed even thinking about it. I'm sure I looked like an idiot yelling at her in the lobby," I cringed. "In front of all those people, too."

"No way, you were great," Jace contradicted. He proceeded to give a blow-by-blow account to his mom.

"I'm glad you stood up to her, Mia," Sarah commented when Jace's slightly embellished version ended. "How about some pointers?" she teased. "I have to talk with her mom about PTA business on Monday. She's the bossiest woman I've ever had to work with."

My smile was only a little forced. "I can believe it," I murmured sympathetically.

Jace looked at me sideways while squirting vast amounts of catsup all over his fries.

"No, I am glad I did it," I insisted. "I just wish I'd done it somewhere else," I added in a low mutter.

Jace gave me a knowing smile. "I get it. You're not so worried about consequences with Randi. You don't want Griff to think you're a spaz. Right?"

"No," I frowned unconvincingly, slamming my shake on the counter.

"Who's Griff?" Sarah wanted to know. "Have you finally decided to try and kiss a toad?"

"Stop ganging up on me," I grumbled, getting up to look for an avocado. "I've never even seen him before tonight. I just hate making bad first impressions. He's too cute anyway. I'd never have a chance with him," I added lamely. And why would I want to go out with him, anyway? I thought. He was out on a date with Randi, after all. He was probably a creep, too.

I started slicing the avocado a little too aggressively. The pit flew across the room as I yanked it out with the point of the knife.

"Sorry." I scrambled after it, trying to grab it before it rolled onto the carpet. Jace was choking back laughter.

"Jason Alexander, don't you dare shoot soda out of your nose onto my jewelry," Sarah warned. Jace hastily stood and went to the sink, coughing and sputtering.

"Mia," she continued. "Stop fretting. This boy will think a lot more of you for standing up to Miranda than if you just stood there taking it."

"I guess." I wasn't sure. And I wasn't sure why I even cared. It's not like Griff would notice me anyway. I knew I was too weird for most boys at school. They couldn't get past my creative outward appearance. If only I could find someone who liked me for who I really was. Like my second family sitting here with me. I knew I could always count on Sarah and Jace. The thought relaxed me. I could feel my frown smoothing out and the tension in my shoulders easing up.

I finished making the sandwich and passed half to Sarah. We all sat and ate in comfortable silence for a few minutes. After I finished and tossed my trash, I fished the broken necklace out of my pocket. "Do you have a new clasp I could buy from you?" I searched the counter.

"You're welcome to whatever you can find. I don't have a big variety right now, though."

I found a silver figure-eight clasp. Sideways, it looked like the symbol for infinity. It seemed appropriate. I wasn't ever taking it off again.

Jace, getting bored with all the girly stuff, got up and switched the TV to some sports channel. He dropped onto the couch with his Oreo Blizzard, long legs stretched out on the coffee table.

I worked across from Sarah, intent on fixing my nan's necklace perfectly. I twisted the last jump ring into place and tugged on the chain experimentally. It felt sturdy enough. This should last for a long time, I thought, fastening it back on.

"Looks good." Sarah was watching me. Her eyes smiled cheerfully, but her skin looked a bit sallow and she had dark circles beneath her eyes. Her hair had grown back. It was short and curly, which still looked entirely wrong. I missed her long, dark, straight hair. I remembered seeing a long braided lock of hair lying on Jace's dresser until Sarah's hair started coming back in after chemotherapy.

"How are you feeling these days?" I asked, concerned. "It's been what, a year now?"

"Almost," Sarah agreed. "I mostly feel pretty good. Still tired a lot. The doctor said it would take at least a year to start feeling like myself again. I think it might take longer." She shrugged. "I'm just glad to be here at all."

I peeked over at Jace. His back was stiff, eyes straight ahead, staring at the game. He hated talking about his mom's cancer, and I almost never brought it up with him around. We suffered mostly in silence, neither of us wanting to discuss painful possibilities, each of us pretending worst case scenarios didn't exist.

"Can you get out and walk now?" I asked. "You were so exhausted for a while, you could barely leave the house."

"Yeah, being able to exercise again is a big plus." She leaned over to me conspiratorially. "Did I ever tell you the sneaky way I got some exercise while I was on chemo?"

"What do you mean?" I asked, curious.

"I learned to lucid dream."

I blinked blankly. "Am I supposed to know what that means?"

"No, not many people do," Sarah admitted. "It's a bit off the beaten path."

I heard Jace snort. He was paying attention after all. "It's loony, Mom," he scolded.

"No, it isn't," she contradicted calmly. "Just because you've never been able to do it…." She shook her head. "It takes a lot of practice, and even then, success is only sporadic at best for most people."

"I still don't know what you're talking about," I interjected.

"Sorry," Sarah stood up. "Let's go to the computer."

Sarah sat down at the small kitchen desk and opened her laptop. While we waited for the computer to start up, she began to explain. "Lucid dreaming means that you are able to realize that you are dreaming and become aware while you are inside your dream. After you become aware, then there are different ways you can affect your dream. Sometimes, you are able to stop a nightmare or change the dream to something less scary. Sometimes, you are able to do things that you could never do in real life. For example, when I have a lucid dream, I usually fly."

"No way." I have to admit I gaped a bit. "Are you serious? You are actually able to figure out you are dreaming, and then you start flying around?" Jace was right. It was kind of out there.

"Sounds weird, I know," Sarah admitted. "But I swear it's completely true."

"Wow!" I was totally fascinated. "So, can anyone learn how? I mean, what you are suggesting seems more like a bizarre fantasy. Hasn't everyone wondered what it would be like to fly?"

"I always have," Sarah agreed. "It does feel like some kind of wish fulfillment. I know that it was a big part of my staying sane while I was going through all my cancer treatments. And it definitely helped stave off depression afterwards. It's not a super-easy thing to learn, though."

"That is so cool." I looked at the computer screen. Sarah had a site pulled up that answered a bunch of frequently asked questions about lucid dreaming.

"Here, have a seat," she said, as she stood and moved back from the desk. "I'll let you read for a minute, if you want."

We traded places and I skimmed a bunch of essays that explained all you could ever want to know about lucid dreaming. As I read, I started to think about the frustrating dreams that had been plaguing me. Lucid dreaming, I thought, might be just the answer I needed. I would never have thought of it on my own. I began fantasizing about seeing who was behind me in my dreams, imagining myself banishing the intruder and flying off on some magical adventure. I blinked. My thoughts were fast becoming ridiculous. An embarrassed laugh escaped me. I hastily covered my mouth.

Sarah looked over at me quizzically from the counter. She had gone back to making jewelry as I took my time reading. Jace threw his mom a triumphant look.

"See, Mia thinks it's stupid, too."

"Do not." I felt my cheeks get pink. "I just got carried away thinking what I could actually do in my dreams. It sounds like way too much fun to me."

I thought of something else. "Don't you wake up tired every morning after flying around all night?" I asked.

"Not at all," Sarah assured me. "Lucid dreams don't last that long. And besides, most people don't lucid dream more than a few times a month." I must have looked disappointed at the time restrictions because she said, "It depends on the person.

Some people can lucid dream almost every night. I have one about once or twice a week."

"I think I want to try it," I said slowly. "You see, I've been having these dreams. They started out as nightmares, the kind that wakes you up crying and freaking out. They have morphed into something else that is still creepy, just in a different way." I looked over at Jace to see if he was laughing at me. He was glued to the game and wasn't paying us the slightest attention anymore. Good, I thought, not wanting to be teased about this.

"I'm betting that lucid dreaming would help you quite a bit," Sarah began thoughtfully. "Dealing with nightmares is one of the purposes of lucid dream therapy and a compelling reason to learn. You might learn faster, since you have such a strong goal in mind."

"The first thing you need to do is get a dream journal going. You need to write everything down that you remember, every time you dream, even in the middle of the night. Then you can look for dream signs. These are things that occur often in your dreams or are common to many people's dreams."

"I don't really get what a dream sign is, though."

"Well, let me see," Sarah said slowly. "Oh, yeah. Once, I was riding on an airplane without a purse or any other carry-on baggage, nothing to entertain the kids, no snacks. I knew that I would *never* go on an airplane trip so unprepared. So, I got up out of my seat, went into the cockpit—which turned into a field—and started to fly."

"Yeah," I laughed. "You are always over-prepared for *everything*. No wonder you knew you were dreaming."

"So what is your nightmare about, anyway?" Sarah asked. "Have you been watching too many scary movies with Jace?"

"No, they started recently. My dream begins differently each time, but soon I become aware of a presence behind me. I try to turn around to see who it is, but no one is ever there. In the first couple of dreams, the intruder was angry and I was absolutely terrified. Then he said my name. The voice even sounded familiar. In my last dream, he was still behind me, invisible, but he was trying to comfort me while my nan's house burned down."

Sarah looked thoughtful.

"Haunted dreams—not as much fun as they sound," I said sarcastically. "I stay up too late, hoping I'll be so exhausted I won't dream." I grimaced, eyeing the clock over the oven. "Want to watch a late-night video?"

"Not me," Sarah shook her head and began organizing her jewelry into a variety of fishing tackle-type boxes. "You could watch the game with Jace."

We both looked over at Jace. His head had flopped over on a pillow, and he was snoring softly, empty cup still clutched in his right hand. "Or not," I laughed. "Guess I have to go face the music," I sighed.

"You know, just talking about lucid dreaming before bed sometimes causes one. Be ready. And if you feel that presence, remind yourself that this is only a dream. Then, purposely turn around and look, expecting to find someone. I'll be excited to hear what happens." Sarah snapped a large case closed. "You know, I've been thinking about your nan's letter, too. I still don't have any good theories."

"Thanks, Sarah. Just knowing you're thinking about it helps."

I reluctantly got up from the stool. Sarah walked over to Jace, removed the cup, and threw an afghan over him. She turned off the TV and dimmed the overhead lights. Walking me to the door, she gave me a good luck squeeze. I hugged her back, not ready to go, but resigned to the fact that I needed to get some sleep. "See ya tomorrow," I waved.

As I crossed the dark street, I noticed that one of the street-lights had busted. I paused, feeling someone looking at me and I thought about my dreams. A chill ran up my spine as I turned around and spied a shadow by a tree. I glanced away, shaking my head, and when I looked back it was gone.

I hurried up my porch steps, shifting my distracted thoughts to dreaming tonight. Maybe I can do it. I felt a determined grin pull at my lips as I set my mind to face the night's unknown adventure.

5

My Imagination

Sarah's prediction turned out to be false. I didn't dream or lucid dream at all that night. Or more accurately, I didn't remember what I dreamed, lucid or not. The next day, I grabbed an empty notepad and prepared to write down every dream, down to the smallest detail. I worked hard every night for the next week. I woke up a number of times each night, writing down various silly or stress-driven dreams, as well as a number of disturbing haunted dreams. But I couldn't seem to become lucid yet.

Sarah gave me encouragement whenever frustration brought me complaining to her kitchen. The week seemed eternal. I always felt on edge because of interrupted sleep and thwarted expectations. The only good moment was when Griff walked by Jace and me during lunch on Friday. He stopped briefly to talk with Jace about photography class and, never one to waste an opportunity, I let myself get a good eyeful while pretending indifference. I was right; he was *way* too pretty for me, but

I sure enjoyed looking. He surprised me by actually seeming nice, too. I wondered why he had been out with Randi.

Randi had taken special care to pretend I didn't exist this week, as if that was a punishment. On the contrary, her lack of attention was the nicest thing she had ever done for me. Not that I would let her know that. I hoped she would keep it up for the rest of the year. My senior year might be bearable after all.

The weekend finally arrived, and I held high hopes for lucid dreams, since I could sleep as long as I wanted. But Friday night yielded nothing. I tried not to set my heart on Saturday night, but I couldn't help it.

I woke up early, disappointed yet again. Grumbling to myself, I dragged down to breakfast, slumming it in worn-out sweats, my hair squashed flat on one side and sticking up like a hedgehog on the other side. My mom and dad were both enjoying a relaxing morning, talking quietly over breakfast. They were surprised to see me up before ten.

I put some toast in the toaster and grabbed the milk jug, lifting it to my mouth. My mom gave me a disgusted, "I can't believe this uncivilized creature is my daughter" look and handed me a mug. I made an immature face while I took the cup and poured.

Dad, having missed the entire exchanged, asked me how my week was.

"Fine," I said curtly, not wanting to get into it with my parents.

"Any plans for today?" he inquired, trying a different subject.

"Nope." I kept my eyes on the toast I was buttering.

Dad gave up and picked up the newspaper as Mom went to load the dishwasher. I sat trying to decide what to do today. I was still sitting there several minutes later when my mom startled me by dropping a heavy photo album on the table.

"Thought you might enjoy looking at this," she said casually, and then walked away, leaving me in private.

I spent an hour leafing through pages of family vacations and school activities, lingering on photos of me and my nan. Memories tugged at me, pulling my emotions into twisted knots. I closed the book and went to lie down on the couch. I remembered reading that lucid dreaming often happens during early-morning naps. I lay my head back and repeated to myself, "I will have a lucid dream," over and over, hoping the power of suggestion would drill itself into my head, paving the way for lucidity.

I FELT THE hot sun beating down on my head and back. My hair felt ready to burst into flames. I saw the tall evergreens ahead, a shady trail beneath, beckoning me. As I headed for the shadowed relief, I stopped briefly to pick several blackberries and pop them in my mouth. The slightly sour juice tasted refreshing and I reached for some more.

All of a sudden, the blackberry bushes shot out large, tangled branches towards me, encircling me with dangerous arms, their sharp thorns snagging on my clothes and tearing at my skin, protected minimally by shorts and a thin t-shirt. I pushed down the panic, trying to hold myself frozen like a statue, afraid the damage would be a thousand times worse if I struggled.

Someone cried my name and I turned, thankful for the rescue attempt. My warning of "Be careful!" died on my lips when I realized no one was there. Maybe they got trapped by the blackberry tentacles, too, I thought wildly. No, wait a minute. My mind fought through the fright, searching for a rational explanation. I'd picked blackberries dozens of times before and the plants had never attacked me. I heard the voice again in my ear.

"Mia."

Everything fell into place with a loud click like the final piece of a puzzle.

"I am dreaming," I whispered wonderingly, hoping not to banish the dream with this exhilarating thought.

I clawed at the branches and noticed the thorns scratches didn't hurt at all. I might as well have been covered in catsup. Once I was free, I took a couple of calming breaths, preparing myself for the big finale. I can do this, I thought.

"Mia." The voice echoed in my ear. I turned deliberately all the way around this time. He was so close that I jerked back violently, tripped, and fell awkwardly onto the dirt trail. I stared up at the figure looming over me. He bent over and grasped my hand, pulling me, stunned and speechless, to my feet.

My eyes were riveted on his surprised face. His hair was longer than I remembered, about shoulder length, various shades of blonde. It curled and waved in rather messy locks. His skin was deeply tanned and his bright, green eyes stood out with shocking clarity against his golden brown skin. He was still taller than me, but not by a lot. He looked a bit older than the last time I had seen him, but he hadn't aged as much as he should have.

"Quinn, was that your name?" I asked carefully, the name rising to my tongue of its own accord.

He nodded seriously. "Mia." His voice was rough and wild-sounding, rusty from lack of use, maybe. He reached out and touched my hair softly. He made an effort to clear his throat. "I can't believe you can finally see me." He shook his head as if he couldn't trust his eyes.

"I've wanted to ask you," he paused. "What happened to all your hair? Did you sleep with gum in your mouth again?" He smiled unexpectedly, his deep dimples an exact imitation of my nan's familiar smile.

My mouth fell open. "What?" I began to doubt my lucidity. This was way stranger than I had suspected. "What's going on?" I gasped. "You look like my nan," my voice broke, "when she smiled," I finished in a whisper.

"Nan," he said thoughtfully. "Oh, you mean Marie. Yes, our smiles are the same."

He looked serious again. "I need to talk to her. But I can't see her anymore. Can you get her a message?" His eyes became intense with worry. I couldn't look away.

"She died," I forced myself to say the painful words, feeling tears building up again.

His response was ferocious. He grabbed my shoulders and began to shake me. "Tell me it's not true," he bellowed into my shocked face. My response was instinctive. I tore my arms free and slapped his face with all my strength. He stumbled and I turned, poised for flight. He collapsed on the dirt, head in his hands, violence gone.

I stood still, trying to figure out what was happening. This was outside my expectations for lucid dreaming. Was I fighting with myself? Was I dealing with my anger over Nan's death? I wasn't sure I liked what was going on. Maybe

I could just fly away from this disturbing scene. Half of me wanted to escape, the other half wanted to know what in the world all this meant.

Quinn crouched at my feet in a dejected lump. I squatted down beside him and put my hand on his shoulder. "Everything is lost," he whispered. "For me, my sisters, my family."

Compassion made me look into his hopeless eyes. "I'll help if I can," I heard myself promise. He reached out to touch me again.

"HEY, MIA." THE voice was loud and persistent. Someone was shaking me gently. I woke reluctantly. "Quinn, wait!" I gasped out loud. But he was gone, and my mom was leaning over me, an annoyed look on her face.

"It's eleven o'clock, for goodness sake. Time to get up." She backed up when my glare settled on her.

"Mom," I cried. "You just interrupted my first lucid dream! How could you?"

She backpedaled immediately. "I'm so sorry, honey. I never considered you might have a lucid dream here on the couch." She looked appropriately penitent. I took a deep breath and unclenched my fists.

"You will never guess who I saw in my dream. It was Quinn."

Mom looked blank.

"You know, from Nan's house. I used to play with him. Well, not usually him. I mostly played with his sisters, Hazel and Eileen."

"Oh," she smiled condescendingly. "You mean your imaginary friends. It's been a long time since you've mentioned them."

Now I pulled the blank look. "What are you talking about, Mom?" I was getting cross. "I played with those kids all the time when we visited Nan. Stop messing around."

Mom tilted her head questioningly. "Mia, you made up those kids. No one else ever saw them. I did love to watch you carrying on extensive conversations and pretend games with them. I used to tell Nan how smart you were. Imaginary friends are one of the signs of intelligence in children, did you know that? You set some high expectations."

"What?"

She frowned, noticing my open mouth, and stopped her rambling.

I couldn't seem to comprehend her words. It sounded like a foreign language. I got up without saying anything and made a beeline for the photo album, ready to prove my point. I flipped page after page. Where were they? I knew they were real. There had to be physical evidence, some proof that I was right. I went through the entire album as my mom looked on silently. Nothing. Not one single photo.

"Honey..." My mom reached over to pat my shoulder, but I shrugged out of her grasp with a jerk.

I couldn't look at her face. "I'm going running, okay? *Alone*," I added fiercely, before she could offer to go with me. I took off downstairs without waiting for an answer.

I tore around my room as chaotic as a tornado, throwing on the first pair of shorts I could find and leaving on my thrashed sweatshirt. I stuffed my feet into whatever socks I grabbed first. They didn't match. I couldn't have cared less. My shoes tied, I snagged my iPod and took off upstairs. I sailed out the door without as much as a "see you later."

Moments later, I was pounding up an unforgivingly steep hill. My lungs were on fire and the loudest, most diverting music I could scrounge up was hammering its way into my skull. I knew I was starting out too hot. I would burn out and end up limping home after bonking royally, but slowing down just wasn't an option.

Images flashed through my head: my nan, my so-called imaginary friends when we were young, Quinn from my dream. I was beyond confused. I couldn't make sense of any of it, so I ran until I felt like falling over. I was starting to wish I had brought some water, when I suddenly became aware of where I was and realized how far I had gone. I hadn't thought to grab my phone, either. Stupid, stupid, stupid! I slowed down and walked, trying to conserve some energy for the run home.

I had run five, maybe six miles. I'd done that before, but not so fast. And now I had the same distance to go back home. Resigned, I started jogging slowly toward where I thought there was a gas station. I was sure Sarah or Jace would come get me, even if I did have to call them collect. "Did gas stations even have pay phones anymore?" I wondered. If so, I hoped it was outside. I wasn't sure they would let me in the station, since I must've looked ghastly by now. I doubted I smelled any better.

By the time I found the gas station, I had given up jogging. If they didn't have a phone, I resolved to beg to borrow a cell phone from the first non-threatening person I saw. My hopes rose at the sight of the phone booth and promptly plummeted when I saw the state of the phone. Guess an outside phone has its drawbacks, I thought bitterly. Not wanting to approach any-one, but knowing I needed to, I sat on the curb, waiting for my face to return to a more normal color than its current bright

red. I felt my hair and gave up any attempt at order. A few minutes later, I made my aching legs stand and I scouted around
for a likely suspect.

A shiny black car, dripping from a recent carwash, glided up
in front of me. I looked in the cab, hoping for a friendly, familiar face and almost passed out. An automatic window slid down
and I wished myself absolutely anywhere but here.

"Hey, you look like you could use a ride." Griff casually
looked me up and down. I was thankful my face was still red
or my blush would have been even more humiliating.

"No thanks," I managed. "I'm waiting for someone to pick
me up." I kept my eyes on my mismatched socks, hoping a
huge earthquake would swallow me quickly, and I could die a
horrible death out of sight of his curious eyes.

"Are you sure?" he asked. "You look pretty beat."

I couldn't help a defiant lift of my chin and found him grinning, as if waiting for a smart reply. "I'm just fine, thank you
very much," I replied through painfully gritted teeth. I stalked
off to the gas station, hoping someone inside would let me use
a phone. Maybe the clerk had a cell phone. Anything but a ride
home with Griff. I would endure any number of torture devices
before setting one foot in his shiny, new car, looking like I did.

"Okay, see ya at school, Mia," he yelled as he swung out of
the parking lot. I pretended I didn't hear and zoomed into the
mini-mart, frantic to get inside and disappear from his view.
This was worse than any nightmare I'd had recently, and I
wished in vain for someone to wake me up. No such luck.

After the clerk took pity on me and let me use her phone, I
waited inside for my dad to pick me up. Jace and Sarah were
too far away to get me. My cooled-down body was becoming

clammy now, and I couldn't face waiting half an hour for them
to arrive. So I settled on Dad, hoping that Mom opted to stay
at home.

My luck held this time. I breathed a sigh of relief and curled
into a ball in the front seat of my dad's Miata.

"You okay?" was all my dad ventured.

"More or less," I replied vaguely and he let me be. Sometimes
I really liked my dad.

6

Unexpected Developments

I spent the rest of the day engaged in mindless chores, allowing my mind to wander. I straightened my room, an unlikely and tedious task, but I could think as I worked. I cleaned out my closet and desk, vacuumed, dusted, and tore everything off my bulletin board. It took all afternoon. I didn't have to answer any questions as I worked because everyone could sense my mood and left me alone.

After my room was perfectly arranged, I picked up an old sketchbook that had been buried under who knows what. I grabbed a pencil and began drawing. I drew Nan's house and backyard, the lake, some little houses I used to build, and lots of tall pine trees—page after page of loose, flowing sketches.

Finally, I felt ready to make the attempt. Quinn. I closed my eyes and tried to imagine his face down to the smallest detail. After a few minutes, I picked up my pencil again. I started with his wide-set eyes and square face. Then I sketched his straight nose and long, curly hair. Finally, I drew his mouth, but I couldn't get the dimples right. I opened my scrapbook and found a photo of my nan smiling and tried to copy the mouth and dimples. When I finished, I tacked my drawings to the bulletin board with Quinn in the middle and sat back.

There, on my wall, was my childhood world, one of love and trust, where I had always felt comfortable and peaceful. Now, in the middle was a lie, a seed of deception that had been planted in my perfect world. How did this happen? I tried to imagine myself back in my childhood. How could Quinn, Hazel, and Eileen not really exist? I thought back. My nan knew their names. I know she did. We used to talk about them. How could she have pretended like that? Was it just a game? No, I know my nan would never have amused herself at my expense. I sat staring at the drawings until my growling stomach distracted me. Still feeling dissatisfied, I went in search of something to eat.

I threw a bunch of stuff in a blender and made a quick fruit smoothie. My parents were working on the bills, so I headed over to Jace's house. I thought maybe I could talk about everything now. Except the part about seeing Griff. That embarrassment would stay mine alone.

My reception wasn't what I expected. Jace was in bed with a fever and sore throat. Tomorrow, he was going to get a throat culture, since he had a tendency to get strep throat. "*Ugh*," I groaned. I hated to think of Jace as a crutch, but school was the pits when he was absent. I began thinking of reasons to stay home as well.

"Have a seat, if you want to risk it." Sarah patted the couch next to her. I sat willingly enough. I'd never had strep throat in my life, but I figured there was always a chance. And if that meant getting sick and missing school, that would be okay. It'd be a good way to avoid seeing Griff for a while.

I stayed for about an hour, discussing my first lucid dream and my so-called imaginary friends. We tossed around theories and ideas. Neither of us could get our head around any of it. It just didn't make any sense. But it was nice to have a non-judgmental listening ear. I returned home feeling better than I expected.

Getting ready for bed, I felt conflicting feelings of anticipation and dread towards the possibility of having another lucid dream. I had to be realistic, though. I had only had the one. I wasn't likely to have another for quite a while. I went to bed and stared at the clock for at least an hour before I settled down. The last thing I saw as I closed my eyes was Quinn's dimpled smile.

I WANDERED AROUND before the morning bell rang, feeling lonely without Jace. My morning classes kept my mind and hands busy, and time didn't drag as much as I had feared. I started worrying about what to do for lunch. I had several friends in my art class who often asked me to sit with them at lunch. I had more in common with them than with anyone else in school, and we had fun goofing around in class together. I was ready to follow them out of class, but decided against it at the last second. With all that I had on my mind, I wasn't really up for all the social chit-chat of who liked whom, and who was dating whom, etc. So I headed out to the grassy quad and looked for a private spot, trying not to care that I would look like a loser sitting alone.

I tossed off my flip-flops and sat on my coat, which I'd carefully laid out the damp grass—no need to go to English with a wet butt. I sat cross-legged in the early fall sunshine, munching an apple and reading a favorite novel I had shoved in my backpack this morning. *Bridget Jones's Diary* always made me laugh, and the quirky dialogue and ridiculous situations effectively distracted me from my irritating thoughts. Like not having a lucid dream last night. I was so absorbed in my book, it took me a few minutes to notice that a pair of black boots had stopped in front of me. When I recognized the boots, my heart kicked into double-time, and I felt my face grow warm. I made myself continue chewing normally and counted to ten before I looked up, trying for casual indifference, but most likely failing miserably.

"Hey," I began a little defensively. "You lose Randi?" I couldn't imagine what in the world he was doing here, except maybe to tease me about yesterday.

Griff laughed and sat down next to me. "Good book?" he asked, avoiding the question.

"One of my favorites," I admitted, showing him the cover. I snuck a look at him out of the corner of my eye. He was way too close for me to carry on a decent conversation. My heart was still hammering away like I'd just run several miles. What was he doing here, I thought again, part of me wishing he would leave, the other part wishing I could say something clever and witty so he would stay.

"So, where's your boyfriend?" His question completely threw me.

"Who?" I asked confused.

"Jace. Isn't he your boyfriend?"

I couldn't help it. I burst out laughing. Feeling as nervous as I did hardly helped matters. Soon, I was giggling out of control. Griff raised an eyebrow at me, and I tried to squash my laughing fit.

"I'm sorry," I choked out. "It's just the thought of Jace as my boyfriend. We've been best friends since I moved across the street from him when I was five. He's like my brother. Boyfriend, *ewww*!" I made a face. "That's creepy."

"*Hmmm*," was all Griff said. I wondered if I'd embarrassed him. I thought about how foolish he had made me feel yesterday, and I sincerely hoped I had.

"Whatever gave you the idea we were together? Just because we hang out a lot? I mean, we don't act like a couple at all."

"Something Miranda said." Griff leaned forward, an elbow resting on one of his knees and cupping a hand under his chin. He tilted his head up towards my face.

I instinctively pulled away, sideways. "You mean, Miss 'I open my mouth and all that comes out is lies and manipulation?' You have a lot to learn about Randi," I smirked. "Have fun with that." I turned back to my book trying to ignore him, but found I couldn't read a single word with him staring at me. Finally, I put aside all pretenses and shot an exasperated look over at him. He seemed cool and relaxed. Not fair, I thought grumpily.

"I can see you made it home alright yesterday." Crap. I knew he was going to bring that up.

"Is that what this is about?" I grimaced. "Yes, I'm perfectly okay, and as you can see, I don't always look like a train just ran over me. It was a bad day, but now I'm fine." I stopped myself from babbling by biting my tongue and looked away, desperate for something else to say. I spied something large and rectangular on the ground beside Griff. "What's that?" I pointed.

He turned and picked it up. "My portfolio. I keep all my photos for class in it. Want to see them?" he offered casually.

"Sure," I replied, welcoming the distraction. I was interested to see what kind of photographer he was, and whether he had a creative side or was just technically adept.

He unzipped the flat case and laid it open on the grass. I leaned forward casually, trying to conceal the anticipation I felt.

"I'd be interested in your opinion. You're an artist, aren't you?" he asked softly, too close for comfort.

"How do you know?" I muttered. He didn't answer so I said, "Fine, I'll give you my impressions."

"Thanks," he smiled. His teeth were very white and his eyes crinkled up when he smiled. I looked down at the photos, feeling unnerved.

"Don't thank me yet, I might hate them. You never know."

"I'll take my chances." He smiled even wider.

Curiosity getting the better of me, I reached for the first photo and held it up.

It was a tree. But it was so much more than just a tree. A large hole was scraped out of the trunk, bark pulled away from the edges and below the hole. It looked like a screaming mouth with a trailing beard. A broken nose made of a stunted branch jutted above, and a hole to the left appeared to be a squinting, eerie eye. The tree was dead or dormant, lightly covered in snow. The effect was truly haunting. I loved it.

"Wow, this is really cool." I couldn't hide my admiration and was rewarded with another beautiful smile. I found myself smiling back.

I leafed through several more photos, all nature themed. All had that same ghostly quality. I was quite impressed. I could almost look past his dating Randi.

"These really are great." I wished I could have one for my room. I'd even splurge for a frame, instead of tacking it on my bulletin board like I did for most of my photos. I especially liked the haunted tree. I went back and studied it closer.

"This one is definitely my favorite." I started to lay it back down.

"I'll print you a copy if you'll help me out," Griff offered. "I need someone to help dust spot some of my photos. I thought maybe you would be good at that."

"I'd love a copy," I said, slowly eyeing the photo. "But I don't know anything about dust spotting. I might be terrible at it. Besides, don't you just use Photoshop for your digital photos?"

"No computers or digital cameras for me. Guess I'm old school. I like using film and printing it myself. But that often leaves white spots from little pieces of dust or lint that need to be hand inked after the photo is printed. Come on, I'll give you a copy just for trying," Griff cajoled. "I'm the worst spotter in the whole photography class, and I could use the help."

"Okay," I agreed. "What do I do?"

"I'll show you. Could you meet me Friday morning in the photo lab? Mr. Cardon said I could come in early and work then."

"I guess so," I started getting nervous again. The thought of working side-by-side with him alone made me excited and anxious. If dust spotting was going to take steady hands, I was in trouble. With Griff leaning over my shoulder, I was pretty sure my hands would be shaking like I was sitting in a meat locker. And I doubted what I would be feeling was cold.

The bell rang. I couldn't believe lunch was already over.

Griff began zipping up his portfolio. I still held the tree photo in my hand.

"Don't you want…?" I began.

"Keep it," he said. "See you Friday morning. Seven o'clock, if that's okay." He was already heading off.

"Yeah, see ya." I needed to gather my stuff, but I still felt dazed at how my lunch had gone. I guess it was a good thing Jace was absent after all. I'd never felt that way before. Huh. That was weird. As I crammed everything into my bag, I hoped fervently that I didn't get strep throat. Maybe I would just talk to Jace on the phone today. He wouldn't care, I rationalized. Would I tell him about Griff? I wasn't sure yet what I'd say.

I SAT ON my floor with my mom's enormous cat, Freddie, curled up in my lap. She was purring like a freight train as I rubbed under her fluffy neck. She was supposed to be my cat, but she always liked my mom better. I don't think she ever forgave me for getting a loft bed she couldn't climb up on.

"So," I asked Jace on the phone, "was it strep?"

"Of course," Jace exclaimed. "That's all I ever get. I still need to wait one more day before I can go back to school. I just started the antibiotic this afternoon."

"School's lame without you there," I admitted.

"You know it," Jace laughed. "Oh come on. Two days. How bad could it be?"

"I ate lunch by myself. I felt like a dork."

"That was dumb. Why didn't you eat with Amber or Skye from Art?"

"I don't know. I wasn't up for inane chit-chat, I guess." I was debating with myself whether to tell him about Griff. I gave in. I could never keep a secret from Jace.

"Umm, Griff came over and sat by me at the end of lunch."

"Well, well, well," Jace drawled. "Isn't that interesting?"

"He asked where my boyfriend was," I paused significantly. "He thought *you* were my boyfriend."

I had to hold the phone away from my ear until Jace stopped laughing.

"I had the exact same reaction," I giggled. "A bit creepy, huh? No offense."

"So was he glad you were available?" Jace teased after he caught his breath.

"How should I know? I can't read his mind," I snapped. "He did show me his portfolio."

"It's cool, huh. He's easily the best in the class."

"He sort of asked me to come to school early on Friday to help him do some dust spotting," I admitted.

"A date in the dark room. Not very subtle," Jace whistled.

"Shut up." I was blushing and very glad I was talking on the phone. "It's not like that."

"So what is it like?" Jace wanted to know.

"I don't know, but it's not a date. He just wants some help. I don't even know how to dust spot, and what if I'm really lame at it, and I look like a fool, and, and... oh, crap," I trailed off.

"This sounds serious. How about some lessons first? You don't have to tell him. Then will you feel better?" I couldn't believe my ears. Jace was actually being cool. I was going to owe him a big one for sure.

"Thanks, but not until you aren't contagious any more. I don't want to get sick."

"Sure thing. I won't be contagious by tomorrow afternoon, but I'll need to get some supplies from school. So, how about Wednesday or Thursday after school?"

"Wednesday sounds great. Then I can have an extra day to practice." I paused. "Don't act like you know what's going on when you see Griff at school, okay?"

"Yes, sir! Any more orders, sir?"

"Shut up," I laughed. "And get better soon."

"I'll do my best, sir."

"Go get some rest, Jace. Talk to you tomorrow, okay?"

"Bye, Mia."

I turned off the phone. Freddie was still curled up in my lap and my legs had gone to sleep. I tried to move her onto my chair without waking her up, but she stretched and stalked off with a haughty look as soon as I placed her on the cushion.

I jumped up and down as my legs woke up, hating the pins-and-needles feeling. I decided to go on a run before doing my homework. Off-road this time, so I wouldn't get lost or see anyone unexpected.

I felt better afterwards and got all my homework done in time to work on a jewelry project before bed. I made a cool, silver-chain bracelet with a turquoise charm. I thought I'd wear it tomorrow. It would be nice to wear something new again. I'd show it to Amber and Skye at lunch. I didn't want Griff to think I was sitting alone waiting for him to come over. No need to seem eager. Friday was soon enough to attempt conversation with him again. I needed some time to psyche myself up for it.

I was thinking more about Griff that night as I laid my head on my pillow. I had found an old black frame in a box. His black and white tree leered at me spookily from the wall next to my bed. *Hmm.* Definitely less appealing at night. Might have to move it tomorrow, I thought, as I drifted off to sleep.

Awareness

A maze of dark corridors lay in front and behind me. A sharp smell of chemicals lingered in the air. I saw wet photos lined up drying on twine along the walls, all of them sinister and foreboding images. I started running to get away from them. A figure was fleeing ahead of me, and I began yelling when I recognized him.

"Griff, wait!" I shouted. "I can't run that fast!" My legs felt like they were dragging through thick mud. Griff turned a sharp corner and disappeared from view. I was sure each of my legs weighed a hundred pounds. Exhausted, I stopped and leaned against the wall, my breath coming in short gasps.

I heard breathing behind me. Yikes! The thought of being followed made me redouble my efforts. I could barely lift my legs, so I started sliding them along the floor. Panic started to envelope me in its icy claws. I opened my mouth to scream when a familiar voice called my name.

"Griff, is that you?" I whispered.

No answer.

"Who's there?"

Still no answer.

Wait a minute. I had an urgent thought. "Quinn?" I called tentatively, "Is that you?"

"Yes." The voice was next to my ear. I deliberately turned, and there he was, right in front of me, so close I took an involuntary step back.

"Are you always so close to me?" I asked without thinking. "Always right behind me?"

"Yes. This is only the second time you've noticed. But I've seen you more times than I can count." He eyes shone a brilliant green in the dark hallway. I couldn't look away.

"I don't understand. Why are you in my dreams? Are you real or imaginary? I mean, I remember you from my nan's house, but my mom said you never existed, that I just made you up. And Hazel and Eileen, too." I ran my hand nervously through my hair and was surprised to find it was long again.

"I can't give you a short answer. Everything is so complicated."

"Can you tell me why you smile like my nan? Is it just wishful thinking because I want to see her again so badly?" I was searching his eyes, as if I could read the answers buried behind them.

"Well, I look like your nan because her twin sister, Anna, is my mother. Marie is," he paused, "*was* my aunt."

"Anna, who disappeared when she was sixteen?" I tried to puzzle it out. "But wait. If she's your mother, why are you so young? Shouldn't you be, I don't know, a grandpa?"

Quinn looked away. I could tell he was wrestling with something. He doesn't know if he can tell me the truth, I thought. He doesn't think I'll believe him.

"Didn't your nan ever talk to you about us?" Quinn's face was drawn, his eyes serious.

"No, she died when I was only twelve. She did leave me a note and her clover necklace. My dad never gave them to me, though. I just found them a couple weeks ago. Her note said she needed to talk to me about something very important." I put a hand on his arm. "She was going to tell me about you, wasn't she? Before she died."

"Probably." His voice was sad. "And about the rest of my family." Then his face cleared and he smiled slightly, with just a hint of dimples. "I knew you had my necklace already. Otherwise I couldn't be here."

I reached up around my neck. It felt unnaturally bare without the necklace. "Do I usually have it on in my dreams?" I asked. "I never take it off when I'm awake."

"No, it doesn't seem to show up in your dreams, no matter where your dreams take you or how you are dressed."

I had an uncomfortable image of my running around in my underwear or worse. I knew I'd had those nightmares before. Had I had any lately, I wondered, horrified. I didn't think I wanted to know. I couldn't meet his eyes. Intense embarrassment was flooding my cheeks.

As if reading my thoughts, not a hard thing to do at the moment, he said, "Don't worry, your dreams have been pretty tame since I've been here."

"Would you tell me if they weren't?" I challenged.

"I'm not a very good liar," he admitted.

"You look more like I remember with your hair like this." He tucked a strand behind my ear, his hand touching my still-warm cheek. My heart gave a funny sort of jump. "Actually, you look nothing like I remember. You were just a child last time I saw you. But your big brown eyes are still the same."

I moved back, trying to think clearly.

"So, umm, where did you go?" I asked, trying to change the subject. "And how come no one else could see you?" That part still didn't make any sense. Did any of this make sense? I was starting to think that none of these dreams were actually lucid. My imagination seemed to be kicked into overdrive.

"I don't really know where to start," he sighed. "You most likely won't believe me anyway. But I will try. It all began with my mother. If she hadn't been on that trail when my father appeared…"

Beep, beep, beep, beep.

"What's that weird sound?" I glanced over at Quinn. He was starting to fade. "No!" I cried, throwing my arms around him in a vain effort to keep him with me.

"Come back soon," he whispered into my hair.

I woke feeling his arms around me, a fresh woodsy scent lingering in the air. My alarm clock blared louder, becoming more and more obnoxious as I failed to push the Off button. I whacked the thing to the floor, wanting to stomp on it and kick it into the wall. Of all the lousy timing! I could not believe it. I lay on my bed fuming, trying to keep myself from yelling my frustration at the ceiling. I was going to learn something truly life-changing. I knew it. I felt ill, thinking about how long it was probably going to take for me to see Quinn again. I closed my eyes, imagining his face, trying to call back my dream, but it was pointless. Even if I had been able to go back to sleep, I knew that my mom would just come in and wake me up if I didn't get up soon. I didn't want her interrupting another important dream, so I dragged myself up and forced myself to get ready for the day.

I was in a bad funk all morning. I barely listened in class and missed several questions asked by irritated teachers. I had a hard time even caring. I tried to pull myself together by lunch time and was able to catch up with Amber and Skye as they headed to the cafeteria. After they bought their lunches, we found a table and spread out our food.

"Cool bracelet. It's so heavy." Skye was studying the pattern of silver rings on my new bracelet. "What's it called again?"

"Turkish Roundmaille. It took a long time to put together, but as you can see, it was totally worth it." Talking about my jewelry always put me in a better mood. I could feel myself relaxing and releasing some of my frustration.

"Could you make one for me?" Skye wanted to know.

"Sure, if I can find some more free time. And if you want it made of sterling silver rings instead of silver-plated, you'll have to give me enough money to cover the cost. Sterling is so expensive these days."

"No problem," Skye agreed. "Just let me know how much it's going to be."

"So," Amber and Skye exchanged pointed looks. "What's Griff like?" Amber started giggling.

"Huh?" I was caught off-guard. I had almost forgotten about Griff after my intense dream the night before.

"We know you had lunch with him yesterday. Come on. What's the scoop?"

"Hey, it wasn't planned," I assured them. "He just came over."

"Lucky you!" Amber sighed. "He is gorgeous."

"Don't you think so?" Skye encouraged.

"It's the long hair," Amber went on. "And don't forget those pale-blue eyes."

I let them ramble on for a while, growing more and more uncomfortable.

Finally I butted in. "How'd you know I had lunch with him?"

"Oh, I heard it from a couple of people."

"Me, too," Amber nodded. "It's probably around the whole school by now. I heard that Miranda is furious," she laughed. "She asked him out, you know, but he hasn't returned the favor yet."

"Yeah, she would have let the whole school know if they were dating," Skye agreed. "She probably can't believe that there might actually be a boy who doesn't worship the ground she walks on."

"How do you know all this stuff," I asked, feeling overwhelmed. I hoped they hadn't heard about my spat with Randi at the theater. I certainly wasn't going to bring it up.

"You just have to keep your ears open," Amber confessed. "It's not that hard."

I spent the rest of lunch listening to an amazing amount of school gossip, more than I really needed to know. But at least I wasn't sitting alone. I did glance around for Griff a few times, glad he wasn't sitting close. I was afraid of what my face might betray if he caught me staring at him.

My life had been much simpler when the only boy I thought of was my best friend. Now, I was preoccupied with the new bad boy of the school and a dream boy I had imagined up when I was a kid. My mind was not going to last long with such constant weirdness. I wondered if it would crack before

I could graduate. That wouldn't be very convenient. I guess I should try to hold it together at least until summer.

As Amber, Skye, and I were walking to our next class, a sharp elbow rammed me hard in the ribs. I shot an angry look at Amber, who was jerking her head to the right, ignoring my grumpy "Hey!"

"What?" I began in an annoyed voice. Then I noticed Griff coming toward us on the sidewalk. I felt my face color and I tried for a casual nod. He nodded back and kept going.

"Thanks a lot," I hissed at Amber. "You made me look like an idiot."

"No I didn't," Amber shrugged. "I bet he thinks you look cute when you blush."

I groaned and hurried off to my next class, Amber's and Skye's giggles following me to my building. I yanked the door open and retreated with relief into the distracting chaos.

MY MOM AND dad both had meetings that night at their schools, and I decided it was time for me to take some action. I needed more information about my nan, and I was prepared to snoop to get what I wanted. I hurried through my home-work so I would have the evening free. I waved goodbye and called my accomplice. Jace walked in five minutes later, look-ing and sounding more like his old self again.

"What's the plan?" he asked, rubbing his hands together and twirling an invisible Snidely Whiplash mustache.

"Sorry," I laughed. "Nothing that sinister, I'm afraid. Just searching through my parents' old stuff. Probably be more creepy than anything else."

"I can handle it. Just lead the way."

We dragged out boxes from my parents' closets and looked through desk drawers. I felt a bit guilty, but as soon as I could tell something wasn't about my nan, I put it away.

"Who's in this picture with your mom?" Jace sat by me on the floor, holding up a folded snapshot from one of my mom's drawers. I glanced at the photo, "Whoa," I gasped, eyebrows flying upward in surprise. "That's my dad, my biological dad," I clarified. "I haven't seen a picture of him in forever. I thought Mom got rid of all of them."

The photo showed a much younger Mom holding a chubby, bald baby wrapped in a pink blanket. A tall, handsome man was smiling down at both of us, his expression adoring and his arm clasped around my mom's waist.

"You know, I didn't even remember what he looked like."

It was immediately obvious where I'd gotten my coloring. Our hair was the same exact color of strawberry blonde. His was long on top and waved back behind his ears, just brushing the top of his shoulders. I also had his golden skin tone, as well as his strong chin and full lower lip. It was weird looking at him like he was a complete stranger. I wondered what he was doing right now, and whether he even remembered he had a daughter.

Jace was holding back, gauging my reaction. "It's okay," I told him. "I don't think about him at all. As far as I'm concerned, I'm living with my *real* dad. Dad adopted me when he married Mom. I was only one when this guy bailed on me and my mom. I can't even think of his name."

I handed the photo back to Jace. "Put it in the exact same place if you can. I don't want Mom to know I saw it."

"Sure." Jace stuck it in an old book and placed it face down in the back of the drawer.

I had never thought much about my biological dad. He ditched us, and my mom despised him, that much I knew. Mom had to finish her degree with a tiny baby to care for and she had barely any money. Her parents helped out a lot, and then life got better once she met Dad. I wondered why she still had that old picture. Not that I would ever ask her. I was not willing to dredge up Mom's painful memories. Besides, I was searching for clues to my nan's past. I needed to focus on that.

I looked at the clock and my heart sank. My parents would be home in about a half hour, and I figured we'd better start cleaning up, just in case they were early. We had stowed every-thing back as neatly as possible when I spied a bunch of letters in the back of my dad's closet. I recognized Nan's handwriting immediately. They were addressed to her son, my grandfather, whom I never had the chance to meet. I barely had time to pick them up when I heard the garage door open. "Hurry!" I exclaimed. "We can't get caught up here." Jace and I raced down two flights of stairs in record time.

Jace sat on my floor panting. "Man, I'm still not back to normal. I think that stupid antibiotic is zapping my energy."

"You just started taking it yesterday, Jace. Your body's still fighting the strep. Take it easy. I'll go get you some juice or something."

"Thanks." Jace laid his head against the wall and closed his eyes. "I hate feeling sick."

"What a wimp," I couldn't resist smart-mouthing as I turned to go. I could see Jace raise his hand, but left before I could be sure of the gesture.

Still laughing, I pulled a couple glasses down from the cupboard. My dad walked in the kitchen and asked how my night was. I made something up about doing homework with Jace and headed back downstairs with our drinks.

While we sipped, I began skimming through letters. At first, I didn't notice anything unusual. But about halfway through, Nan made a couple of references to someone she just called "A."

"I'll bet she's talking about her sister, Anna."

Jace shook his head. "She could be talking about anyone. She isn't saying anything important about A. Does it even say if A's a girl or a boy?"

"No," I said, feeling discouraged. I glanced over at Jace. I could tell he was getting bored and wanted to go home. He looked pale and wiped out.

Taking pity on him, I said, "Hey, I'm done for the night. Why don't you go home and get some sleep?"

He didn't even hide his relief. He stood immediately, and grabbed his sweatshirt. "I'm staying after school tomorrow to play ball. But I can come over with the photo supplies after dinner, okay?"

"Meeting Michelle?" I teased.

"Hey Miss Pot, you aren't calling the kettle black, are you?"

"Alright, alright," I laughed. "Look at us, all goofy and infatuated. I'm quite embarrassed for us. Who would've ever thought?"

"Hey, I could go out with any number of girls any number of times. You're the picky one." He smiled slyly. "I can't wait to see the look on Randi's face when she finds out about you and Griff."

"Stop jumping ahead," I warned. "He hasn't even asked me out yet."

"Don't worry, he will. I'll be sure to tell him all kinds of stuff about you in class."

"Like what?" I threatened menacingly.

"Wouldn't you like to know?" Jace winked as he strolled out the door. "See you tomorrow."

"Keep your big mouth shut!" I yelled as he walked up the stairs. I stared around me in disgust at all the letters. I shoved them into a pile and stuck them in one of my desk drawers. What was I doing? Going through my parents private things. Spending all this time on dreams and old letters. Maybe I should just give up this pointless search and try to live in the present. I was a senior in high school and a cute boy asked me to hang out with him. Enjoy yourself, my mind told me. Stop trying to make life more complicated than it already was. I pep-talked myself into bed and kept up the steady stream until my eyes closed and Quinn's face came unbidden into my mind.

Ah, Quinn. That gorgeous hair and beautiful, brown skin. Was he real or not? Would I ever find out for sure? Did I really want the truth, or did I want to believe the lie? Or maybe I was crazy. Or Nan was crazy, or, more likely, senile. I imagined my nan's kind, lovely face flashing that dimpled smile I loved so much. No way was she crazy or senile. There had to be another explanation. Something was going on, and I had to find out what it was, even though I was years too late to do anything about it.

8

Darkroom Drama

Friday morning, I dragged my butt out of bed way too early, not sure if even a boy as cool as Griff was worth getting up that early for. After a long shower, I put on a funky thrift store t-shirt with my favorite gypsy skirt. I gave my hair special attention, but as always, my hair ignored me and did whatever it felt like doing. It wasn't a total loss, though. My skin was clear and the rings under my eyes had faded with extra sleep. Armed with the knowledge I'd gained from Jace about dust spotting, I felt fairly confident. Turns out I've got a knack for spotting, at least that's what Jace said. But who knew if I could pull it off with Griff looking over my shoulder?

Mom gave me a ride to school on her way to the junior high, since I wanted Jace nowhere near me and Griff. I would be nervous enough without Jace making cheesy faces at me whenever Griff was looking the other way. Not that Jace offered to drive me. He never got up until the last second, anyway; I think it took him all of ten minutes to get ready. He was sure to still be snoozing while I sat in the photo lab, trying to act cool and calm and totally relaxed. Yeah, that was a good one. I was bouncing around like someone washed my clothes in itching powder.

"Good luck on your makeup test." My mom had no idea I was meeting a boy before school. "You look nervous. Did you study enough?" That was my mom, always concerned about my academic achievements.

"Studied for hours, Mom. I'll be fine," I lied guiltily, not meeting her eyes. "See you tonight."

I took a calming breath and squared my shoulders, walking determinedly toward the building with the photo lab. It was 6:55 a.m., and no one else was around. The deserted school looked vaguely threatening, and I was glad I didn't have to come early all the time. I reached the lab, but the door was locked. I knocked with shaky hands, waiting for someone to let me in. No answer. I knocked a second time, louder than before. I was beginning to think I'd gone through a lot of trouble for nothing when the door swung open and Griff stuck his head out.

"You made it. Come on in." He held the door wide enough for me to slip in past him.

"I was just in the dark room. Sorry it took a minute to get to the door. It's hard to hear anything back there."

"What are you printing?" I asked, not looking at his face.

"Come and see." He led me to the back of the room, past a heavy, light-deflecting curtain and into a smaller room. It was dark except for an eerie red light glowing on the wall, and the pungent tang of chemicals reminded me of my dream.

"Check it out." Griff pointed to a container where a photo was being rinsed, swirling around in some kind of liquid.

"What do you think?"

I was having a hard time formulating words, what with standing so close to him in the dark. "Snap out of it," I told myself severely.

The picture floating in the solution caught my eye. It was a carved stone gargoyle, cracked and weather-beaten, balanced precariously on the corner of a rundown-looking roof. The photo was printed in brown tones, which made it seem old and mysterious, and, like his other photos, haunted.

"Where was this taken? Not around here, was it?" Hey, I had put some words together and they had actually made sense. Maybe I could do this after all, I thought.

"It's pretty close if you can believe it. People call it the gargoyle house. Not very imaginative, but accurate. There are probably a dozen different gargoyle statues all around the house and grounds. I shot a whole roll of film last time I was there. I could drive you out there sometime, if you wanted to see them."

Good thing he turned around to check his work, because my mouth was hanging open. I closed it quickly and tried for a casual, "Okay, sure." It sounded like someone else's voice, but he didn't seem to notice. He had taken his photo out of the solution, and I followed him into the outer room, where he was putting the photo through a drying machine.

"You ready to try dust spotting?"

"Are you going to show me what to do?" I asked, not wanting him to know I had spent a ridiculous amount of time practicing for this moment.

"Come on over. I set things up already." He led me to a desk and chair. There was a light clamped onto the desk, spotlighting the work area, several colors of ink, and a delicate-looking brush. "Have a seat," he gestured. He leaned over behind me and explained the process. My mind wandered as I peeked at his profile, watching the words come out of his mouth, hardly aware of what they meant. He handed me a practice photo and moved aside considerately, to let me make an attempt.

"I'm going to print a couple more pictures while you learn, okay? If you feel confident enough, try spotting the one I just dried."

"I'll try," I smiled.

He went through the curtain and I was able to relax enough to finish the practice photo fairly quickly, my hand trembling only slightly. Feeling brave, I started on the gargoyle photo. I hadn't tried to spot a brown-toned photo before. The paper was different, too. It felt heavier, thicker. I liked spotting on this kind of textured paper much more than on the glossy photos Jace had given me to practice on. I was enjoying myself, humming a tune, lost in the work. All at once, I realized Griff was standing behind me watching my progress. I put down the brush hastily.

"Am I doing okay?" I asked awkwardly, wishing I hadn't been caught humming.

"You are definitely a natural." He had a hand on the back of my chair and was leaning over so close, I couldn't think. "You should say 'thanks' or something," my brain was trying to tell me. I couldn't make the words come out. He turned his head and looked straight in my eyes. My tongue became tied in the worst way. He smiled and I smiled back.

"So," he said softly. "What kind of an artist are you? This spotting seems like cake for you. Do you paint?"

"I, um, mostly make jewelry," I managed to whisper. I lifted up my arm to show him my new bracelet. "Like this."

"Really?" He sounded interested. "That's amazing." He actually took my hand, holding my wrist up closer to his face so he could study my bracelet.

"How about the necklace you're wearing?" he asked, still holding my hand.

"No," I shook my head. "That used to belong to my nan; she was my great-grandma."

"It's beautiful. Do you mind if I have a closer look?" he asked, his face way too close to mine.

Without thinking I reached up to take it off.

A knock on the door made us both jump, as if a spell had been broken. I glanced at the clock. "Is that really the time?" I gasped. Talk about time flying. I could hear Griff swearing under his breath.

"Guess we better clean up fast. Class is going to start soon." He sounded disappointed.

I handed him the gargoyle photo. My brain was switching back on, it seemed. "I finished this one already. I can do more sometime if you can let me have some of the inks and one of those tiny brushes."

"Thanks. I'll get some supplies together and a few more photos and give them to you at lunch. Is that okay?"

"That's fine. See you then." I snagged my bag and pushed open the door. I needed to get out of there. Ah. Fresh air. I took a long, deep breath to try and steady my nerves. That was certainly interesting, I thought, as I ran off to the next building. I wasn't sure how soon I wanted to do that again. Yikes. I didn't like feeling so out of control.

But, wow, talk about charming. Normally, I didn't turn into a big pile of mush when a cute boy talked to me. What's up with that? I may have to avoid Griff for a while to try and get some of my self-respect back. Of course, I just told him he could come by at lunch. I'd let Jace do most of the talking, and I'd sit back and play it cool. I thought I could manage that, out in the sun, with company and with a bit more distance between us.

Who was I kidding? I knew if he asked me out, I'd say yes in a heartbeat. What a pushover I was.

I scolded myself all the way to my first class.

JACE TORTURED ME all through lunch, asking me question after question about my so-called photo lab adventure. I didn't want to get into it, in case Griff suddenly showed up, and I told Jace I'd spill the beans after school. Guess I should have talked, because the final lunch bell rang and Griff was a no-show. I was a bit relieved, to tell the truth, but Jace kept complaining that I'd stalled for no reason and now he'd have to wait until the drive home for details. I snarked at him to stop being such a gossipy girl and was rewarded with a very unladylike remark.

We bickered all the way to English class, where I endured multiple nasty "if only looks could kill" stares from Randi. I wasn't sure if anyone saw Griff and me coming out of the photo lab around the same time this morning. But judging from Randi's looks, I'd say it was highly likely that someone did and then blabbed the news around school. Hmm. I wondered what was being said, and if Griff had heard any rumors, and how he felt about being the object of so much speculation. I bet I would be bombarded with questions in Art tomorrow. "But how would I answer?" I mused.

I was leaning against Jace's car with my eyes shut, feeling very tired after such an early and emotionally charged morning, when a familiar voice startled me.

"Not a morning person, huh?" Griff drawled.

"You have no idea." I straightened up self-consciously. He was so much taller than I was. Must be over six feet. Even taller than Jace.

"I brought some photo supplies, if you're still up for helping me out." He held a manila envelope in his hand. "You don't have to, you know. I feel like I'm asking for a big favor."

"That's okay." I reached for the envelope. "It's not a big deal, really, unless you've put a whole semester's worth of photos in here." I paused, feeling the thick envelope. "Then you might have to owe me." I raised my right eyebrow, feeling brave.

"And what would you like for payment?" Griff teased.

My stomach lurched at the tone of his voice and I hastily looked down, all smart comments banished from my mind.

"I hear there's an anime festival this weekend. How about I take you to a movie to say thanks?" He certainly had my attention now.

"I read about that festival in the newspaper. I'd really like to see one of the Miyazaki films. I think *Nausicaa* is playing tomorrow night. Or maybe it was *Princess Mononoke*. I wouldn't mind seeing either one on the big screen."

"Sounds good. Can I call you after I check the times to let you know and to get your address?"

I gave him my cell number so I wouldn't have to let my dad talk to him on the phone. Or worse yet, my mom.

"I'll be at work tomorrow until five, so hopefully the movie starts later than that. You might have to pick me up straight from work if the show starts early."

"I'll call you tonight when I find out for sure." He smiled, and I bit my lip trying to tame my goofy grin. "Talk to you later, then."

As he turned to leave, Jace sauntered up, smirking like crazy. "Hey, Griff."

"Jace," Griff acknowledged, and kept on going.

I watched him walk away as Jace unlocked the doors muttering, "my, my, my."

"Shut up," I retorted good-naturedly, as I got in and opened the manila envelope. I sorted through the photos, handing them off to Jace. "I'm doing him a favor and spotting all these, so he's taking me to the anime festival," I announced triumphantly, letting my smile go all dreamy.

"Hey, I thought we were going to that," Jace complained. "Michelle hates anime."

"How can you like someone who hates anime?" I was putting the photos back into the envelope, and Jace was backing up. "That's just wrong."

Jace just shrugged his shoulders, looking grumpy.

"I'll go with you and see whatever is playing tonight or Sunday, okay?" I said, trying to placate him. "Let's look up what's playing when we get home."

"Alright," Jace agreed grudgingly, "but you better tell me all about you and Griff in the photo lab this morning."

"Fine." I spent the rest of the trip home trying to explain what happened without going into all my giddy, head-in-the-cloud emotions. It made the story rather boring and uninteresting. As usual, Jace knew me better than that and wanted to know what I was leaving out.

"Nothing," I claimed. But I finally admitted that I kind of lost my head around Griff, getting all scatterbrained and flustered and not feeling myself at all. "I guess I'm pretty infatuated," I sighed, not unhappily.

Jace gave me an assessing look but said nothing.

"I'll go look up times and then call you about what's playing when, okay?"

Jace just shook his head. "Maybe Sunday," he said sulkily. "I'm not in the mood tonight." He let me out and zoomed over to his driveway.

I walked inside feeling unsettled, and went straight to my room, wondering about all the ways my life was changing right now. I had been in a very comfortable rut for quite awhile. But now the wheels of change had started, and I wasn't sure I was ready for whatever lay ahead. Even though Jace and I were like brother and sister, and we had casually dated other people before, neither of us had ever felt head-over-heels about anyone until now. I wasn't sure how much this would affect our friendship. I knew that no matter what, I would always care about Jace and had hoped that after high school we would remain close. The thought of losing that closeness made me feel sick. I swore to myself that if it was up to me, I wouldn't let it happen.

I went upstairs in a sullen mood. I grabbed some snacks and settled back into my room, ready to scour the rest of the letters from my nan. That would keep my mind from wandering, I hoped. I started where I had left off, with the mention of someone named A. I skimmed page after page of mundane trivia that a mom would think would interest her grown-up son. They painted the deck, got a new stovetop, went to the lake. My eyes felt like they were glazing over. I mean, I loved my nan and missed her dearly, but this was even more information than I wanted to know about her everyday life.

I stifled a yawn and skimmed more quickly. Suddenly, there was another reference to her friend A. She had a baby named Quinn. I read the line again. Could that really mean what I thought it meant? But what year was this? I glanced back and read something about my dad being in kindergarten. Whoa, hold on a minute. How could this be my Quinn? He looked all of, well, I didn't know, eighteen, I guess. Teenaged anyway, not in his twenties, I was pretty sure. So, none of this was going to make sense, I decided. I sat back against the wall and rubbed my tired eyes, trying to figure out what I was doing. I was dreaming about someone I had seen at my nan's, but my mom had never seen him. My nan had gone along with my childhood imaginary scenario, and had written about someone very similar being born forty years ago. And this all had something to do with my necklace.

Okay. I decided I must have been a little delusional at this point because I was still trying to work out how all this was possible. I didn't like to think my nan was senile or that I was hallucinating, as a child or now, in my dreams. So, as insane as this all sounded, I knew there had to be a rational, or maybe not-so-rational, explanation. And I was going to find it.

I was wrangling with my thoughts when my phone's ringtone made me jump. I listened to it for a second—I loved that song—and then looked at the number. Not recognizing it, I answered cautiously. My heart sped up considerably when I heard Griff's voice. The movie started at six thirty, so he wanted to pick me up at work so we could get something to eat. I gave him the address to the bead shop, and he told me he'd be by at a quarter to five, if I could get off a little early. I told him no problem, and we said goodbye. He was definitely not a phone guy, not into chit-chat or shooting the breeze. All business, but that was fine, since I really wasn't in the mood to try and be clever and cute.

Now I had to figure out what to wear to work all day that would also look good for a date afterwards. I definitely had my work cut out for me, knowing I'd probably try on every outfit in my fairly limited closet. I could really use a close girlfriend right about now, I sighed. No use asking Jace's opinion, or worse yet, my mom's. I'd just have to guess. Man, I sucked at guessing. Oh well, better get started. This could take all night.

Some Food For Thought

Darkness filtered through my blinds and seeped down inside the window wells of my basement bedroom. It was late. My clothes, which took forever to finally choose, were draped over a chair for tomorrow, and I lay back in my bed, my gaze alternating from the haunted tree photo to the childhood collage on my bulletin board. My eyelids drooped in exhaustion, and I gave up and closed them against the confusion caused by the two sets of pictures. I repeated the words I used every night, hoping to persuade my mind to have a lucid dream. I had so many questions for Quinn, or for my subconscious. No, I wasn't going to think that. Please, let me see Quinn, I thought, as I sank into sleep.

The football stadium was crowded and noisy. I needed to find Griff. We had tickets next to each other, and for some reason I couldn't figure out the numbering system. A large man strolled past in a white, sequined Elvis costume. Huh. That was odd, even for a football game. Looking around, I realized that everyone swarming past me was wearing an outrageous costume. Was it Halloween? I couldn't remember. The crowd parted before me like a theater curtain, and my eyes became riveted on the gorgeous guy in front of me. Or at least on his abs. I blinked in surprise. It was Griff, and he was wearing some sexy costume that showed off his stomach muscles. I stood fascinated, with my mouth hanging open, not able to look away. Was this my lucky day or what?

My gaze was abruptly jerked from Griff's muscles to the girl at his side as she grabbed his hand. It was Randi, also dressed to kill in some little number with thigh-high boots. She gave him a way-too-intimate-for-public look and dragged him after her into the crowd.

What was going on? I thought Griff was meeting *me* here. Where did Randi come from, and how come everyone was dressed incredibly, except me? Where was my costume? I looked down in frustration at my stupid t-shirt and boring jeans.

"Hey," I started to go after them. I looked at the ticket in my hand and searched around for the corresponding gate, but the one I wanted was blocked off. Frustrated, I tried to get the attention of some of the stadium workers. No one would look at me. It was like I was invisible or didn't exist. *Argh!* I was getting really ticked off. Forget it, I thought angrily. Griff's welcome to skanky old Randi. I didn't care anymore. Spinning on my heel, I made to storm off and go home.

"Mia." I heard my name.

"Finally," I thought in relief.

"Griff, I can't find my seat." But Griff wasn't there, and now that I thought about it, that wasn't his voice at all. The voice was definitely familiar, though. I racked my brain for the face to go with the voice. Adrenaline surged through me as I made the connection. This was just a ridiculous dream. *Sheesh!* I couldn't believe it took me this long to figure it out.

I spun around and cried "Quinn!" feeling elated and excited.

He was there, smiling and looking gorgeous. I almost threw myself into his arms, but checked myself at the last second. He, however, didn't seem to have the same reservations as I did and scooped me up against his chest whispering, "Mia, you're back." We stayed that way for a few moments, until, feeling suddenly self-conscious, we broke apart. My face was flushed and I kept my eyes on my toes.

"Let's get out of here." Quinn took my hand and pulled me to the edge of the stadium. Yikes. We were higher up than I had realized.

"Come on," he urged, and began climbing over the railing.

I knew it was a dream, but it still looked frighteningly high. I thought about Sarah claiming that she was able to fly in her dreams. I desperately wished I knew what to do.

Quinn tried to pull me up and over the rail, but I panicked, yanking myself back. "I can't do it," I admitted miserably.

He stepped back down. "It's just a dream, remember. You can do anything."

"But I don't know how," I stalled.

"Okay, can you get us somewhere else without flying? I don't want to talk here." He was still holding my hand. I pulled away nervously and stuck my hands in my pockets, thinking about what I had read about lucid dreaming. Sometimes people could change their environment by going through a door. I turned around and spied a door marked Private. I would try that before I jumped off a three-story wall.

"Follow me. I'm going to try something else." I strode purposefully towards the door. I stopped briefly in front of it, imagining my nan's backyard on a warm summer afternoon. I reached for the doorknob and pulled it open expectantly.

As if in a trance, I crossed the threshold into that very familiar place, eyes raised to the beautiful trees that towered over me. I could feel Quinn behind me and heard the door click shut, blocking out the noise and confusion of the stadium. I felt the peaceful wind as I watched some playful grey squirrels chase each other up the side of the largest evergreen. I sat on the porch bench, happy to be here again. Quinn sat down next to me, straddling the backless bench. He took one of my hands, and I realized by his melancholy expression that this place didn't bring him any peace—if anything, it made him more distressed.

"I'm sorry, I thought you would like coming here," I sighed. "I can see I made a mistake." I figured I could open a door here and lead us to a more comfortable place easily enough. I started to stand, but he pulled me gently back down.

"No. This is the right place. It's painful, but it will help me tell you what you need to know." His expression was determined, his voice resolved.

My attention was glued to his green eyes, although his warm hand gripping mine was a bit of a distraction. "Tell me," I asked eagerly. "Hurry, before something wakes me up."

"Where to start?" he mused.

"Who are you? How old are you? Are you real or imaginary?" I began spouting questions until he held up his free hand.

"If you remember, it all started when my mother met my father. She was walking along a trail somewhere near here many years ago. My father had just left home. He was trying to escape being forced into a loveless marriage by his family. Refusal wasn't an option, so he left."

"Forced into marriage?" I interrupted. "I didn't know that even happened in the last century."

"It was very common in my father's family." Quinn squeezed my hand. "He was born into a very powerful and influential family where disobedience carried serious penalties. My father was an intelligent, independent thinker who didn't care about the consequences. When he refused to follow the path chosen for him, he had to flee from everything he knew and loved. But freedom, he thought, was worth the heavy cost.

"Then, by chance, my father met Anna. In spite of, or maybe because of, extreme circumstances, they fell in love. My father knew his parents would be furious, but he married her anyway. He could never give her the life he felt she deserved because they had to live in secret, always worried that his family would discover and separate them."

"Anna's family thought she was dead." I pulled my hand away rubbing the goose bumps springing up on my arms. "How awful for them, and for her," I murmured, trying to imagine what life would have been like for that young couple on the run.

"My mother had a terrible choice to make," Quinn nodded. "She had to choose between the man she loved and her family. After a while, her family gave up looking for her and even had a funeral, thinking she must be dead. They all accepted her supposed fate except for Marie, your nan.

"As twins, they were always incredibly in tune with each other. Marie insisted that Anna wasn't dead, claiming that she would have known in her heart if Anna had died. My mother soon realized Marie would never give up on her, and would have spent all of her time searching for her, wasting her life away. That was unbearable to my mother, so she revealed herself to her twin and told her everything."

I caught myself chewing on my lower lip and quickly stopped. "So Nan knew about your father's family, and she helped hide you. But then what happened? Where did your family go and how in the world are you able to visit me in my dreams?"

Quinn leaned forward on the bench, rubbing his forehead and running his fingers through his wild curls. I had to consciously keep my arms folded in order to squash my instinct to reach out and touch his hair.

"It's so complicated and the details are fuzzy, but I will try to explain what I can. I think my parents were found out, or someone they trusted betrayed them. They had a few friends who were helping them stay one step ahead of my father's family. One day, my parents took my sisters and me into deeper hiding than usual. They claimed it was just a precaution, but looking at their faces, I knew better.

"I refused to stay hidden at first. I wanted to go with my parents. They finally persuaded me it was necessary for me to protect my sisters. It was only supposed to be for a short time, a few weeks, maybe." His fists were clenched tightly, his body stiff and rigid with anger. "But obviously something went wrong. So wrong that my parents never returned, and now Marie is gone. Damn it all, I don't know what to do."

"But that was eight or nine years ago," I stammered in horror. "They've been missing that long? That can't be good," I finished in a hushed tone. I looked at his bowed head and gave in to my urge to touch his hair. "Quinn, I want to help," I said softly. "Please tell me what I can do."

My breath caught in my throat as he lifted his grief stricken eyes to mine. I was mesmerized, and I knew at that moment, without a doubt, that I would do anything to help this beautiful, melancholy boy. He took my hand from his hair and laid it against his cheek, closing his eyes.

"That means more to me than you know. Thank you." His voice was husky and warm, and sent a thrilling chill through me.

"The thing that worries me the most right now is the whereabouts of my sisters. We were separated, and now they are lost, as well as my parents, and Marie is dead." The tortured look in his eyes was devastating. "I am alone."

"Oh Quinn, I'm so sorry," I said gently. "But you aren't alone. Just tell me how I can help."

He looked intently at me for a moment then looked down. He opened his mouth as if to speak, and then he seemed to change his mind. He was squeezing my hand so fiercely without realizing it; I finally had to pull it away with an apologetic "*ouch.*"

"Sorry, Mia. I didn't hurt you, did I?" He took my hand back, rubbing it gently where he had gripped it so tightly just a second before.

"It's okay, really," I managed, feeling quite distracted by his massaging fingers.

Eventually, Quinn lifted his gaze back to my face. "Mia, do you remember seeing a bracelet and ring that matched your nan's necklace?"

"No. I mean, I remember them, but I haven't seen them lately. Nan didn't send them to me, just the necklace. I can search the house tomorrow if you want." Suddenly, my dad's promise sprang to mind. "Hey, next month my dad and I are going back to Nan's house to clean it up and go through some of her old stuff. If I can't find the ring and bracelet at my house, I'm sure they will still be at Nan's, don't you think?"

"You're going to Marie's house? There's a chance my parents have been trying to find me, but they didn't know where to look. Maybe they don't know where I am. How close do you live to her house?"

"Not very close. It'll probably take two days of driving to get there, unless we fly. Where was your father's family from anyway? Did they live close to Seattle?" His fingers, still rubbing my hand absently, made coherent thoughts a bit more challenging.

He laughed bitterly. "Not really."

"What?" I cocked my head and pulled my hand away. "There's a whole lot you aren't telling me, isn't there?"

He looked down, guilt etched into his expression. "Yes," he admitted. "But it is so hard to explain, so completely unbelievable. I'm afraid to tell you. Afraid you will wake up and rationalize it all away, and never even try to talk to me again."

"You trust me so little," I exclaimed, hurt.

"I trust you completely." The force behind his words took me aback for a moment. "I just don't know how to convince you that, when you're awake, I am still real, as real as you are."

"It *is* confusing when I wake up," I acknowledged. "But if you tell me more, it would make more sense in the real world, I think. Wouldn't it?" I was starting to fret, and began trying to tuck strands of my short hair behind my ears like I always did when I was nervous.

His eyes were drawn to my unconscious movements. "So why did you cut off your hair? I remember you crying when you had to cut off a big chunk of hair that had gum stuck in it." His eyes, studying me so closely, started to make me embarrassed. "It's such a remarkable color," he added softly.

Nice way to change the subject, I thought, feeling myself blush. "Hey, I happen to like short hair." It came out more defensively than I meant it to. "Besides, it really ticked off my mom when I cut it. She actually cried when I got back from the salon, can you believe it?"

"You had long hair in your last dream when we met. Could you do it again?"

"I don't know," I admitted. "Maybe, but why should I?" I demanded. "I like my hair this way." He was grinning at me mischievously, an eyebrow cocked. "Hey, I don't change my hair for anyone but me." His challenging smile got bigger.

Feeling rather ridiculous, I gave in. "Oh, fine. I'll try." I closed my eyes and imagined myself with long hair again, the way it waved down my back and how it felt when the wind blew it. I opened my eyes. Quinn looked like he was trying not to laugh. I shook my head. Nope, still short. I shrugged.

"I still don't know exactly how this lucid dreaming works. I guess I don't care about long hair that much. Too bad. You'll have to deal with the short version." I scrunched up my nose and made a face. "If we're playing change-the-subject, why don't you show me how flying works? It looked like you were ready to take a flying leap out of the stadium." I stood up with my hands on my hips, deciding to turn the tables back on him.

Smiling smugly, he stepped up onto the bench and I gasped out loud as he rose gracefully into the air. I don't know what I expected. Awkwardness, arm-flapping, or something silly, I guess. I was surprised at the elegance of dream flight. He was amazing to watch. No wonder lucid dreaming had helped out

Sarah when she had cancer. Flying like that was bound to make you feel free and alive.

Watching him show off at a distance, I was able to think clearly for a minute. He was obviously an expert at manipulating dreams, and I wondered again how he was able to enter *my* dreams. I remembered reading some theories about astral projection on a couple of free-thinking lucid dream websites. Could that be what he was doing? But what did that have to do with my nan's necklace? I realized I needed to hurry and ask him more questions before this dream ended.

I waved to get his attention. He grinned back and held out his arms to me. I expected him to land next to me on the bench, but the next thing I knew, I was swept into the air. I cried out at first, squeezing my eyes shut in fear, trying to overcome my irrational fear of heights.

"It's okay," Quinn whispered in my ear. "You are safe with me. I won't let you fall. Let me show you how wonderful it can be."

My heart pounded a desperate staccato in my chest while I pried open my eyelids. Expecting an overwhelming vertigo, I was not prepared for the beauty of what I saw. The treetops blowing in the wind, the houses spread out below. The feeling of freedom. I slowly released the death grip I had around Quinn's neck, and began to enjoy the magnificent view.

"Quinn," I breathed. "It's the most wonderful, I mean incredible..." I stopped. Nothing I could say would describe the way this felt. I looked at him, trying to convey my feelings. Our eyes met and he understood.

I never want to wake up, I thought. Please let this dream last forever. How could real life compete with something like this? I sighed, and buried my face in his shoulder, enjoying his clean, woodsy scent. I wanted so badly for Quinn to be real. "Quinn," I pleaded. "Won't you please tell me the truth about what's going on?"

Quinn landed us lightly on the porch again. His arms were still around me, clasping me tightly to him, my arms still encircling his neck. "Haven't you figured it out yet?" I shook my head mutely. "Think about it. When did I start visiting your dreams?"

"After I found my nan's necklace," I murmured, spellbound by his nearness.

"Exactly." He brushed back my bangs with a light touch of his fingers. "Don't you see? I'm trapped in your nan's necklace." He leaned over and touched his forehead to mine. I closed my eyes, trying to absorb what he had just told me, rational thought vanishing away as he held me close.

"I need you to free me, Mia. Will you help me?"

"But how? I don't understand." My voice faltered as his hands moved to my face, tilting my head up toward him. My eyes flew open wide in surprise. "Oh, my gosh! He's going to kiss me." I thought my heart was beating fast before, but that was nothing compared to what it was doing now. I thought it was going to fly straight out of my chest. Quinn looked down at me, a question in his eyes. He was asking if this was okay. My throat closed up; words were impossible. I closed my eyes as he leaned forward and laid his lips softly on mine.

My eyes flew open in bewilderment, and then snapped shut in angry frustration. I was awake, and I was alone in my room. My heart was still hammering painfully in my chest, but Quinn was gone. I had gotten so excited, I had woken myself up. I sat up in an angry stupor, my arms wrapped around my legs, my face buried in my knees. "Quinn," I whispered. "I promise I'll help you. Oh, please be real," I repeated over and over. "You have to be real." I sat there for a long time before my alarm finally went off.

Conflicting Feelings

I arrived at work a little late the next morning. Luckily, no one seemed to notice and the store was still empty of early-morning customers. Good thing I had picked out my clothes the night before, because I got ready like a zombie. My mind was trapped in last night's dream, and I was having a very difficult time keeping my focus here in the real world. Fortunately, my dad dropped me off at work, since I was in no position to be behind the wheel of a car.

I headed straight for the back room, hoping to help with inventory or restocking bins, since I was afraid my attitude to the customers would be surly at best. Yup, today I'd be hard pressed to be perky and polite—better to hide instead. Luckily, the store wasn't too busy, considering it was a Saturday; most of the customers were attending the scheduled class and didn't need my help. I skulked in the back and straightened up for a while until I felt ready to work a register.

I showed off my new bracelet to the other employees, who all wanted the pattern. My boss suggested I work up a proposal for a chain-making class, if I wanted to teach some Saturday in the spring or maybe next summer. My mood rose with my ego being stroked, and I forced myself to think about my date that night. Before my dream last night I was so excited. Now I felt ambivalent, conflicted. Was I betraying Quinn if I went out with Griff? And was it fair to Griff if I was pining away after my dream guy? What a mess this had become in the last day.

Time seemed to be set on fast forward since I was anxious about the evening. What was up with that? Time usually went so slowly at work. It was four thirty before I knew it, and I went reluctantly to the bathroom to check how I looked. I raised my eyebrows a few times, trying to ease my frown lines away. I freshened up my mascara and put on lip gloss. I practiced smiling a few times, but my smiles looked awkward and false. "Whatever," I shrugged.

I glanced down at Quinn's necklace. After last night, it was hard to think of it as my nan's anymore. I had hardly left it alone all day, touching it constantly, trying to connect it to the boy in my dreams. I kept trying to imagine Quinn somehow trapped inside, waiting for me to get him out. It sounded ridiculous in the daylight, but I could feel something when I held tight to the clover charm, some kind of emotional remnant left over from the night before. Somehow, I knew it was true. I just didn't know how yet.

The bathroom door flew open and my friend Jane burst inside. "There is a gorgeous guy outside asking for you, lucky girl," she grinned. I pasted a smile on and followed her out the door.

"See you later," I called over my shoulder as I pushed open the heavy front door.

"Have a good time." I tried to ignore the giggling.

Griff was leaning against his car, looking bad-boy beautiful with his dark, long hair tucked behind one ear and his black leather jacket and boots. I had to admit I felt a thrill just seeing him here, but it was tempered by my confusion over my feelings for Quinn. What was I going to do? My mind told me to forget my dream and have fun. My heart warned me to be careful. I tried to ignore them both and remain casual, calm, and unflustered. Yeah right. That was going to be a piece of cake.

Griff eased himself up and opened the door for me. I had a mind-flash of the last time I had seen him in this car. I flushed a bit, remembering the state I was in, and was thankful that I had taken the time last night so I could make a better impression today.

"Nice jacket," was the extent of his notice. That figured.

"Thanks," was my brief reply. I had found my short black jacket in a vintage clothing store as part of a two-piece '50s-style dress. It looked really cool over a pair of jeans and white t-shirt. I swung into his black Mercedes, way nicer than most of the cars parked in the school lot, and thought this boy might look tough, but he definitely came from some money. I wondered where we were going to eat.

His camera, sitting between us, gave me an easy topic for conversation. "Take some pictures today?" I picked up the heavy manual camera, carefully checking out the huge lens. That had to be expensive. "A few," he replied evasively. "I was hoping to take some more before it gets too dark. Is it okay if we get our food to go? I thought you might like to see that gargoyle house."

"Sure," I agreed, surprised at the evening's turn of events. "Will we have time before the movie?"

"It's not that far." He pulled into a Mexican restaurant. "Is this okay?"

I nodded, and we stood in a quick-moving line; he ordered a burrito and I got a taco salad. Back in the car, sipping a couple of sodas, we headed out into a part of town that I wasn't familiar with. Most of the houses were very old and rundown, but a new trend was emerging and several homes had been purchased by those wealthy enough to restore the houses, top to bottom. The area was an eclectic mix of battered and beautiful.

The gargoyle house hunched gloomily at the end of a cul-de-sac with a For Sale sign protruding from its lawn. We sat in the car and ate since the wind had picked up and it was too cold to eat outside. I didn't mind. This was much better than a dark Italian restaurant, where I would feel awkward and uncomfortable—and be forced to look Griff in the face while I ate.

We munched mostly in silence, both of us studying the foreboding-looking house. Griff told me he had discovered it when his parents were searching for a new house in this area. He had made friends with the selling agent, and she was cool with him coming over to take pictures anytime. I was glad about that, not wanting the evening to end with us being caught trespassing and running from the cops. Although that would be more memorable than most dates I'd been on.

After stuffing our trash back into the carry-out bag and tossing it on the back seat, we got out to check out all the gargoyles. The sun was setting and the dusky sky made an appropriate backdrop for the spooky house. Griff snapped a couple of photos as we picked our way through the overgrown grass and weeds. The garden in the back had taken over completely, running amok through the whole yard. Several gargoyles peeked sinisterly from behind untidy shrubbery.

I stood gazing at the gargoyle on the roof, remembering the photo I had dust spotted and comparing the picture to the real thing. Out of the corner of my eye, I caught a movement and turned to see Griff lowering his camera.

"Did you just take some pictures of me?" I accused huffily. "I thought you were taking pictures of gargoyles. Wait," I held up my hand at his grin. "Don't answer that. I just set myself up for that one, and I don't need the punch line."

He came up close, still smiling. "I couldn't resist the expression on your face, so I just started snapping. Sorry. I should have asked first."

"That's okay," I muttered. "Just don't be disappointed. I'm not that photogenic."

"I don't believe that," he asserted confidently. "Not with your cheekbones and eyes."

"*Pfff*" I snorted, trying to blow off his compliment. He probably used that photography line on dozens of girls, and I wasn't going to fall for it.

"Here, I'll take some more and prove it to you." He raised his camera and I darted away. "No thanks. Why don't you show me which one of these is your favorite instead?"

After a short pause, he agreed. "It's over here, by what used to be a pond." We carefully followed cracked stepping-stones to the remains of a decorative pond. The water had dried up long ago, and scraggily weeds grew haphazardly in and around it. In the middle, on a large stone, crouched a very small gargoyle. It was still in good condition, I was surprised to note, made from a lovely white stone I thought might be marble. Despite the beauty of the stone, the gargoyle's appearance was particularly hideous, and I felt a chill creep up my spine.

Griff took a few photos in the final bit of light. We'd have to get out soon, before it became too dark to find our way through the maze of weeds without a flashlight. I rubbed my arms, trying to fend off the cold and creepy chill that had gathered around me. I closed my eyes, waiting for Griff to hurry up and finish. Unconsciously, I reached for the charm on Quinn's necklace. Feeling strangely comforted, I opened my eyes and again realized Griff had been shooting pictures of me.

"Stop that," I ordered, irritated. "I didn't agree to have my picture taken." I knew I sounded grumpier than called for, but he was making me feel very uncomfortable.

Griff studied my annoyed face and said, "I thought you were just acting coy. Most pretty girls I've met go out of their way to have their pictures taken. I didn't expect you to be any different."

Now he was really bugging me. "Yeah? Are you lumping me in the same category as Randi? That's insulting, you know." I turned sharply before he could reply and started to stalk back to the car, done with this little outing.

I flipped open my cell phone to check the time. We would have to hurry if we were going to make the movie in time. I hoped he had the foresight to get advance tickets; otherwise, this would be a very short date. Maybe that would be just as well.

I was concentrating so hard on wading through the tall, snarled grass that I almost didn't spot them. Two figures standing still by the side of the house. I froze, not knowing what to do. Strangers lurking in the shadows of an empty house could only mean trouble. As the panic set in, I turned blindly and ran smack into Griff. He grabbed my shoulders, steadying me.

"Someone's by the house," I whispered fiercely. "What should we do?"

"Where?" He had his arm wrapped protectively around my shoulders.

"Right over there." I paused. "Oh crap, they're gone. No wait, they're over there." The figures were edging around the side of the fence slowly.

"What can you see?" Griff asked confused.

"Those two guys. They're trying to get behind us," I hissed urgently. "We need to get out of here, now!" I pleaded. I took his hand and yanked him toward the front of the house. I stumbled over a tree root sticking out of the ground and would have fallen except for Griff's support. We tore through the front yard to the car, which Griff unlocked on the run. We dove into the car, Griff floored it, and with a squeal of tires, we were away.

I rested my head on the headrest, still shuddering in fear and panting in relief. "We got away," I gasped. "I didn't know if we would."

We stopped at a red light and Griff looked over at me. "What exactly did you see?" he asked curiously.

"Didn't you see them sneaking around?" I saw his frown and added, "There were a couple of guys creeping into the yard, I swear."

"Hey, it's okay. I believe you." He looked more thoughtful than concerned, though. Someone honked behind us. The light had changed to green, and Griff eased out into the intersection. I sat back moodily. He didn't believe me, I could tell. This night was turning into a mess. I decided to keep my mouth shut the rest of the way to the theater.

We made it just in time for a quick bathroom break and a bucket of popcorn before the movie started. Not wanting to explain my disgust of popcorn, I said I still wasn't hungry, but made sure I had a Diet Coke. I could use a caffeine boost, now that the adrenaline from our impromptu run had died away. We managed to find a seat in the back of the theater on the side, and although we had to climb over several people, at least the movie hadn't started yet. I hated coming into a movie late.

Griff was making a concerted effort to be nice. I'm sure he was wondering how his trip to the gargoyle house had gone so wrong. I tried to make nice as well, but I'm just not very good at hiding my feelings.

Luckily, the movie was amazing on the big screen. Griff had never seen anything by Miyazaki, and it was fun to watch the film again with someone who didn't know what to expect. I felt the tension flow out of me as the movie progressed. The quality of the storytelling and animation carried me into another world of magic and adventure, and I succumbed to the emotional rollercoaster ride. When I leaned over and whispered to Griff that the scene coming up was my favorite, his amused blue eyes caught me by surprise.

"What?" I whispered distractedly.

"Nothing," he whispered back. "I've never seen anyone so into a movie before."

I rolled my eyes and shushed him in time for my favorite scene. But his comment made me feel self-conscious about my reactions. During the rest of the movie, I kept giving him sidelong glances to see if he was watching me or the movie.

As the credits rolled and the soundtrack played, I sighed happily, glad we had made it to the movie in time. "So, what did you think?" I ventured at last, breaking the mood.

"I think I might have to watch some more anime," Griff smiled. "But it wouldn't be as much fun without you beside me."

I knew it was childish, but I couldn't stop myself from sticking my tongue out.

"Is all anime this good?" he asked, laughing.

"Depends on what you think is good. There are all different levels of quality, like in any other genre. Some is good, some is awesome. My favorite is Miyazaki, because I love his sense of storytelling and all the magic, of course."

I kept up a steady stream of animated babble all the way to the car. My mood having shifted dramatically, I felt like this date had been alright after all. I didn't feel so giddy about him anymore, which was nice, and my guilt about my feelings for Quinn was assuaged. I talked with him like I would have talked to Jace, sort of, as long as I didn't look at him. His good looks still made me a little crazy. But I was handling it in a way I hadn't before. That had to be good, right?

I handled it all the way home. We chatted about anime and avoided any mention of the gargoyle house misadventure, and I was lulled into a comfortable frame of mind. It wasn't until he parked in front of my house and turned toward me that the nerves kicked in again. Those light-blue eyes surrounded by thick dark lashes made my stomach do flip-flops. I looked hastily away, my long earrings swinging against my shoulders.

"Did you make your earrings?" he asked quietly in the dimly lit car.

"*Mm-hmm.*" I still wouldn't look at him. "Silver and moonstones."

"Quite pretty." I could tell he was trying to get me to look at him, but I didn't trust myself. I thought about Quinn instead.

He tried a different tactic. "Thanks for coming with me tonight. The night wasn't a total loss, was it?"

I glanced up quickly, and then stared at my hands in my lap again. "It was fine. And the movie was great."

Then he leaned closer. "I really do believe that you saw someone at that house, you know."

My eyes flashed up again. "I don't think you do. You didn't seem worried at all. Well, let me tell you, I'm not in the habit of seeing things that aren't there." I stopped babbling, realizing what I just said. Damn it, Quinn is *not* imaginary, I thought angrily. I shut my eyes.

Griff distracted me by touching my shoulder. "Hey, I'm not making fun of you, if that's what you think." He looked closely at my expression. "Are you okay?"

I nodded glumly.

"Despite everything, I had a really good time with you. You are hands-down the most interesting girl I have ever met." His teeth looked very white as he smiled at me. "I shouldn't have brought up what happened earlier. I'm sorry." I gazed into his sincere-looking eyes and felt bad for causing a scene. What did it matter if anyone was there anyway? We were safe, right? Wait, did he just call me interesting? Yikes! I really needed to get out of there; his smile was starting to set off my alarm bells.

"I'm sorry, too. Let's just forget it." I put my hand on the door handle. "I'll, um, have those photos of yours done as soon as I can. Probably a few at a time, okay?"

I scrambled out the door before he could answer and started heading up the driveway. He had hopped out his door and caught up with me, quick as lightning. I turned and said, "Hey, thanks for the invite. I'll see you at school on Monday."

He tilted his head and gave me this enigmatic half-smile, as if he could read my thoughts and confusion. "You are quite refreshing to be around, did you know that?"

I had no response to that, so I shrugged, inching my way up the path to the front door. "Thanks again," I repeated, trying to end the conversation as he followed me.

"Are you scared of me?" he asked with one eyebrow quirked.

That did it. "No," I stopped inching and faced him defiantly. He was so tall I had to look way up. "Why would I be?"

"I don't know. It seems like you're running away from me." He leaned against the porch rail and tucked a strand of hair behind his ear.

"Nope," I denied. "Not running away. It's just late and I, uh, thought you might want to get on your way," I finished lamely, realizing it probably wasn't even ten.

"You don't want to invite me in," he reasoned. "That's fine." He straightened up.

I looked at him suspiciously. "You know if I invite you in, you'll have to meet my parents. Not really on the favorites list for most guys."

"I don't mind, unless you don't want me to." He waited patiently for me to make up my mind.

"Well, okay," I conceded. "But they'll be kind of nosey. Hope you don't mind Twenty Questions."

"No prob," he grinned. "I can take it."

"Just don't say I didn't warn you," I muttered as I opened the door.

I could smell something delicious baking as I walked into the hall. My stomach actually growled in response, so loudly I'm sure Griff could hear it.

I decided on a preemptive strike. "Mom, I brought home a guest. I sure hope that cake's about done."

We entered the warm kitchen, still cluttered with bowls and spoons and measuring cups. My mom was leaning over, unloading the clean dishes from the dishwasher. She paused, a cheerful smile on her face, and wiped off her hands before coming over to us. "Hi, I'm Sharon. You must be Griff. Come on in." She gestured to the bar and we both sat down. "Sorry, this is still a mess. I was watching one of those cooking shows and I had to try out one of their recipes. I don't know what came over me. I'm not usually much of a cook."

"It smells great to me," Griff smiled, oh-so-charmingly.

"Well, I guess we'll find out in about twenty minutes," she smiled back, thoroughly charmed. I rolled my eyes. This was not going to be fun, I could tell.

I sat back and watched Griff banter easily with my mom about cooking, her work at the junior high, and where he was from—which turned out to be California. He was good, I had to admit it. He didn't falter until he asked where my hair color came from. My mom is a natural blonde. "From my first husband," she said, lightly enough, but I detected an edge in her voice. Griff must have heard it, too, because he changed the subject immediately.

After what seemed like an eternity, the cake came out of the oven. It smelled heavenly, and we each ate a huge slice with ice cream melting on top. "*Mmmm*," I murmured. "Mom, that was so good. I hope you wrote down the recipe, because you *have* to make that again."

"I printed it out from the show's website. Griff, would you like me to make a copy for your mom?"

"That would be great. I think that was the best piece of cake I've ever eaten. Thanks, Sharon." He was still on a roll, and my mom was eating it up.

"Sure thing. I have a couple of things to finish upstairs, so I'll bring a copy down in a bit." Oh crap, she was trying to give us some alone time. "I can get it, Mom," I offered.

"Not to worry," she chided. "I'll be down in a few minutes." She gave me a little wink before heading upstairs. I groaned inwardly and got up off the stool. "Want some more?" I asked, snitching a lick from the knife.

"I'm good." Griff stretched and ran his hand through his hair. Don't even look, I scolded myself sharply, and dropped the knife into the dishwasher. I began loading the dishwasher to keep my hands occupied, and Griff started handing me things from the counter. Thanks a lot, I thought sarcastically, as we were done in no time. Now what?

I spun around to wipe my hands on the dishcloth hanging on the oven and I bumped right into Griff, not knowing he was right behind me, my dripping hands leaving marks on his t-shirt.

"Sorry. I'm sure it will dry quickly. It's just water." Flustered, I backed away.

"Don't sweat it." He brushed at the dampness.

I grasped at an idea. "Would you like to see some of the jewelry I make?"

"Do you have a portfolio?"

"More like a cardboard box. I'm not very organized," I admitted. "I'll go get it," I said, thankful to have something to do.

I dug around in my closet until I found the right box, snatching it to take upstairs, when I discovered Griff leaning in the doorway, gazing around my very messy room.

"I see you found a frame." He nodded toward his tree picture on my wall. Then scanning my walls, he noticed my bulletin board. "You're a good sketch artist. Who is this? Someone from school?" He pointed to my sketch of Quinn.

There was no way I was going to discuss my dreams with Griff, so I lied. "A friend from Washington." It wasn't really a lie, I guess. But I could feel my color rising. "I found my box. Let's go upstairs. There's nowhere to sit down here." I used my box to push him out of the room and toward the stairs.

We sat back down at the cleaned-off counter and I showed him my jewelry. He admired them all, but hardly touched anything. What was it with boys and jewelry?

That giddy feeling crept over me again and I felt clumsy and flustered. I wished Griff wasn't sitting so close. Even though he was being extra-complimentary about everything, my emotions were shot, and I could tell I wasn't going to last much longer. Tonight had been emotionally charged, to say the least. Not to mention my dream the night before, and getting up so early. I was so worn out, I really wanted to go to bed.

He leaned over close, and before I knew it, he had reached out to touch Quinn's necklace. It was way too intimate a gesture for me, and I pulled back nervously, my eyes startled into looking into his eyes.

"Where did you get your necklace again?" he asked quietly.

I found myself answering, "It belonged to my nan."

"Can I see it?" I couldn't seem to look away from those intense blue eyes.

"I don't like to take it off," I stalled, for some reason.

"Please," he insisted.

"Well, I don't know," I said, but my hands were creeping up around my neck. I had just undone the clasp when I heard my mom coming down the stairs, announcing loudly that she had the recipe. I re-clasped the necklace and scooted off the stool quickly.

Griff slowly slid off his stool and my mom handed him the recipe, then apologized that it was getting late and time for guests to be getting home. "Go, Mom," I thought. She discreetly went back upstairs. I made myself busy packing things up.

"Thanks for the great night." My voice sounded shaky, even to me. What had just happened? I wondered. My brain still felt fuzzy and I blinked several times.

"Was it?" Griff asked.

"Sure," I turned around against the counter and looked him in the face bravely. "I'll see you Monday." I slipped past him and went to open the front door, hoping he'd take the big fat hint.

"See you, Mia," he said quietly, and paused in front of me. I dropped my eyes quickly to the floor.

"Bye Griff," I whispered.

He stayed still for several seconds, and then he ran a finger softly down my cheek to my jaw line. By the time I had a chance to shudder, he was gone. I closed the door and leaned against it in relief.

"Talk to you in the morning," I shouted to my mom so I could make my escape without interference. I was so exhausted that I barely made it down the stairs. I threw off my clothes and dove into bed, practically passing out the second my head hit the pillow.

Hide and Seek

I woke slowly, feeling drugged and slow. I had been running from shadowy men through a dark street. I pounded on doors for help, but no one would answer me. None of the people I passed on the street could see anyone following me, and they scurried away from me as if I had a contagious disease or something. I would have been put out if I hadn't been so scared.

The light coming through my blinds teased my tired eyes. I felt frustrated that I hadn't seen Quinn in this latest dream. How equally frustrating it must be for him to watch me in all manner of ridiculous situations, and only occasionally be able to talk to me. And touch me. And—oh, stop! I wasn't going there. Well, maybe just for a minute. "Ah, Quinn," I breathed, wishing I could go back to sleep.

Eventually, I looked over at my clock—10:45. Nice to be able to catch up on my sleep a bit. Yawning and stretching, I climbed out of bed and hunted for my running shoes.

I needed to get some exercise and let my brain sort out last night's adventures.

The weather had warmed up enough that I didn't need to bundle up. And so, dressed in shorts and a sweatshirt, I took off into the foothills, welcoming the burn in my lungs and the pull on my muscles. I ran until my head felt clear, and then turned around, mulling things over on the downhill.

My initial infatuation with Griff seemed to have cooled off. He was still quite a treat to look at, but he seemed sort of hazardous to my state of mind. I kept trying to figure out why. He certainly acted nice enough, especially with my mom. So what was my problem? I didn't know. Maybe I just needed some space. My independence felt threatened by his ability to turn me into a giddy girl, which in turn made me feel vulnerable and helpless. *Argh!* I didn't like that one bit.

As I stretched my legs in the front yard, Jace wandered over. I hoped he wasn't still sulking. He sat next to me on the grass. He was wearing baggy jeans and a t-shirt. His normally spiky black hair was drooping over his forehead into his eyes. He brushed at it absently.

"So, I was kind of a jerk Friday. Sorry." He had apology written all over his face.

"It's cool," I smiled. "Still want to see a movie tonight?"

"You took the words right out of my mouth. You know, that's kind of a gross saying." He started miming the action.

I laughed. "And people say I'm weird. So, what's playing?"

"How about *Steamboy*?" I've never seen that one, and it's supposed to be really good." Jace lay back in the sun, head cradled on his hands.

"Sounds fun. Just tell me what time." I had finished stretching and I lay on the grass next to him, crushing dried crunchy leaves under me. It was a gorgeous fall afternoon, still warm enough to be hanging outside, and the trees were stunning, sporting colorful leaves. Piles of pumpkins were stacked on our neighbors' porches. It was definitely my favorite time of year. I sighed contentedly.

"How was your date?" Jace ventured tentatively. I told him about the strange trip to the gargoyle house and getting mad when Griff took my picture. I tried to explain the creepy men, but it sounded so stupid in the sunshine. He wanted to know about the movie, and I told him that was the best part of the evening.

"I wanted to see that movie, you know. I'm jealous you got to see it on the big screen. So what did you do after?"

"Griff wanted to come to my house, even if it meant meeting my parents. Isn't that odd?" I rolled to my side, my head propped on my arm.

"I know I'm never anxious to meet a girl's parents," Jace confirmed.

"He was Mr. Charming to my mom, of course. It made me really uncomfortable. I was actually very relieved when he left."

"I thought you were crazy about him? Sounds like that's past." Jace eyed me thoughtfully. "It's because he's acting like he likes you now. That always scares you off, doesn't it?"

"No," I glared back. "Well, I don't know. I have to admit, I hate feeling dependent on anyone but me. It's annoying to have someone have power over me, making me all giddy and goofy. And sometimes Griff makes me nervous. He's asked to see my necklace twice, and even though I've sworn never to take it off again, both times I found myself ready to hand it over. I would have, if we hadn't been interrupted. I don't like that at all."

"*Hmmm*," was the total of Jace's helpful advice.

"Whatever. I think I'll just avoid him for a while. I need to get a handle on how I feel."

"He might not let you ignore him," Jace speculated.

"He only asked me out to pay me back for helping him. He'll probably be asking someone else out next week." I wasn't sure how I felt about that, either.

"As far as I know, you're the only girl he's asked out since moving here. If you remember, Randi asked *him*."

"That's not helping," I sighed. "Man, I *so* need a shower." I stood up and began walking to the house. "What time is the movie?" I asked over my shoulder.

"Nine o'clock. Let's get something to eat first, okay? Come by around seven or so." Jace got to his feet and started heading home. "I have to finish that stupid English essay before we go."

"'Kay, see you then." I hopped up the steps in a much better mood than when I woke up.

As I ate a late afternoon lunch, I listened to my mom go on and on about what a nice boy I had brought home last night. All I had to do was smile and nod and make a few monosyllabic remarks to keep her happy. I think she worried about me not dating much. Not that she would really get it; she was the cheerleading, drama club, student council type. I'm sure she never lacked for a date. I headed downstairs with her gushing enthusiasm clinging to me like lint.

After I showered and finished the last bit of my homework, I spread out Griff's photos on the floor. He'd given me fourteen, and while most were fairly clean, there were a couple that I knew would take a while to spot. I still had a couple of hours before going over to Jace's house, so I got started. The sooner I finished these and gave them back, the easier Griff would be to avoid. Maybe I would chicken out and have Jace take them to

Griff in his photography class. That would be lame, but probably safer for me. No. I could at least take them to him in person. I wouldn't be *that* rude.

I spotted ten of the fourteen and then cleaned up for the movie. I had hoped that my mom and dad would go out today, so I could search the house for the bracelet and ring Quinn had asked me about, but no luck. I thought again how someone could be trapped in a necklace, and it still didn't make any sense. I felt like my mind was in some kind of holding pattern, reserving judgment until more information was collected. But wow, Quinn had kissed me. Granted, I had woken up before it got anywhere, but that was definitely the most exciting moment in my life so far. *Hmm.* Kind of pathetic that it was in a dream. That would change soon, I told myself sternly. We would meet in real life soon. I just knew it.

I wished I could tell someone. Not Jace or my parents. Maybe I could talk to Sarah, but I wasn't sure what she would say. And what would I say? "Guess what? I'm totally infatuated with a dream boy. Isn't that great?" I thought maybe I would keep that information to myself a little bit longer.

JACE AND I were eating lunch inside against the blowing wind, discussing every detail of the movie from the night before. Things seemed back to normal somehow. We had come to school a little early that morning so I could have Jace's support as I handed off Griff's finished photos. I wasn't in the mood to face him alone yet. He was in the lab early, of course, and I gave him the ten prints I had spotted, promising the rest by the end of the week. Before a whole conversation could ensue it was time to go to class. *Whew!* I felt relieved to have gotten that done so smoothly. Now I could pretend he didn't exist until the end of the week.

I laughed as Jace mimed a scene from the movie, glad that things were back to normal with us as well. I couldn't stand the thought of being separated from Jace for any length of time. He could always make me laugh. And I could relax and just be myself around him.

"What should we do for Halloween this Saturday?" I asked when he sat down.

"No way, is that *this* Saturday? Let's go to that big farm with the corn maze and haunted house. I hear it's really scary, at least for chicks," he grinned at me.

"Not me," I argued. "Those things are so fake."

"But this one isn't just a haunted house; part of it is out in the woods and the guys who dress up and run the show actually grab people. Michelle's friend got picked up and thrown over a guy's shoulder. She totally freaked out when he started carrying her into the woods."

"No way!" I was outraged. "They can't do that. They'd get their butts sued if anyone got hurt."

Jace shrugged. "That's just what I heard. I don't know how they can get away with it. Still want to go?" Jace made an evil leer at me.

"I'm in," I said, punching Jace in the chest. "If anyone touches me they are gonna be totally surprised," I threatened.

"Not with a girly punch like that," Jace teased. "They'd just fall over laughing. Of course, then they'd be too busy laughing to carry you off into the forest. Good strategy."

"You are *so* going to get it." I started punching Jace again until we both cracked up. "Okay, this week you'd better teach me some self-defense moves. I know you took karate for, what, ten years?"

Jace raised his eyebrow at me. "I thought you were Miss Pacifist."

"It couldn't hurt to be prepared." I folded my arms and thought of those strangers at the gargoyle house. The bell rang, breaking my train of thought, and Jace and I took off for English.

All that week I dodged Griff. I was always pleasant and friendly when I saw him, but I made sure I was never alone with him. I was creative. Grabbing a friend to talk to, pretending to forget something at the library, staying after school to talk to a teacher. I thought I was so clever.

Friday after school I was hiding—I mean relaxing—in Jace's car, waiting for him to finish up, when a knock on the window made me jump. I rolled down the window, reluctantly, as I recognized Griff. I tried to act casual, but I knew my cheeks were pinker than usual.

I turned down the CD and Griff said, "That's a great song."

"I love this CD. Have you heard the whole thing yet?" I asked, finding my tongue worked.

"I haven't bought it yet." Griff leaned his arms on the open window and I pulled back, fiddling with the volume.

"Jace and I were talking in class." A red flag went up in my head. That couldn't be good. "We were thinking of maybe making this Halloween a double-date. He's asking Michelle and I could drive, since my car is bigger. What do you say?"

There was no way to get out of this gracefully, and he knew it. I could tell by the amused look on his face. He waited patiently for my response, watching my emotions play over my face. Fine, I thought. He wasn't going to make me stay home on Halloween. So I gave in.

"That sounds like fun."

"Good." His smile was assured and confident. I wanted to wipe it off his handsome face. He knew I'd say yes, and that made me mad.

As if reading my thought, Griff stood up. "One more thing." He handed me a manila envelope from his portfolio. "These are for you."

"I'm not finished with the others," I protested.

"They aren't for you to spot unless you want to. They're for you to keep."

He winked at me and walked away.

I sat there frozen for a second. Did he actually wink at me? He was *so* infuriating. I tore open the envelope in a snit.

I was still looking at the photos when Jace finally got into the car. He looked worried. "So did Griff talk to you?"

I nodded.

"So are you cool with it?"

"I guess," I replied distractedly.

I was rereading Griff's note as Jace picked up one of the photos from my lap.

Mia,

I knew you would be photogenic when I took these, but I had no idea just how beautifully

they would turn out. The camera loves you. Sure you don't want me to take some more?

Griff

I swallowed hard, lifting up one of the photos. It was me, and yet, not me.

"Are these the photos Griff took? The ones that made you so mad?" Jace turned to me. "Because these are the best pictures I've ever seen of you. They hardly even look like you. Uh, no offense." Jace grabbed one of the other pictures. "I think you owe Griff an apology."

"Maybe," I hedged. They had turned out amazing, although I'd have preferred it if he had asked to take my picture first. The quality of the photos had a strange effect on my image. They gave me this ethereal, haunted look, like the rest of his portfolio. I had to admit that they made me prettier than I thought I could be, but the mood of the photos made me uneasy.

I stuffed them back into the envelope along with the note, not wanting to talk about them anymore. There were other things to discuss with Jace.

"How could you set me up like this?" I grumbled. "I had to say yes. What did you and Griff talk about anyway?"

Jace at least had the grace to look guilty. "Griff asked me about you. He thinks you're playing hard to get, you know, with all the avoidance and games."

"What!" I exclaimed, slouching back into the seat with my arms folded across my chest. "He is so completely full of himself," I seethed.

"I told him you don't play games. Not sure he believed me, but I did try." Jace started the car. "He wanted to ask you out again for Halloween, and I thought you might be more comfortable if it was the four of us. Was I wrong?"

"No," I admitted. "Thanks, Jace. I really do appreciate your sticking up for me," I sighed. "And thanks for the double idea; I don't know how I feel about Griff right now, but I do know I don't want to be alone with him if I can help it."

"I think the haunted house and corn maze will still be fun. And scary," he teased. "You'll have to resist the urge to cling when things get freaky. Hopefully, Michelle won't feel the same way, though," Jace chuckled.

"Please! Girls *know* the only reason boys take a date to a haunted house is so that they'll have an excuse to cuddle. Give us some credit."

"And they like the excuse just as much. That is, if they are going with the right person." Jace glanced at my sour face. "Come on, a few days ago you would have been happy to cuddle a bit. Maybe you misjudged him. He still seems pretty cool to me."

"We'll see." I kept silent the rest of the way home, an ominous feeling building up inside me.

12

The Whole Truth

The dry dirt flew everywhere as we kicked through the corn maze. I was regretting my tendency to always wear flip-flops. My feet were filthy. As I stared at my feet in disgust, my friends vanished behind the next turn. I followed slowly, embarrassed, and wishing I owned a pair of high-top tennis shoes. It was getting dark, and I must have missed which turn they took. "Hey guys," I yelled. No answer. "That's not funny!" I yelled louder. Still nothing. Annoyed, I hurried around a bend—smack into someone. I overbalanced, and while I was steadying myself, the stranger twisted my arm behind my back and told me to keep walking with my mouth shut.

I screamed instead, and he yanked my arm up higher, until I could only whimper. "Griff, help me, please," I whispered, tears streaming down my face.

"Mia." The voice flooded me with relief.

"Quinn," I gasped and closed my eyes and turned around. The stranger was gone, and I collapsed into Quinn's outstretched arms.

He picked me up gently, and flew upward out of the forbidding field. We landed in a sunny little park and he set me down under a tree. I was still shivering. He held me close and stroked my forehead, softly murmuring reassuring words in my ear.

I finally snapped out of it and leaned forward, putting my head in my hands. "I keep having this dream, don't I? Where I'm being chased."

"I'm glad I was able to rescue you at last." Quinn looked worried. "What brought on these dreams? Was it what I told you about me and my family last time?"

"Partly," I thought about it. "Also, the other night when I was out," I paused uneasily, reluctant to say I was on a date. "I saw a couple of strange men in the dark and I thought they were coming after me. I don't think the person I was with could see them. I don't know. It made me think about how I could see you and your sisters, but my mom thought you were imaginary. It's all very confusing."

I lay back against his chest and his arms encircled me, comforting me. "You want to know why you could see us," Quinn said quietly. "But I don't know myself. Nan only saw us if we let her."

I turned around needing to see his face, his eyes. "How could that be?" I persisted. "Tell me all of it, please."

"In a minute. I want to ask you something first."

"Allright," I agreed leaning back against his shoulder looking up at his face.

"Who's Griff?"

I blinked. Oh dear. This was awkward. I quickly tried to think of what to say.

"I just wondered because you dream of him a lot lately." He added into the silence.

"I do?" I was surprised. I didn't remember any vivid dreams about Griff. Yikes. Who knows what my subconscious had been working through? "He's just a boy from school. I've gone out with him once." I wasn't going to mention I was going out with him again tonight.

"Do you like him?"

I choked a bit. "Are you always this direct?" I countered.

"Yes. So do you?" he persisted.

I lowered by eyes, trying to think. "I don't know. I met him a few weeks ago. He's, um...interesting." I peeked up at Quinn who was frowning slightly. I blundered on, not knowing why I should. "He is nice-looking, but he also makes me nervous."

"Do I make you nervous?" Quinn asked softly.

"Of course not," I denied immediately.

"Good." Quinn looked relieved.

"You are mysterious, and I still don't know much about you, though," I said, happy to change the subject. "Like, how in the world could you be trapped in a tiny little necklace?"

"Well, that's a good question," he agreed thoughtfully.

"And are you going to give me a good answer?"

He laughed, and I could feel his chest moving under my head. "I promise it will be a truthful answer, although I don't know if you will find it good. My father's family, you see, is not like yours. My father grew up in a home filled with people who were extremely prejudiced against people like you."

I felt my back stiffen in anger. "Because we aren't wealthy, is that it? Is this a snob thing?" My voice came out in an offended squeak. "My parents work very hard but they are both teachers, so we don't have a huge amount of money."

Quinn got my attention back by placing a finger on my lips. "No, it has nothing to do with money. How can I say this?"

He took his finger off my lips and started running it through my hair. I realized it was long again. What was up with that? Wow, his fingers felt so nice. I closed my eyes.

"My father and his family could do things that would seem highly unusual to you." His words snapped me back from distracting thoughts.

"Like plopping someone inside a necklace."

"Exactly, something that would seem like magic to you."

"Magic, like, illusions a magician would perform? Or do you mean witchcraft kind of magic?"

"Neither, really. Do you remember all the fairy tales and stories that Marie used to tell?"

"Sure, she drastically influenced my reading from a young age. I loved *Lord of the Rings* instead of *Little Women* or *Little House on the Prairie*, much to my mom's dismay," I sighed. "Nan used to read to me in the backyard or at the lake. Those were good times."

"Well, did you ever think about where all the legends and tales came from?"

"From a time of storytellers and superstitions, I guess." I shrugged my shoulders.

"And what if they were based on actual facts from long ago?"

"Really, are they? That would be amazing." I sat up straight and turned around to face him, sitting cross-legged so I could look closely at his face. He was really going to tell me every-thing this time. I was sure of it.

Quinn smiled. "A very long time ago humans lived with other beings. People who had power given to them by the earth and could perform magic that would seem like miracles to humans. Everyone lived together fairly peacefully for many, many years.

"But soon it became apparent that humans, in general, lived quite differently from the rest. Humans lacked respect for the earth, became involved in territorial wars and cruel conquest, believed in the power of machines rather than the power of the earth.

So these other beings split themselves off from the humans into another time and dimension here on the earth. They vowed to protect their own earth and reject all things human. They called themselves The Terrara, or 'Earth Protectors.' Humans became *Nequam*—'the worthless.'"

He paused, checking to see what my reaction might be, but I didn't want the interruption, even if I did think "worthless" was a mighty broad title for *all* of humanity. I waved my hand to encourage him to continue.

"My father came from a powerful family of Terrara. His name was, I mean *is*, Grayson. Because he was the firstborn son, he had many expectations and obligations laid upon him. However, he hated politics and power. His passion was for exploration and discovery, a type of scientist, I guess you could call him. His parents hated his choice of lifestyle, and tried to tie him to the family through a politically arranged marriage. My father, as you know, rejected his family and this situation and left home.

"Even though travel to the human world was forbidden, my father was willing to risk the consequences. He found a place where the passage between the worlds was thin, and he discovered a way to travel back and forth without anyone being the wiser. It was during these explorations that he met Anna, my mom, and they fell in love.

"Now the penalty, if you are caught even associating with humans, is death. Can you imagine the fury and outrage his family would experience if they found out he had fallen in love with a human girl? The shame and dishonor he brought on them would have been too much to bear; the family would have hunted them down and killed them in order to remove all trace of this disgrace. So my father was very careful, and lived apart in a self-imposed kind of exile."

"How did Nan find out about your mother and father's situation?" It was hard to imagine that my always-sensible Nan knew any of this, much less *believed* any of it.

"My father and my mother, when they came to see Marie to tell her that Anna was still alive, had to explain to her why she couldn't reveal this knowledge to anyone. They told her the truth."

"So Nan knew about where your father came from? She knew about the Terrara and everything?" I was having trouble wading through all this strangeness. I felt like I was inside a novel, my mind trying to grasp the reality of his words.

"She did," Quinn smiled. "It would be much easier to show you proof if we were in the real world. Anything I do here, you would think is just part of your dream and would therefore be unbelievable."

"What did your father do to convince Nan back then?" I wanted to know.

His smile grew sly. "He flew."

"You mean, you can fly in the real world. You are kidding me?" My head was swimming from information overload. Weird information overload. "So that's why you're so comfortable flying in my dreams. It's already second nature to you."

"I've been flying for a very long time."

"And how long would that be?" I frowned again. "As near as I can tell, you should be old enough to be my dad. That's kinda creepy, you know."

"The Terrara have a different age span than humans. I am still quite young, as far as my people are concerned. Well, not exactly my people." His voice became gloomy. "I am a product of two worlds, and I belong in neither one." His face reflected his lonely words. Quinn leaned over and rubbed his forehead, his beautiful hair capturing my gaze, his words filling me with compassion.

I reached out, smoothing his curls. "Quinn, how did you become trapped in my necklace?" I asked, my voice thick with worry.

Quinn grabbed my hand and squeezed it with both of his. "Remember when I talked about going into hiding when my father thought he was betrayed?"

"Yes." Wait. I suddenly got it. "The necklace was a hiding place?"

"Uh-huh. My parents were able to construct a special necklace, ring, and bracelet to be used as a temporary—so they thought—hiding place. My father cast a transference spell, and my sisters and I were each hidden inside one of the pieces of jewelry. The set was given to Marie to protect until my parents returned. As you know, they never did return." His voice betrayed his misery.

My voice stuck in my throat, and I tried to swallow.

"So did you find my sister's ring and bracelet yet?"

"Oh my gosh," I gasped. "The ring and bracelet have your sisters inside. I've looked through my house pretty thoroughly, but I haven't been able to find them. Now that I know what they contain, I'll look even harder. And, of course, they might still be at my Nan's house. My dad and I will be going there soon, remember?" I was babbling, trying to convince Quinn how much I wanted to help him.

Quinn looked depressed. "That's okay. Thanks for trying." He tried to smile. I felt like I had failed him, even though I knew it wasn't my fault. "We have to get you out of that necklace." I declared forcefully. "You must have some idea of what to do, right?"

"I don't know much about that kind of magic." Quinn admitted unhappily. "It is very advanced."

"But your parents had to have had a contingency plan, something for Nan to do just in case something happened to them. Your father must have known the danger and he would never have allowed you to remain trapped." I was twirling a chunk of my hair round and round with my fingers. It was something I hadn't done since I was a kid, but it felt completely natural doing it again.

"I'm sure they did have a plan, but when they didn't come back, Marie probably panicked, not knowing what to do or who to trust. It must have been terrifying for her."

"Well, there must be a way." I stood up and began pacing around beneath the huge maple tree. "Maybe there are some clues at Nan's house. I'll make sure I comb the place thoroughly, searching everything I can find for some answers. In the meantime, you need to go through your mind, remembering every single detail about the spell that you can. Try to remember words, descriptions, tones, hand movements, I don't know, anything that might have some relevance to the entrapment. We need information before we can proceed."

I almost bumped into him, when he got up suddenly and placed himself in my path. I looked up into his grateful face.

"You are amazing." He smiled, this time the smile reached his eyes.

I relaxed. "Nope, just being practical. One of these ideas is going to give us the answers we need. I'm sure of it."

"You are taking all these revelations more calmly than I would have expected of most people."

"I'm not most people." I tilted my head to the side, a wry smile touching my lips. "Most people think I'm a bit odd, so I guess I'm much more likely to believe some pretty odd things myself." I shrugged. "Besides, I trust you and I believe what you are telling me is the truth… no matter how outrageous it seems."

"I don't know what I'd be doing without you." Quinn pulled me into a warm embrace, and I lay my head against his shoulder.

"When we get you out of here, you're gonna owe me some magic tricks, you know. I want to fly for real."

"We'll have to be extra careful. If you remember, I can hide from normal humans, but you can't."

"Are you calling me abnormal?" I huffed teasingly.

"No," Quinn laughed. "Just think what would happen if someone spotted you flying around. That would be difficult to explain."

"You think?" I couldn't help laughing too, imagining the mess that would cause. But the thought of being with Quinn in the real world with me gave me a jolt of happiness. I wished I were going to my Nan's house sooner. I wanted to get started on this spell-breaking stuff right away.

How strange, I thought. None of this was what I expected in the least. I really hoped I could take the feeling of trust and belief into my waking consciousness. Without Quinn next to me, this feeling would fade. I sighed, worried.

"Everything feels like it will be okay when I'm with you," Quinn breathed into my ear. "I wish you could stay here."

"Me, too." I hugged him tightly, trying to plant myself in this environment permanently, but as if in answer to our wish, Quinn began to fade and I felt myself being torn from him, back to reality.

"Come back soon," Quinn cried urgently, as he disappeared.

I found myself gripping my pillow fiercely and released it, feeling rather foolish. Reluctantly, I sat up, the sudden loss sweeping over me more intensely than I thought I could endure. I glanced over at Quinn's sketch and made a silent vow to get him out as soon as possible. Then I lay back and went over all the strange things he had revealed to me, and tried to assess how I felt about it all.

I was still puzzling it over when my alarm went off. Frustrated, I got up and began getting ready for work.

13

Halloween Surprises

"You are going to knock their socks off," my mom enthused over my shoulder, while checking her work in the mirror. I tried not to roll my eyes. My mom, the drama queen! At least today it came in handy, since everyone at work was supposed to dress up for Halloween. As I scrutinized her handiwork, I had to admit she was still good after however many years since college. I was feeling excited to get to the bead store and show off my new look. Of course, I was bringing regular clothes with me because there was no way I was going out with Griff, not to mention Jace and Michelle, looking like this.

My mom gushed a steady stream of enthusiasm all the way to work. I kept nodding and grinning foolishly, hoping the ride would end soon. I swept out of the car dramatically as my mom pulled to the curb, to the applause of Jane and Wendy who had also just arrived.

I'd found a 1930s black glamour dress that fit perfectly, and my mom had done very cool makeup on my neck. Two serious looking wounds oozed fake blood, and I had to keep reminding myself not to itch them. My face was pale with heavily shadowed cheekbones and deathly under-eye smudges. The only thing missing was Bela Lugosi.

Mom had made me wear heels, so after my dramatic posing, I ruined the effect by practically killing myself tripping up the steps. Wendy looked fabulous as a medieval princess, hair piled up high and intertwined with flowers and jewels. Jane had dressed as a 1920s flapper with salon-styled wavy hair and funky jewelry.

My necklace had threatened to get in the way of my bite marks, so I had wrapped the chain a few times around my ankle instead. It felt strange not to have the necklace easily accessible, and I found myself reaching for it numerous times during the day, and being startled for any split second that it was gone.

The day was a hoot. We were acting in character with our costumes; even my uptight boss let go as a '60s style go-go dancer. I couldn't believe she could pull that off. We were having so much fun that I wasn't paying attention to the time, and Griff arrived before I could change my clothes. When I saw him I froze, staring slack-jawed and wide-eyed. Then I knew what my meddling mom had been so thrilled about.

Griff's 1980s *Lost Boys* vampire outfit was a fun compliment to my 1930s style vampire victim costume. He leered at me, showing a bit of fang as he strolled into the store. I had to admit it—he looked *incredible*. But there was no way I was going to the haunted house in this inconvenient, not to mention cold, costume, Besides, my feet were killing me.

"I guess I can thank my mom for this?" I asked, hand on my hip.

"Are you mad?" he mocked back.

"No, but I'm not going out in this," I replied firmly, waving a hand down myself. "I'd freeze and probably break my ankle."

"That would be too bad."

Seeming to like what he saw, Griff came closer, inspecting my neck, and admiring my bare shoulders and back. "I think we can modify it enough that it will work out."

I stepped back glaring. "What are you talking about?"

"Your mom gave me a bag with some boots, a wrap, and long gloves. They're in the car. That's why I came early, so you wouldn't have already changed." He grinned confidently. "Jace and Michelle are dressing up, too."

I was backed into a corner. Having been clearly manipulated by so many people, I felt quite out of sorts. But after a few seconds, I determined not to be a spoiled sport; this was my favorite holiday, after all. I made myself smile and said, "Well, let's see what you brought."

Raising an eyebrow in surprise at my complacent acceptance, Griff led the way to the car and pulled out the bag from my mom. He hesitated before giving it to me, though. "How about a couple pictures? You're first."

I thought about it briefly, and decided, since he'd asked nicely, that it would be okay. I'd like to remember this outfit anyway. It was definitely the best costume I'd ever worn.

"Where?" I asked, eying the parking lot dubiously.

"Over there by the bricks," Griff pointed. "Under the street light."

I leaned against the light post while he fiddled with his camera. I reached down to adjust the charm on my ankle, and realized he was already snapping. I'd always posed for pictures before, but Griff just seemed to snap at random. I wasn't sure what to do.

"Just relax," Griff encouraged. "Touch your neck, get into the part."

Feeling self conscious, I closed my eyes and touched my neck. I gave myself a few minutes to play act, and then the goose bumps got the better of me.

"I'm cold," I complained. "Can we stop now?"

"Okay, maybe we can take more later," Griff grinned. "You were getting into it, weren't you?" he teased.

Blushing, I grabbed the bag and went back inside the store to finish getting ready. Amid giggles and suggestive comments, I took off my heels—glad Griff was waiting outside. I was stunned when I pulled out the expensive black leather boots. They were soft and supple and went all the way up to my knees. I might have new favorite footwear besides flip-flops, I mused. *Mmmm.* Even the leather smelled good. As I slipped them on, and they felt as good as they looked. I wondered when my mom had gotten these for me. I owed her big time.

I slid the long gloves way up my arms and pulled on a fake fur cloak that was worn low enough that it would leave my neck makeup alone. I tried to figure out what to do with Quinn's necklace. It hadn't felt comfortable around my ankle inside my boot, so I asked Wendy to wrap it around my wrist and over my glove. I had a pang of guilt shoot through me. I was on a date, a rather exciting dress-up party, with an extremely handsome boy. I shook my head, trying not to feel guilty. There was nothing I could do for Quinn tonight, so I might as well have fun on Halloween.

Wendy gave me a hug and mugged, "Be good, Daarrling. But not *too* good."

I gave her a dramatic air kiss on each cheek, and flounced out of the store with a wink and a wave.

Griff opened the door for me. I got in carefully, arranging my dress while he deposited the bag in the trunk.

"You're in a good mood." Griff glanced at me after starting the engine.

"I love Halloween," I said simply, as if that was the only answer needed.

"You look extraordinary." His eyes skimmed over me.

Again I flushed. "You make a quite an impression yourself," I conceded. I kinda have a thing for vampires, as my mom knows very well. Darn her.

Griff looked even hotter than usual, if that was possible. I had a hard time tearing my eyes away. Good thing Jace and Michelle were coming. I was going to be way susceptible to Griff's oh-so-powerful charm tonight. *Better be careful, girl!* I warned myself.

Trying to lighten the mood, I asked, "How can you talk normally with those fake teeth in?"

"The teeth aren't a huge mouthpiece—just individual fangs that you can glue to your incisors. See?" He opened his mouth.

"I've never seen those. That's pretty clever." They looked completely real.

He leaned closer, getting into the part. I squirmed. "Hey, no biting, for real." I tried to sound like I was joking, but my voice was a bit on the breathless side. Stupid charm, I thought, as my cheeks turned pink yet again.

Laughing, he backed out the car and we headed off to Michelle's house.

THE FOUR OF us drew stares as we cruised around the farm. Griff and I looked good together—even Jace and Michelle commented on that. Jace confirmed the fact with much smirking and winking when Griff's back was turned. It was hard not to slug him.

Jace and Michelle also created quite the pair in their pirate outfits. Jace's hair was spiked, he wore one of my huge hoop earrings, and with his eye patch he looked roguishly wicked. He was actually wearing a white puffy pirate shirt and new brown leather pants that must have cost a fortune. Michelle had her long hair done in intricate exotic braids, with multicolored beads clicking together as she shook her head. I wondered briefly about how long that must have taken to style. Add in her torn short skirt, flowing blouse, and tall boots, and it wasn't hard to tell how she felt about Jace.

After grabbing some snacks from the concession stand, we went to check out the corn maze. I couldn't help thinking about my dream from the night before—glad I had boots on this time. And I stuck close to the others, trying to keep my fears at bay. Sensing my mood, Griff draped his arm around my shoulders. I gave in to the urge to lean against his side.

The sky was dusky blue and the moon had risen over the mountains, a bright sliver winking down on us. The corn maze took on an eerie quality. I was surprised that Griff hadn't started taking pictures with the camera he refused to leave in the car. It was bouncing against his chest while he walked, at odds with his vampire costume.

As if reading my mind, he stopped and offered to take pictures of Jace and Michelle, and then Jace shot some of Griff and me. I forced myself to relax as Griff pulled me close. Jace took some serious ones and then Griff had to ham it up and pretend to bite me. Yikes. Jace just kept on shooting as we play fought. Oh my, I thought, imagining how those would turn out.

The four of us laughed and joked the rest of the way through the maze, which turned out to be much less challenging than the sign claimed. The maze had been used far too much already, having been open since the beginning of the month, and the right path was easy to find, along with several short cuts that had been forced through the dry corn stalks by bored people too lazy to find their way out. After exiting the maze and brushing and stomping off as much dust as possible, Jace and Michelle went for drinks, while Griff and I held their places in the long line for the haunted house.

Alone with Griff, even in a crowd, my brain froze and all small talk was banished from my mind. Now that we were standing still, I had to hug myself to try and stay warm, extra glad for the boots, gloves and cloak. Griff came up behind me and wrapped his arms around mine, snuggling me against his back. I closed my eyes and enjoyed his warmth, trying not to hyperventilate.

"Having a good Halloween?" he asked softly, his chin resting on the top of my head.

"*Mmm-hmm*," my intelligent reply.

"Aren't you glad you stayed in costume?"

"Sure, did my mom prep you on what to wear?"

"You don't really mind, do you?" He was rubbing his hands up and down my arms, and I couldn't focus very well on his words.

"Nope," I whispered softly, feeling dangerously good.

"I can't figure you out, Mia," he murmured against the hair above my right ear. "One minute I think you like me, and the next minute, you act like you can't wait to get away from me."

I stiffened, my mellow mood blown. He was crazy if he thought I was going to discuss how I felt about him after only two dates, especially here in public. I refused to answer, my jaw tightening painfully.

He forced me around in his arms, and my jaw clenched even more. I looked at his neck, refusing to meet his eyes.

"If you're wondering, I like *you* very much. You're the only girl I've asked out for a long time." At my look of disbelief, he added, "I only went on that one date with Miranda because she asked me. And I thought Jace was your boyfriend." He leaned down and caught my gaze. "I was glad to hear you were just friends."

There he stood like the fulfillment of all my teenage vampire fantasies. The teeth, the leather, the long dark hair. Holy crap. I felt split down the middle. Half of me was screaming, "What about Quinn?" My other half was urging me to throw my arms around Griff's neck and lay one on him right there in public. I stood there like a deer trapped in headlights, not knowing what to do.

A high-pitched shriek right behind me jerked me into motion, and I launched myself out of Griff's arms in a panic. I was breathing like a sprinter, and I tried to blame it on the scream. I spun around and came face to face with one of the so-called monsters that roamed the lines, trying to get everyone into the right mood.

"Hey baby," he sneered at me grabbing my arm. "You look good enough to eat." My alarm bells already ringing, I reacted instinctively by snagging his other arm and performing a self-defense move Jace had recently taught me. Before you could say *Boo!* the poor kid in the costume was flat on his back, dazing at the stars.

I gaped in distress, embarrassed at my overreaction. Griff leaned over my victim, helping him stand up. "You might want to keep your hands to yourself from now on." He gave the bemused kid a push on his way. Around us, the crowd burst into whistles and applause. I smiled hesitantly.

"Remind me not to get you mad at me," Griff smirked.

"What's going on?" Jace and Michelle walked up as the clapping died out. "What did we miss?"

Griff answered for me. "Mia just threw down some guy in a costume that was bugging her. Laid him out flat on his back. It was pretty funny."

Jace handed me a hot chocolate, sloshing it as he started cracking up. "So, you're using those moves I taught you already, huh? I thought you said they were for an *emergency*." He laughed harder as I stuck my tongue out at him. "Now you're throwing down any old guy you feel like. Wish I'd seen it."

Michelle was giving me an appraising look, like she never expected violence from someone like me. She laid a hand on Jace's arm. "Maybe you could teach me some self-defense moves, too." Effectively pulling his attention back to her, she and Jace started chatting quietly, heads together.

Shut out of the conversation, I sighed and turned away. The hot chocolate was warm against my gloved hands, and after blowing on it, I took a small sip, careful not to burn myself. Adrenaline flowed out of me and I began feeling tired. I wished I had a bench or something to sit on; I'd been on my feet since ten that morning. Griff put an arm around my shoulders and I leaned against him, gratefully.

"Tired?" he asked.

"Yeah, it's always a long day when I go out after working all day. Don't you have a job?" He seemed like a rich boy, but I guess you never knew.

"Sort of." His answer surprised me.

"Really, what do you do?"

"Hard to explain," he hedged. "So, did you like the photos I took of you last week?" he asked, changing the subject.

"Well," I tried arranging my thoughts. "You made me look a lot prettier than I usually do."

He raised his right eyebrow at this, but didn't interrupt.

"I was spooky looking, too. I mean, I love the eerie quality of your work when you photograph trees and gargoyles. It was sort of strange seeing myself that way, like it wasn't really me." I glanced up. "Did that even make any sense?"

"If you thought those were spooky, how do you think you'll look in the ones we took tonight?"

"But these are different," I argued. "These are fantasy, meant to be supernatural looking. The other photos were just me, being me, and yet they weren't me." I grimaced apologetically. "Sorry, I don't think this was the answer you were wanting. The style and execution were wonderful, just the subject matter was uncomfortable for me."

Griff was looking down intently at me. "You constantly surprise me."

I had no response to that, which made me frown slightly. He was always turning the conversation on its head, leaving me floundering for something to say. I felt like I was missing something, but I didn't know what.

"Hey, look, we're almost at the door," I blurted out. What a relief.

A few minutes later, we were ushered into a dark, creepy barn. Griff held my hand as we strolled through rooms of affected scenes of violence and, well, just plain grossness. I was okay with that. Over the top gross-out stuff never scared me— it always looked so fake. It was the things jumping out that I couldn't seem to guard against. I threw myself into Griff's arms more times than I'd like to admit.

Leaving the barn, a small group of us were herded into the woods behind the barn to a small stage where a band was dressed up, playing supposedly spooky music. It was actually pretty lame, and we all rolled our eyes at each other as we moved to the back of the crowd, hoping it would be over soon so we could move on.

"Hey, I'll be back in a sec," I told the others, as my eyes scanned the crowd. "I see Skye over there with a guy." I smirked at Jace. "I've gotta go check out who she's with." Griff reluctantly let me go, and I crossed behind a bunch of bored looking teenagers, quickly heading towards Skye. Suddenly, I felt myself yanked roughly and dragged away from the crowd into the dark woods. A hand clamped over my mouth and someone hissed at me, "Keep your mouth shut." The situation was so like my dream from last night that I was astounded for a few seconds, and then I started fighting like a crazy person, kicking and biting.

I viciously pulled the little finger of the hand over my mouth. He let go with a shout of pain and I screamed, "Griff! Jace! Help me!" until another assailant backhanded me across the face and I collapsed on the ground. I was crying in fear now, worried no one could hear me over the loud music.

I began crawling away from the voice swearing close to me, and then I heard something else that froze me in place. Shock made me stay limp, as someone tried to lift me, but fear snapped me out of my paralysis and I went for my attacker's eyes, scratching and tearing.

An angry voice was yelling at me in a language I couldn't understand. I was sobbing, calling out for help, despair almost overcoming me, when someone finally came to my rescue. It was so dark I couldn't tell what was going on. I heard screams and cries of pain. At last, Griff was lifting me up, cradling me close, as I wept my gratitude into his chest.

I believe that I was hysterical for a short time; maybe I fainted. I don't remember much about what happened next. When I opened my eyes again, I was stretched out on the ground and my head was in Jace's lap. Michelle was pacing and talking on her cell phone. Griff was gone.

"You're going to be okay," Jace soothed. I touched my sore mouth and realized I was bleeding where my teeth had cut into my lip. So, it wasn't a dream this time. Someone had grabbed me for real? What the...? I tried to get my head around what was going on. I attempted to sit up, but Jace held me down.

"What happened?" I stuttered.

"You tell me. One second you'd gone off to talk to Skye, the next, Griff is shouting that you're missing and taking off like a maniac."

"Where's Griff now?" I asked urgently.

Jace shook his head. "The idiot went back to find the guys who hurt you."

"What!" I broke free of Jace and scrambled wobbly to my feet. "Why'd you let him go?"

"Let him?" Jace asked in disbelief. "He came back to the show, thrust you into my arms and said, 'The guys who did this are going to pay.' He looked freakin' scary, so I let him go, while Michelle and I tried to take care of you. Believe me, there wasn't anything I could do to keep him here."

I swayed on my feet, not knowing what to do, when Griff strode into view. Jace was right, his face was terrifying, and I sank down as his glower settled on me. He squatted down on his haunches next to me, his expression changed. He gingerly touched my lip, and then pulled me into a gentle embrace.

Feeling vulnerable and grateful, I slid my arms around his neck and whispered my thanks into his ear. He raised me to me feet and began inspecting me for further damage. Besides having a throbbing, bloody lip, my eye was tender—probably a black eye in the works—and some of my nails were ragged from scratching, poking out from the ruined tips of my gloves. My arms were sore. I figured a number of bruises would be obvious as soon as I peeled back my gloves.

Tears threaten my eyes as I noticed my ruined costume. My fur cloak was dirty and matted, my dress had blood stains from my lip, and my delicate gloves were messed up beyond repair.

"Guess it's a good thing you took pictures earlier," I said weakly. "Oh no. You didn't lose your camera, did you?" I looked anxiously into Griff's face.

"It's fine," Griff scolded. "You don't need to worry about anything except *you* right now. Looks like you're going to be bruised and sore for a while, but nothing more serious than that." His face looked very angry still, and even though I wanted to ask more questions, I wasn't sure if I dared.

I was rubbing my hands together trying to warm them up, when I suddenly realized Quinn's necklace was missing. I began a frantic search on my hands and knees, panic welling up inside of me. This could not be happening. What if…? No, I couldn't think that. I wouldn't let myself.

"What's wrong?" Griff and Jace asked at the same time. "My nan's necklace," I stammered in fright. "I can't find it. It was wrapped around my arm like a bracelet so it wouldn't get in my make up. It's gone. I can't lose it." My voice was going into an annoying high-pitched whine, but I couldn't stop it. I wasn't going to leave this spot until I found it.

Everyone began combing the ground for me. I thought about where I was dragged. It could have fallen off out in the dark where they... I started shaking. I think I was going into shock. Before I could pass out again, Michelle leaned over and plucked something tangled in the fur of my cloak. Tearing it off, she held it up for my inspection. Relief flooded over me like a warm shower.

"Thanks, Michelle," I whispered, clutching Quinn's necklace to my chest, rocking back and forth. "Sorry I messed up your date with Jace." She waved her hand, as if to say, "Forget it," and instead turned to the boys, taking charge. "We need to get her out front. The police are on their way and want us to make a statement, if possible."

The rest of the evening was a blur. I told the police what I could remember. I had no descriptions to give them, since it was so dark. They were baffled when I told them my assailants were speaking a language I had never heard before. By the time they were done, I think they were convinced that it was just some drunk kids getting out of hand. Griff looked on furiously. He briefly told them how he had heard me, had chased off the attackers, and brought me back to my friends at the stage.

My mind balked at this, knowing he was leaving stuff out, but I kept silent, determined to ask him about it later. An ambulance had been called, and I sat still in utter embarrassment while they determined that I just needed an ice pack and some rest. When we were finally able to leave, everyone was as exhausted as I was. The ride home was silent, except for some whispering from the back seat.

Griff kept glancing over at me. I sat staring into the windshield, seeing nothing, shivering occasionally, and gripping my necklace tightly in my right hand. We dropped off Michelle first; I kept my eyes down as Jace walked her to the door. He came back after a few minutes and we drove to my house. I sat, dreading the scene awaiting me when I walked in the front door.

Griff helped me up the steps. Jace went in first to warn my parents before they got a good look at me. I took off my ruined cloak and lay down on the couch. Mom cried and fussed over me like I was four, zipping off my boots and pulling off my gloves, but I didn't mind. Jace and Griff explained the situation as best they could, and my normally subdued dad used a few swear words that made my eyebrows fly up in surprise. Mom didn't even scold him. I caught Jace trying to hide a grin.

Griff and Jace stayed to see me settled, I guess. But they looked so awkward sitting across from me on the matching floral armchairs, I told them they should go home and get some sleep. Jace came over and gave me a careful hug. I gave him a painful, lopsided smile and he winced slightly.

"I'll be over tomorrow to see how you're feeling, okay?"

"Have a raw steak ready." I pointed to my already closing eye.

He rolled his eyes and then said seriously, "I'm glad you're okay."

Griff looked like he wanted to stay and talk, but I was being smothered at the moment by too much parental concern. I took care of it.

"Can you get me some ice in a bag?" I asked my dad. "And Mom, can you bring my sweats and stuff upstairs? I want to wash my face and sleep in the guest room. I'm not up for a loft bed tonight." As they disappeared on their appointed tasks, Griff came over and sat next to me.

"I'm so sorry," he said softly.

"Not your fault." I tried to grin again, but it stung and I gave up. "Besides, you saved me." I leaned against him.

"I took too long to find you. You got hurt." I could hear blame in his voice.

"I'll mend." I took a deep breath, and asked the question that had been bothering me. "What happened to those guys?

Griff narrowed his eyes, his mouth a grim slash.

"I know you aren't telling me something," I pressed again, wanting to know the truth, even if it was ugly.

He opened his mouth, making an exasperated sound and I noticed something, "Hey," I blurted out, startled, "Where did your fangs go?"

Griff stared at me in astonishment. Before he could answer, my dad came back in with a bag of ice wrapped in a dishtowel. Griff got up and walked to the door. "I'll call you tomorrow, okay?"

I nodded, realizing this was neither the time nor place, and eased the ice over my eye, trying to stifle a groan of pain. Griff's face hardened. He left without a goodbye.

As I lay, at last, in the guest room, in comfortable clean clothes, aching all over, I kept reliving the night's insanity. I hated the fear, the pain, and the embarrassment equally. But the one thing that stuck in my brain like a painful sliver was the word that I had caught among the jumble of foreign words. The word that had stunned me almost into submission, spat out in anger, by someone I couldn't see: *Nequam.*

Denial and Disappointment

I slept like a dead person, remembering none of my dreams, and woke stiff and sore in the same position I fell asleep in. My body felt like I imagined a kickboxing bag would feel, if it had any nerves. Sitting up made my head zing with pain. I could barely open my right eye. Hobbling to the bathroom, I caught a glimpse of my reflection and gasped in surprise. I looked even more hammered than I'd thought.

Mom must have heard me moving around, because she showed up soon after I came out of the bathroom, asking how I felt and if I wanted any breakfast. I ate some soft buttered bread, popped some ibuprofen, and drank a ton of ice water, my throat feeling rough and raw from screaming and crying. Then Mom filled her huge bathtub for me and I eased my sore body down into the steaming hot water. I closed my eyes and listened to music for at least an hour. When I got out, I felt almost human again.

Still not wanting to think about last night, I curled up in bed and read. My mystery novel effectively kept my mind from wandering, and I ate the lunch my mom brought up to me in bed, not wanting to move. Next, I made her hand over the leftover Halloween candy, and by the time Jace came over, I was hopped up on sugar, having eaten half a dozen little chocolate bars.

"Your face looks like a rainbow—an evil, painful rainbow. I never knew rainbows could be evil," Jace teased gently.

"Yeah, that's me, the puffy-faced evil rainbow fairy." I made a wild-eyed grimace, and Jace put a hand to his heart.

"So, you can at least joke about it now?" Jace asked, looking more closely at me.

"Well, actually, I'm trying out denial. It's working out pretty well so far," I said cheerfully.

"Is the subject off limits, then?" Jace was unwrapping candy bars and tossing them back as fast as I was earlier.

"I guess not. I just didn't want to think about it when I was alone. And I definitely didn't want to discuss it with my parents."

"You're okay talking about it with me, then?" Jace was trying so hard to be tactful and polite; I reached over and punched him in the arm, making him drop his candy on the carpet.

"What?" he grumbled.

"I'm not made of glass, you know. And I'm not going to fall apart and start bawling again. What's wrong with you?" My lopsided smile didn't hurt so much today. Thank you, ibuprofen.

"You didn't see yourself last night," he reminded me. "It was scary for us, too."

"Sorry, it seems sort of surreal now. Kinda blurry and fuzzy to me. I guess it's a bit clearer for you, though, isn't it?"

"Too clear." Jace frowned. "Was it really just a couple of drunk kids looking for trouble?" His forehead creased in worry. "It was the weirdest thing, Mia. One minute you were walking through the crowd, the next you were gone."

"I don't know," I said, my voice distant as I remembered that disturbing word.

Jace looked suspicious. "You sound like you have an idea."

I sighed, wondering how I could talk to Jace about Quinn and his family and the necklace without him thinking I needed to be committed. Everything I had learned from Quinn had taken on more significance since I heard that word during my attack. His story became scarily plausible, instead of just hopefully probable.

I decided to take the proverbial plunge and tell it all; whether Jace believed any of it was going to be up to him. "Okay," I said, "I hope you don't need to go anywhere soon, because this might take a while."

Jace, looking curious, settled back against the wall with the bowl of candy. "Fire away. I'll listen to anything, if there's candy."

So, I started at the beginning, reminding him of my haunted dreams and how I had met Quinn when I became lucid. Explaining Quinn's ties to my nan's sister and then the whole Terrara background proved difficult, though. Jace kept asking questions that I didn't know the answer to. I couldn't tell if he believed me, or if he was enjoying the scenario like he would a book or movie.

Then I told him about the word, Nequam. "I couldn't understand most of what my attackers were saying. They spoke a bit of accented English to me, ordering me to shut up, but mostly they were talking and yelling in some kind of foreign language. I am positive I heard the word *Nequam*, though. It sounded like a swear word or something. I was so stunned I almost forgot to fight." I shuddered, remembering more than I wanted.

Jace looked like he was still trying to digest all this information, so I kept hypothesizing on my own. "What if they knew I had Quinn's necklace? What if they snatched me to get it? And the bracelet and ring, of course." My mind had been trying to ignore this possibility, and now that I had said it out loud, my stomach felt sick, the candy I had eaten churning sickeningly.

"You're jumping to too many conclusions," Jace warned. "How do you know any of this is real? It's so completely far-fetched."

"I know it seems that way at first, but I have had more time than you to think about it. And Quinn," I paused, slightly embarrassed. "He genuinely needs help. I just know it. I remember him from when I was a kid. How could I be making this stuff up? It's too weird, even for me."

Jace put aside the bowl of candy and sat beside me. "Do you think the guys at the gargoyle house had anything to do with all of this craziness?"

"Oh my gosh," I gasped. "I never thought of that. Hey, if they were Terraran, then that explains why only I could see them. No wonder Griff couldn't figure out what I was talking about."

I reached up and held onto Quinn's necklace, feeling ill again. "What am I going to do? It's not like anyone will believe me about any of this." I looked up, doubtfully. "Except you, right?"

"I'm believing more and more every second," Jace said grimly. "I just wish I knew what to do about any of it."

Jace put his arm around me and I leaned against him. I felt incredibly exhausted after all the talk and theorizing. My mind wanted to struggle through and come up with some kind of solution, but my body just wanted to go to sleep, spiraling downward after my giddy sugar rush. Jace noticed me nodding my head.

"You definitely need to lie down again." He pushed me back down onto the pillow. "I'm going to think about this stuff at home. Can I tell my mom what's going on?"

"Sure," I mumbled. "She's good at figuring stuff out. We'll see if she thinks I'm nuts."

"Nah," Jace smiled. "She's the lucid dream queen, remember. She owes you, after all. It was her dream ideas that opened up this can of worms in the first place."

Jace walked to the door. "Get some rest. I'll come back later tonight."

"Bye," I managed, before I conked out.

HOW DID I get here? I asked myself, bewildered. The black sky was pressing down on me, the moon's crescent providing a feeble light on the unfamiliar landscape. All at once, a dozen figures melted out of the forest in front of me, sharp teeth gleaming in the moonlight. I pressed my back against a rough tree trunk, my leg muscles tensing, ready to sprint. My breath came in heavy, frightened gasps; my hands clenched in defiance. What was happening? Suddenly, I recognized the foremost figure as he stepped close, and my eyes widen in horror. It was Griff, his mouth open, teeth glistening.

"No!" I shrieked in panic, lunging to the side, tripping on a tree root and landing painfully on my knees and hands. A voice in my ear cried "Mia!" and I collapsed in relief. Just a dream, I thought wildly.

Someone was holding me gently. "Quinn," I breathed softly.

"Wake up," the voice beckoned softly in my ear. I opened my eyes, but it wasn't Quinn's face next to mine; it was Griff's. He was sitting next to me on the guest room bed, holding me and stroking my hair. Still half in my dream world, I tore myself away from him and jumped out of bed like it was on fire.

Griff put his hands up and talked slowly and calmly, like he was talking to a frightened animal. "Mia, everything's okay. You were having a nightmare. You're safe at home." My eyes focused on the room, and reality came back to me in a rush of embarrassment. Griff was here? Sitting by me in my bed? Yikes. I had to get out of here.

"Um, I'll be right back," I stammered and turned and ran down the hall into the bathroom. I leaned against the closed door, feeling on edge from my freaky dream and its unexpected resolution. I looked in the mirror. What a mess. My eye was half-swollen shut, my bottom lip was puffy and scabbed, and my hair looked like I styled it using my finger and an electric outlet.

Well, I could at least have fresh breath. Going to sleep after eating lots of chocolate had made my mouth taste especially nasty. I brushed out my frustration on my teeth and gargled, having a hard time spitting around my big swollen lip. I straightened my sweats and tried to get my emotions under control. Taking several deep breaths, I braced myself and forced myself back into the guest room.

"Sorry about that," I apologized upon entering. "You kinda freaked me out."

Griff smiled, seeming to understand my state of mind. "Not a big deal. How's your face healing?"

"I think it looks worse than it feels, actually." I touched my lip carefully.

"The swelling should go down soon. Are you keeping ice on it?" Griff came closer, peering intently at my eye and lip. I made myself stand still, trying for nonchalance—trying and failing miserably, of course.

"Nope, no ice since last night," I admitted. What was he doing playing doctor, and in my room, too? "How'd you get in here, anyway?" I asked, my defenses rising because of his unexpected nearness.

"Your mom let me bring your dinner in to you." I noticed for the first time a plate of food sitting on the nightstand. The sky was darkening outside my window.

"Oh," I said in a small voice, sitting down again. "Thanks."

Awkward silence.

"Since you were sleeping, I was just going to leave the food and go. When I set down the plate, I could tell you were having a nightmare, so I tried to help you wake up." He sat down next to me. "I'm sorry about last night, Mia. Those bastards hurt you. And now you're having nightmares." He shook his head, setting his long hair in motion. I looked away.

"It certainly wasn't your fault, Griff. You were the one that helped me. If it wasn't for you, I don't know what would have happened." I found myself reaching out for his hand and he covered it with his other hand. I felt safe all of a sudden, his strong hands enclosing mine.

"Are you going to tell me what happened when you found me last night?" I asked softly. "How come they let me go? I mean, you looked pretty scary when I saw you, but there were two of them…" I trailed off, as I saw his brows lowering and his mouth tighten.

"They ran away. I think they thought more people were on the way."

"Did you get a good look at them? Do you know what language they were speaking?"

"It was too dark to tell and I didn't hear them speak," he answered shortly.

I was disappointed. I really needed more information to work on one of my theories. "That's alright." I looked into his eyes and I don't know how, but I knew he was lying. Why? Did he think I couldn't handle the truth? He seemed to catch my thoughts and he glanced down at our entwined hands.

"I have to go out of town with my family," he said abruptly. "I might be gone for a while. I wanted to check on you before I left."

"Oh, okay." I swallowed. I don't know why I felt a wave of disappointment flood over me. Especially after he just lied to me. What was wrong with me? I'd been avoiding him all week, and now hearing he was going on vacation made me want to cry. I guess all a guy has to do is save my life and I'm all his. No questions asked. Okay, I'm an idiot—a beat up, pathetic-looking idiot.

"I'm going to miss you," Griff said quietly. He took my chin and lifted it gently with one finger until he was gazing right into my miserable misty eyes. "Don't worry. You'll be safe while I'm gone. I promise."

He ran his thumb lightly over my swollen lip and I shivered, eyes closing automatically, emotions flying in all directions.

"I'll be back soon, Mia," he whispered. "Don't forget about me."

His lips brushed my forehead and then feathered gently over my sore lip.

My mom's voice floating up the hallway broke the spell. Griff pulled back quickly, rising to his feet. My cheeks were burning and I just stared up at him, memorizing his beautiful face. What if he didn't come back?

"You have to go?" I whispered at last. Was I talking about now, or with his family? I didn't know. I just knew how wretched I would be if I couldn't see him again soon.

He nodded silently, watching as a tear escaped my lashes and trickled a betraying streak down my cheek. He looked like he wanted to say something else, but after a moment, he just said, "Take care, Mia."

"Bye, Griff." I watched him turn and walk out of the room. When he was gone, I curled into a ball and stared at the wall blankly, with unseeing, wet eyes.

More Proof

A little while later my mom came in and sat by my bed. She began rubbing my back and smoothing my hair, not saying anything for fifteen minutes or so. I could hardly believe she could hold her tongue for that long. I was impressed. Finally, she asked if Griff and I had a fight.

"No," I murmured reluctantly. "He's just going out of town with his family."

She seemed surprised. "Where are they going?"

"I don't know. It didn't come up."

"Funny time to take a vacation; Thanksgiving break is coming right up. Why go now?" she mused. "Did he say when he'll be back?"

"Nothing specific. Do I have to go to school tomorrow, Mom? I look like a freak." I made a pitiful scabby pout.

"As long as you can stay caught up," Mom gave in. "Have Jace pick up your homework, okay?"

"Thanks, Mom." I felt better with that weight off my shoulders. "If Jace comes over, send him on up."

"Sure. What about more ice or a hot bath first?"

"I'll be fine, Mom. I just want to rest and try and forget all about what happened." Don't I wish? I thought.

Mom looked at my cold plate of food. "You at least want me to warm that up?"

"Nah, I'm not hungry."

Worry written all over her face, she picked up the plate and headed downstairs.

Jace called an hour later, saying he hadn't had a chance to talk to his mom yet, and maybe it would be better if we did it together. I could tell he was having second thoughts about the whole thing. I told him that I wasn't up for it tonight, and that maybe we should wait a little longer before we told anyone else. He seemed relieved. I couldn't blame him. I still had my doubts, sometimes. I also asked him to get my homework tomorrow, and maybe the next day, depending on how I was feeling.

He wanted to know if he and Michelle should keep quiet about what happened. The quieter, the better, as far as I was concerned. I didn't need any extra questions and strange looks. But maybe the news had leaked out already. I was glad I wasn't going to have to face anyone tomorrow.

After I hung up, I grabbed the mystery I had been reading earlier, trying to calm my mind and ease it to sleep. I didn't want to think about the attack or the possibilities it represented. I really didn't want to dwell on Griff leaving or how I felt when he gave me that very soft, almost real, kiss. Stop that. I hated to think about the gossip that could be flying around school the next day. And what would I tell Quinn if I saw him tonight?

What I dreaded the most was the nightmares. Man, I hoped this book was good, because I needed a supremely enthralling, action-packed, can't-put-it-down, all-night distraction. Luckily, the book fit the bill. It wasn't until three o'clock that I finally slid into a painless sleep, with no nightmares, or lucid dreams, or any remembered dreams at all.

I stayed in bed all the next day, more out of pity than pain. I still ached a bit, but I think my spirit was more busted up than my face. When Jace came over with my homework, I got up and tried to act like everything was fine. He knew better.

"So, Griff wasn't at school today."

"Not much with the subtle, are we?" I shot back.

"Is that why you're so bummed?" That was Jace, as perceptive as always, unfortunately.

"Yeah, I knew he was leaving. He came over yesterday and told me he was going on vacation with his family."

"So, now that he's gone, I'll bet you wished you hadn't ignored him all last week."

"Thanks for rubbing it in. I really needed that. Way to kick a girl when she's down." I made a face at him. "Like to smack me in the eye, too?"

"Okay, okay. Chill." Even Jace could see I was not in the mood today. "Do you just want me to go?" He pointed to the pile of papers. "I picked up what homework I could." He stood up.

"No, please stay. It's cool. I'm just on the grumpy side."

"You need to burn off some angst. How about learning some more self-defense moves? I'm thinking they might come in handy. I mean, I hope not. But, um…" Jace trailed off.

"It's a good idea," I agreed. "Show me anything you think might help."

For the next hour, I worked off some stress and gave myself a mental boost. If I could really get good at some of these moves, I would feel a lot safer. Practicing everyday would give me something positive to focus on until Griff came back. And it would be fun to show off once he returned—whenever that was going to be.

Using my muscles felt good. I thought by tomorrow I would be up for a run, and knew that the endorphins would do my attitude more good than just about anything. A hot shower and a couple hours of homework later, I found myself hungry for the first time since the attack. My parents were thrilled when I came down to dinner. My dad's famous chicken enchiladas disappeared in no time at all.

My mom pushed for me to go to school the next day, but with my dad on my side, I got one more day of respite. Still dreading sleep, I read until very late, hoping to bypass any nighttime horrors. However, my subconscious had ideas of its own.

THE WIND WAS whipping my hair into my mouth as I tore up the steps to the shaky, crumbling porch. I had to get out of this storm. The front door was securely locked. I rang the doorbell half a dozen times before kicking it in frustration. I braced myself for a dash to the back door. Jumping off the side of the porch, I raced around the side yard and ran smack into a giant stone gargoyle. I pinballed off of the statue into a prickly shrub, gasping in surprise and shock.

The gargoyle twisted its thick stone neck and glared down at me. I squawked in astonishment and scrambled out of the bush, backpedaling across the yard. In a matter of moments, two smaller gargoyles sprung out of the darkness and trapped me, their cold claws digging into my arms. I began trembling, not able to move or utter a word of protest.

It wasn't until the creatures began dragging me into a basement window that I let loose the mother of all shrieks. "Mia," my name, floated in my ear, bringing knowledge and release. I had started to feel faint when I turned and saw Quinn, arms out to catch me as I collapsed. He freed me from the nightmare and brought me to that peaceful park again. I sagged in relief as I escaped my self-conjured terror.

"Finally," Quinn said fiercely. "You've been having horrible dreams and I haven't been able to do anything to help you. It's been making me crazy."

Quinn looked down at me. I was lying on my back letting the sun's rays soak into me, trying to erase the previous horror. "I'm a bit crazy, too." I mumbled, not wanting to move.

"What's going on?" Quinn touched my arm, calling back my attention.

"Do I have to talk about it right now?" I moaned. "I just want to lay here in the sun and forget."

"Please, Mia." Quinn brushed back my hair. "You might wake up any minute."

"Oh, okay." I sat up grumpily. I didn't want to remember.

"Did something bad happen?"

I rubbed my forehead and reluctantly began to speak. I explained in painful detail my near abduction and how I heard the word *Nequam*. I related Griff's rescue, and how I was battered and bruised, but otherwise okay.

Quinn was silent and still. I started getting nervous.

"Say something in your Terraran language, Quinn. You can speak more languages than English, can't you?"

Quinn began speaking rapidly and angrily in a fast-paced musical language. I recognized it immediately. "That's the language my attackers spoke," I whispered, hands reaching up to cover my face. All doubts vanished.

Terrarans were real, and they were responsible for my attack. How was I going to deal with this? There could be no police involvement. I couldn't talk to any other adults. I didn't have any idea how to protect myself. The only person who understood what was going on was trapped inside a necklace.

I was in such big trouble.

Quinn touched my arm and I jumped, having been so caught up in my own paranoid meanderings. "What?" I asked dazed.

His eyes were narrowed, his expression fierce. I was so startled by his appearance I gaped at him.

"I said, *'How did Griff save you, exactly?'*" Quinn growled.

"I don't know," I admitted. "He wouldn't tell me in detail. He said he scared the attackers off, but there were two of them, and, well, that doesn't seem very likely, does it?"

I looked at Quinn's severe face. "What is it?" I asked. "What are you thinking? You look so angry." I took his hand to distract him. "You're scaring me, Quinn."

"I'm not sure." Quinn squeezed my hand a little too tight and I eased mine back. "I don't trust Griff," he said slowly. "A human couldn't take on two Terrarans and come out of it unscathed. You said he wasn't injured, right?"

"Not that I saw." I was getting angry now. "But Quinn, no way can you suspect Griff of anything. He saved me. If it weren't for him, I would have been captured for sure. And you would probably be dead, your necklace destroyed," I finished brutally.

"Why are you so positive that Griff is innocent? I think your emotions are clouding your judgment," Quinn snapped, daring me to disagree.

"Look, I don't care what you think about Griff," I spat. "What am *I* supposed to do to stay alive? That is a pretty big priority for you, isn't it? You still need my help, don't you?" I folded my arms and glared at him.

He ran his hands through his hair and took a deep breath. His voice was more calm and controlled when he spoke. "Mia, I'm sorry. I was out of line. I'm just worried about you and, I suppose, a little angry that I wasn't there to save you myself."

I relaxed a bit. "It's okay. We're both on edge. Things are pretty scary, aren't they?"

"I feel so helpless trapped in here," Quinn whispered harshly. "I've got to get out."

I could feel the desperation behind the words, and I went over next to him and put my arm around his shoulder.

"We're going to figure this out. In the meantime, any advice on what to do if someone from Terrara comes after me again? Any plans of attack, weaknesses, Kryptonite loopholes, or the like?"

"Huh?" Quinn looked confused.

"Never mind. Just tell me if there's anything a human can do against a Terraran."

"I'm not really sure. My parents didn't confront their enemies. They hid," Quinn said bitterly. "I will try and think, but my knowledge is so limited."

"I guess I'd better hope they don't know where I live." I sighed and lay back, face lifted to the sun. This situation was getting worse and worse.

"Wait. *Iron*. My father couldn't touch iron. It was like a symbol of the machines that humans chose over magic. You can protect yourself if you carry around something made of iron." Quinn looked relieved to have remembered something useful.

I looked doubtful. "That sounds like part of a fairy tale I heard when I was a child."

Quinn raised his eyebrows.

"And I guess that's where those tales come from, isn't it? That is so weird." I rubbed my eyes. "Well, I guess I'll be making some iron jewelry soon. I hope that's even possible. What's made of iron these days, anyway?"

"You're asking me?" Quinn grimaced. "Since I'm only half-Terraran," Quinn continued, "I don't think I'd be affected much by iron if I was free of my necklace. But I am afraid if you wear something made of iron, that it might limit my coming into your dreams. I don't know. We'll have to try it though. You have to be safe."

Quinn came over and lay beside me. "I really do care about you, and even though it makes you mad, I still don't trust Griff. Maybe I'm just being overcautious and probably a little jealous, I admit it. But I need you to be safe. And not just so that you can help me."

I looked up into those earnest green eyes and my last trace of anger dissolved. I knew he was truly worried about me. I reached out and brushed those irresistible curls. "I care about you too." I let my arm fall back over my eyes, blocking out the sun. I was so exhausted. What happened if you fell asleep while you were lucid dreaming? I wondered. Would you wake up, go into another dream, or start a non-dreaming cycle of sleep?

Quinn wrapped his arms around me. I snuggled up close to him. The next thing I was aware of was the sun streaming in through the blinds in the guest bedroom window. The clock on the wall said eleven. My stomach growled. My first thought was I've got to find me some iron.

MOM AND DAD had left for work so I could raid the house without their curious looks and raised eyebrows. First, I moved my stuff back down to my room, feeling sick and tired of the sterile-feeling guest room. Then I rounded up any decorations that seemed to be made of cast iron, a candlestick, a small side table and some antique golf clubs. I arranged the table near the front door, the candlestick by the back door, and the clubs by my bed.

Then I started scouring the Internet for whatever information I could find on iron, whether it was jewelry, scrollwork, antique beds, etc. I needed something to carry with me. I settled on a meteorite charm that was very cool. I had forgotten that most meteorites were made of iron. I smiled, as I realized my Kryptonite crack was less of a joke than I had thought. I also found a set of vintage iron tools, including a small hammer with a loop for a handle, and several wrenches. I'd carry at least one in my backpack or purse, maybe another in a pocket if they were small enough.

I'd found out that some of the precious stones that I used in my jewelry contained iron, like tiger iron. Duh. And hematite. I pulled out my jewelry box, figuring that keeping my hands busy would be a good way to deal with my distracted mind. I had a bracelet made of hematite that a friend had brought back from somewhere in South America. I thought I might take it apart and make something new.

As I worked, even though I tried not to, I thought about last night's conversation. Quinn had been so angry, and I had been so defensive. Griff had been the catalyst. I still felt confident about Griff's behavior, though. He *was* trying to protect me, I was sure of it. And yet those seeds of doubt were sown, and once planted, they were so hard to dig up. I knew Griff was keeping something from me. But what?

I sighed, finishing up the clasp on my new bracelet. When I had hooked it around my wrist, I felt a sense of security, false though it probably was, but at least I had something physical to give me a feeling of hope and protection.

After I cleaned up I really wanted to go running. But since I had stayed home from school, I felt like I had better not get caught running through the neighborhood, so I had to settle for the old treadmill in the unfinished part of the basement. I plugged in my iPod and ran for an hour, listening to an audio book. My bruises had faded to yellow, and bothered me only a little as I ran. Afterwards, I practiced what I could of Jace's defensive moves, without a partner.

A long hot shower, which I let run into a soaking bath, turned my mood even more hopeful. I thought I could reasonably face school the next day without panicky nerves. Jace brought me more homework, and I made sure I was fairly caught up before I went to bed that night. As I climbed up into my loft, I dragged one of the old golf clubs up with me and lay it on the side of my bed within easy reach. Just in case.

16

The Lull before the Storm

My stomach was queasy as I rode to school with Jace the next morning. He had told me that no one had heard about my "mishap," so not to be nervous. I couldn't help it. I wished for the umpteenth time that Griff was going to be there, and wondered yet again when he'd be coming back.

I flipped the mirror down for the second time, checking out my array of faded bruises.

"Just tell them that some kid beat you up and stole your Halloween candy."

"Har har."

"I seem to remember someone trying to do that to you when we were in elementary school. You really let him have it. I can still picture the kid running home, crying like a baby, even though I can't remember his name."

"Travis Johnson." I ran a finger over my lip; the scabs were almost gone. "No way was I going to let someone get away with all my hard-earned candy. So I smacked the snot out of him. Mom was going to ground me until she found out he jumped me first. My dad laughed all night and called me 'Mighty Mia.'"

"With all the self defense I'm teaching you, maybe you'll actually start deserving that nickname." Jace glanced over at me as we pulled into the school driveway. "So, any news? Have you seen anyone hanging around?"

"Nope, I've got some protection now, though. And they've lost their element of surprise. They won't catch me unawares next time." My gaze was determined and grim.

"Geez, you sound like some paranoid schizophrenic. I can't believe you are carrying an iron candlestick in your book bag. Doesn't it weight a ton?"

I shrugged. "Who cares, as long as it works? I'm getting some lighter stuff in the mail in the next couple of days."

As we walked to class, I felt the eyes of numerous students scanning my face. I tried to mentally shut down, ignoring their questioning looks, striding quickly to my classroom.

I made it through to the weekend, dodging questions and catching up on homework, practicing self-defense and checking the mail. My vintage tools came on Friday, and they were every bit as cool as their photos claimed. I stuck a wrench in my book bag, replacing the heavy candlestick, and put another small one into my jeans pocket. The hammer with the looped handle was awesome, and I was trying to figure out what to hang it on when my mom walked in.

"What kind of hammer is that?" she wanted to know, getting a bottle of water out of the fridge.

"Just something for my jewelry," I lied quickly. Maybe it wasn't a lie. I'll bet it would be great for pounding silver wire into fun shapes, I thought, hefting it and whacking it into my palm.

My mom looked at me closely. "Mia, I'm a little worried about you."

Uh-oh, I thought. Now, I'm going to pay for not having spilled my guts about my *feelings* after my attack. But what was I going to say about it? There was too much I couldn't tell, even if I had wanted to.

"I've been talking to my friend Diane," she said cautiously.

"The shrink?" I tossed her a glare, my voice antagonistic. "I don't need to talk to anyone. I'm fine." I tried to keep my voice level. It wasn't easy.

"Look, it wouldn't have to be official." Mom could tell I was mad, and was using her soothing, pleading voice. "I thought I'd have her over for dinner next week."

"No way, Mom." I said clearly and calmly. "I'm not talking about it any more. I've said all I have to say, and everything is fine. You can invite her over if you want, but I'll go to Jace's."

I packed the bubble wrap back into my box and stuck the whole thing under my arm. I turned to go downstairs. "You don't need to worry about me, Mom," I threw over my shoulder. "Let's not make a bigger deal out of this than it is, okay?" I paused on the top step, giving my mom the most charming, genuine smile I could dig up.

Mom still looked doubtful, but at least she smiled a little in response. I kept my fingers crossed all the way down, hoping she bought it.

By the end of the following week, I was pretty sure I had my mom convinced of my stability. Life had gone back into a very familiar routine. School, Jace, homework and work. I saw no strangers hanging around the house or school. I don't know if it was the iron, but I hadn't had any lucid dreams for a while. And Griff was gone. Life was the same as it had been for several years. And I hated it every stupid minute of it. I smiled and made nice with everyone in public, and when I was alone it all came crashing down. My life felt empty without Griff, and without Quinn. Normal things were tediously dull. Not that I wanted to be attacked again. But my life felt *wrong.*

I worked out fiercely, taking out all my frustration on Jace as he taught me, or on the trails as I ran after school. Jace was pretty good-natured about it, and mostly just complimented me on my vast improvement. My boring life started making me think I was doing all this for nothing. Maybe I *was* need-a-shrink crazy, after all. But I kept working out like a maniac, anyways, my subconscious telling me it was just the lull before the storm.

Saturday night I came home fried from work. Things were getting busy at the jewelry store as the holidays drew near, just a week and a half before Thanksgiving break, when my dad and I would be heading to my nan's house. I laid my leather jacket over a kitchen chair and made myself a cup of hot chocolate. Sipping it brought back memories of Griff and me in line for the haunted house. I remembered his arms around me as I leaned against him. I shook my head in annoyance and climbed down the stairs to my room.

On my desk was a manila envelope with my name on it and no return address. My heart gave a funny lurch in anticipation, as I suspected whom it was from. As I sat cross-legged on the floor, I ripped the top and pulled out several pictures. The one on top was of Griff and me goofing around in our

Halloween costumes. I smiled, as I recalled Griff pretending to
bite me, leaning over my neck, fingers gripping my shoulders.
Our costumes looked fabulous, and Griff was make-my-heart-
stop gorgeous, of course, even though he was mugging it up
for the camera.

Beneath that photo were a couple shots of Jace and Michelle
in their pirate costumes. They both looked fantastic. I thought
how happy Jace was going to be to get these. He was already out
on a date with Michelle tonight, so I'd run them over tomorrow morning. He'd love another excuse to go to Michelle's
house tomorrow. He was so crazy about her, and luckily she
seemed to feel the same way.

The next photo was a serious pose of Griff and me. My
adrenaline started pumping, just looking at it. Griff was behind
me, gazing down at me. He had his arms wrapped around my
waist, and I was resting my head against his shoulder, tipping
my head back to look up into those way-too-pretty eyes. The
chemistry sparking between us was obvious even in a two-
dimensional print. Oh my. I could feel myself blushing, just
looking at the picture. Apparently, as soon as Griff printed this,
he knew *exactly* how I felt about him, even though I refused to
say the words. What was that corny saying about a picture and
a thousand words? Damn. Guess it was true.

I flipped over to the last picture. It was one Griff had taken
of me by the lamppost. I was glancing up over my bare shoulder,
having finished adjusting Quinn's necklace around my ankle.
Again, there was that haunted, distant look on my face, and
with the '30s-style dress and makeup, wow! I looked like some
old movie starlet from a horror flick. No way was that of me.

On the photo was a sticky note:

Mia, you are the most incredible girl I have ever met. You have no idea how hard it was for me to leave. Please be careful. I will be back as soon as I can.
  Griff

MY HEART POUNDED fast and furiously. And it was trying to make a choice I didn't think I knew how to make. No matter how much I cared about Quinn and wanted to help him, I wasn't sure any emotion could top what I felt for Griff at that moment.

I lay back on my floor pondering my fickle emotions, wondering if by my next lucid dream my heart will have flip-flopped again. If both boys were here in the real world, I wouldn't be in such a predicament, I felt sure. Could someone be in love with two people at the same time? If love was the right word— *infatuation* perhaps? Obsessed by handsome faces and pretty words? "Enough of this," I scolded myself. "I have other things than boys to worry about right now, like the fact that someone from another dimension might, right this minute, be stalking me, hoping to steal a set of jewelry containing three people who were only half-human."

That's it. I sounded like a raving lunatic. I tossed the way-too-distracting photos onto the desk, and tromped up the stairs to the family room. What was wrong with my life? Why couldn't I just be normal? And why, when my life did seem to go back to normal, did I feel so dissatisfied? I sighed and turned on the TV, trying to forget everything by turning my brain to mush for a couple hours.

IT WAS THE Tuesday before Thanksgiving and my mom and dad and I sat down to an early feast. Since Dad and I were going to Washington, my mom decided to visit her sister in San Jose for the holiday. Dad was taking her to the airport tomorrow morning before we left for Nan's house.

"Pass the mashed potatoes?" I asked my dad.

"You look like you could use a few more helpings," my dad teased. "Have you been dieting?"

"No." I admitted truthfully. With so much exercising and working out, I had lost a few pounds, but I thought it looked good. I had more lean muscle than I ever had before. I felt strong and confident—ready—in case of any trouble. "I've been running a lot, I guess."

"You look very pretty." My mom had been extra watchful since we had our little chat, and I made sure to act upbeat and happy around her as much as possible.

"Thanks, Mom." I made the effort.

"Have you heard from Griff?" she asked, a little too casually.

"Just the one letter." I finished my second helping of mashed potatoes, pushing my plate away and feeling too full for pumpkin pie just yet. "Maybe he'll be back after the break," I said more optimistically than I actually felt.

"You excited to see Nan's house again?" Dad asked. "I'm afraid it's not going to be the same." He sounded like he was warning himself more than me. It was the house he grew up in, after all.

"It will be nice to go through all the memories and pictures." I got up and put my hands on his shoulders. "Thanks for planning the trip, Dad. I really am looking forward to it." I gave him a hug then reached down for his plate. "Are you done?" At his nod, I took it over to the sink, rinsed and loaded it into the dishwasher. I helped with the rest of the dishes, and then went downstairs to pack.

"Save me some pie," I yelled from the bottom of the stairs.

I had just zipped up my suitcase when Jace came strolling in with two plates of pie and whipped cream.

"*Mmmm.* Good timing," I smiled, reaching for a plate.

"Hey, these are mine," he teased. "Go get your own."

"Don't make me hurt you," I threatened.

"Holy crap! Show me your bicep again," Jace said. I proudly flexed.

"Here, just take the pie. I don't think my ego could take getting my butt kicked by a girl." He pretended to quake in fear.

"Stop it," I laughed good-naturedly, pleased by his compliment.

We sat and ate for a while in silence. My mom's homemade pumpkin pie made Thanksgiving dinner feel complete, even though it was two days early. My dad and I would be reheating leftovers on the day of, or maybe eating hamburgers. It didn't matter, as long as we were at my Nan's house. I couldn't wait to get going.

"So, no activity on the supernatural front?" Jace wanted to know.

"Nothing serious, obviously," I confirmed. Although, I was pretty sure that someone had been shadowing me for the last few days. I could never catch sight of anyone. It was just a feeling, but it was a strong feeling. I kept all my iron handy, just in case.

"I'm excited to look for clues at my nan's house." I was watching Jace run his finger around the plate, getting up all the last bits of whipped cream. "You want another piece? I'm sure Mom would be happy to give you one," I said, eying his movements.

"In a minute," Jace replied. "What do you think you're going to find?"

"I really want to find some clue to help get Quinn free. If you could see him, then you'd know I was telling the truth." I felt a little bad that Jace still acted like my imagination was running wild. He believed that someone had singled me out, but still couldn't come to terms with my explanation. I figured I'd get proof for him one of these days. I really hoped my proof wouldn't be painfully procured.

"I believe you," Jace insisted, but I rolled by eyes.

"So, are your brothers coming home for Thanksgiving?"

"Yep, all four of us will be there to drive my mom nuts. She'll love it. Plus Mike's bringing his wife and the twins. So it will be a madhouse. Too bad you'll miss it."

"Say hi to everyone for me." I was jealous of Jace's family get-togethers. They were completely insane, with four brothers, but in a good way. From the time I moved into the neighborhood and made friends with Jace, I was always included. It was nice.

"Any plans with Michelle?"

Jace frowned, "No, she's off to Mexico with her family. Hear anything more from Griff?"

I shook my head.

"You taking his photos with you?" Jace smiled slyly.

I blushed. "None of your bee's wax."

"Thought as much. I hope he comes back soon so you can be done with all this pining."

I reached over and smacked him. "I don't pine for anyone. That's ridiculous."

Jace gave me an annoyingly knowing smile.

"Besides, he's probably forgotten all about me." I worried about that a lot. "He might not even come back at all."

"You've got to be kidding me. You are so blind. He *totally* likes you."

I smiled over at Jace. "I really hope so." Then I blushed again. *"Argh,* I hate liking someone."

"Oh, get over it," Jace laughed. "I'm getting more pie. Want some?"

"Just a sliver." I handed over my plate. "Thanks."

I looked over my room, making sure I didn't miss anything important. On impulse, I grabbed the sketch I had made of Quinn and tucked it into my suitcase. I hadn't had a lucid dream for so long; I was tempted to take off my iron jewelry before bed. I waffled for a minute, and then decided to wait until I got to Washington. I'd have more to tell Quinn in a couple of days, I reasoned.

I went upstairs and ate another piece of pie with Jace and my dad. I hugged Jace tightly as he left, which made him snort and exclaim, "Don't get all mushy on me!" after which I punched him in the stomach. Laughing, he went on his way with a third piece of pie on a paper plate, claiming it was for his mom.

Pftt. I knew him better than that.

Nan's House

The two days on the road blew by faster than I would have thought. My dad is so carefree and comfortable to hang out with. And more importantly, I had loaded my iPod to the max. We went through every album by Social Distortion and the Ramones, courtesy of my dad, and I introduced him to a few bands that he acted like he enjoyed just as much. I had bought several audiobooks for the occasion as well, and we listened to *Lucky Jim* by Kingsley Amis, my dad's favorite book of all time. I definitely scored points with him for bringing that. And we started *The Lord of the Rings,* which brought back wonderful memories of summers with Nan.

We took turns driving my mom's Volvo, since the Miata was too small in case we wanted to bring anything back home. I hoped what I found would be so small my dad wouldn't notice. The crucial clue…the key to it all! I couldn't help getting my hopes up. They sped along with me as I drove, picturing Quinn, free of his necklace, able to be reunited with his family. I was basking in my future success as I zipped down the familiar street and parked in the steep driveway blanketed with pine needles.

My dad and I exchanged goofy grins while we unbuckled our seat belts. He fished through his keychain for the right key, and we both restrained ourselves from running to the door. The yard was trimmed neatly, kept up by the company my dad had hired. The tall trees hovering over the house looked comforting and familiar, and I stopped for a moment to take a deep breath of the humid, pine-scented air. Smiling, I hurried up the steps, excited to go inside.

I bumped into my dad's back. He was frozen in the doorway.

"What's up?" I demanded. He didn't move.

"Hey, Dad." I pushed him gently into the hallway. "Let me in."

As I moved past him, my eyes took in the scene of devastation and I, too, stood stock-still, my brain refusing to accept the reality of what I was seeing. The living room looked like a tornado had come down the chimney and tossed the entire room into chaos. Furniture was upside down, shelves emptied, their contents strewn willy-nilly, lamps broken, books ripped. My stomach heaved violently, and I ran to the bathroom, legs giving way in front of the toilet. Luckily, I hadn't eaten for a while and there wasn't much to come up. I sat on the floor for several minutes, too nervous to stand up.

Dad appeared in the doorway, still looking stunned. "Mia, are you okay?"

"Yeah," I managed. "Is the whole house wrecked?"

"I'm afraid so." Dad rubbed his forehead. "I guess I'd better call the police. I can't even tell if anything is missing, though."

My stomach twisted again painfully, as realization poured over me. "Nan's ring and bracelet," I gasped. "Dad, do you know where they are?"

"Huh?" Dad just looked blankly at me, like I'd said something in a foreign language.

"The bracelet and ring that match this one." I held out my necklace. "Do you know where they are? Were they in this house?" I almost shouted in my panic.

"Yes," my dad answered slowly, as if just making the connection.

"Where were they?" I asked desperately. "Are they still here?"

I got up from the floor and grabbed my dad's arm. "Show me where."

Please let them still be here, I thought, anxiously. But I had a sickening feeling that they would be gone.

Dad led me to my nan's room in a silent stupor. He picked up a drawer that had been dumped on the floor. An empty box lay underneath it. "Last time I was here, they were in this box."

"No!" I cried out, holding the box in my trembling hand. What was I going to tell Quinn? Tears welled up and I brushed them away violently. What could I do? I couldn't even tell how long ago this had happened.

"Maybe she moved them?" I asked my dad, not really believing the possibility.

"It's my fault," my dad whispered.

"What?" I was confused. "How could this be your fault?" I knew what had happened, but I was pretty sure my dad had

no clue what was going on. This must seem like a random bur-
glary to him—a cruel yet arbitrary act of violence.

"I need to sit down," my dad said shakily, and led the way
down the hall. We rearranged the mess in the living room and
found places to sit on the trashed floral couch. I hunched in the
corner with my arms wrapped around my legs, trying to figure
out what to tell my dad, where to start.

"Nan tried to tell me some things before she died," my dad
began unexpectedly. "She told me she had some valuables that
needed protection, things like her bracelet and ring. She gave
me the necklace for you at the same time in that envelope."
Dad hesitated. "She told me I needed to hide them, but be
ready to hand them over if someone named Grayson came to
get them."

My head shot up at the mention of Grayson, Quinn's father.
"Did you do it? Did you hide them?" I asked earnestly.

"I thought she was sick and talking out of her head. I
brought them home and put them away in her dresser jewelry
box. I remember thinking that I would go check later if that
secret place really existed, but then she had her second stroke
and I never got around to it. There were so many other things
to do." His voice broke. "I'm still not certain if this–" he waved
his hand at the mess, "is even connected to her request." He
put his head in his hands.

"It's okay, Dad." I touched his arm lightly. "Do you remember where she wanted you to put her jewelry?" I had to know.

"She told me she had a hidden place under the carpet in
her guest room, left corner under the bed. Can you imagine
Nan dragging a bed out of the way and tearing up carpet and

flooring? Sounds crazy, right? Why in heaven's name would Nan have a secret stash?"

"Let's go find it and see if the thieves got into it." I was on my feet and tearing down the hall before I finished my sentence.

The guest room was in shambles, mattress tossed but the metal frame was still in place. That gave me hope. Dad and I wrestled the heavy bed frame out of the way and then carefully pulled back the corner carpet. There was a hole cut into the floorboards. I pried it open with the small screwdriver on my dad's Leatherman keychain. Inside was a heavy box. It looked and felt like cast iron. With the huge iron bed frame above it, it was no wonder it had been missed.

I lifted it out carefully and we took it into the living room for examination. I studied the box from every angle, but couldn't find a way to open it. I raised my eyes to my dad. "Did she tell you how to open the box?"

He fidgeted uncomfortably. "Well, she told me a word would open it. Like magic."

"So what's the word?" I asked without blinking.

"It doesn't make any sense. It's an old Latin word meaning 'worthless,' or 'good for nothing.'"

"*Nequam*," I said, firmly. The box sprang open with a slight snap, followed by my dad's loud gasp. Inside were many notes and letters, all of which I hoped would be vitally useful.

There was no ring or bracelet.

"What is going on?" my dad demanded quietly.

"Boy, Dad, that's a loaded question." I made a rueful face. "I don't even know where to begin, especially since I only know part of this very confusing story."

My dad folded his arms and put on his best looking-down-his-nose professor face, as if to say, "Try me. I'm smart enough to keep up." What he actually said was, "Tell me everything you know now, before we call the authorities about this."

I had to smirk, thinking about what the authorities would make of the truth I was about to relate to my dad.

"Okay, Dad," I agreed. "But you have to promise not to judge what I say until I am completely done. This is not going to be something you will enjoy hearing. You're going to think I'm crazy. But I swear it's the truth I'm telling you, okay?"

Dad nodded his head and gave me a polite listening face. I sighed and began. I talked about the necklace, the lucid dreams, Quinn (both young and now), his parents, Nan's help, and the Terraran mythology. Then I retold the story of the recent attack in light of this new information. It took a very long time, and it was dark when I had finished.

Dad just sat there, staring into space. I figured it was going to be a while before he could process any of this, so I suggested we go out and get a hamburger or something to eat. He got up numbly and we got into the car and drove away. I pulled through the drive through, and within a half an hour we were back at the house with hot food. Dad still hadn't said a word. I let him be.

As we ate I decided it would be a good time to look at the papers from Nan's box. I unfolded some letters from Anna to my Nan. They confirmed what I had just told my dad and I handed them over after I finished them. The letters made me sad, reading about Anna and Grayson's difficulties, hiding, trying to raise a family, always plagued by the fear of being caught.

Finally, I found something I could use. It was the letter talking about the jewelry. Anna asked her sister to carefully guard her children. And she made careful instructions in case she and Grayson were not able to return. There were words to a spell,

I guess, written in a language that I could not read. I figured that Anna had taught Nan some Terraran during the years. I hadn't thought about the language barrier. I knew I would have to memorize the words so I could write them out for Quinn in my next lucid dream. Oh boy. There were a lot of words. I'd have to get started tonight before I went to sleep.

I began searching for loose pieces of paper to start writing down phrases. I memorized best if I wrote things over and over until I could do it without thinking. It was the key to most of my good grades. My dad watched what I was copying. Finally, he spoke.

"As a professor of classics, I teach mythology all the time. But this tale you've told me is just too much. A new mythology. Magical beings that exist outside of legends and fables. My head is struggling to go along with it all, Mia."

"It was easier for me, since I learned only a little at a time." I wrote the first sentence out five times. Then started on the next.

My dad stood by the window, gazing out into the dark backyard. I thought about someone staring back in at us, and the hair on the back of my neck rose. "Here, Dad. Take this." I handed him a wrench from my pocket. He looked at it suspiciously. "It's iron," I said. "It provides some protection against Terrarans, remember? Just put it in your pocket, okay?"

My dad slipped it into his front pocket reluctantly. "I never called the police," Dad murmured. "I guess I'll do it in the morning. I don't know what I'd say to them at this point." He moved to the hallway. "I'll try to fix up some beds for us to sleep in."

I looked around, thinking that I'd rather go to a motel. I felt exposed here. Vulnerable. In fact, I doubted I'd be able to close my eyes, much less get any sleep. I was about to open my mouth, when my dad turned to me and said, "However, if you are right in your theories, maybe it would be best to go somewhere else tonight."

Relief in my eyes, I stood up gratefully and gathered what little I had brought in initially. I stuffed the letters back in the iron box and scooped it up as well. "Let's go." I stared at the large dark window in the living room. "I'm starting to get creeped out."

We drove to the closest motel and I made sure we got a room on an upper level. Not that a second story really mattered if Terrarans could fly, but at least they might be slightly discouraged by the fact that someone might spot them, *hopefully*. Once inside, I took a shower, feeling grimy from the long day on the road.

While my dad showered, I finished copying my notes. I was completely fried. I took off my iron meteorite bracelet and lay it on the bedside table next to my other little iron wrench, hoping I would lucid dream so I could give Quinn the information I had memorized. I dreaded telling him about the missing jewelry and Nan's ransacked house, but I longed to see his face.

I sighed, turning over on my side, pushing the nasty bedspread away from my face and wriggling uncomfortably on the rock-hard motel mattress. Nothing was turning out the way I had imagined. I closed my eyes and wished I were curling up in my Nan's house, snuggling under her extra soft down blankets, all safe and secure. I had felt so confident on the way here. Now I didn't know what to think anymore. Puzzling over what had happened, I fell into a restless sleep before my dad turned out the lights.

THE WOODS CLOSED in eerily around me. I was lost. I heard the scream of a wild animal behind me. I darted down the dirt path, feet slipping on the loose rocks and pinecones. Someone was chasing me—I could feel it—but I couldn't hear any footsteps. Suddenly, my legs flew out from under me and I slid down the hill painfully on my butt. As I frantically scrambled to my feet, I quickly brushed my hands over my cut and trembling legs. Something was swooping down from above. I screamed and cowered on the trail when, through my panicky gasps, I heard a familiar voice.

"Quinn!" I called out. Turning, I reached out shaky limbs for his familiar embrace. "I missed you."

His arms held me firmly to him. I relaxed, listening to his heartbeat through his shirt. I knew I had so many things to tell him, but I just needed a minute to forget all the difficult things and enjoy his closeness. After a few moments, Quinn released me.

"It's been so long," he sounded frustrated. "What's been going on? I was so worried."

"Let's find a place to sit down. I have some important things to tell you."

We walked through the woods into my Nan's backyard. I went up the steps and deliberately opened the back door. The house was back to pristine condition and I looked around wistfully, taking in the scene I had expected to find when I arrived at Nan's real house. I sat on my Nan's floral couch, style straight out of the '60s, the blue and brown color scheme now back in vogue. I leaned back, resting my head on the oversized cushions, not wanting to be the messenger of bad news.

"Tell me everything," Quinn urged.

I took his hand, preparing how to break the news in my head. There wasn't an easy way to put it, so I ended up just spitting it out.

"My dad and I reached Nan's house today. The house had been torn apart, and, Quinn, I'm afraid your sisters' jewelry is gone." My voice broke; I couldn't help it. "I am so sorry, Quinn. I will do whatever I can to get them back."

Quinn had gone motionless. His eyes glazed over in misery. I tentatively stretched out my hand, but he arose swiftly, anger distorting his features, and let his fury destroy the room around us. I cowered as he drove his fist through the windows, swept decorations off the mantelpiece, turned over tables, and ripped down curtains. After several terrifying minutes, he dropped down onto the floor and covered his face in his hands and wept like a broken child.

Carefully picking my way through the mess, I knelt beside him and stroked his hair, murmuring sympathetic words in his ears, letting him empty himself of grief. I hated being the one to crush his fragile hopes of reuniting his family. I was a bit stunned at his loss of control, although I really couldn't blame him. The thought of losing my mom and dad made me sick. Just the sight of my Nan's destroyed house had me running for the bathroom. And now his weeping was tearing me apart. I had to do something to help ease some of his pain.

"I think I found the formula to free you," I said gently, trying to insert the only sliver of hope I had. Quinn's body went suddenly still but he didn't raise his head. "I discovered an iron box which contains lots of letters, including one with a lot of stuff written in Terraran. I didn't know how to read it, so I memorized the written words. Here, I'll write them down for you."

I got up and searched the kitchen for some paper and a pen. The telephone table yielding what I wanted, I sat crossed-legged next to Quinn, who was still huddled in a tortured ball with his head bowed between his tucked-up knees. I wrote quickly, my fingers flying across the page. As I continued writing, Quinn raised his head, pushing back his tangled hair. He began reading the words aloud in his beautiful language, although his voice was harsh and rasping.

Moved by the sound of his voice, I looked up entranced by his dilated pupils focused on words I had just written. "More please," he begged, when he had finished all I had written.

Startled, I picked up where I had left off. I felt as if my hand was guided by something other than my memory, for in places where my mind froze, forgetting the letters, my hand continued confidently, spelling out unknown phrases and sentences.

At last I dropped the pen. Quinn's face had become hard and resolute, and he stared at the words like a lifeline, determination sweeping away the traces of pain and grief. I couldn't stop myself from gently wiping away a stray tear that lingered on his cheek. He grabbed my hand and brushed his lips softly across my knuckles.

"Does this letter help?" I asked earnestly. "Please, let me help you."

"I'm so sorry, Mia," he whispered, "I was out of my head, not able to think of anything except my sisters being gone. I hope I didn't scare you." He turned away and surveyed the room, looking embarrassed.

"Forget it. No harm done." I squeezed his hand and he glanced at me again. "This house is only a dream. And, hey, I wasn't very good at cushioning the bad news. I'm really sorry I was so blunt. But this letter I found—it's good news, right?"

"Very good," he agreed. He managed a small smile. "These words promise a way out. But I can't do it by myself; I will need your help more than ever now."

"Of course," I agreed quickly. "I'll do anything."

I studied his green eyes, feeling relieved that the anger had faded. I still felt anxious, though, like he had thrust his violent emotions away, but they were still bubbling just under the surface like a sleeping volcano, ready to burst forth at the slightest provocation. I wondered what he would do once he was free from his necklace prison. Maybe I didn't want to know.

"I need you to memorize these words," he continued. "I will say them to you so you can hear the stresses and intonation. You will need to practice them over and over until you can say them without flaw. Can you do that?"

"I'll do my best." I scrunched up my nose. "I've never been good at any of the foreign language classes I had to take in school. I hope this is easier than French."

"I have a feeling you will do fine. You can see us when no one else can, which makes me suspect that you will have a knack for our language, as well."

"Guess we'll see," I said hesitantly, not really buying into that theory. "We better start, though. I want you to go over this with me as many times as possible before I wake up."

We moved into the family room, away from all the broken bits and pieces. Sitting across from each other at the small dining room table, we began practicing. After many tries, I finally got the hang of the inflections and the words began to feel natural in my mouth. Quinn was as patient and calm as he was angry and violent earlier. I felt the tension easing out of me with each sentence successfully learned.

The dream stretched on and on. It felt like the longest lucid dream I had ever had. I wondered if it had anything to do with being near Nan's house. Maybe lucid dreaming would be easier here. Or did I have some kind of automatic access to Quinn here on his home turf? The thought did give me some comfort.

We finally finished the whole paragraph. I read it out loud several times to make sure I had everything down just right. Quinn gave me an enthusiastic smile. "You speak Terraran like a native." I flushed with pride, beaming at him.

"Too bad I don't know what I'm saying," I laughed. "So, what's the next step?"

"You will need to be able to say these words when you are awake, of course. I'm not sure of the rest of the circumstances. We might need to try it a few different ways before we can get it right. I think, first, just holding the necklace. Then if that fails, we will have to get more creative. Were there any other letters that you haven't read yet?"

"Yes, quite a few. I knew this one was important so I copied it before I read everything else. I will read them all tomorrow. Maybe, there are more clues to tell us if breaking the spell is more complex than just saying the words."

Quinn rubbed his forehead, frowning slightly. I leaned my head against his shoulder. "We are almost there. Don't stress it. In a very short time you will be free. And I think you owe me a ride. In the sky, at dark, so no one can see us." I smiled at the thought.

"I'll owe you more than that," Quinn said softly. "You have helped me so much. Just having someone to talk to has been more than I could have hoped for." He reached across the table and pushed my hair back from my forehead, tracing a finger down my cheek. I sighed deeply, happy and content here in my Nan's house with Quinn sitting so close to me.

"Teach me how to say something else in Terraran."

"Okay." He thought a minute, and then said something short and melodic.

"*Mmmm.* That was beautiful. What does it mean?"

"Thank you," Quinn's eyes were shining and very intense.

"Say it again." He did and I repeated it slowly until I had it right.

"Soon I'll be able to tell you that in the real world." Quinn got up and stood next to my chair. He reached down and pulled me firmly to my feet. He leaned close and bent his head toward me, his intentions obvious. I have to say I had a flash of panic, thinking of Griff. My thoughts tossed around madly in my head for a split second and I hesitated almost too long. At the last moment I turned my head slightly, and his lips landed on the corner of my mouth. They lingered there briefly, and then he raised his questioning eyes to mine.

I felt my cheeks fill with color, my tongue awkward in my mouth.

"I don't know what I'm feeling," I stammered.

He put a finger on my lips. "It's okay," he assured me. "I'll be out of here soon, and then we will see what happens. I apologize if I made you feel uncomfortable."

I slid my arms around him and lay my cheek against his chest. "I do care about you very much, Quinn. Things are just terribly confusing right now. In so many ways."

"Soon," he murmured, fingertips on my neck, "I'll be in the real world and things will be better."

"I hope so," I murmured, a chill running down my spine that had nothing to do with his fingers. "I really, really hope so." Somewhere in the back of my mind an annoying little voice taunted that we were nowhere near the end. That we were at the beginning of a dangerous race, and the finish line hadn't even been announced yet.

18

Madness in the Woods

I woke up clear-headed with foreign words on the tip of my tongue. I repeated the Terraran phrases to myself that morning as I showered and got dressed. My dad got ready slowly. I knew he was depressed at having to call the police and report the disaster to strangers, who would likely feign concern for a few a moments, then leave with no realistic help offered. I wasn't sure if I could handle their visit, either.

My dad and I discussed our story as we drove over to the house to meet with the detectives. No mention of the hidden box, but we would report the missing jewelry. Not that we thought there was a chance in a million the police would be able to recover the bracelet and ring.

I squirmed in my seat, feeling uneasy and frustrated. I wanted to go for a run, doubting I'd get a chance to, but still longing for the chance to stretch my muscles and clear my head.

Thirty minutes later we sat across from two officers who looked barely interested in the damage done to the house. The older of the two—a puffy-faced and large-mustached man—asked questions. Meanwhile his partner, a blonde, muscular-looking woman with a square jaw, took notes. When it became obvious that my presence was unnecessary, I told them that I would be walking on the trails behind the house.

"Are you sure that's a good idea, Mia?" My dad pointedly inquired.

"It's daylight," I reminded him, "and a public trail. I'll only walk on the path directly behind our neighborhood." I took my cellphone and waved it around. "You can call me if you need me, okay?" I hoped they wouldn't, though. I wanted to walk and forget.

The police officers nodded, and my dad relented.

I left through the French door in the dining room, crossed the backyard to the gate in the back fence. I unlatched it and followed the small path from our gate to the main trail. The narrow path had become wild and overgrown, and I stepped over piles of dead leaves and broken-down branches until I reached the groomed trail. I took off briskly down the familiar lane, smiling at remembered walks with Nan, picking blackberries, kicking pinecones, and avoiding the giant slugs that made me gag whenever I accidentally stepped on one.

"Hello, Mia." A voice startled me out of my daydreams, and I froze in horror at my carelessness.

I backed up in a panic, fumbling for my cell phone, as I tried to identify the person in front of me. I thought how foolish I had been to think I would be safe alone and outside. The public trail now felt isolated, with tall trees blocking the view of neighboring houses and the grey sky above me glaring down, unfriendly and threatening.

"Don't you remember me?" The man in front of me raised his arms in a peace offering kind of way and made no attempt to come closer.

I forced my trembling legs to remain still while I studied the stranger. He had longish blonde hair, pulled back from his tanned skin. His eyes were a familiar bright green. "Grayson?" I asked, hesitantly.

He smiled slightly and nodded. "I haven't seen you here for a very long time. You're all grown up now."

My body sagged in relief, rejecting the powerful surge of fight-or-flight juice coursing through my body. "You're safe," I smiled. "Quinn will be so happy."

"You know where my son is?" He stepped closer, looking at me intensely.

I tried not to cringe away, nerves still zinging a bit. "He thought you were dead. Anna, too. I've been looking for his sisters. But my Nan's house has been searched and the ring and bracelet are missing."

Grayson frowned. "We will find them," he declared, his voice thick with emotion. "You must tell me where Quinn is."

Almost of its own accord, my hand reached up and pulled the necklace out from the neck of my t-shirt. "I have him with me."

Grayson raised his eyebrows. "But you can converse with him. How?"

My eyes narrowed. *Wouldn't* he *know this?* I wondered. "Don't you know?" I asked, stepping back carefully.

His eyes flashed in irritation. "Give me the necklace. My son needs to be with me. Thank you for keeping him safe." He took several steps toward me and I stumbled backward, fear and doubt beginning to surface again.

"Tell me where you went after you left your children with my Nan," I said, stalling for time. "And where is Anna?"

He paused, tilting his head to the side. "You don't want to know," avoiding the question.

I tried again, "Is this the trail where you met Anna?"

A slight hesitation. "No," he then said, eyes far away. "Close to here, but not on this trail."

I relaxed fractionally, shaking my head. I was just being paranoid, I thought. But even though Quinn belonged with his father, my mind rebelled against handing the necklace over. He was my friend; I couldn't just let him go. I didn't know what to do.

Sensing my reluctance, Grayson changed his approach. "I can see you have become attached to my son. Why don't you come with me? You can help me release him from the necklace." He smiled kindly down at me. "Then we can talk together."

"Where do we need to go?" I asked warily. "Can't we do it right here?"

"Sure," he agreed immediately. "Hand me the necklace. I know what to do."

Feeling compelled, I undid the clasp and pulled the chain off my neck. I looked longingly at the charm for a moment, then forced myself to move in front of Grayson. I gazed up into his face as I lifted the necklace toward him. His eyes followed the necklace intently, then widened in surprise as he spied the meteorite charm dangling from my hematite bracelet. He hissed and his face seemed to blur for a few seconds, revealing another face: angry and fearful, and definitely *not* Grayson.

I snatched my arm back, shoving the necklace into my pocket. It slid to the bottom, past the little iron hammer, which I grasped in panic. My mind was spinning recklessly. I frantically considered my options.

This is not going to end well, I thought.

Grayson's face had turned hard and furious. He advanced threateningly. "Don't even think about running." His smile smug, his expression arrogant.

"You can't have Quinn's necklace," I ground out, through gritted teeth.

"Do you think *that's* all I care about? You don't know *anything*."

My panic meter rose another notch. What was he talking about?

I had had enough talk, and my legs made my decision for me by sprinting off down the trail. I had only gone a few yards when I was grabbed from behind. I spun out of the grasping hands, whipping the iron hammer around.

I heard the *crack* of impact as I smashed my hammer into this man's jaw and teeth. I winced in horror at what I had done.

His hand drew back from his face—now clearly *not* Grayson's—covered in blood. He flexed, ready to smash his fist into my face, but I was already ducking, ready to dodge his blow. My hammer fell like lightning against the side of his kneecap, and with a grunt of pain, he collapsed to the ground. I aimed at the back of his head, shocked when my arm was caught mid-descent in a powerful grip.

Screaming out my fear, I grabbed at the arm that held me, clutched at his chest, pivoted, bent and *pulled* with all my might, sending my second opponent into the dirt. *I've got to tell Jace about this*, I thought.

Then, for the first time, I saw the face of my second assailant...and almost passed out.

"Griff," I choked out, about to kneel down next to him. Then
my instincts took over. "You aren't real," I cried out defiantly.
"Just another dirty trick!" I spun around and ran as fast as I
could, tears blinding me as my feet slipped on the gravel and
bark in the path.

I was almost there. I could see the path to my Nan's backyard and I sprinted even faster, my lungs burning, anxious to
reach somewhere familiar and safe.

But how safe could it be?

My dad will be attacked too, I thought. I couldn't endanger
him. I wavered momentarily, hoping for the help of the cops.
But what could they really do? They couldn't get involved in
all this. Something worse would happen, I just knew it. At the
last minute, I skipped the path and kept going down the public trail, not having any idea what to do next.

Then someone grabbed me from behind.

As I cried out, strong arms lifted me into the air, zoom-
ing us off the trail and into the tall trees. I dangled helplessly,
venting my rage with every swear word I knew. I struggled and
thrashed my legs while we weaved and veered through the air,
until finally I hung exhausted and panting. Forcing myself to
stay still, I tried to keep a little strength in reserve for when he
finally let me down.

After what seemed like hours — but was really only a
couple minutes — we came down, awkwardly, behind some
huge trees with massive amounts of undergrowth. He suspected resistance, and not one to disappoint, I threw myself
into attack mode. In a flash, I had my back pressed against
a gigantic tree, a hand clamped fiercely over my mouth. I

looked at my captor's face and couldn't help my muffled gasp of dismay. I knew as long as the glamour held, my efforts would be half-hearted at best. Somehow, I couldn't bring myself to bash a hammer into Griff's face. I went limp, and would have fallen if he hadn't been holding me up. His hand let go of my mouth.

"Please, change your face," I whispered.

"Mia, *shush*. We are in terrible danger."

"What?" I gaped at him in astonishment, completely unable to grasp what was happening.

"I can't explain now," he whispered into my ear. "Please, trust me."

"You can fly," I said stupidly, my brain falling to pieces. "You're one of *them*." "Oh, no." I sank down onto the forest floor, feeling my world collapsing in on itself. I couldn't breathe. I couldn't think. Three words looped through my brain, over and over: *Griff wasn't human.*

"They'll be here soon," he said, urgently. "We must make it look like you escaped. Hit me with your hammer. And draw some blood, dammit!" He lifted me up and shook my shoulders.

"I can't," I protested weakly, my brain all undone.

Griff picked up my arm and forced my nails to gouge through the skin of his cheek. This snapped me back to reality and I tried in vain to pull away. "Stop, please," I cried. And he thrust his hand into my mouth, pushing my jaw shut with his other hand until I tasted blood. Horrified, I spat on the ground after he pulled away with a grunt of pain. I could hardly keep from gagging. Then he picked up my hammer.

A speck of reason burst into my brain. "Wait, you can hold iron?" I stammered, wiping my lips with the back of my shaking hand.

"Obviously," he stated grimly. "I'm only half-Terraran. Now hit me."

"I can't." I began to cry, stinging angry tears of frustration. "You can't make me."

"We are both going to die, if you can't hit me," Griff hissed furiously. "Now!"

His voice slapped me into attention. I took a shaky breath and swung out in desperation. Griff leaned into it, and I felt the impact against his temple, his ear tearing, then gushing blood. He swayed, then grinned a wild, ferocious smile. "Stay here and be quiet. If I'm not back in an hour, run like hell." He crushed me to his chest for a split second then he was gone. I wobbled, my feet tripping against tree roots and I fell against the tree, my head bouncing off the rough bark. My vision swam and colors danced in front of my eyes before darkness rushed over me.

MY EYES BLINKED, trying to focus. My brain felt sluggish and stupid as I squinted up at the tree branches above me. A hand was stroking my hair. I tipped my head back to see Griff's worried face leaning over me. "You were on vacation," I muttered foolishly. Emotions and images came tumbling back over me, one chasing the next around my brain, leaving me gasping with confusion. Griff was silent as I tried to put together what had happened.

"What the *hell* is going on?" I finally demanded, pushing myself into a sitting position, facing Griff with an accusing expression.

My gaze fell on his bloody ear and scratched cheek, and my anger flip-flopped to alarm. "Oh my gosh. What did I do?" I cried out, sickened as I recalled smashing the hammer into

Griff's temple. I covered my face with my hands, horrified by my handiwork.

Griff gently pried my hands away from my face. He cupped my chin in his hand and my eyes flew open as he kissed me, lips pressing urgently against mine. My breath caught in my throat for an instant, then I found myself responding, passionately. Every rational thought disappeared, with all my focus centered on his mouth, his hand stroking my neck, and his other hand holding me close to him.

After several long moments he pulled his head back. I could hear my breath coming in ragged gasps. My cheeks burned. Griff put his head in the hollow of my neck. I could feel him struggling to even out his own breathing.

"I'm sorry," he said softly, his breath tickling my throat and sending shivers rippling through me. "I thought we were both going to die."

I was still not sure I could form words. My heart was going faster than when I had been running for my life. I didn't want to talk. I didn't want to know all the details of what had happened. I just wanted this moment. I slid my hands into Griff's beautiful hair, thinking of nothing but the soft feel of it running through my fingers. But he flinched and made a little sound, effectively breaking my dreamy mood.

I pushed his head to the side to see what damage I had inflicted. "Oh, Griff," I whispered. "Why did you make me do that?" His ear needed some serious medical attention. There was so much blood; I had to close my eyes. I started twisting my hands guiltily in my lap. "How long have you been bleeding? We have got to get you to a doctor."

He took my hands and brought them to his lips. "I'll be fine. I heal quickly."

It was like a bucket of ice water dumped straight over my head. I gasped, snatching my hands away and stood up shakily.

"You aren't human," my voice sharp with hurt.

"No," he agreed, standing up slowly beside me.

"I don't understand," I pleaded, clenching my teeth. "You were a student at my school."

"I was sent there."

"Because of me?"

"No, just chance." Griff touched my arm but I moved away hastily. His touch made me forget important things. Mixed me up. *I need to think clearly*, I said to myself.

"So why were you here? In the human world?" I had to know the truth, no matter how painful. I thought of Quinn's distrust of Griff and immediately tried to squash the feeling of betrayal.

Griff stayed silent and instead sloughed off his jacket and tugged his shirt over his head. Yikes. I took a step back. Before I could demand to know what he was doing, he turned and I saw a silver tattoo shining on his lower back. It was an intricate design of a sun and earth entwined. Above the symbol I noticed scars criss-crossing his back, and I shuddered.

He turned back, his face bitter. "I do what I am told to do. You see, I am only half-Terraran. I am considered *tainted*. My only purpose is to serve others. A slave who follows orders…or pays the price." His hand reached behind him as if to touch the symbol, then pulled away as if burned. Griff raised his stricken eyes to mine. "I have always obeyed, until I met you." He added softly.

I could hardly comprehend what he was telling me. "But you have a car, and a camera. All those beautiful pictures…" I trailed off.

"It was part of the identity I carefully cultivated while I was living among humans. I needed to blend in."

"It was all an act." I sat down again, the enormity of it all weighing me down. I fell for it like an innocent child. Sure, he had made me nervous occasionally, warning bells had lit up, but I never listened, and now I would pay the price. Fool that I was.

"So, how old are you really?" I asked in a tired voice.

"Do you really want to know?"

"Yes."

"A hundred and sixteen, I think."

I felt like I'd been punched in the stomach. I sat curled up into a ball, hugging my legs, closing my eyes against Griff's very distracting bare skin.

"Why did you ask me out?" I choked out the words. "Because of Quinn's necklace?" I dreaded the answer. Everything that had passed between us had become poisoned. A lie.

"No," he sat close to me, his leg brushing mine, but I refused to look at him. "You are the most fascinating human I have ever met. You mesmerize me. I'm not supposed to make close connections to any humans, but I couldn't help myself." He traced a hand down the back of my neck. "Please, Mia. Look at me."

I shook my head, ignoring—or at least trying to ignore—the hand on my neck.

"Was that before or *after* you saw my necklace?" I asked bitterly.

"The necklace was an extremely unfortunate coincidence, as far as I was concerned. I knew it was Terraran the second I saw it. I kept it a secret from those I report to for as long as I could. I was only planted in your school—as I have been in many others—to search for others who are part-Terraran. To make sure our secret is protected."

"How did they find out about my necklace?"

"They sent others to check on me. They saw the pictures I took of you and your necklace. Remember, you saw them at the gargoyle house. That's my home, by the way, while I stay in the human world."

I glanced up in surprise. "You live in *that* spooky place?" His eyes were staring hard into mine, as if he could drill understanding into me. I retreated into myself again, swearing I wouldn't look him in the face anymore. Instead I said, "You pretended you couldn't see them." My voice an accusation.

"I did not," he argued. "I was startled and worried that you *could* see them. I wasn't sure who you were or what your ability to see them meant."

"I have always been able to see Terrarans," I confessed. "But I don't know why, either. It wasn't until recently that I even learned anything about Terrara. I wish I was still ignorant. Ignorance being bliss and all."

"You saw Grayson's family, is that right?"

The name struck a nerve. "Are you still collecting information for *them*?" I spat, suddenly furious. "I'm not letting them kill Quinn, or enslave him, or whatever they're planning on doing to him."

"I'm doing everything I can to protect you *against* them!" Griff practically shouted. "Can't you believe me? If my dodge hadn't worked back there, we would both be captured and maybe even dead by now."

"How can I trust you?" I demanded. "Everything about you is a lie. For all I know you are still working for them, gaining my trust, seducing me into giving you the necklace." My voice trembled with the emotions spilling from my pathetic, wounded heart. I had fallen for Griff so hard. I could hardly stand to think that he had used me, was still using me. I huddled tighter into my ball of self-pity.

"They want more than the necklace, Mia. For some reason they want *you*." His voice was ice. "I never lied about the way I feel about you. You need to understand at least that much."

Against my better judgment, I allowed myself to peek up at him. I wanted to believe him so badly. His hand still lingered on my neck, a warm contrast to his frozen words. "Griff," my voice broke. "I want to believe you. I really do." I slumped over onto his shoulder, longing to be convinced. To have all doubts removed.

He drew me close, wrapping his arms around me. His warm skin felt smooth and strong under my cheek. "Mia," he rubbed his chin against my hair. "I wish things were different. That I was an ordinary human boy at your school, and we both knew nothing about Terrara."

"Me, too." I was so drained. My arms ached, my head pounded. I drifted into a strange, dreamlike state. Maybe I was in shock. I don't know. I was aware of my surroundings, but my mind floated away, leaving all the stress and emotional trauma behind.

Suddenly, my head did that weird little jerk that it does when you start to fall asleep sitting up. *Please don't let me have drooled on Griff's naked chest*, I thought, lifting a hand to touch the side of my mouth. It was bad enough that he was still shirtless. He needed to get dressed before I embarrassed myself. Despite what he had told me, I was still deeply attached to him. I pulled back and tore my eyes from his beautiful, golden brown skin.

Griff was watching me warily. "Let me see your mark again," I asked quietly. He seemed startled, but leaned over obligingly, and I lightly touched the intricate silver design. "What makes this shine?"

"It's made with iron. If I fail in my duties, it can be used to punish me. As I'm half-human, I can hold iron, but this mark be made to be white-hot. It's extremely unpleasant."

"Oh, Griff. That's barbaric." I ran my eyes over the pattern of old scars above the iron mark. *I have it so easy*, I thought. My parents had never even spanked me. I shuddered, imagining life as a slave. Without thinking I lowered my head and pressed my lips gently to the horrible mark. An electric spark zapped my lips, like you get when you drag your feet over the carpet and then touch a doorknob. Griff jerked and I was on my feet in an instant, realizing the intimacy of what I had done. I rubbed my lips as I snatched up his t-shirt and tossed it in his general direction, muttering something about how cold it was.

Back turned, I checked the time on my cellphone. Only about an hour had gone by. *I bet Dad isn't even worried yet*, I thought. I wondered if it was safe for me to go back there. I needed to come up with some kind of plan.

"Are you supposed to be searching for me right now?"

Griff came up behind me and placed his hands on my shoulders. "Yes."

"And the people you work for know who I am now, and where my Nan lived. How I'm connected to Grayson's family and that I have Quinn's necklace."

"I'm afraid so," Griff agreed grimly.

"Do they know my home address, too?"

"I haven't given it to them, but they know where you go to school. They know that I know you, but I've been vague about our relationship."

Our relationship, I thought. *What is it exactly?* "Someone was following me for a couple of days before I came here. I could feel it." I tipped my head back. "Was that you?"

Griff nodded. "I was trying to keep you safe. Ever since Halloween night, you have been in danger. I was called home the next day. My master was interested in you, having heard from another source about your attempted abduction. He wanted to find out what I knew about you. I told them as little as possible. I hated leaving you, but I had no choice."

"Who were the men who grabbed me at the barn and what did you do to them? Are they dead?"

"They did not work for my master. I had never seen them before. And no, they aren't dead, but they were in no position to tell anyone what happened, either."

My stomach knotted with this revelation, even though I had expected as much.

"So, some other Terrarans know about me and my necklace, too. Why would anyone even care?"

"I don't know why others are getting involved, but the Terrarans I work for are interested in your necklace because they are political rivals with Grayson's family. If they could get their hands on Grayson or his half-Terraran children, they would have incredible power over Grayson's family."

Griff's words chilled me. The thought of my childhood friends enslaved and used as pawns in a political game made me sick. My hand went automatically to Quinn's necklace, still resting safely in my pocket. I needed to get Quinn safe. Should

I try and release him from the necklace, or was he actually safer hidden inside?

"Everything is so difficult." I rubbed my temples trying to think. "First, I need to go back to my dad. Do you think the house is being watched?"

"Probably."

"Would they harm my dad?" That was the thought that really frightened me.

"I don't think so," Griff grimaced. "But they don't tell me everything. After all, I'm only a slave."

His bitter words made me flinch. "I'm going back. I have to get my dad out of here."

"I can't be seen helping you," said Griff.

I put my hand on his cheek. "I know. Do you think you could fly me closer, though? Without getting caught?"

"I think so."

"What will happen if you *are* seen helping me?" I had to know.

"I will be punished, probably killed." Griff's eyes stayed blank as if he were commenting on the weather. I gulped.

"Griff, is there any way for you to be freed?" I asked. "Any way at all?"

"I can be freed only by my master's death, if he does not transfer my bonds to someone else before he dies. But his death cannot be by my hand, or I will die as well."

"What is your master's name?"

Griff's eyes narrowed and he remained silent.

"Tell me," I insisted. "Please."

"Daniels."

"Okay, good to know."

Griff captured my hand in his, anger flashing in his eyes. "I forbid you to get involved in my situation. You need to get away and be safe."

My defenses flew up. "You can't tell me what to do or whom not to help."

"Mia," he pleaded, anger ebbing and concern sharpening his look. "I *have* to know you are safe. That you are not hurt because of me."

"Safe?" I snorted. "How is *that* going to happen? Besides, I won't do anything rash. I just like to know who all the players are. See if you can find out who else is interested in the necklace."

"I get the feeling that someone is interested in you, not the necklace."

"That's ridiculous. The necklace is the only tie I have to Terrara." I raised my eyes to his. "Except for you, I guess."

Griff frowned at that. Since he was still holding my hand, I pulled on it, getting his attention. "Come on, we aren't going to figure it out right now. There are too many pieces missing from the puzzle. Can you fly me over, now? I'm really worried about my dad."

Griff, after pulling on his jacket, picked me up. I slid my arms around his neck, ready to go. He held me for a long moment without moving, just staring at me, until my cheeks started heating up. "*What?*" I asked, slightly exasperated.

"I don't know when I will be able to see you again."

"Oh." I hadn't thought of that. "Will you be under surveillance from now on?"

"I don't know, but it is getting harder to slip away to see you, or protect you. I will do my best. That is, if you want me to." He looked down at me. "Do you still want me around, or, now that you know the truth about me, can you hardly wait to be rid of me?"

I gaped at his directness. What was I going to say? I studied his beautiful blue eyes which were filled with pain, and I realized I couldn't add any more to what he had to bear. It wasn't like I could blame him for being a slave. My heart hurt just thinking of his shame. "I will always want to see you," I said simply, staring into his haunted face. "In spite of what I may have said earlier because I was hurting, I still trust you." I ran a finger down his cheek. "I can't help myself."

His eyes flashed in relief at my words and I thought he might kiss me again. Much as I wished for such an incredible distraction, I needed to get back to my dad. I buried my face in his neck, winding my hand into his hair on the unhurt side of his head. I softly breathed, "Please fly me back, Griff. Please." It worked. We soared through the trees while Griff held me close to him. I enjoyed myself a lot more than I did last time; it was over before I wished.

"This is as far as I can go."

I nodded, as he set me down just off the dirt path. "Thank you, Griff. Please don't get yourself in trouble because of me. I couldn't…" I stopped. I could feel my eyes starting to fill with tears. Crap, I didn't want to do this again. I *hated* saying goodbye. I had already done this with Griff a short time ago, but *this* goodbye seemed more permanent and scary. I made as if to take off without another word, but he yanked me back into his arms and kissed me until my knees started to buckle.

He drew away and I stared at him like an idiot. Damn, he was good. How was I supposed to move, let alone *run*, after a kiss like that? "Not fair," I chided. "You've had like a hundred years to practice." I ran my fingers down his dark brown hair.

He laughed softly in my ear. I had forgotten how wonderful his laugh sounded. It had been so long since I had heard it. "I don't want to let you go." He pushed me reluctantly away. "You better hurry, Mia, before I change my mind." I moved halfheartedly toward the path, my feet dragging me through the brush.

"Goodbye, Griff," I whispered.

"Goodbye, Mia. Be safe." He took several steps as I watched, and then turned back. He mouthed something softly, too far for me to hear the words. It looked like, "I love you." He put his fingers to his lips, and then disappeared into the trees.

Decisions

I must have stood staring open-mouthed after Griff for a full minute, regardless of anything around me. Blinking, I tried to be sure of what I had seen. Good thing no one decided to attack right then. I was way too distracted to do a single thing. Forcing my emotions to the back of my head, I made myself creep up the trail to my Nan's path. I crossed quickly and fumbled with the gate, thinking someone might jump out at any moment. I reached the back door and ran inside.

I decided yelling would be stupid, so I carefully checked through the house for my dad. I was starting to panic until I noticed a note on the counter. It read:

> *Mia,*
>
> *The police found out disturbing news while they were here. I have gone to Nan's gravesite. Meet me there if*

you get this in time. If I'm not there, I'll be at the police
station making a report. Call me if you can get a signal.
  Love, Dad

There were two addresses scribbled at the bottom and some
sketchy directions. I folded the note and stuck it in my pocket.
I knew we needed to get far away from this house. My nerves
told me to hurry and I rushed around, gathering anything we
brought with us, as well as several items that I couldn't bear
to leave behind.

I was on the porch, punching in the locking button in the
middle of the handle since I didn't have the key for the dead-
bolt, when a noise behind me made me whirl around. Someone
was coming around the side of the garage. It looked like a
neighbor, but with glamour powers available to Terrarans, I
wasn't going to trust my sight.

I scrambled into the car and started the engine. I cracked
the window and waved hello. I figured if it was a Terraran in
disguise, the metal car would be too much for them to handle.
I was right. Angry words flew at me while I gunned the engine.
Probably stupid of me, but I couldn't help flipping the creep a
rude gesture as I escaped in my iron machine. Heart pounding, I raced down the street to the cemetery, wondering what
other horrors awaited me there.

My cell phone signal kept flickering. When I finally reached
a spot where I could get a strong signal, I pulled over and dug
my dad's note out of my pocket. He answered on the second
ring, his voice agitated with worry.

"About time you called. I was starting to think something
bad had happened."

"I'm okay, Dad." I decided to save the truth for later. "Where are you? What happened?"

"I'll tell you when you get here. I'm at the police station. It's off 42nd. By the library. Come over and pick me up."

"I'll be there in a few minutes," I promised. "See ya."

"Bye, Mia."

I dropped my phone into a cup holder and headed toward the center of town. There would be lots of people and lots of metal. I held my breath, hoping for some luck.

DAD AND I were seated in the back of a very crowded restaurant near the police station. He was drinking a large cup of Coke and I was picking at a salad while we waited for the rest of our food to arrive. I felt off-balance. My dad had just explained why he had taken off with the cops. They had made a connection between my dad and another crime. A grave had been defiled. My Nan's.

I had choked when he had said the words. Nauseated beyond belief at the thought of someone desecrating my Nan's resting place, probably to find her ring and bracelet. I despised the Terrarans before for their cruelty, but this was too much. How could anyone stoop so low?

My dad had gone and checked the gravesite. I was glad I hadn't gone, even though he hadn't had to identify the body, or more likely, bones. I don't know how fast a body decays. I clenched my hands furiously, angry that someone made me think about my Nan's body decaying. I hated them. I pushed my salad away, sickened.

My dad's face was pale, his expression lost and helpless. I couldn't blame him, since he'd had to deal with everything in only a day or so. Denial seemed more plausible than acceptance this early in the game, no matter what the evidence. *I wished I could still go back to the denial stage,* I thought, sighing.

I had told my dad an abbreviated version of what had happened to me. Without the kissing. But I included Griff's place in this turn of events, and the knowledge that the Terrarans knew much more about me and the necklace than I would have hoped. Neither of us had the foggiest idea what to do next.

As we sat at the booth and nodded in a polite daze to the server who brought out our food, I searched my bag for the letters from Nan's iron box. Maybe there would be some clue as to what to do next. I spread the papers all over the table, trying to put them in some sort of order. Most of the letters were from Anna to her sister, telling all the details of her life on the run. A few were from Grayson to Nan. And then there was the one in Terraran, which told how to break the spell.

I located another small, hastily-scribbled note stuck to the back of an envelope. It had no date on it. The handwriting looked like Grayson's, and warned my Nan that someone was after his family and that he would be coming soon for his children. He would have to come at night. He told her not to use the spell to release Quinn and his sisters because they would be much easier to take with him in their hidden jewelry form. He gave Nan a password so that she could identify him and not be fooled by someone glamoured to look like him. The password was "Love endures."

I blinked as I thought of all that Grayson's family had endured, and was still enduring. My life had been a charmed fairy tale in comparison. I had never before realized how lucky I was to grow up safe and secure with a mom and dad who love me, and I felt embarrassed about all the things that I had taken for granted. I didn't think I would look at my life the same way again.

"Find anything helpful?" my dad finally asked.

"Not much more than before. But I did find out the password that Grayson was supposed to give Nan so she would know it was him. It's 'Love endures.' We might need that sometime, if we ever find the real Grayson, which I really hope we do soon. I'm running out of ideas. What do you think we should do?"

I made myself take a bite out of my hamburger, not that I was hungry. But I figured that I should get some fuel in my body. After a few small nibbles, my stomach took over and decided it was glad to have food after all, and I finished the whole thing in record time. I started on my fries before my dad made any comment.

"I think we should go get your mom," Dad raised his anxious eyes to me.

I froze, a fry halfway to my mouth.

"You don't think Mom is in any danger, do you? Won't we just be bringing danger to her?" The thought made me queasy and I dropped my fry back on the platter.

"Mia, I really don't know what to think. But I worry about her being by herself. It will only take a day to drive there. I'd feel better if we were all together. Preferably in a place far away from here *or* home."

I was contemplating what my dad was suggesting when my cell phone rang. Surprised, I glanced at the number. It was Jace.

"Hey, Jace." I tried using my casual voice, to see if it was working.

"Mia, I need to tell you some kinda bad news."

I sat up straight in the booth chair. "What's wrong?" My dad looked alarmed.

"It's not that bad. No one is hurt, Mia. It's just that your house was broken into last night. Someone totally trashed it."

I rubbed my eyes, feeling frustration burning behind my eyelids.

"What is it?" my dad rasped harshly.

"Our house was ransacked last night," I related to him, covering the mouthpiece of my phone. I watched as his shoulders sagged and he put his head in his hands.

"How did you figure it out?" I asked Jace. "Oh, feeding Freddie. Is she okay?"

"She's more pissed-off than usual, and wouldn't some out from under your mom's bed, even for some fresh food. But she's not hurt, if that's what you mean."

"So what's the damage?"

"Hard to tell. Mostly it just looks like it was searched. I didn't notice anything in particular missing. But lots of things are broken, I'm afraid. Does this have to do with you-know-what?" Jace lowered his voice.

"Probably," I admitted, and I related the happenings since we arrived in Washington as briefly as I could. It still took several minutes.

"That's harsh." Jace's voice was full of concern. "So, does your dad believe?"

"He's trying to. It's a bit of a shock, as you can imagine. How about you? Is your skepticism finally disappearing?"

"Guess so," Jace said in a quiet voice. "What should I do about your house?"

"Call the police." I glanced at my dad for confirmation. He nodded dejectedly.

"Shall I give them your cell number?"

"My dad's." I gave him the number. "Thanks for calling, Jace. I'll call you soon when we have any more information, okay?"

"Sure, I'll let you know any developments over here. And Mia, be *careful*. This is getting scary."

"I know. Thanks, Jace. Bye." I hung up.

I looked over at my dad. "Sounds like calling Mom was a good idea."

Dad glowered at his half-eaten hamburger.

I kept going. "Tell her we're on our way. And to not leave the house by herself. Or maybe you shouldn't tell her that, because she'll want know all the details, and we have to do that in person." I stopped rambling, noticing the desperation on my dad's face. "Do you want me to call her and make something up? A little white lie? Anything to cover up the real reason we are coming?"

My dad made himself sit up. His face became serious. "No, Mia. I can do it." He fished his phone out of his front pocket and punched in the number.

I was proud of my dad. He used his calm and mellow nature to his advantage. He was cool and composed as he told Mom about the two break-ins and the grave desecration. He soothed her fear and let her know we were on our way to pick her up. He didn't talk long, telling her we had some errands and such to take care of before we left, but that he would call her again soon.

"Wow, Dad, you handled that way better that I ever could have."

He smiled grimly. "Your mom's not stupid. As she starts to think about it, she's going to figure out I left out a lot of details." He stood up. "Let's get going as fast as we can. How do you feel? Tired?"

"A little," I admitted.

"Good," he said. "I feel wide awake, so I'll take the first shift. I'm going to want the last shift, too," he warned. "Mom and her sister went up to Redwood National Park. So I want to be behind the wheel on Highway 101. Wish we brought the Miata."

He put on his parka and left a decent tip on the table while I shrugged into his old leather coat and took a last sip of soda.

On the way to the highway, we topped off the gas and bought tons of snacks to munch on and keep us awake for the next ten hours or so. No big stops, we decided. Just bathroom breaks and gas. After a quick look at the atlas to check directions, we were off.

I fidgeted, trying to find a comfortable position to nap. I was sitting shotgun since the back seats were full of scattered knick-knacks and suitcases that I had haphazardly tossed into the car when I fled the house. Neither my dad nor I wanted to take the time to organize anything, so I was left to twist and turn in the front bucket seat. I unbuckled my seatbelt, but hastily refastened it at my dad's growl of disapproval. *Fine*, I thought, stuffing my coat into a ball and shoving it against the door as a makeshift pillow.

My thoughts flitted through all the painful details of the last couple of days. I still felt anguish over the destruction of Nan's house, and could hardly think of the pain to come when we saw our own home in shambles. I was glad I had snagged all the pictures of Griff and me and my drawing of Quinn. At least they wouldn't have any obvious clues staring them in the face.

Who was it that had been at our house? Was it the same Ter-rarans who had been at my Nan's, or someone else? What were we going to do now?

I thought again about Quinn's life on the run, and despair filled me at the thought of our predicament. There was no easy answer to our situation. Our best hope was to find Grayson. But how?

My mind wandered back my conversation with Griff. I pressed my hot face into my coat as I remembered the kisses we had shared. *Please be safe*, I thought, wondering when I would ever be able to see him again. Had he really told me he loved me? *My mind must have imagined it*, I scolded myself. After all, he wasn't human, and was like, a hundred years older than I was. But one look at his face and all those things became insignificant. *What a basket-case you are*, I told myself, giving myself a mental slap. *Think about more important things, like what are we going to do after we meet Mom.*

I tried to concentrate on pertinent ideas and plans, but my mind kept reliving those oh-so very pleasant moments with Griff. In spite of everything, I drifted off to sleep with a smile on my face, listening to my dad singing along with the radio, as off-tune as always.

A Practice Run

The empty hallway was dimly lit and all the doors were shut, classrooms darkened. "What time is it?" I wondered. "And where is everyone?" I was getting creeped out, and I couldn't remember where the closest exit was.

As I hurried to the end of the hall, I heard angry voices coming from one of the classrooms on my right. I peeked into the small, rectangular window on the door, squinting into the bright, lightly lit room.

My hand flew to my mouth to cover the gasp of shock.

Griff was writhing on the floor – face down—as someone stood over him, pointing and screaming, his face red with rage. I burst through the door, ready to swing a chair at Griff's tormentor if I had to, but the instant I saw his face I froze in shock. My dad glared at me with livid, red eyes, his mouth spouting unfamiliar words in Terraran, while the tattoo on Griff's back blazed a liquid iron glow. Griff continued to cry out in pain, while I stood there staggering in disbelief.

"Mia." The word echoed in my brain and I latched onto it with hope. *Please let this be a nightmare. Please.*

"Quinn," I choked out desperately. "Is that you?" I spun expectantly, and breathed a huge sob of relief when he was standing right behind me, arms out to steady my shaking body. He led me from the disturbing scene to an empty classroom down the hall. We sat down at a couple of desks, and I rested my aching head on the cool wooden surface.

He reached over and rubbed my neck gently while I tried to calm down.

"Are you okay?" Quinn asked softly.

"I *really* didn't like that," I mumbled.

"That was Griff," Quinn stated. "Again." He sighed, and I wondered how often Griff starred in my dreams—and in what capacity. This time he had been the victim, but had he sometimes been the romantic lead? *Poor Quinn*, I thought. *This must be extremely annoying for him, especially since he already distrusts Griff.*

"Yeah, that was Griff all right. I just learned some important things about him. You should probably know, too. You were right; he's more than just a boy at my school."

Quinn gave me a triumphant look. "I knew it."

"He's not a bad guy, Quinn. He's a victim, just like my dream was showing us. He's half-Terraran, like you, and he's enslaved to some family that is a political rival of your father's family. To a master named Daniels. He has an iron tattoo that is used to torture him if he disobeys."

Quinn raised his eyebrows. "*He* told you this story?"

I gave him a withering look.

"What?" Quinn sounded exasperated. "How do you know he's telling the truth?"

"Because he saved my life again," I answered coolly, "and he showed me his tattoo." I continued to tell him the complete story of the past day or so. Well, with a little strategic editing. I'm not *that* mean.

"So, now Dad and I are driving south to pick up my mom." I stood up and began nervously pacing between the rows of chairs. "But I don't have the faintest idea what to do once we find my mom. Where do we go? What do we do?"

Quinn came over to me and took my hands. "Get me out." His eyes were fiercely determined. "I'll help protect you and your family. We can look for my father together."

"But Quinn, I think you're safer hidden away," I insisted.

"No!" Quinn's voice was firm. "I'm done with hiding. I feel like a coward in here." He gripped my hands tightly, and I squeezed them back reassuringly.

"Okay," I sighed. I could tell he was serious. And I *had* promised to help him. "I'll try." But, to be honest, I wasn't sure if I'd be able to do it.

Quinn seemed confident enough, though. "Come on. Let's practice now. Before you wake up."

"Sounds good to me," I agreed. "Let me see if I can make my mind conjure up a necklace." I closed my eyes, imagining the necklace in all its intricate detail, the silver chain, the clover charm, the small gemstones. Opening my eyes, I walked to the nearest desk and lifted up the lid. I stared in amazement, as Quinn's necklace lay there winking up at me.

Quinn came over and picked it up reverently. "You did it, Mia. It looks perfect."

I smiled, pleased with my effort. This lucid dreaming thing was starting to get easier.

Quinn held the necklace up. "Here, hold it with me."

We both wrapped our hands around the clover charm. "Wait. Let's sit down," I said. I wasn't sure how steady I was going to be on my feet. Quinn pushed the desks out of the way and we faced each other, sitting cross-legged.

We held the charm in front of us, and Quinn began to recite the Terraran words. He spoke the first line, and then I repeated it back. He had no problem remembering the words, it seemed. His voice became stronger, louder with each sentence. My echo also became more powerful until we came to the final line. He looked at me and I understood. We'd say the last words together. It was like I saw the words floating in the air above me. As if with a single breath, we released the last part of the incantation and time felt suspended. We both froze as if afraid to move. Then the mood faded, and we both began gasping for air. Colors twirled around me and my vision exploded into darkness.

I sat up, coughing and spluttering, like I'd inhaled a huge gulp of sea water. When I could finally catch my breath, I realized I was awake and inside a moving car. My dad was glancing at me in dismay, still trying to pay attention to the road. I tried to give him a thumbs-up sign, since words were pretty much impossible. Eventually, I managed a husky, "I'm okay," and he relaxed, marginally. When he reached a likely spot, he pulled over and gave me his undivided attention.

"That was quite a bad dream." Dad reached over and laid his hand on my arm, concern etched in his eyes. "You're still shaking. Mia, are you okay?"

I pulled my legs up onto the seat and wrapped my arms around myself, trying to settle my quaking body. I felt like energy was radiating out of me in all directions. It was unlike anything I'd ever experienced.

"Whoa, Dad. Can you feel the air in the car? It feels thick, full of something. Magic, maybe, I don't know." I waved my hand in front of my face experimentally.

"The air seems just fine to me, Mia. What's going on?"

"In my dream with Quinn just now, we practiced breaking the spell keeping him in the necklace. It was amazing, Dad." I leaned my head back and breathed deeply, enjoying the rich smell of the air. I rolled my tight, tense shoulders and cracked my knuckles, making my dad wince. He hates when I do that.

"I'm not sure I'm ready to try the real thing yet, though. It was pretty intense." I started scrounging around the back seat. "Man, am I starved. Apparently doing magic, even practice magic, gives you the munchies."

My dad gave me a weirded-out look and settled back into the driver's seat. "I think I'm going to need a break soon. How about I drive while you eat, then we switch places?"

"No problem, Dad. Just let me get some sugar and caffeine and I'll be good to go." I tore open a package of string cheese and started peeling off tiny strings. I never got this kind of cheese except from gas station mini-marts anymore. It reminded me of being a kid.

I chowed down all manner of junk until my energy level perked up. Then, with a Diet Coke in the cup holder, I took over the driving. It was getting dark and I loved driving at night, especially when I could listen to my favorite tunes. The time seemed to fly by. My dad snored and snorted occasionally in the corner, head flopped against the window, oblivious to the pounding music. I relaxed, and I drifted off into one of those driving dazes, where you can drive perfectly well while your mind wanders off in all directions.

I relived the feeling of doing magic. The way it made goose-bumps fly across my arms, and the hair on my neck stand up straight. The look in Quinn's face as we spoke Terraran together. The dancing colors at the end. I could hardly believe it was all just a practice run.

When we stopped for a break later that night, I decided, I'd try the spell for real. I wondered where Quinn would end up materializing. In the back seat of our car, I hoped. Good thing he was only half-Terraran, or the car would be bad news.

Then, the million-dollar question: where would we go once we found Mom? Of course, convincing her of the truth would be a heck of a lot easier with Quinn free. I couldn't wait to see the look on her face when he showed off how he could fly.

Flying. I sighed, remembering the last time I had flown. My heart sped up just thinking about it. I hoped that Griff was safe, and that his helping me had gone unnoticed. Our luck had lasted so far, but something told me it was going to run out in the near future. I had to find a way to get Griff free. After I freed Quinn, of course.

I nearly laughed out loud at my train of thought. I used to worry about getting good grades on my tests and papers, not to mention wishing for a date for Friday night. Now here I was doing magical spells and plotting slave rebellion, escaping kid-nappers and fleeing danger. High school problems seemed far away and insignificant. Who knew if I'd even be back in time to graduate?

What a turn my life had taken: some of it scary, some of it exciting. I hoped with all my heart that a reasonable solution could be found for all this drama soon. There were elements of it that I didn't want to give up. I wasn't sure how to incorporate those elements into my ordinary life, and found myself wondering if it was even possible to *have* an ordinary life after all this. Doubtful.

I finished off my Diet Coke, a feeling of worry and frustration settling on me.

Around nine, I found a rest stop and pulled into the surprisingly full parking lot. I had forgotten it was Thanksgiving weekend. After a quick pitstop and several vending machine purchases, we checked the map. My dad wanted to drive since we were coming up on the split-off to Highway 101. I tried to explain that it wouldn't be the same as driving it along the Southern California coast, especially in the winter and during the middle of the night. But he would not be denied.

"Hope you're not setting yourself up for disappointment," I warned.

"Thanks for the advice, *Mom*," his sarcasm a bit thicker than usual.

I rolled my eyes. "Whatever. Just let me do the spell before we start going, okay? If all goes well, we're going to have another passenger." I looked into the back seat. "We'd better rearrange things first."

We drove the car to a more secluded area and made room for another person in the back seat. Then as my dad nervously watched, I pulled out my Terraran notes and began the spell. I clutched the necklace in both hands. I focused my mind on Quinn and his release into this car. I took a steadying breath and recited the first line.

I hadn't gotten very far into the spell before I realized something was very different. My voice was flat, without power. I peered closely at the necklace. It appeared to be the same as always, and yet something was definitely wrong.

I sat back, frustrated. What was going on? Did I use too much magic last time? Had I wiped out my supply? Did I even *have* a supply? I was human, after all. Maybe I couldn't do it without someone who had experience with this sort of magic. Oh Quinn, I thought. What can I do to help you?

I frowned over at my dad. "It's not working, obviously. I guess we'd better go get Mom. I'll see if I can talk to Quinn while I sleep and see if he knows what's wrong."

I couldn't tell whether my dad was more anxious or relieved that the spell didn't work. "Is there anything I can do?" he asked, trying his best to be supportive.

"Nope, just get us to Mom." I curled up in the front seat, irritated at my lack of success. I went over everything in my mind. Nothing stood out as being outrageously wrong. I was extra careful in my pronunciation. No stutters or mistakes. *Argh.* I couldn't figure it out.

I leaned my head against the cold glass of the window and watched the dark scenery go past. I finally closed my eyes, as my stomach rebelled against the whirlwind images. Shaking myself mentally, I tried not to dwell on my failure. Quinn's melancholy face swam in front of my eyes, and with an apology on my lips, I sank into a troubled, uncomfortable sleep.

A HORRIBLE SCREAM drove itself into my head. My body was thrown violently, slammed back into the seat with an air bag. A screech of metal shrieked in my ears, and I felt a biting wind rushing by my right side. I was slipping sideways, falling into dark nothingness. I flailed my arms in panic and managed to grab onto the flapping seatbelt. I was dangling and twisting and gripping with all my strength.

All of a sudden, as I hung there, everything switched from fast blurred images into eerie slow motion. I looked around me and saw my mom's Volvo rupturing out of a torn guardrail, a large redwood tree – we must have hit that—hanging over the edge of the cliff blocking the road, my door clinging to the rest of the car by only by a tiny bit of metal.

My mind absorbed all of this in a split second and then I peered beneath my legs at a black, salty-smelling void.

"I don't want to die." My terrified voice was whipped away by the freezing, rushing air. I couldn't see back into the car to see if my dad was hurt. "Dad," I tried to shout, "help me!" No answer, except the tearing sound of metal as my broken door swung violently in the fierce wind.

"Quinn!" I screamed my next horrible thought. If I fell, his necklace would be lost with me and he would die as well. The thought of someone else's death besides my own snapped me into even more desperate action. I couldn't let this happen.

Instinctively, my hands began twitching. I tried to suppress the movements, worried I would let go of the seatbelt. At that instant, the car door was hit by a huge gust of wind and slammed into me, whacking me against the side of the car. My hands slipped. They continued the motions, even as I started falling backwards toward the rocks and ocean. I watched my hands detachedly, as if they belonged to someone else. My mind was definitely going to pieces.

The thought of Quinn popped into my head again. "Save us, please," I sobbed, a sense of reality sweeping over me. "Grayson. Please. Come find your son. I don't want to kill him."

The world began to fade and I hoped I would pass out before I hit. Just for a moment, I saw Griff's face whirl into view. His arms stretched out like he was trying to catch me.

An instant later, I smashed into something. It wasn't a pointed rock slicing my skin or ocean water, unyielding because of my long fall. When my dazed eyes had a chance to focus and I regained the breath that had been knocked out of me, I found myself staring at a polished wooden floor.

"Wh-wh-what?" I stammered, in shock and pain.

"Mia." A comforting voice calmed my fear. Gentle hands turned me over. My eyes fell upon a familiar face. "Quinn," I gasped. "I thought this was real." I looked over his shoulder. "Wait, how come your father's in my dream?"

"Mia," Quinn whispered softly. "You aren't dreaming. I can't believe you're really here."

"Huh?" I whispered as Quinn tried to lift me up. My head was throbbing where it had smacked the floor; my stomach heaved violently. "Don't move me," I warned. "I'm going to be sick." Quinn gently lowered me back to the floor.

"Ohh, please, make it *stop*," I choked out, before my voice failed. Overwhelming nausea took hold and I curled myself into a ball, trying to control my stomach enough to not throw up all over Quinn.

"You'll be okay, Mia. It's just a side effect." Quinn's voice was muted, as if coming from far away. Finally, things became too much for me and I checked out of this painful reality into blessed oblivion.

Reunions

A cool cloth on my forehead felt soothing and comforting. I shifted my sore body and found that I was lying on a soft bed with a quilted blanket tucked around me. Groggily, I opened my eyes and attempted to focus them on the figure above me. A cry of surprise escaped my lips as I discovered a face I hadn't seen for years.

"Hazel? Oh my gosh. *Hazel.* You're safe."

She smiled a little shyly at me. "I'm glad that you remember me. It's been a long time."

She looked maybe sixteen, but I knew she was much older, and was wearing an attractive bronze-colored sweater and black pants. Her curly blonde hair was every bit as lovely and unruly as her brother's, and flowed down past her waist. She tucked a stray strand behind her ear and reached over to take my hand.

"We were so worried about you. Thank you for taking care of Quinn. We've been searching for him for a long time." She squeezed my hand gently.

"So all this is real?" I tried to sit up. "Quinn's free. And I didn't crash into the ocean. What in the world happened?" I felt a little dizzy still and quite nauseous and I reluctantly lay back down on the pillow with a groan.

"Here, drink this. It will help settle your stomach." Hazel handed me a teacup with a murky brown liquid inside. I forced the cup to my lips. The concoction was nasty and I shuddered as I made myself take a small sip.

"You're sure this is going to help?" I made a face.

Hazel laughed. "It smells hideous, I know. But it will stop the nausea, if you can get enough of it in you."

I grimaced and took another shuddering gulp. I handed the cup back to her and lay down. I felt so drained and weak. "Is your sister Eileen here, too?"

Hazel smiled. "She is, but she's off in 'I'm getting married so no one else in the world exists' land. She says she's happy Quinn is home, of course. It just doesn't really show, because she's so distracted." Hazel kept going on about the wedding and the lucky guy and all the wacky arrangements. My tired brain started zoning out.

Coming back into focus, I asked the question that had been bugging me.

"Hazel, where's my dad?"

Her eyes grew troubled and she turned away. "Umm, I'm going to go get someone who can give you more answers."

"Wait," I said, but she was already out the door.

I looked around the simple bedroom while I waited. It was painted a pale blue and had two small windows with plain white curtains tied back on the sides. Outside, the sky looked dusky and I saw a few sprinkled stars. There was a fire in the fireplace at one end of the room that had burned down low, and the room was getting a little chilly. I pulled the blanket up to my chin and snuggled down in the soft mattress. My eyelids felt so heavy, I think I fell back asleep.

I awoke a while later and the nausea seemed to have past. Thank goodness. I stretched and sat up, wishing desperately for a toothbrush and a shower. I reached up and felt my hair. It was doing all manner of stupid things.

"How are you feeling now?"

I jerked in surprise, my eyes flying to a handsome, serious-faced man standing in the doorway. I couldn't help cringing back into the bed once I'd recognized him. The last time I'd "seen" him, I had ended up bashing him a number of times with my hammer.

He must have noticed my distress because he immediately said, "Calm yourself, Mia. I truly am Grayson. Thank you for returning my son." He made me a courteous bow, and then sat down on the tall wooden chair beside my bed. Taking my hand he said, "Love endures, Mia. Love endures."

I couldn't help it. All the stress of the last little while welled up inside me and came spilling out. Tears started streaming down my face and I bawled like a little kid. Grayson handled my outburst with consideration and grace. He patted my shoulder, handing me tissues and murmuring soft words. When I finally pulled myself together, hiccupping and blinking, and trying to gain back a bit of my lost composure, I said, "I have so many questions."

"I'll answer them if I can."

"Where's Quinn?"

"He's resting. He needed a lot of recovery time after his release. You accomplished the impossible, you know." He tilted his head. "The two of you were able to break the spell, and in a dream, no less. It was quite extraordinary."

"We *did*?" I shook my head. "I knew I felt something, even though we were only supposed to be doing a practice run. But where did Quinn *go*? I had no idea it really worked. I guess I expected something more dramatic, like Quinn falling out of the necklace onto the floor at my feet." I grimaced. That sounded ridiculous.

"No, he came here. The spell was designed so he would return to his family when it was broken. You can't imagine our astonishment when he appeared on his own, after all our searching." Grayson smiled at the memory. "It was the most amazing surprise." He regarded me seriously. "We will always be in your debt, Mia."

I felt my cheeks flush and I stammered, "I would do anything for all of you. You are my Nan's family, after all." I sighed. "Even after all this time, I still miss her."

"So do I," Grayson's eyes tightened with painful memories.

"What about Anna?" I asked tentatively.

He shook his head. "She is gone. She was human, you know." He got up and went to a window, his heartbreaking gaze looking out into the darkness.

"I am so sorry," I whispered. Grayson just nodded. An uncomfortable silence lengthened. Unable to bear the painful quiet, I brought the conversation to the present.

"Can you please tell me about my accident? It's all very fuzzy. And where's my dad?"

He remained silent, so I kept rambling on. "I mean, I thought I was a goner, sailing over that cliff. Speaking of debts,

I think I'm the one that owes *you* for saving *me.*" Grayson was studying me thoughtfully, and then he turned and beckoned to someone who must have been standing out in the hallway.

I thought my quota for shock had been all used up, but this one blew all the others away by a long shot. My voice fled as my jaw just about hit the bed sheets, I was so stunned.

"Hello, Mia. You've become quite a remarkable young woman." He sat on the edge of my bed, and I couldn't help pulling my feet up away from him as I struggled to sit cross-legged, backing myself up into the corner where the headboard met the wall. I couldn't seem to catch my breath. My heart was slamming against my ribs in confusion and alarm.

"I see you recognize me, so I don't have to explain who I am." He smiled grimly. "I can tell you aren't going to like this conversation. If it had been up to me we never would have been in this situation at all."

My astonishment warped instantly into anger. "What the *hell* are you doing here?" I spat out through clenched teeth. "You left Mom and me when I was just a baby. So, yeah, I'm sure you aren't excited to see me. And I'm sure not happy about talking to you, either. Now where is my *real* dad?"

My biological father winced. Footsteps sounded in the corridor, and Quinn came tearing into my room. "Mia, are you okay?" He sat down at the head of the bed and wrapped his arm around my rigid shoulders, glaring around the room with an accusing eye.

"Quinn," Grayson said evenly. "You know Lord Kyan. He is the head of this household, remember."

I sat in stubborn silence, not knowing what to think or say.

Quinn nodded respectfully to Lord Kyan. "Why is Mia so upset?" He glanced from face to face. "What am I missing?"

"Lord *Kyan* is apparently my biological father," I seethed. "Which would make me *part-Terraran*, correct?" I glared at the man in front of me. He looked as young as he had in the photo I had found in Mom's drawer. I wondered if she had had any clue who or what he was. I doubted it.

"Hey, that explains a lot." Quinn actually had the nerve to look *happy*. "No wonder you were so good at speaking Terraran, and we broke the spell in your dream. That was unheard of, I've been told." He trailed off as he caught a glimpse of my face. "Of course, that would be quite a shock. Thinking you were completely human this whole time."

I was still glowering at Lord Kyan. "Did Mom know?"

"No." He at least had the grace to look uncomfortable. "Unfortunately, the risk of bringing her—and you—into this situation became far too great. I made the decision I thought best: I left, and I tried to make it so you could grow up as a normal human girl."

"Best for *whom*?" I snarled. "A young mom with a tiny baby to raise on her own?" I know it wasn't exactly fair, now that I knew the danger involved with the Terrarans, but I couldn't help it. I waved my hand over at Quinn's dad, still leaning against the wall next to the window. "Grayson here thought the risk was worthwhile. He didn't abandon Anna."

Grayson broke in uncomfortably, "Things were harder than you know, Mia. I'm not sure if I would do the same thing again, given the choice."

Quinn looked upset with his dad. "It *was* worth it, Dad. We're together again, aren't we?"

Grayson smiled at his son, but it was a sad smile. "I'm very thankful that Mia brought you back."

My anger had begun to simmer down and I repeated myself, "Is *anyone* going to tell me where my dad is?"

Quinn and Grayson glanced at Lord Kyan. *Uh-oh*, I thought. *That doesn't bode well.* "Is he hurt?" I asked, starting to panic. "He's not..." My throat constricted, I couldn't finish the words.

"He's not here," Lord Kyan said gently. "We don't think he's seriously injured. But I'm afraid he thinks you fell out of the car and died in the ocean. He doesn't know yet that you are alive and here with us."

"You mean you saved only *me*?" I asked incredulously. "Why would you do that?"

"Actually, Mia, *we* didn't save you at all." Lord Kyan put out a hand to touch me then pulled it back when he saw the look on my face.

"We would have tried, if we had known what was going to happen. But we didn't. We were a little preoccupied with Quinn appearing. Your release spell must have been felt all through Terrara like a beacon screaming, 'Powerful magic, right here!' Someone answered the signal with a horribly, devious attack: tossing a tree in front of your car." His face twisted in anger. "Their objective was thwarted, however, when you fell off the cliff. They wanted you alive."

"But if you didn't save me, what happened?" I was totally confused.

Quinn leaned over and his eyes seemed to dance with excitement. "*You* did it Mia. You are a *traveler*."

I just stared blankly.

"A *what*? Is that supposed to be good?"

Lord Kyan continued. "I am also a traveler and since you are my daughter," he shrugged, "it is not a big surprise to me, although I had spelled you to reject your Terraran talents before I left. For your protection, of course."

"I've been under a spell since I was a *baby*?" I asked, disbelief flooding my voice.

"To make sure you blended in to your environment," Lord Kyan said, defensively. "What would have happened if you had started flying around? You probably wouldn't have developed any Terraran talents until you were a teenager. That's what usually happens to unknowing part-Terrarans, but I didn't want to take any chances. I didn't want you to be anything other than human."

"Wait a minute. I can fly?" This was just getting weirder and weirder.

"But traveling is a lot cooler than flying," Quinn insisted. "Very few Terrarans can do that. You can go back and forth between the human world and Terrara at will. You must have come here because you were looking for me. Is that right?"

"Yeah," I said slowly. "I remember panicking and not wanting to die. But I also didn't want your necklace lost either. I think I wanted to find Grayson." I smiled at Quinn's dad. "I didn't realize that the necklace was empty." I made a wry face. "Good thing, too, or I really *would* be dead."

"Your instincts took over," Grayson nodded.

"So can you tell me how I did it?" I tried to be polite as I leaned over toward Lord Kyan. "I really need to go back and tell my dad that I'm alive. He must be devastated." I looked around at the others. "I mean, I don't remember exactly what I did. It's all kind of a blur."

Quinn looked apologetic. Grayson gazed at the floor.

"Mia, that's not a good idea," Lord Kyan frowned.

I bit out my words carefully. "Are you telling me that I can't go see my *dad*? That he has to go on thinking I'm *dead*?"

Lord Kyan folded his arms across his chest and put on an imposing face. "Mia, it would be *extremely* dangerous for you to go back to your dad right now. The others will be searching for you. We don't know if anyone witnessed what you can do. But the scent of magic that remained after you traveled will have been strong, so they will most likely guess you are still alive. Going to see your dad would be walking into a trap."

I choked back an angry retort and Quinn pulled me closer to him, trying to offer some comfort.

I closed my eyes, thinking of my dad and mom. I *had* to find a way to tell them I was okay. I was not going to let them go through this kind of pain. I *couldn't*. I leaned my head against Quinn's shoulder and felt tears prickle behind my eyelids. I'd go along with this…for now. But I'd find a way to reach my parents. *Soon*, I promised myself.

Controlling my emotions, I opened my watery eyes.

I was surprised to see traces of pain on Lord Kyan's face. I turned away. *What does he care about me and my family?* I thought coldly. But I knew I needed to play nice to him, so he would show me how to use my new talent. He might be the only one who *could* teach me.

I took a deep breath and brought out the puppy dog eyes. I knew they'd be even more effective full of tears.

"Please. I'm so confused by all this. Can't you show me what I am? And how I can do all these Terraran things? I need to understand myself. I promise I won't do anything foolish."

The eyes worked wonders on Quinn. If he'd been a puppy, his tail would have been going a mile a minute. Even Grayson looked willing to go along with my request. Lord Kyan, however, looked faintly suspicious. Damn. He was a smart one, and I had been less than subtle. I lowered my eyes and tried to tone down my obviousness.

"It would help me understand who I am, really. It's overwhelming, finding out I'm not completely human." That part was certainly true. It made me angry that my heritage had been hidden from me. If not for the chance finding Quinn's necklace, I might never have known the truth. I had to bite my lip to hold back my irritation. The part of me that was kissing up was warring with the side that wanted to yell and scream at this insane turn of events. I felt torn in two, as well as absolutely exhausted.

I laid my head back on the headboard and waited for someone to answer. Quinn and Grayson were deferring to Lord Kyan. It figured.

"Let's see how you are feeling tomorrow," Lord Kyan said slowly. "I think you need some rest and time to think. And right now, you definitely need something to eat and drink. We'll talk again tomorrow."

With that, he stood and the discussion was apparently over. With a final look at each of us, he swept out of the room. *Humpf.* Guess it's nice to be a Lord, whatever that means.

Quinn scooted off the bed, promising to bring back something to eat. Grayson caught me smiling after his son and I blushed a bit. I cared about Quinn very much, but I didn't want anyone to get the idea that it was more than that. I was still conflicted because of my feelings for Griff. I looked down at my hands.

"Traveling has left you weak," Grayson said. "You need more food since you threw up everything in your stomach after you got here. You need time to rest and regain your strength."

My face must have shown the horror I felt, because Grayson continued, "Don't worry; the few who I've known with that talent all react the same way to traveling. It's a serious drawback. So, even though it seems extremely convenient, it's only used rarely, since one is rendered quite helpless for a time afterward."

I ran my tongue over my teeth. No wonder my mouth tasted so nasty. "Are there any toothbrushes here? And what about a place to shower and clean up?"

"Hazel will help you after you have had something to eat. Then you will need to get some more rest. We all will. It's still the middle of the night here."

"And where is *here*?"

"You will see in the morning. Or afternoon, more likely. *Ahh.* Here's Quinn and Hazel. I'll see you tomorrow, Mia. Thank you again for returning my son." He turned and walked gracefully out the door as the others walked in.

Quinn brought back three plates piled high, the smells making my stomach growl. The food was warm and delicious, and I have to admit, I ate like I hadn't eaten for days. I guess traveling left you starved, once your appetite came back. The chicken and rice tasted mouth-wateringly good, rich and delicious with unfamiliar spices. I was so thirsty I must have drunk a half-gallon of water.

Quinn and Hazel sat with me on the rug in front of the fireplace. They were so chatty and friendly that before long, I felt completely natural around them. Childhood memories blended into the present. They both seemed so happy that I was part of their world that I couldn't find a way to complain about the difficulty of my sudden life-changing discovery. So I put on my cheerful face and went along with all their excited talk.

Inside, however, I was nervous and afraid of what this revelation would do to my relationship with my parents. Would it freak them out? Would they believe me, or even care one way or another?

And right now they believed I was *dead*, thrown to violent death off a cliff. All at once, my food went from delicious to disgusting. I forced my eyes from the remaining scraps on my plate.

I *had* to find a way to get in touch with my parents, whether Lord Kyan approved or not. But, for now, I was so tired I could hardly think a straight thought, much less form a plan.

Pushing my plate aside, I brought myself back to the here and now. I asked Hazel if I could get cleaned up somewhere.

"Sure." She stood up and waved for me to follow. "Girls only," she told Quinn firmly, and he held up his hands in an innocent gesture. His smile, to me, looked a bit mischievous, though. "Go to bed, Quinn," Hazel scolded. "You can see Mia tomorrow."

He got up, saying, "Okay, okay." As he walked past me he gave me a swift kiss on the cheek. After giving a quick sly glance at his sister, he strode out the door.

Hazel raised her eyebrows to me and I tried to send her my own innocent smile, but I don't think she bought it. "Follow me," she smirked.

After brushing my teeth, I enjoyed a long, hot shower and Hazel thoughtfully loaned me a soft, long nightgown. It wasn't really my style since I usually sleep in shorts and a tank-top, but I was grateful not to have to sleep in my grungy jeans and long sleeved t-shirt. Hazel took all my clothes off some place to have them washed. Those pieces of clothing had seen a lot of action, from hammer fights in the woods to stolen kisses, magical spells and unintentional cliff-diving off Highway 101.

I finished cleaning up and found my way to my room. My fire had been built up and was crackling happily. I ran my fingers through my short hair as I sat in front of it for a few minutes, trying to give my locks some kind of sense of direction before they were smushed into my pillow for the night. I almost fell asleep on the hearth rug.

Forcing myself away from the comfortable warmth, I crawled into my bed and slept soundly for the first time in a very long time.

A Safe House, a Reckless Plan

Tears streamed down my face and my pillow was soggy as I dragged myself out of my nightmare. I could still see my mom's face while she came tearing down the road to the accident site. My dad was covered in blood, and then they were holding each other, crying and grieving inconsolably over the loss of their only child.

I punched my wet pillow angrily. I couldn't do this. I couldn't stay here. Everything felt wrong. I had to get back to my parents. I picked up my cell phone on the side table by my bed. It was still juiced up, and I glared at the "no signal" message in vain, wishing for some way to communicate that I was alive and safe.

I was, of course, happy and relieved to have helped free Quinn and reunite his family. In the process, however, I had lost myself. I felt emotionally adrift. I had been separated from my parents not only physically, but also culturally. Now

I belonged to a completely different world than they did. My own familiar world was gone forever—blasted into a million tiny fragments, scattered over a cliff and into the ocean the second I had done that strange, otherworldly spell to save my life.

It was odd to think that my mom had—although she didn't know it—had a part in all of this. How would she feel about it? Even though I knew she loved my dad, I really didn't want her here, seeing her ex-husband, stirring up old feelings and memories. That worried me.

No, I was the one that needed to get away. Far away, so I could figure this out.

I let my mind relive those horrible moments falling off the cliff. What *was* it that my hands had done? I let the images wash over me, trying to remember. I still couldn't tell. It was pure instinct, mixed with a healthy dose of adrenaline. I couldn't repeat the process, even if I wanted to. I would have to have someone show me what to do next time.

I let myself think about my biological father, Lord Kyan. Who was he? What kind of a house was this, where he housed so many people? Were we in Terrara, or my own earth? How did he feel about seeing his daughter? Was I his only daughter? That didn't seem likely. I'll bet he was way older than he looked. So, did he have lots of other children? That made me start. Did I have half-brothers or sisters? Wow.

I closed my eyes. "I shouldn't even go there," I chided myself. Way too many chances for pain and disappointment.

All this was too much for one person to handle at once. I flipped over my soggy pillow and tried to huddle on my side into a comfortable position.

After a while, I gave up.

The windows showed a moonlit sky. Was it still the same night, or had I slept through the next day into the next night? I had no idea.

I got up and found the bathroom. Then, tip-toeing awkwardly in my borrowed nightgown, since that was all I had, I decided to wander the halls a bit, check things out. My worry had left me wide-awake and I needed to move around.

I wished I could go for a run because that was usually the most helpful solution to a restless mind. I needed adrenaline, and some endorphins. Well, some snooping in the middle of the night would have to be good enough; the possibility of getting caught might at least result in some sought-after adrenaline. I just hoped I wasn't caught for real.

I passed many closed doors until I reached a long, steep staircase. I gingerly stepped down the wooden stairs, hoping that there wouldn't be any creaks or groans under my weight. I made it to the bottom without any disastrous sounds, and I kept creeping, guided by the small amount of light coming from a room in front of me and to the left.

I slipped inside the cracked door, peeking around in wonder at the huge array of books along the walls lined with shelves, top to bottom.

I browsed the nearest shelf. An assortment of books both human and Terraran caught my eye. Large volumes with dusty covers, emitting that slightly musty smell I have always liked. On one wall, next to a window covered in a velvety red curtain, hung a familiar photo, which made me pause uncertainly. I ran a finger along the frame, gazing at the young man and woman beaming at a chubby bald baby.

Feeling awkward, I turned to the fire at the far end of the room and I moved to the chairs placed comfortably near the hearth. I froze mid-step, as I noticed someone sitting in one of the chairs. He was watching me, unsurprised, a book lying neglected in his lap.

"I expected you sooner." Lord Kyan closed his book and looked at me with a half smile on his lips.

I tried to act as if I had planned this all along. "I still have a lot of questions."

"I'm sure you do. Have a seat." He indicated the chair across from his. "Use the blanket, if you're cold."

I settled into the armchair and wrapped the soft blanket around my legs and feet.

"You have my hair and coloring." He looked thoughtfully at me. "But you have your mother's lovely brown eyes." With those words, his gaze went to a far away place.

"Did you ever regret your decision?" I had to know, even if the answer was painful.

"Not many days go by without my thoughts turning to the two of you. But as much as I miss Sharon and regret not seeing you grow up, Mia, I was always able to console myself that you were safe and better off without me." He looked at me a bit wistfully. "Your visit here has made me wonder if I did the right thing."

I blinked in surprise. This certainly wasn't the answer I had expected. I didn't want to feel anything for this man who had abandoned us so long ago. I just wanted him to teach me to use my powers, so I could leave. This confused things.

I squirmed in my seat, feeling bad for what I was going to do. "Don't you think Mom should know that I'm safe? Can't you imagine what she is going through right now? I need to go back."

Lord Kyan grimaced. "You're not very subtle with your manipulation tactics, are you?"

I blushed.

"I told you that isn't a good idea. Others will be waiting for you. Your parents are safer now, thinking you are dead."

I crossed my arms in annoyance. "That is too cruel," I complained. "I'm their only child."

"Sharon didn't have any more children?"

"No. After three miscarriages, she decided that she couldn't handle any more disappointment."

Lord Kyan nodded and looked away.

"Do you have any other children besides me?" I blurted out, before I could stop myself. Yikes. I wasn't sure if I wanted to know the answer.

"No, just you." His face reflected an intense loneliness.

"But how old are you? Didn't you love anyone else? You must have had lots of opportunity since you seem to be such an important person." I bit my tongue. *Stop getting involved,* I told myself sternly, and glanced toward the fire, rather than at his face.

He sighed deeply. "Do you really want to know all this about me? I think the reason you sought me out is for information about your powers. Am I right?"

I tried not to look guilty as charged.

"Of *course* I want to know about my powers, but I'm interested in your life, too," I admitted. "I never expected anything like this to happen to me. I thought I was just a regular, ordinary girl. A human girl. This all seems like some crazy dream." I leaned my head back on the soft chair. "For one thing, you're my father, but you don't look that much older than me. That's a bit unnerving, ya know."

He actually laughed. "I'm quite a lot older than I look. Would you like me to sprinkle some grey in my hair? Add a few wrinkles?"

"Okay," I smirked. "Let's see it."

One minute he looked twenty-something, the next, forty-something. "Whoa," I laughed. "That definitely looks more middle-aged. But you need a few extra pounds around your gut."

He raised his eyebrows.

"Not willing to go that far, huh?" I sniggered, not believing that this conversation was taking place. I think we must have both been loopy from lack of sleep. Or maybe it was just me. "So, can you glamour yourself to look like someone else?"

"No." He changed back to his young self. "Only full-blooded Terrarans can appear as completely different people. I can merely change my own appearance, like the length or color of hair, my skin tone and texture, height, things like that. I am half-Terraran. I had a human mother, like Quinn."

"So, I'm a quarter-Terraran. What does that mean?"

"Each case is different, of course. Though you *do* seem unusually powerful for having only a small part of you Terraran. However, we come from a very important and influential family line."

I tried to worm more information about our family tree from him, but he clammed up and would say nothing more on the subject. Still, after much more pleading and convincing, I finally got him to agree to show me how to access some of my powers.

"You promise not to travel to the hospital, that you won't travel anywhere near your parents," he said, looking me sternly in the eyes. I stared back calmly and promised honestly that I wouldn't do any of those things. I had another plan forming in my head...and I wouldn't have to break my word to do it.

He relented, reluctantly. "I'm only teaching you because I think you might need all your powers in the near future, to stay safe. Things are coming to a head, and I can't predict their outcome. But I *do* want you to survive, Mia. I know you don't believe it, but I genuinely care for you and your mother."

I nodded, not knowing how to answer, feeling uncomfortable and inexplicitly choked-up.

Lord Kyan studied my face thoughtfully for a moment. "Let's get started, then. This might take a while."

He stood up, and held out his hand.

"COME ON SLEEPYHEAD. You've been sleeping for hours. You need some food."

I groaned and turned over, pulling the covers over my head. The sunlight coming through the windows was making my tired eyes smart. I felt like I had barely returned to my room.

"Go away," I mumbled, irritated that anyone could be so cheerful in the morning.

I heard a plate or cup clink onto the side table, and thankfully, the annoying voice went far, far away. I sank back into a blissful slumber.

When I woke again it was dark outside. I seemed to have gotten my days and nights all mixed up.

I thought back to the night before with Lord Kyan. He had been as good as his word, and I was fairly certain I could pull a traveling trick if I needed to. I also practiced flying. Well, at least some *hovering*. I was still a little hesitant to let myself get too far off the ground. Probably one of those things best learned when you were a kid and still thought of yourself as completely invincible. Oh well, I'd hopefully get over my phobia soon. Flying would be *totally* useful. Not to mention fun—if I could just let go.

I drank the cup of water I found on my table, and as my stomach growled, I wished that I hadn't rejected the food offer from earlier that morning. After using the bathroom and taking a quick shower, I noticed my clothes, cleaned and folded, on the floor beside my bed. It felt good to be back in my normal clothes. That long nightgown was so *not* me. I tousled my wet hair, wishing for some gel. Shrugging, I decided to get out of this bedroom and go exploring again. *Please let me find a refrigerator*, I thought.

I rounded the first corner, straight into Quinn.

I barely muffled my gasp of surprise, stepping back a couple of steps. He gave me a glimpse of those adorable dimples as he smothered a laugh.

"Hey, sleepy. I've been waiting for you to wake up." He slouched against the wall casually. "Which is a nice change, actually. I used to always hope you'd hurry and go to sleep, so I could see you."

I cocked my head and put my hands on my hips. "How long have you been waiting? That wall doesn't look like a very comfortable spot."

"I heard you moving around earlier. I've been waiting just a few minutes for you to come out of your room. Figured you'd be starving."

"You figured right," I laughed quietly. "Got anything stashed away?"

"Just follow me." Quinn took my hand and led me down the hallway. Somehow, holding hands in real life affected me differently than it did in my dreams. Yikes. I wasn't so comfortable with it anymore. But I couldn't pull away and be rude either, so I allowed him to keep it up while we went along, feeling my cheeks heat up and hoping he wouldn't notice.

Alone with Quinn, in the dark. *What was I doing?* When were we going to get to the kitchen? I needed something to do that did not involve close contact.

"In here," Quinn whispered. We entered a small sitting area with a couch, and small tables, and a large glowing fire in one corner. I could see some baskets with fruit and other food items, and my stomach rumbled urgently in response. Quinn cracked another smile.

"I'll get us something to drink. Be right back."

I curled up on a couch and started munching a juicy pear. I didn't think I'd ever eaten such a delicious piece of fruit. I was looking around a bit desperately for a napkin to catch the juice running down my fingers to my wrist when Quinn returned. Luckily, he had some cloth napkins, along with a couple of glasses of water.

I started on a second pear as he joined me on the couch.

"These are by far the best pears I have ever eaten," I began gushing. "Are Terrarans the best gardeners, or what? Is it magic that makes them so sweet and juicy?"

"Don't know. Everything tastes extra good to me, too. Remember: years without eating. I'm not sure how a spell could keep me alive that long without food. But, wow, now that I'm free, I can't seem to stop." Quinn picked up a pear and almost half of it disappeared in a single bite.

"We're like two little kids sneaking into the fridge at night. Is anyone going to come and get mad?" I asked, glancing at the door.

"Hope not," Quinn smiled, eyes looking mysterious in the firelight.

And I suddenly got a whole lot *more* nervous. Eyes down, I finished my pear and wiped my fingers off, using a napkin with a little water dripped onto it. There was another bowl filled with nuts, and I grabbed it and settled it into my lap, as I scooted into the corner of the couch and pulled my legs up. Quinn settled back into his corner and eyed me silently.

My ears filled with the crunch of almonds, the soft chewing of fruit, and the hiss and crackle of the fire. In the dimly lit room I could feel the awkwardness sliding up over me like a scratchy, uncomfortable blanket. I refused to break the silence first, waiting to see what he wanted to say…but also *worried* about what he would say, as my brain relived a few very friendly dream moments.

Eyes firmly fixed on the fire, I kept chewing.

"Things are different now that I'm free, aren't they? Now that we're both part of the real world."

"Kind of," I hedged. "But I'm so glad you're free, of course," I added quickly.

"Me, too. Mostly." he said rather wistfully. "The closeness we shared in your dreams is gone. That time is fading like all normal dreams, I guess. And I find that I miss you."

"I'm still here," I began awkwardly. He raised his eyebrows, and gave me a rueful smile.

"You're right. It's not the same. I don't know why." For a minute, I let my eyes run through his loose blonde curls that glowed with the warmth of the firelight. Finally, I tugged my eyes away.

"I think I do. The real world has more consequences. You can't be so free and spontaneous with your feelings." He turned to gaze at the fire, his profile becoming a burnished bronze that reminded me of several classical statues that I had admired at my favorite museum. I smothered a sigh.

"I thought we might have been falling in love in those dreams, but now that we are both back here in the real world, that doesn't seem to be the case. At least not for you. Or am I misreading your emotions?" He turned and captured my gaze.

I almost choked, his words snapping me back from my museum fantasy. What is it about Terrarans? They have no concept of subtlety and beating around the bush. I hate talking about things in such a scary, straightforward manner when I'm not ready.

I made myself take a deep breath. "Quinn, I haven't even spent that much time with you. I know I care about you. I'm very happy I helped free you. But love is a pretty big deal. I mean, do we have to decide all this right now? Can't we just go back to getting to know each other here in the real world? I'm only seventeen, you know." Everything came out in a rush. I closed my mouth, my emotions still spinning around wildly.

"Yeah, I'm forty. I know." He gave me a smile in spite of the serious conversation. "That's not old at all, by Terraran standards."

"You're right," I said, trying not to think about Griff's age. "But I *am* young. And I'm confused about so many things besides my feelings for you. Not that those feelings aren't important, Quinn. They are. But there is so much stuff I'm being bombarded with at the moment." I began twirling my short hair in agitation. "It's incredibly overwhelming."

Quinn looked at me closely. "I'm sorry. I'm not being fair to you. I had forgotten all the new situations you are dealing with. I was selfish even to bring it up. I just have a hard time being with you without remembering what it was like before."

"Me, too," I admitted. "I will always remember those dreams. They may fade a little, but never completely. They changed my life. You changed my life, Quinn. If I had never found that necklace, I wouldn't have found out all the other things about my life. I'd be a totally different person."

"Not only good things have happened, though," Quinn frowned. "Your parents think you're dead."

"That's true." My temper flared for a second; I pushed it back down. "But, bringing it back to the bright side, now *you're* reunited with *your* family. So that's good. And I'll see my parents again. It will just take a while to work things out." Unwisely, I began thinking about my plan.

Quinn picked up on it right away. "You're scheming, aren't you?"

"No," I denied. Too quickly.

"I'll help, if I can. You helped me. I feel I owe you." Quinn reached over and took my hand in his. "Listen, I know that your *father*..." (I scowled at that word) "...I mean *Lord Kyan* forbade you from visiting your parents. So I'm thinking you've come up with a sneaky way around his restriction."

"Quinn, I'm not involving you. You could be in big trouble." I squeezed his hand nervously. "Look, I need to find a way to let my parents know I'm okay. I will be safe. I've thought it through."

"You're going to see your other family, aren't you? Jace and Sarah."

I gaped at him, pulling my hand away in surprise.

"How did you…?" I stopped. "Crap, you learned a *lot* about me from my dreams. Quinn, I *can* trust you not to say anything, can't I?" I looked him straight in the eye. "Please."

"Mia, I swear. I won't give away your plan unless it's obvious that you're in trouble. Can you give me a timeframe so I can know when to start worrying?"

"I don't know. A day or two? I still don't know all the ins and outs of traveling. Lord Kyan showed me the basics. I'm sure he suspects trouble. I'll bet he's just sitting there, waiting for me to make my move. But I can't help it. I *have* to take care of my family."

"Family comes first. I understand completely."

"I was thinking of leaving tonight. Which reminds me. I still haven't seen this place in the daytime. Are we in Terrara or on Earth-side?"

"This home that Lord Kyan has made is on Earth, which makes it harder for us to stay hidden from humans, but it's worth it. We are far north, inside forested wilderness areas. We don't need electricity or other human conveniences, so we can be far away from human settlements. We can use our powers for gardening, fuel, and such necessities. We are relatively safe from Terraran purists here."

"*Hmm.* I would have liked to see it in the light. But I feel rested and well-fed. *Eww,* that is actually more of a drawback, isn't it? Thinking back, I must have spewed my guts out when I got here." My nose wrinkled up as my imagination supplied the gory details. *Ugh.* "Sorry about that."

Quinn scooted over and put his arm around me. "I didn't care one bit. I was *so* happy to see you. And we were all astounded that you could travel. You shouldn't be embarrassed about being able to do something only a tiny percentage of Terrarans can do. You should be proud."

I hugged Quinn on impulse. He was giving me the pep talk I needed, and I really appreciated it. "Thanks, Quinn. I'll come back as soon as I can."

"Be careful, Mia." And he leaned over and kissed my cheek. I sighed and rested my head on his shoulder. He began running his hands through my hair.

Which had become long again.

"How did that happen?" I asked.

"You're forgetting," Quinn laughed. "Since you are part-Terraran, you can change your appearance, too. Like the color and length of your hair, eye and skin color, and age, of course. I happen to like your hair this way."

I smiled up at his grinning face, feeling torn about leaving him.

Then he spoiled the mood by saying, "I know you're going to try and rescue Griff."

I stiffened, clamping my mouth shut. He was *way* too perceptive. Dammit. "Seriously, Mia," Quinn said. "Think about what you are *doing*."

"I'm not talking about him. You don't like him or trust him." Of course, then I went right on talking about and defending him. "He's trapped like you were, only worse. Quinn, he's being *tortured*. I can't walk away from that."

"*He* might be a trap." Quinn's face became stone like as he stared at me.

"You can't talk me out of it," I said, rising to the challenge.

"Why not?"

"He saved my life. Now I have to try and save him. That's how it is. End of discussion."

"What discussion? When is there ever a discussion with you?" Quinn sighed deeply and took my stiff, defensive body and held it tight. I counted to three and made myself relax. "I just want you to come back," he said, simply.

I forced a determined smile. "I have no intention of screwing up. Somehow, I'll make it work. Just wait and see." I ran my finger down one of those appealing dimples. "You don't need to worry about me, really."

Quinn nodded, but still looked unhappy. "Can't help it," he muttered.

With a slow reluctance, I moved away from him and sat crossed-legged on the rug in the middle of the room. I felt Quinn's emotions trying to draw me back to him. But my courage was up and running. My emotions were charged up. I needed to go before I wimped out.

I looked up at Quinn's fretful face, and tried not to feel guilty. Or scared.

"Please. I know you're mad, Quinn, but will you cover for me for just a little while? I swear I'll be careful."

"Only for a short time. Then I'm letting everyone know where you went," Quinn promised.

"Okay, just give me a chance to do it myself first. You know, I miss not having you with me anymore. I still wear your necklace for luck, see?" I held up the charm; Quinn gave me a reluctant smile.

"I'll be back soon, Quinn."

"I hope it really does bring you good luck, Mia."

I blinked my eyes a few times, focusing on the words that Lord Kyan had taught me, on the intricate hand motions. Once I started, they came back to me as if I had done this kind of spell my whole life. My last view was Quinn's worried face as the room blurred into a thousand colors. The next thing I knew, I was laying on the tile floor in Sarah's kitchen, groaning and crawling around, frantically opening lower level cupboards searching for a bowl to throw up in, while Jace and the rest of his family stared at me like I was an alien who had just landed in their kitchen and was now looting their cupboards.

23

Out of the Frying Pan

I woke up, in yet another unfamiliar bed. How long had it been since I slept in my own room? Not that many days, surely, yet it felt like *forever*. I struggled against the nausea, clamping my jaw together, willing my body back to normal as I tried to sit up.

My mind remembered the few minutes of hysteria when Jace's family realized the sick creature who had just spontaneously appeared on their floor was actually a real person they knew and loved. I was still rooting around a cupboard when Jace yelled, "Mia, where did you... Oh my gosh! We thought you were dead!"

Sarah just kept repeating my name like a chant, over and over. I attempted a smile, and then promptly threw up in the mixing bowl I had discovered. Before I passed out I managed to say, "Don't tell anyone I'm here yet. Please. Danger." Then I barfed up another lung (at least, that's what it felt like), and everything went black.

"MAN, I'VE NEVER thought I'd be happy to see someone spewing all over the kitchen floor. You can barf like a champ, you know." Jace's face hovered over mine.

"Thanks," I whispered. "Still nauseous."

"Mom made you some tea, but it smells *really* nasty so I brought you some Coke. Room temperature. It always helps me when I have the flu."

I took a small sip, trying in vain to cover up the disgusting taste lingering in my mouth. I wished I was up for standing at a sink and brushing the taste out completely. *Not yet,* my stomach told me, queasily.

"So I guess you can pull a Harry Potter now, huh? You totally freaked my family when you popped out of thin air. I assume this is a Terraran thing?"

I nodded faintly. "I'm part-Terraran. My biological father. Remember his picture?"

"Whoa." Jace looked stunned. "You mean you're not completely human?"

I studied his face nervously, waiting for him to freak out.

Jace peered at me closely, squinting his eyes. "No wonder you've always been so weird."

Half-relieved, half-irritated, I stuck my tongue out at him. I would followed up by tossing my pillow at him, but I was still too weak.

Jace gave me that goofy grin I loved so much. "Mia, that's the coolest thing ever." Then his face grew serious. "But wait, what happened in Washington? Do your parents know you're alive? They called about a car crash. It was one of the worst phone calls ever." He shuddered.

"They don't know yet," I said. "I want to tell them, but I've been warned that it's too dangerous. So I came here instead."

I coughed and took another sip of soda. "It makes me sick to think of them suffering. I want to talk to them so badly. Yet if I do let them know what's going on and then something bad happens to them, well, how could I live with that?"

"You are not in a good place, Mia. Definitely stuck between that stupid rock and that crappy hard place. Let's think, though. There's got to be something we can do."

"Somehow I need to get my parents a message. I can't do it. Maybe you can. But the message has to be subtle. Ears may be listening."

"Well, do you have any code that you guys have used before? Like a safeword for allowing a stranger pick you up from school? You know, it's okay if they have the family password. My mom used to have one for me and my brothers. Don't think we ever used it, though. But you know my mom, she worries about everything." Jace rolled his eyes.

"No," I said slowly. "We never did the family password thing. However, Dad and I found a letter in my Nan's stuff. The letter was from Grayson, Quinn's dad, and he had a password so that my Nan could be sure she gave the jewelry to the right person. The password was 'Love endures.'" I sat up straight, ignoring my irritatingly light head. "You could tell my dad that you realize this is a horrible time, but to understand that *love endures.* I'm pretty sure he will get it. He has to." I sat back miserably, rubbing my aching forehead.

"Hmm. It sounds kind of iffy. What if he asks point-blank questions? I'd have to lie. I would *hate* doing that. And my mom is going to hate it even more than I do. In fact, she might have already called your parents." Jace jumped to his feet. "Crap. I'll be back in a second." He sped out of the room before I could open my mouth.

I closed my eyes. *Please, oh please. Sarah, I hope you didn't call my parents.* I kept repeating this thought over and over, until Jace came back with his mom in tow.

"Mia, honey, why in the world am I not allowed to call your parents?" She bustled over and sat on the bed, checking my head, presumably for a fever.

"I'm not sick or delusional. I swear. My parents are in big-time danger, and even though I want to tell them I'm okay, I can't. Seriously, Sarah, it's life or death."

She stared at me. "If I hadn't seen you fall onto my kitchen floor out of thin air, I never would believe you, you know. That was so unreal; my mind still keeps trying to rationalize what happened."

"It isn't as much fun as it looks," I grumbled. "The side effects suck."

Sarah burst out laughing. "Be glad you weren't the one cleaning up the kitchen floor. At least you didn't land on the carpet."

I slid down in the covers, cringing. "You're right. Cleaning up someone else's barf totally trumps being the one doing the barfing. Sorry about that."

Sarah grabbed me and pulled me into a hug. I swallowed back some lingering nausea, head feeling woozy, full of cotton. "Mia," Sarah said, "I would clean up after you *any* day. I am just so happy to see you alive. We were sure you were dead."

Tears came into my eyes and I blinked several times, relaxing into Sarah's maternal embrace.

"Mom," Jace warned, "you're smothering her. She's gonna barf again."

"I'm okay," I managed to croak. But my stomach was relieved when Sarah let me lay down again. "I think I need a bit more sleep. Then I'll be back to normal."

I started fading immediately after my head sunk into the pillow, but not before I heard Jace smirk, "Normal. Since when have you *ever* been normal?"

"I STILL DON'T think this is a very good idea," Jace said, sounding like a broken record, or skipping CD, or whatever.

"Just wait and see," I told him again.

"You know, I might never forgive you for making me go shopping for gross girl clothes on Thanksgiving weekend. Do you have any idea how long I had to stand in line? I was totally humiliated."

"You are the best friend a girl could ever have, Jace," I cajoled. "I'm going to owe you a huge favor. When all this is over, I'll pay up, I swear."

"*Humpf.* I'll have to think of something really good," Jace growled.

Then I walked out of the bathroom, struck a prissy little pose, and then spun around so he could get the full effect.

I have to say it: Jace goggled.

"So, still sure it won't work?" I mocked.

For the first time since forever, no words came out of my best friend's smart mouth.

"You might want to pop your eyes back in, 'cause we've got places to be." I couldn't help laughing.

"But…" Jace sputtered.

"Just a bit of magic makeup. Think anyone will recognize me?"

"No way," Jace snorted. "I take it back. This might work after all."

I went out the back door and snuck around to the front to test my theory.

I stood on the front porch, shivering, as I waited for Sarah to answer the door. She opened the door and eyed me warily, completely without recognition. It was hard to keep a straight face. "Could I borrow your phone, please? My car broke down just down the street." I had made my voice deeper, huskier, older.

Sarah looked me over for any signs of danger. She always liked to be a good neighbor, but she was fiercely protective of her family as well. Inviting a stranger in her home went against most of her instincts. I lowered my blue eyes and fiddled with my long blonde hair. My pastel pantsuit was about as threatening as a bar of soap. I looked like a young businesswoman who was late for a lunch date.

Suddenly, Jace threw the door open wider behind his mom, and let out a loud guffaw. Sarah gave him a "stop being so rude" look. But try as I might, I couldn't stop myself from cracking a huge grin.

Sarah's confused gaze swept from Jace to me, and back again. "I'm sorry, Sarah." I struggled to keep my face straight, ignoring Jace's now booming laugh. "It's me, Mia. I had to test my disguise and see if it worked."

I walked past Sarah's astonished face into the living room and sat down primly, folding my hands demurely in my lap.

Jace about fell over, he was laughing so hard. "Guess it works pretty well. As long as a certain bigmouth doesn't give me away," I said as glared pointedly at Jace, who was struggling to control himself.

"How in heaven's name?" Sarah began.

"Just a perk of my mixed heritage," I smiled. "Now, I need a ride to the nearest hotel. I'm going to make a couple phone calls from the lobby. Oh, and can I borrow one of your fancy winter coats, Sarah? I need something to go along with this outfit. Got anything that will work?"

Sarah came back in a daze with a pretty camel-colored three-quarter length coat that matched quite well. Normally, I would never have been caught dead in it, it was so proper. "Perfect," I enthused, catching sight of myself in the hallway mirror. How bizarre. I sure hoped this would work. I couldn't wait to change my clothes into something less hideous. "Sunglasses?" I asked hopefully, and accepted a pair of gold metal-framed monstrosities. "The final touch." I nodded thankfully.

"I'll give you a call when I'm done. Thanks for all your help." I gave Sarah a hug.

She still looked a bit baffled, but she went along with it. "Let me know what else we can do, dear. Are you sure I can't call your parents?"

"Not yet," I said seriously. "Soon, though. I promise."

I SAT WITH my hands folded neatly in my lap as Mrs. Smythe, the real estate agent, chatted a nonstop string of praise for the falling mortgage rates, the desirability of the neighborhood and the bargain price of the house. I let her ramble on and on, encouraging her with an occasional nod or smile. I was barely able to make chit-chat, much less execute a well thought-out conversation. All I kept thinking was, *I really hoped this works.*

The agent whipped through a four-way stop, barely avoiding a parked car as she gesticulated enthusiastically about some aspect of the location. I smothered a gasp and tried to look pleasantly interested. I admit I'm not the best driver, but this disregard for even the most basic rules of the road was getting me wound tighter than I would have thought possible. I breathed a sigh of relief when we pulled into the driveway of the gargoyle house.

Looking at the house made my stomach turn over. I didn't know for sure if Griff was going to be anywhere near this house. He had once told me that he lived here when he was on Earthside. All I could do was hope that he was around, and that other Terrarans weren't. Of course, that was the whole point of the disguise, and the real estate agent. I had to look like a normal human buyer who had nothing to do with Griff, or Terrara, or anything unusual.

I accompanied Mrs. Smythe to the front door, and nonchalantly eyed her movements as she punched her code into the key box hanging around the front doorknob. I was pretty sure I had her number. I ingrained it into my brain for future probable use. She swung the front door open, immediately pointing out obvious features of the place. I turned to her as politely as possible, and smiled the sweetest smile I could.

"Could I please have a little privacy? I need to get a feel for the *spirit* of the place. Talking makes it hard to listen to what the house has to tell me."

Mrs. Smythe raised her painted-on eyebrows. She must not have heard that one before. She touched a hand to her stiff, hair-sprayed helmet of a hairdo, before answering.

"Well, I don't know. You might miss something important."

I went on smoothly. "Maybe you could look in the backyard for me and take stock of all the gargoyles. My father wants a complete list of all the statues. I have to have his blessing before I can buy it for restoration. It's his money that will pay for all of it, of course." I tried to smile a "daddy's little girl" smile.

Mrs. Smythe decided to take the hint without argument, thank goodness. She bounced down the steps, searching for pen and paper from the bottom of her purse.

The moment the door closed, I started rushing room to room. "*Griff?*" I whispered. I knew it was dangerous, but I couldn't help it. I got to the last bedroom at the end of the hall. I opened the door, my heart pounding in my throat.

No one was there.

No! He *had* to be here. *Somewhere.*

I hurried back to the kitchen, checking doors. Finally I found it: the door to the basement. I pulled a string and a dim, yellowish light bulb cast a slight glow down the wooden stairs. Biting my lip, I edged my way down to the bottom of the stairs, turning to the framed (but not finished) room on my right. I found another hanging bulb and pulled a metal chain.

The eerie light swept around the cement walls and shadowy two-by-fours. I jumped about three feet when an indistinguishable face peered from around a corner. My heart leaped. In utter panic, I tried to look (but not look like I was looking) and see who was watching me silently. "Is s-some-one there?" I stuttered cautiously. "I'm here with a real estate agent. Looking to buy a house, but not a haunted one. Although I do have a thing for haunted photography," I continued carefully.

The figure stepped out into the light. He did a little trick with his fingers and I felt the disguise I'd worked so hard on fall away.

I was Mia once again, in a ridiculous outfit, staring at Griff's extremely pale face. His hollow eyes blinked in surprise, and then his whole body collapsed back against the cement wall, sliding down in a graceless heap.

"Griff!" I rushed over to him, taking his pain filled face into my hands. His long hair was tangled and matted. I gently brushed through it with my fingers. "Oh my gosh. What have they done to you?"

"It's really you?" he slurred. "You can *travel*. You're part-Terraran, a *powerful* Terraran. I didn't know. Why didn't I know?" He was shaking his head over and over.

"Griff, stop it." I held his face in my hands, studying his bruised and cut face, wincing as I imagined him being tortured because of me. "I didn't know either. I just found out."

"I saw you fall. I thought I was too late. That I couldn't save you." He reached out and ran a hand down my cheek, making me shiver. His hands were freezing.

"Was that real?" I wondered aloud, thinking back. "You were there?"

"Then, before you hit the rocks, you vanished." His cold hands grabbed my hands from his face and held them tight. "I was *so* relieved. I couldn't believe it."

"Oh Griff, we have to get you out of here. Someplace safe. Where no one can hurt you."

"I can't leave. They'll find me. *You* have to go. *Now!*" Griff was starting to get agitated. He pushed himself away from the wall, as if only just now realizing that I was real, not some kind of fantasy. "Mia, you have to get out of here. They are looking for you even *harder* now that they know how powerful you are."

"Griff, I was careful. No one saw that it's me. No one knows I'm here."

He got to his feet unsteadily. "Mia, you have to travel away from here, now!" His voice was becoming steadier now. He took me by the shoulders and started to shake me insistently.

"Stop it, Griff!" I grabbed his arms and stared into his intense blue eyes, wide open in worry and concern.

My focus narrowed; all I could think about was the boy standing in front of me with his hands on my shoulders. "Oh Griff, I missed you so much." Without thinking of consequences, I stood on my tip-toes and planted a fierce kiss in the middle of his tightly drawn mouth.

He hesitated a split second. Then his arms wrapped around me tightly and he kissed me back, as if he couldn't help himself. A long, desperate kiss that left me breathless when he buried his face in my neck. "Mia," he sighed unsteadily.

I held him close, so overwhelmed by the emotions I was feeling: relief, excitement, happiness. He was whispering lovely things in my ear. I turned my head, half in a daze, and our lips met again. I gave myself over completely to the moment. Nothing else mattered.

"How very sweet," a voice mocked behind me.

Griff and I tore ourselves apart. We were both disoriented for a second, and my face must have been several shades of red.

I stared into the eyes of a tall, dark-haired man. He was dressed in an elegant suit and shiny black shoes. His wavy hair was styled back off his thin, pale face, his cheekbones sharp and angular, with thin slashes of black for eyebrows. His thin mouth curled up in a sneer, and his grey eyes flashed coldly as they ran over me.

In a panic, Griff grabbed me and shoved me behind him. "*Now, Mia, go!*"

I was stunned into inaction.

"Oh, I'd stay if I were you, Mia." The stranger in front of me flicked his wrist and Griff fell on the floor in agony. "We have so many things to discuss."

"No!" I screamed. "Please stop!" I crouched by Griff, trying to hold his shaking body, protect him somehow. It was no use. I knew this was Griff's master, Daniels, and that there was nothing I could do to block the pain he was sending through Griff's iron tattoo. After what seemed like hours, not seconds, Griff was released, and he lay still groaning weakly on the floor in front of me.

Tears streaming down my face, I began the spell to travel as fast as I could, hoping fervently Griff would be able to come with me. Immediately, the words choked in my throat and my hands were seized in a vice like grip.

"Now, now. None of that. Do you want to spoil my plans?" His hands were like steel and in a matter of seconds, Daniels had wrapped something around my wrists that prevented any movement of my hands.

Struggling in frustration, I cried out. "Mrs. Smythe, help me!"

"Oh, I'm afraid you are wasting your time. Mrs. Smythe thinks I'm your father. That I surprised you by getting into town earlier than expected, and now we have all the time we need to look over this lovely house before we make an offer." He smiled with glee. "You know, that pink outfit looks atrocious with your red hair. But I guess you were a blonde when you arrived, weren't you?"

"How did you know I would come here?" I spat out, feeling outrage at the ease of my capture.

"My dear *innocent* child. Griff is the perfect bait. Tall, dark, sexy, and in trouble. I knew you wouldn't just leave him behind. He's very good at what he does. Because of you, he's earned his freedom this time." He looked down at Griff, and then glanced back at me.

I stared at him, aghast. A trap? *Griff* was the trap? Could I have been that blind?

My heart felt like someone was squeezing it unbearable tight. I couldn't breathe. *No*, a voice in my head screamed. *No way!*

"Oh, you are delightfully gullible, my dear. Falling for such a cliché. The look on your face is absolutely priceless." He smirked nastily at me.

"Griff would never do anything to hurt me," I whispered vehemently, as I scooted my trapped arms under Griff's head, pulling him awkwardly onto my lap to give him some relief from the cold, hard floor.

Daniels' smirk shifted into a frown. "No, Griff seems to be quite taken with you, and has done all manner of things to keep you from me. He will be duly punished." He paused, considering. "However, he was useful in bringing you to me in the end, so maybe he won't suffer as much as he would have otherwise."

As soon as Daniels confirmed that Griff hadn't really betrayed me, that he was just making some horrible joke at my expense, I was able to catch my breath. With oxygen feeding my brain again, my mind was able to snap back into action. I twisted and strained against the strange restraints. Nothing. I felt my pockets, surreptitiously, with my elbows. I still had my iron weapons. Not that I could reach into my pocket with my hands tied together. Dammit.

My head was pounding in fear as I tried to come up with a new plan, all the while berating myself on the stupidity of my old plan.

A hand slapped me sharply across the face. "Pay attention." Tears stung my eyes and I gazed belligerently up at that horribly smug face.

"That's better." He wiped a couple of tears away with his fingertips and I shuddered away from his touch involuntarily. He smiled even wider. "Your eyes are quite lovely, my dear. I can see why Griff became distracted."

His hand slid down my neck and pulled Quinn's necklace out from under my blouse. "And you brought the necklace. Even better." He slid the chain around my neck until the clasp was in front and delicately undid the clasp while I writhed and flinched in panic. "Keep your hands off!" I cried.

"Finally," he chuckled menacingly, holding up the necklace. "I'll have the upper hand at last."

All at once, he froze, looking closely at the charm. "Why you conniving little..." he lapsed angrily into Terraran for several sentences. "You will be very sorry for what you did."

I barely had time to see him raise his arm. The pain was sudden and intense, and the world exploded into black despair.

I LAY ON a small, narrow, uncomfortable bed. *Yet another bed—the worst one by far*, my confused mind realized. *That makes how many?* I sat up, and my head swam. I touched my cheek delicately, and felt a crusty scab forming over a long painful cut and bruise. *How long have I been out?* I wondered. My eyes adjusted to the low light coming in through a couple of tiny narrow windows, and I scanned the room for clues to where I had been taken, but the bare walls and plain tile floor gave me little to go on.

How much time had passed? And where was Griff? Not here. My body was stiff from lying in one position, and my toes and fingertips were icy cold. I was glad for the coat Sarah had lent me, though regretful of the condition it would be in by the time I was able to return it. *Oh please, let me have a chance to return it,* I thought, as I stuffed my hands into the deep pockets.

I got up and started pacing the small room, maybe six feet by fifteen feet. I was feeling overwhelmed by how ridiculously easy it had been to capture me. What an *idiot* I was to think my plan was somehow original. That I could outwit someone way older and craftier than me, using powers of disguise that Terrarans themselves had been masters of for centuries.

All I had wanted was to get Griff somewhere safe. It seems that I was extremely obvious in my emotions and intentions. I felt young, foolish, and very human. I clenched and unclenched my hands in worry. *Argh.* Now what was I going to do?

I guess that would depend on where I was, and who was around. I suddenly realized that my hands weren't tied, and I made desperate movements to travel back to Quinn.

I stopped midway through.

What if I led some of the Terrarans to that sanctuary that Lord Kyan had hidden for so long? I couldn't do that. I had to assume that they had put some kind of a trace on me. I would not endanger anyone I cared about. Not Jace, or Sarah either.

Instead, I thought of a neutral place. A park, next to a police station where I used to play as a child, with large white pavilion and a blue playset. I concentrated on that place and my hands started moving of their own accord. I finished the spell with a grimace.

Nothing happened.

Something was inhibiting my power to travel. Damn. Now what?

I patted my pants pockets. All my iron was gone. Even my meteorite bracelet was missing from my wrist. I felt around my neck and a huge sense of loss swept over me. I knew Quinn was safe, but losing his necklace was a nasty blow.

I sat back on the bed, feeling hopelessness creep over me, sending shivers down my spine that had nothing to do with the temperature of the room. I leaned back in a funk, trying to think of something – *anything*—to do, when the door quietly opened and a girl who looked a few years younger than I did walked uncertainly into the room. I caught a glimpse of another figure lingering in the hallway, an immense shadow in dark clothes with fierce eyes, and then the door slammed shut behind the girl, who jumped anxiously at the loud noise.

The girl was small and fair-skinned, so thin that her plain clothes drooped on her tiny frame. Her brown hair curled in tight ringlets that could only be natural—no perm could form such perfect curls.

Her hair was tied in a loose ponytail that reached to the middle of her back. She was carrying a heavy pail of water and several articles of clothing. She set the pail down quickly, and lay the clothes down carefully on the end of the bed, looking warily at me, trying to gauge my mood. I stood up and crossed my arms, waiting for what she had to say.

"I'm here to tend to your wound and help you get ready to be presented," she said cautiously, as she moved to the window and lit a couple of small candles that perched on the sill.

I touched my cheek and winced at the soreness. "What do you mean, *presented*?" I wanted to know, eyeing the clothes on the bed doubtfully. "Those look like dresses, and there is no way I am dressing up for a psycho like *Daniels*."

The girl gasped, and wrung her small hands pitifully. "*Shhh*. He might hear you."

I cocked my eyebrow at her, trying to act unafraid. "What is going on?" I demanded. "Where am I? Do you know where Griff is?"

"He is healing. You must do as our master says if you really care about Griff. There is nowhere for you to go."

I spluttered in annoyance and anger. "He's not my master! *No one* is my master, and there is *no way* I'm going to wear something like that."

She looked at me closely and put a finger to her lips, then took a dress off the pile and showed me a pocket tucked into the side of the dress. Inside the pocket rested my meteorite bracelet and my iron hammer.

I stared at her in amazement.

I reached in the pocket, but she batted my arms away, shaking her head emphatically. I pushed her arm aside and slipped my hands around the comfort of my familiar little hammer, lifting it and sliding it into my pants pocket. The frantic girl pointed at the large lump it made. I tried putting it in my coat pocket, but she kept shaking her head and pointing to the dress.

"Oh fine," I conceded, placing it back in the dress pocket in irritation and flopping down on the bed. "What's your name?"

"Caryn," she whispered, as she dunked a cloth into the pail, and gently began washing the blood off my cheek.

I jerked away from her hand, and took the cloth away from her surprised hand. "I can do it myself," I explained, feeling the gash and wiping the dried blood away from the lower part of my cheek.

"You missed some." She grabbed the cloth away, and finished the job as I scowled. I didn't like feeling like a little kid. Then she spread a sweet-smelling ointment on my cut, which burned and strung. I closed my eyes. Next, Caryn produced a comb from her pocket and began brushing through my short hair, dipping it in the now-dirty water, trying to tame it into some semblance of order.

"My hair obeys orders about as well as I do," I said, getting up and away from her outstretched arms.

"Now the dress," she said, holding a bronze-colored gown high up for my inspection, as I glared distastefully at the shiny material with the narrow waist and yards of fabric poofing out from underneath.

"Oh gag. I can't wear something like that." Even if the stupid thing fit me and hid my weapons, I could hardly hope to use most of the defensive moves that Jace had taught me. I'd trip over the ridiculous skirt for *sure*. The waist looked too tight, and even though the front was fairly high with straps tying around my neck like a fancy halter top, the back dipped suspiciously low. The exposure of my back gave me a sick feeling in my stomach. I didn't like the look of that space at all.

It took me awhile to convince myself that I had no other choice but to wear the gaudy dress. Caryn helped squeeze me into it and tie the back pieces around my neck. I felt exposed, and freezing, and extremely nervous.

Caryn held up a pair of high-heeled shoes and I laughed. "No freaking *way*," I growled and slipped on the conservative loafers that matched my pantsuit. At least I could run in those. I'd break my leg in those heels. Caryn looked worried, but I refused to change my mind and finally she turned to go. She gave me a brief uncertain smile.

I sat back on the small bunk, patting my pockets. I asked her quietly, "Why are you doing this?"

She stopped partway to the door and hesitated. "For Griff." Her cheeks flushed darkly. "He has taken care of me since I came here. And now I want to do something to help him."

I didn't know what to say.

She smiled faintly. "Griff says you are very powerful. If you escape, let me come with you, please. I miss my family." She breathed these last words so quietly; I almost couldn't make them out. I blinked at her trust in me and sighed, doubting I could live up to such hope.

"I'll do my best." I tried to smile.

A sharp knock on the wooden door made us both jump. Without another word Caryn turned, and picking up the extra clothes and the bucket, walked to the door.

"She's ready," she announced in a loud voice.

The door was flung open, and Caryn disappeared into the dark hallway. The door stayed open and a large man in a dark-colored suit came in and took me by the arm, just as I had managed to slip Sarah's coat around the voluminous dress.

"Hey," was all I got out before he shoved me in front of him.

"Walk," he said.

"Okay, okay," I muttered, as I hurried out the door before he could touch me again. My mind was going a mile a minute as I tried to think of an escape plan. Just as I was trying to convince myself that traveling away without Griff—or Caryn for that matter—was not a cowardly plan, my wrists were seized in another strong grip and bound behind my back.

I struggled against the binding, but it was painfully tight; I couldn't budge it. *I am so screwed* was all I could think as I trudged along the cold hallway. No windows. Only a few closed doors. Nothing useful to see or remember.

Now what?

I was pushed toward a set of stone steps, and found it difficult to climb with my hands behind my back. I stumbled several times over the hem of my ridiculous dress, making me extra-glad I had ditched the heels; they would have been ten times worse. Once the man caught me when I was about to fall, shoving me forward and causing me to rip the edge of the stupid gown. I fell, banging my shin on one of the stairs. I swore nastily at him, but either he didn't understand me or didn't care.

The stairway seemed interminable. By the time I reached the top, I was breathing hard and wishing I could rub my bruised leg. I stood at the top and rubbed my left calf against the sore spot on my right shin, while I leaned unsteadily against the wall. I could feel a bump forming.

My guard, a blonde brute with frizzy long hair, who looked like an ad for a pro-wrestling show except for his conservative suit, leered at me and lifted my skirt a little. "Want me to check that for you?" he asked in heavily accented English. I snatched myself away and he laughed.

As fast as I could, I twisted around and kicked him in the side of the knee with all the force I could muster with my hands tied. I slipped and fell hard on my butt, grimacing in pain. He grunted, and took a surprised step backwards. His arms floundered a little, as he balanced on the edge of the top stair. I lashed out with my foot and knocked his left foot off the step. He teetered briefly, but pulled by the weight of his huge, muscled body, toppled over backwards, and thudded noisily down the steep stairs.

I scrambled awkwardly to my feet and took off as fast as I could. I tore down the hallway, looking for some way out. I finally came to a large window. I gulped as I saw how high up I was. Treetops were waving in my face. Very tall pine tree-tops. Yikes.

Maybe I could fly, though, if I really focused my energy. I frowned in concentration, and I rose a few inches off the ground. My tied hands were making things harder than usual. I squeezed my eyes shut and I flew up to the height of the window ledge. I carefully stepped onto the sill, and a powerful force flung me back into the wall on the other side of the hall. My head bounced and my arms were twisted behind me in such a way that when I hit the wall my shoulder popped right out of its socket. I screamed shrilly and involuntarily, as I slid to the floor in a daze.

Into the Fire

I heard feet pounding up the hall. I fought grimly to keep from losing consciousness, though the world seemed vague and blurry. *How many times have I passed out lately?* I wondered. *My brain's going to become permanently scrambled one of these times.* Someone pulled me roughly from the floor and I bit back a back scream of pain as I was dragged down the corridor into a large, open room.

I was dropped unceremoniously on the floor, in front of several stone steps. I gritted my teeth as I saw big black boots stop in front of me, and a cruel hand reached down and hauled me to my feet.

"You are quite troublesome for your size, aren't you?" Daniels smirked.

"May I present Mia Stone, Your Majesty?" Daniels continued. "The resemblance to your nephew is striking, isn't it? And she has his power and resourcefulness, as well. Even though she's grown up thinking she's only human."

Daniels ran his eyes scornfully over me, and continued, "She may not look like much of a threat, but she dispatched the guard and would have flown out the window even with her hands secured, if the windows hadn't been spelled against escape."

"Welcome, Mia." The voice cut through my thoughts like a sharp, sinister knife. "I am so *very* pleased to meet you."

I gazed through a haze of pain into an uncomfortably familiar face. Strawberry blonde hair waved down his shoulders. He had a full, red beard and rosy cheeks. His clothes were made of dark, maroon velvet with some fur trim. A long cloak was clasped at his neck with a huge jewel. His booted feet were crossed in front of him, as he lounged in an intricately carved wooden chair.

He looks like a young, thin Santa Claus, I thought, *except for the dead, pale blue eyes.*

Those eyes latched onto me and I felt fear drift up my spine like a slithering snake, almost obliterating the blinding pain of my dislocated shoulder.

"I believe I have, *finally*, something important enough to get Lord Kyan's full attention," he smiled at me, while I struggled not to pass out.

Crap. I was in such big trouble.

Daniels' hand bit into my arm and I jerked away, which caused me to gasp in pain again, and even though it was the last thing I wanted to do, I found myself begging to have someone fix my shoulder. "It popped out of its socket," I groaned pitifully. "Will you get these restraints off, so I can put it back in place?" I couldn't think straight about my surroundings, or make escape plans, or kiss myself goodbye—which was definitely a more likely scenario—until my stupid shoulder was back where it belonged.

"Mia," Griff was suddenly at my side. I couldn't help notice that he looked much better. His hair gleamed and his clothes were clean, although his face was drawn with doubt and worry. He turned to Daniels. "She needs help. Let me remove the wrist guards." He bowed his head. "Please," I heard him whisper.

"Griff, don't," I managed to gasp.

"Hmmm. I don't know," replied Daniels. "I rather like her helpless and fragile. She's less likely to make trouble. But she wouldn't be as much fun, either, I suppose."

With a quick movement of his hands, Daniels made my restraints disappear. He then pulled off my bulky coat, grasped my forearm, and swiftly yanked my dangling arm up and out to the side, forcing the bone back into place with a sickeningly loud pop. I screamed, first in shock, and then gasped in stunned relief, as the intense pain shifted to a dull ache and throbbing.

My vision cleared and I was able to take in my surroundings. His Majesty, my great uncle—*was that really what I had just heard?*—was sitting forward, watching the proceedings with an eager gleam in his cold eyes.

No way was I related to *that* creep. How wrong is it to have a ruler who looks like an evil Santa? Something was definitely screwed up here.

Cradling my tender arm, I turned toward Griff. I wanted to talk to him, but I knew that it was useless in front of a crowd of people. My eyes slid from him to the several dozen people lining the walls of the room. They were all dressed to the teeth, letting me know this nightmare was some kind of formal get-together. They were arranged in pairs and small groups, and most had their eyes fixed on me. I had a sudden case of stage fright, mixed into my already high level of just plain fright. *I'm in for more than just a talk with His Majesty,* I thought. That didn't sound good.

"Come closer, Mia." His voice was low and friendly, compelling in a way that clashed strongly with his scary-looking eyes. I found myself walking closer to the man on the wooden chair than I thought was wise, but when I tried to stop, my legs refused to listen. I concentrated hard and my legs slowed, and finally they stopped several feet in front of the three stone steps leading up to his chair. It still felt too close.

"Interesting." He paused, and studied me with those pale, unfeeling eyes. I made myself stare back, and forcibly suppressed a shudder. I wondered if, maybe, like in those vampire shows I was so fond of, I should beware of his gaze. However, I couldn't bring myself to lower my eyes first. I was having the longest staring contest I'd had since elementary school, and for the first time in years, I was glad I used to be a champ.

Before either of us could fold, we were rudely interrupted. Daniels, apparently insulted by my lack of fear and cowering, shoved me to my knees and said, "Bow before your King. And lower your eyes in respect."

"Not my King," I muttered defiantly.

"Daniels, your obsequious behavior irritates me." Sparks seemed to fly out of His Majesty's voice, which froze a hand ready to strike me for my insolent remark.

I couldn't help (and didn't even try) but smirk at Daniels as he backed away, apologizing.

"Come closer," the King barked. I could feel his will pushing into my head.

Slowly I stumbled up the stairs, almost tripping over my long skirts that I refused to lift up, because I kept telling my legs not to go up the next step. But after some long drawn-out moments, I stood facing the King, my hands clenching in frustration at my stolen will.

"Mia, I am your great uncle, Lord Aiken. Your father Kyan was the son of my youngest and most irksome brother, Daynen. Had your blood not been fouled by the human women they each chose, you could have had a place here in my court. But now you are no more than a political pawn. Lord Kyan has been evading me for years, choosing humans over Terrarans, and causing me no end of harassment for the death of his father."

My eyes must have shown my dismay when I realized he had murdered his own brother, because Lord Aiken laughed. "Don't expect sympathy here, Mia. We may be related, but I care little for those who have been tainted by human blood. Even if you are more powerful than I'd thought possible."

"Why do you hate humans so much?" I asked, my voice much more respectful than I felt. I had no idea what to do, so I thought keeping him talking was the best plan for the moment. "You Terrarans split off so long ago. What's it to you, anyway, if some of your people want to reconnect with the past? We, I mean, humans and Terrarans, must have got along at least a little bit before the split, right?"

"No!" His thundering reply made me jump back quickly.

"Humans are *Nequam*—worthless, foolish beings—full of hate and waste. We never 'got along,' as you say, and we never will!"

"I know a whole bunch of people who feel differently about that," I muttered.

"Yes, finally, we get to the heart of the matter." A smile pricked the corners of his bearded mouth, and I swallowed hard. Me and my stupid, big mouth.

"You will now tell me the location of Lord Kyan and his followers." He looked at me with such an expectant expression, I found myself opening my mouth.

With an effort, I closed it, then glared back with all the determination I could muster. His eyes narrowed, and I felt sweat break out over my forehead. My lips clenched in a painful line. I wrenched my eyes away, and backed up, inch by slow inch, to the top of the steps.

I wanted to scream out my defiance, to spit in that obnoxious face, but I was afraid of what words might spill out of my mouth once I opened it. I ground my teeth together in fury. I could hear the sickening squeal of enamel rubbing together. *Eww.* If I eventually made it out of here, my dentist bill would be *huge.*

I stepped gingerly down onto the first step. Then the next. Miraculously, I reached the bottom without falling over my skirt, and no one had tried to stop me. Lord Aiken, I had to admit, though, when I hazarded a glance at him, looked royally pissed. He must have thought I wouldn't be able to resist his mind control. What a conceited jerk.

I started sliding my feet along the stone floor like they were wading through thick, knee-deep mud. Griff came and took my arm, his face showing a mixture of astonishment and concern. "*How* are you opposing the King?" he whispered.

I shook my head mutely, still not trusting my voice. I didn't know myself. But the King was *not* going to make me tell him where my friends were hiding. I couldn't live with myself if I betrayed them that way. *My mouth's staying* shut, *no matter what*, I resolved grimly. *It's not like I'll be any safer if I tell my secrets.* On the contrary, as long as I had valuable information, I was hoping I could stay alive.

"Shall I help things along?" inquired Daniels, grasping my right hand and pulling me away from Griff. My instincts reacted, overriding my good sense; I used one of the moves Jace had taught me, tossing Daniels over my shoulder, and onto his back.

The whole room went eerily silent. I felt the King's focus falter in surprise, and I took off running to the door, dragging a shocked Griff by the arm. The next second, Griff was convulsing on the floor beside me, and I was screaming at Daniels to stop, calling him every horrible name I had ever heard, with tears coursing down my cheeks.

"You coward," I panted. "*I* was the one who humiliated you. *Stop hurting Griff!*" I threw myself at Daniels without deciding what I was going to do. I could hardly see straight, I was so furious and terrified.

I scratched my nails down his left cheek, three angry bloody stripes that made him flinch and draw back a fist. I sidestepped, and dodged his blow. My eyes flashed on Quinn's necklace swinging around his neck, and I lunged for it, fuming that he was wearing my Nan's special gift to me around his own sorry neck like a trophy. I was almost spitting, I was so enraged.

I snagged it and ripped it away, but the sight of it had distracted me long enough that a couple of guards had raced over to protect Daniels. I had no sooner stuffed my prize in one of my pockets, when my arms were seized by a couple of brutish-looking men with muscles larger than life. I struggled uselessly, while Daniels seethed in front of me, wiping his cheek with a prissy-looking handkerchief, and adjusting his crumpled clothes.

I didn't regret what I had done...I just wished I could have done *more*. My face must have reflected my feelings, because Daniels wrapped his hand around my chin in a vicious grip, snarling into my face, "I'm going to enjoy this." I tried to bite him, but he let go before I could sink my teeth into his nasty little hand.

"The bench, please," he commanded loudly, and a tall, padded bench was brought out into the middle of the room. The guards yanked me down until I was bent over on my stomach, my toes barely touching the floor, my bare back exposed and vulnerable. I fought like a wildcat, knowing with a sinking feeling what was going to happen next. The guards forced my hands into stiff plastic-like cuffs on either end of the bench, so my arms were stretched out to their full length. My shoulder – so recently dislocated—screamed in protest, but there was nothing I could do against those giant muscles.

"With your permission, your Majesty." Daniels bowed before the King, who glanced thoughtfully at me and then made a gesture to continue. "My tools," Daniels called loudly, and someone left the room in a hurry. "We will see how much pain you can handle before I crush your spirit," he whispered in my ear. "I hope it's a lot."

"Griff, come here. You can be a witness to this process. See what you have accomplished by keeping Mia from us." The same two guards dragged Griff across the floor and left him in a heap in front of me. He still looked stunned. His hair was hanging loosely around his strained face, his shirt was torn, and his hands were shaking as he reached up to touch me.

"Mia, I tried everything I could think of to prevent this."
His voice was barely a whisper. He knelt in front of me and
I lifted my head from its dangling position over the bench,
straightening my neck awkwardly to meet his gaze. He cupped
my face softly with his warm hands

"I'm just stupid and stubborn, I guess," I said, trying for a
smile. I didn't want him to blame himself. It was *my* plan that
had backfired. None of the guilt should be laid on him. "It's
not your fault. *I* was the one that came and found *you*. It was
a dumb idea. I'm so sorry, Griff." I searched his alarmed face,
his blue eyes so close to mine.

Even in this horrible situation, I felt my heart jump. He was
already so beautiful and his concern for me made him all the
more attractive. I closed my eyes, trying to focus on my situation, rather than his hands stroking my cheeks. Griff's nearness
always made it hard for me to think clearly. His touch made
it almost impossible. Crazy as it might seem, the room started
fading away.

"You were safe. Why didn't you stay there?" Griff whispered.

My eyes opened in surprise, the answer so obvious I wasn't
sure about putting it into words. "But *you* weren't safe," I said.
"I couldn't just *leave* you. Not after what you had done and
how I feel about you..." I trailed off. I couldn't believe I was
talking about this in a public—not to mention, horribly life
threatening—place.

Griff's look intensified, his blue eyes becoming even more
bright and vivid than usual. My cheeks flushed.

"Somehow, I'll get us out of here," he swore under his breath,
his fingers tracing down my cheek.

"Things aren't looking so good," I murmured faintly, pulling
against the tight-fitting cuffs. Suddenly, the door banged open

behind us, snapping us both to attention. I shuddered as someone stomped swiftly across the wooden floor. "I'm thinking things are about to get a lot worse before they get any better," I said. *Or maybe they won't ever get any better,* I thought to myself. *Maybe this is it.*

My mind was torn from the spell of Griff's touch, and I was starting to freak, thinking about knives and liquid iron. Even Griff was starting to lose his cool. His head jerked up when Daniels came over and leaned down, maliciously twirling some kind of small tool in his hand. A wooden handle fastened to a long, sharp shard of crystal.

"You aren't going to make a scene, are you Griff?"

Griff shot to his feet, but the guards were ready for a display of resistance. Viciously smiling, one guard smacked Griff back down. The other locked his arm around Griff in a chokehold that was painful to even witness, taking savage delight in the situation. I recognized his frizzy blonde hair—the guard I had pushed down the stairs. His nose was busted, but his body seemed to work just fine. He gave me a nasty, twisted smile. So much for taking care of things myself.

The guard began squeezing Griff's windpipe with his brutal weapon-like arm, his grin widened evilly. I began a wild protest, watching Griff's thrashing body, when I felt something cold and sharp graze my lower back. I had to bite my lip in order to stifle a cry.

"Now Griff, I remember your branding day like it was yesterday," Daniels voice had a sickeningly fond, almost reminiscent tone. "I'm certain you do, too. So you know how Mia is going to feel and you know that the more she fights the more painful the process will become. You should be helping her, not making things worse."

Daniels squatted down between us, leaning his head into my line of vision, looking back and forth between us. "Now, Griff, wouldn't you like to comfort her, instead of having her watch you choke until you pass out? Though I have to admit: Mia's added suffering from watching you being strangled might make her experience all the more exquisitely painful. I might enjoy that, too. Oh, it's *so hard* to decide which would be more satisfying."

He laughed, and I thought my head was going to explode with anger.

"I can't believe you think *humans* are worthless!" I shouted out. "You Terrarans are completely *demented*. I can't believe I'm even *partly* related to you." I was so angry and frightened and tired I couldn't hold my tongue any longer. "I don't care if you brand me to the *moon;* I'll never do a thing you say. And I swear, you will pay. Maybe not right now, but pay you will. Soon. *In full!*"

I stopped, realizing what I was saying. Damn. Was that me making a speech or something? Too bad I wasn't some kind of general, or ninja, or superhero. Maybe I might have a prayer of backing up all these threats.

As it was, all I got was a cruel smirk and rolled eyes from Daniels. I couldn't keep back a snarl, I was so furious. I pulled uselessly against my restraints, and gritted my teeth in frustration. In desperation, I tried to grab Daniel's hair, which was dangling tantalizingly close to my pinned hand. But he just casually moved away, sneering, his focus back on Griff.

"So, Griff, what's your choice?"

My guard—Frizz-head—released Griff's neck enough for a few gasping words to be heard.

"Let me go. I won't interfere."

Daniels waved a hand, and Frizz-head dropped his arm and stood back, his arms folded across his chest, eyeing Griff doubtfully, as if not convinced that Griff would behave himself. "If he tries anything, choke him into submission," said Daniels. "I don't want to be interrupted. I mean it."

Griff tried to catch his breath. His face was still red, and he rubbed his throat as if trying to coax some needed air down into his lungs. "Daniels, please," he began.

"Stop, Griff. Don't say anything you'll regret," I cut in, still seething, but hugely relieved that Griff was free.

"*Shhh*. Mia." Griff barely glanced at me. "I will do anything. Mia doesn't deserve this. Let her go. I won't defy you anymore. I will do whatever you ask, as long as Mia is safe."

A booming laugh made Griff jerk his head behind him. If you can believe it, I had almost forgotten the King.

"Daniels doesn't have the ability to save Mia. She is *mine*. Daniels is branding her for *me*, so nothing you say can change his mind, or mine. So sit back and take a last look: Mia will be a different girl once she has been tamed by pain."

The King nodded toward Daniels. "Get on with it. I'm starting to get bored of all the drama and delay."

Griff sunk to the floor in resignation. I could see the look of defeat in his eyes. It scared me more than the pain I had been promised. Griff's face seemed to change—the light faded from his eyes, and his tanned face became pale and stricken. I watched him turn an unhealthy, pasty color, as if from a long time illness, which transformed his face into a barely recognizable, empty shell. I was staring at a mannequin wearing Griff's face.

I opened my mouth to say something, anything to get his attention, to bring his familiar face back, when a white-hot fire suddenly struck my lower back. A wave of nausea swept over me like a blast from an oven. I panted and tried to control my mouth, forcing it shut, working to block the scream loosened by the intense pain.

All at once Griff was right next to me, his hand stroking my hair, whispering soothing words in my ear. My mind was too preoccupied to hear the exact words, but his presence helped control the trembling in my neck and back. I concentrated on breathing, like I was meditating in front of one of my mom's yoga DVDs. Breathe in, breathe out. I imagined releasing the pain through the top of my head.

The pain surged up my spine, like a gigantic swarm of black crows streaming out of the crown of my head. It was like I could see them flapping frantically, furious to free themselves from my suffering body. I focused my mind on the rhythm of my breathing, eyes unfocused, and ears barely comprehending Griff's sympathetic words.

Time passed. Whether it was one minute or one hour, I don't know. But miraculously, the pain started receding. The fiery strokes were becoming warm now, not so unbearable. I could feel each individual slice, and I could see the image that Daniels was forming, as if he were drawing it right in front of me, instead of carving it into my back. I could see the liquid iron forcing its way into my skin, but suddenly, I felt my body accepting the intrusion. Welcoming it, even.

I had no idea what was going on; I was just happy to have the pain recede. My relief was total and intense. My body, which had been taut like a guitar string, relaxed in a single fluid movement onto the bench and I heard Daniels ask Griff if I'd fainted. "Not as much of a fighter as I had expected," Daniels sighed, obviously disappointed at my lack of screaming and begging.

I let my eyes roll up and my lids close, going along with his belief that I'd passed out. Griff cradled my face in his hands and ceased his fervent whisperings. I waited until his ear brushed past my lips and made a faint noise. He froze for a second, and softer than butterfly's touch, I mouthed, "My right pocket. My hammer. Not yet."

Griff continued his caress of my face, softly whispering, "It will be okay. I *understand* how you feel. I promise you'll be alright."

Behind my closed eyes, I watched the tattoo continuing to form. The bright image etched itself onto my eyelids. When the design was finally finished, I realized that Daniels was about to add the name to which I'd be linked. He paused briefly, readying his tool to carve my master's name in tiny letters around the outside of the circular tattoo: Lord Aiken.

I jerked in resistance. That, I would *not* allow.

Daniels laughed, thinking I had come back to consciousness. "Not quite through, yet. But soon, we will give you a chance to feel the power of iron. Since you are so anxious, I'll give you another demonstration."

Griff gave a cry and fell away from me convulsing painfully.

"No!" I yelled. "He didn't even do anything, you bastard!" This wasn't the plan. Griff needed to be able to reach my hammer. I watched for an endless moment as Griff writhed on the floor, his face twisted into a terrifying grimace.

And then, something inside me snapped. I felt like a volcano as all the pent-up anger inside me blew out of the top of my head. My hair stood up on end, like an electric charge had just run through me. I heard someone gasp, as my body began expelling the hot iron that had just been tattooed into me.

There was deathly silence in the room, broken by Daniels saying, "What the hell?" followed by the sound of something dropping onto the stone floor. I was vaguely aware of voices all around me.

"What's happening?"

"How did she do that?"

"*Nobody* has that power."

Mostly, though, I focused on the dazzling symbol that had—moments before—been buried in my back. I could feel it flowing out of my skin like a long silken thread pulled out smoothly by an invisible hand.

The strand reformed its original design in the air before my eyes, hovering over Griff, who stared with a kind of fascinated unbelief from the floor.

Griff struggled to his feet as the guards backed away slowly, their eyes riveted on the still-glowing iron. Griff brushed past me, scooping the hammer out of my pocket and hiding it somewhere I couldn't see.

He tried the restraints, pulling on them with his bare hands, when someone grabbed him and I heard a scuffle from behind. Someone seemed to have snapped out of the trance my iron trick had placed everyone under.

I concentrated hard on the liquid iron, closing my ears to the sounds around me. I imagined the cuffs being split open by the hot strands, but gently, so as not to burn my skin. Then, I directed my gaze to the side of my body, and watched in fascination as the iron unraveled from the edge of the design, and flicked a long strand—like a fiery whip—toward my wrist. I couldn't help a panicky flinch. Maybe that was a really dumb idea.

The next thing I knew, the cuff fell open, and I pulled my sore arm free. A second later, my other arm was free, and I stood, doing my best to ignore the searing pain in my back, and looked at the chaos around me.

In the space of a few seconds, the room emptied. As people fled, Griff was using my hammer to great effect against the frizz-haired guard, who now had one arm dangling uselessly, and his nose, which I had broken earlier, was again dripping with blood.

I turned to Lord Aiken. Daniels was talking fiercely with the King, almost pushing him off the stone dais, urging him out of the room.

I stepped toward them and they both turned to look directly at me.

I let my face split into a smirk. These men were going to be sorry they messed with me. I glanced up at my new iron weapon hovering in the air, thinking how best to use it to my advantage, when the small ceramic bowl holding Daniel's molten iron jumped into the air and came flying directly at me.

I put up my arm and turned my face just in time.

Hot fire spread across the left side of my body, scorching my bare arm, shoulder, and side. Screaming in shock, I stared down at the burned areas, frantic. I concentrated on the hot metal, which leapt off my skin and formed a bright ball of iron, hanging in the air next to my iron design. With a surge of raw anger, I fired the ball across the room directly at Daniels, then staggered backwards from the force of my throw and the pain of the burns.

Somehow I hit Daniels smack in the middle of his chest, the iron burning through his clothes. He was panicking and tearing off his shirt, but his actions weren't fast enough to prevent the iron from singeing his skin.

The King, who had been staring at what I had just done to Daniels, tore his eyes away and bolted for the door. "Hey!" I yelled. *No way are you getting out of here unpunished*, I thought.

My fiery design flew after Lord Aiken, stopping in front of the door, right at eye-level. He backpedaled away, and I kept the hot metal only inches away from his face, shadowing his every dodge and duck.

My arm and back both felt like they had burst into flame, but I tried to block the pain as I concentrated on the flying iron. I thought about the whip end that had released me from my cuffs, and sent a fiery lash across my great uncle's right cheek. He bellowed in shock and rage, then yelled a command at me causing me to freeze my actions: his will bursting into my head.

"No!" I screamed back, and fought his will with all the force I could muster. *Let's see how you liked being branded*, I thought, fighting his will, and somehow – slowly—bringing the pattern closer and closer to his face.

"This is *not* over, Mia!" Lord Aiken yelled, no doubt feeling the heat of the iron that was now less than an inch from his face. "You *will* be sorry for what you started."

Then he disappeared.

The design, suddenly released from his resisting will, went sailing past the spot he had been and straight into the wall. Smoke billowed as the iron burned the pattern into the wooden paneling.

I turned around desperately, but realized he could travel just as easily as I could, and could be *anywhere* by now. *I hope you're puking your kingly guts out in some horrible place*, I thought. I yanked the iron out of the wall with a thought, and looked for Griff.

When I saw him, I almost collapsed in panic. "Griff, stop!" I yelled.

Griff was kneeling on top of Daniels, his knees trapping Daniels' arms and hands to prevent any spell movements, with the hammer's head thrust into Daniels' open mouth. I saw smoke rising up from the burning flesh, and the smell made my stomach roll over.

"Griff, don't kill him. You'll die as well!" I screamed, rushing to his side. As I ran, I tripped over a bundle of clothes and landed awkwardly on the floor. I glanced at the obstruction for a split second, uncomprehending, then froze, my eyes arrested by the horror in front of me.

Caryn lay face up, unmoving, her eyes glazed over in her too-pale face. I knew instantly that she was dead. "No," I gasped, trying to lift her to me, my mind refusing to accept the obvious. She was an innocent girl who had helped me. I had no doubt that her efforts in getting me my weapons had been the cause of her death, and I started gagging and crying, my guilt surrounding me like a black cloud.

As I rocked her in my arms, my vision focused back on Griff. He was spitting out words of hate into Daniels' face. I realized that Caryn's death must have snapped the last bit of his control and he was going to kill Daniels, even if it meant his own death as well.

I gently laid Caryn down on the floor and crawled over to Griff.

"Stop!" I cried, pulling on Griff's arms. "Listen to me. You can't do this. Please Griff. You can't die. I won't let you." I wrenched his face over so he had to look at me. His eyes seemed unfocused and wild with vengeful anger.

"Griff, please. For me." I tried to rub his cheeks with my hands, pull on his hair, anything to get his attention back to me.

Suddenly, Griff's eyes rolled up in his head and he slumped on top of Daniels. "No!" I screamed, and looked down at Daniels. He wasn't moving. I pushed Griff off him, terror coursing through me. I felt for pulses in each of their necks. I found nothing on Daniels. Griff's was weak, his heart barely beating at all.

What could I do? Was there anything I *could* do? I pulled a plan together after a few seconds of turmoil. I wasn't sure if it would work, but I had to try.

I laid Daniels' head back and put my lips to his blackened mouth. My instincts kicked in and I began CPR, just as I had been taught when I had swimming lessons so long ago. Breathe, then to the chest. Push. Push. Push. Oh gross, his chest was covered in horrible burns—burns that I had inflicted myself. Don't think about it. Back to his mouth. Try not to gag. Do it for Griff. You must bring him back, or Griff will die.

I don't know how long I knelt there in that empty room, giving the kiss of life to a man I hated more than almost anyone in the world. Finally, though, I heard a weak gasp and sat back, hoping against hope that I had done the right thing. I looked over at Griff. He was breathing shallowly as well. I felt tears of relief fill my eyes, and I moved over to Griff's side, all the while keeping a close eye on Daniels.

I stroked his forehead. "Are you alright? Can you hear me?"

He whispered my name, and I told him everything was going to be okay.

I was wrong.

My nose twitched and I realized the room was filling with smoke. My iron weapon—which in my panic I had left unattended—had somehow settled on a drapery and set it to flame. The wood-paneled walls had caught fire as well, and the place was becoming smoky and scary.

"What have I done?" I yelled, yanking Griff to his feet. "We have to get out of here!"

"I have to get Caryn," Griff whispered. "I won't leave her body here. Daniels can burn. I won't die if I don't inflict the death," He growled mercilessly.

I hated Daniels, but I wasn't sure if I could just leave someone to burn to death. I vacillated, watching Griff gather Caryn's limp body up into his shaking arms.

"Let's go." Griff strode out of the room without a backwards glance at Daniels, the master he had served for dozens of years. Could I do this?

I hesitated.

Without warning, Griff dropped Caryn with a sickening thump and fell, convulsing, to the floor.

"If I die, so do you," Daniels cried out weakly.

I acted without thinking. I raised my hand and Griff's tattoo, hot as fire now, came whipping out of his back like a striking cobra. It flew – a bolt of iron lightning—at Daniels, neatly slicing off the hand that had been making motions towards Griff. I watched in horrid fascination as the flesh was immediately cauterized closed by the hot iron. Daniels passed out in pain and I ran to Griff. He was panting on the floor, a stunned look on his face.

"Is it gone? Is it really gone?" His fingers fumbled at his back.

"It is," I whispered. "Does it hurt? I'm so sorry." I stayed down by him, trying to keep under the layer of grey smoke that was building up around us. "We need to crawl out of here. Now. I'll help with Caryn."

I glanced back, trying not to make the same mistake as I did before, leaving a hot iron symbol floating around the room. I gestured and Griff's iron design, along with my missing iron, came slowly back to me, hovering brightly in the smoky air above me.

Griff and I dragged Caryn across the floor and out the door. My guilt over leaving Daniels had dissolved with his last attack. He would kill if he survived, I was sure of it. I guessed I'd have to live with what I had done, but at least I'd be alive.

And Griff was free.

25

Outta Here

When we crossed the threshold, a voice came echoing down the hallway.

"Crap," I muttered, readying my iron while Griff stood defiantly, holding Caryn's body against his chest. He looked like he was getting to the end of his strength. I felt the same. If we faced a whole group of enemies, we were done for.

I leaned wearily against the wall, staring up at Griff's haggard face, and wondered if these were our last moments.

"Griff, in case we don't make it out of here," I began, but he interrupted me.

"*Shhh*, Mia. We're getting out." His face was now empty of any emotion but grief.

At that moment a figure came tearing around the corner. I flung one of my hot iron symbols directly at him. He ducked at unearthly speed and my weapon went sailing right over his head, singeing some blonde, curly hair in the process.

I screamed at my error. "Quinn! Oh my gosh! Quinn, is that really you?" I got my iron under control and ran to him, shaking at how close I had come to taking off his head. I held my iron bracelet up to his face to make sure. His face remained unchanged while he reached out and pulled me into a tight embrace.

"Mia, you're alive. I'm so relieved." I flinched and cried out when he rubbed against my burned arm and he immediately released me, studying my injuries.

"You need medical help. Come on. The others are making a way for us to escape." I took Quinn's arm and gestured behind me.

"Quinn, this is Griff. And he's holding Caryn. She isn't… she wasn't…" My voice caught and I couldn't continue. I blinked back miserable tears.

Stroking my neck in a soothing gesture, Quinn assessed the situation with a glance. "Here, let me hold her. You look like you're about to fall over." I winced, knowing that was the wrong thing to say.

Griff's eyes hardened. "I'm just fine." He walked quickly and confidently past Quinn. "I know the fastest way out. Follow me."

"You don't know where the reinforcements are stationed," Quinn insisted. "We need to get to the west entrance. My dad, Lord Kyan, and several others are keeping the guards busy. We need to get there as fast as we can."

Griff nodded. "Keep going straight, follow the stairs down and then left."

We took off and met no resistance for the next few minutes. We made it to a large banquet hall before we met anyone at all. Some servants saw us and cowered at one end of the room, clearly conflicted about what to do. I wanted to take as many slaves with us as would go, but they refused to follow us even when we offered sanctuary, pointing to their iron tattoos.

I paused and tried quickly to pull out their tattoos, but nothing happened. I thought maybe the iron had to be hot—liquid—for it to work. I didn't know how to activate the tattoos, and even if I did, I didn't want to hurt anyone by experimenting. Besides, we needed to keep going.

I promised to remove their tattoos if they came with us, showing them the former tattoos that still floated behind me, hot and fiery in the air.

To my relief, several men and a couple of women decided to trust me and followed us to the sunlit hallway. No sooner had we left, though, than angry voices bounded down the hallway.

We fled down endless corridors, around dozens of corners seeking the west entrance and the rest of our company. Feet flying, we tore down a large, ornately decorated hall, luxurious carpets muffling our footsteps, and came to a large entryway. A huge chandelier dangled above our heads, long white-tapered candles burning brightly. A tall double-door towered over us: the last barrier to our escape.

Noise from a different direction caused us to jump in panic and my iron weapons flew to attention, waiting impatiently for the identity of those arriving.

"You're safe!" a familiar voice rang out, freezing my motions of offense, and wringing an emotional cry from Quinn.

"Father, is everyone here? I found Mia and a few others willing to leave."

"Hurry, we don't have much time. We have kept the guards busy, but they will organize again soon. We need to be away from here *now*."

"Where's Lord..." Quinn was cut off by an ear-splitting shriek.

As the rest of us jerked abruptly toward the sound, we found an angry, imperious looking woman leaning against the exit doors with her arms outflung, barring our way. She had not been there seconds before.

"Where is my son?" she screamed, her long, dark hair disheveled, her green eyes wide with fury. "Tell me where Daniels is!" Her mouth was twisted up in a snarl, her teeth almost bared, like an outraged animal.

I looked at her, horrified to realize that the man I had just maimed and left to die had a mother who cared about him. A mother who looked like a savage banshee right at the moment, but still, a mother.

"I will not let you leave," she continued in a vicious tone, unconcerned that we greatly outnumbered her. "You are disgusting products of Nequam filth." Foamy, white spittle was forming on the corners of her mouth, making her look rabid, and I flinched at the hate in her wild eyes.

She settled her scary gaze on Griff, still cradling Caryn's limp body in his arms.

"You cannot leave. I will not allow it." She pointed a shaking finger at them, stepping a few steps away from the door.

"You cannot stop me, Adrianna." Griff smiled grimly. "I no longer serve you, and Caryn is dead by your son's own hand. She comes with me now. I will never forget what your family has done to her and so many others."

"What do you mean you no longer serve us? My family owns you," Adrianna spat nastily.

Apparently trusting us to protect him from possible harm, Griff turned his back to Adrianna, and lowering Caryn, reached behind him and pulled up the tatters of his shirt.

Adrianna gasped, "It cannot be. How is this possible?"

I felt it was my turn to step in.

"Your son picked on the wrong human. Or I guess I should say, *part*-human."

She actually hissed at me. "You dare interfere in my house?"

"I was dragged to this house against my will," I said. "Your son just tried to *enslave* me in this house," and I spun the hot metal symbols towards Adrianna.

She drew back against the door, and I caused the design to unwind and knit itself into a net. I eased the glowing iron close to her, trying to intimidate her away from the door. She closed her eyes, stubbornly refusing to move, blocking our way out.

I let the iron hang inches from her skin, watching the heat cause sweat to break out on her forehead and drip down her cheekbones, and finally, trickle from her chin to the floor. Damn, she was stubborn. Nasty as she was, though, I didn't really want to singe her face, but the seconds were ticking away.

I glanced desperately over at Quinn and his father. My eyebrows said, "Now what?"

Before they could answer, a loud, growling sound from outside the door made me gasp. My focus broke and the floating iron slipped and burned a stripe down Adrianna's cheek.

"The black hounds," Griff yelled. "She's stalling us while the hounds get organized. We have to go *now!*"

"No!" screamed Adrianna suddenly and my net faltered again, slicing through several locks of hair. "Do it," she taunted me. "What, are you afraid of me? You'll have to kill me if you want to leave."

I stared at her, horror written across my face, knowing I couldn't kill her, when something streaked past me, pushing Adrianna aside with a powerful thrust. She crumpled on the floor, a large, obscenely ornate picture frame laying smashed on the floor next to her. That the portrait was of the King was just visible from the colorful shreds.

"I'm not afraid of you," Lord Kyan growled. "And finally, a good use for that pompous portrait."

He eyed all of us with irritation. "Everyone out! The armed guards are right behind me."

As if freed from a trance, everyone behind me sprinted for the door. Lord Kyan grabbed my hand. "Nice toys," he quipped as he glanced at the white-hot iron patterns floating alongside me. "What are you going to do with them?"

"Not sure yet," I admitted, and let him pull me out the door, trying not to stumble. "They're a bit of trouble to keep track of."

A huge, black dog lunged into our path. He was taller than five feet at the shoulder, with savage teeth and long, curved claws.

Lord Kyan thrust me behind him as he directed a flash of light into the dog's eyes. Another dog leaped to our left, and Grayson directed a heavy branch, snatched by magic, into the dog's open jaws, down his tender throat. The hound whimpered and collapsed.

More dogs circled around us, snarling and drooling.

"Into the air!" Grayson yelled, and Lord Kyan pulled me up with him. Everyone else jumped to follow suit, springing over the huge guard dogs' heads. I saw one man get his leg torn by a huge claw, as he leaped up. The man flew erratically, blood flowing down his leg and foot onto the hound's heads, whipping them into a frenzy. Quinn caught the hurt man in his arms and soared higher away from the wild dogs.

Lord Kyan still held my hand, in case my flying technique had not improved since he had seen me last, but my fear of the hounds had released me from my fear of flight, somehow. I let go of Lord Kyan's hand and tore through the air, savoring the feeling of freedom for a full ten seconds before Grayson shouted, "Down to the trees. Get under cover! Not too close to the ground, keep away from the hounds."

Dropping like hawks, the rest of the company dove for cover. My inexperience caused me to falter, long enough for an arrow to slice past my cheek. Another scraped my burned arm. With a cry of shock I also dropped, but not in the graceful dive of a bird of prey, more like the tumble of a wounded sparrow.

I heard several others around me cry out in pain. No! More people were getting hurt because of me. I saw Griff launching himself downward, still holding onto Caryn, an arrow sticking out of his left calf.

My stomach clenched in fear. My confidence leaked out of me, and my exhausted brain froze in a terrified stupor. I told myself not to black out, that this was very bad timing, a really stupid moment to finally lose it, but I seemed to have reached my threshold for pain and shock.

"Stay with me, iron," I murmured weakly. Weaving and veering chaotically, I tried to control my free fall, but the tree was suddenly right in front of me. "Oh, crap," I muttered, before an explosion of pain sent me reeling into blackness.

I WAS SITTING on a dirty blanket on the sidewalk of a busy street. People of all shapes, sizes, and colors were hurrying past me, turning their heads aside, as if I was an embarrassment. I looked around, and I had dozens of former iron tattoos lying on the blanket around me with small price tags hanging off each one.

I picked one up and examined it closely. The name Daniels, still visible on the edge, made me suspect this one was Griff's former tattoo. What was I doing trying to sell them?

A woman appeared in front of me. She looked vaguely familiar. Someone's mother, I seemed to remember. She wore a dirty white dress and her eyes flashed with a fierce light. Before I could say anything, she raised a crossbow and aimed it at my chest. I froze with my mouth open. I heard the click of the release, but suddenly I was flying, a hand on my upper right arm, pulling me out of the way.

My first thought was Quinn, and that I was lucid dreaming again. But Quinn was released from my necklace, so that didn't make any sense. I craned my neck back, and again my mouth fell open. No words made it past my lips.

My rescuer and I flew down to a large sprawling city park, and we landed gracefully on the edge of an enormous fountain. The spray from the cool water hit the back of my neck, bringing me back to my senses.

"Sarah, are you really here?" I finally forced the words out.

"Mia, you've had us all sick to death. Where have you been? Your parents are home planning a funeral. And Jace and I didn't have any way to contact you. We were so worried and had no idea what to do. We became desperate. So I took matters into my own hands."

"How are you here?" I was still goggling. I couldn't help it.

"Mia," Sarah sounded exasperated. "After all you can do, you're baffled by a bit of astral projection?"

"*Umm.*" I thought about it. "Okay, you're right. This is pretty commonplace compared to how weird *I* am."

Sarah put her arm around me and pulled me against her. "Mia, where are you? Are you coming home?"

Oh boy. What to answer. I didn't know myself.

"Let's hope this dream lasts a while," I began. "This is going to take some time."

I explained, as best I could, about my attempt to help Griff get away from those who had enslaved him, and our rescue by Lord Kyan, who was really my father, and that I was on my way back to his sanctuary, most likely, and I didn't know when I would be able to come back home.

"I'll talk to Lord Kyan when I wake up. I assume I'm not dead, since I'm dreaming, so someone must have had pretty fast reflexes and caught me before I did a major splat."

"Mia," Sarah gave me a little shake to get back my attention. "What about your parents? Jace gave your dad the message 'Love endures,' but he is still in too much shock. I don't think he got it. Your mom is going through all the motions, but it's like all her life energy has been completely drained."

I swallowed back the enormous lump in my throat. I had to get back. No matter what the consequences. I would have to bring my parents to the sanctuary. That was it. I could bring them to me. Then I would have time to explain. Then they would be safe.

"I'll come back and get them," I promised. "Try and tell them that things will be okay. Don't try and explain how, though. I'll do that. But do try and get through to my dad, if you can. He knows a little about what is going on. He should be able to figure it out. I'll explain myself to Mom. She won't believe anything 'til she sees it with her own eyes. Too stubborn," I broke off, tears starting to leak out of my closed eyes.

I leaned against Sarah, letting my grief flow out of me in a gushing flood. I thought about my parents mourning me, I thought about Griff grieving over Caryn, I thought of Daniels' mother rage over Daniels, and my part in his horrible death. I hated that he had forced me to hurt him. I kept telling myself it was all self-defense, but my heart still sickened with guilt over what I had done.

Sarah held me and let me work out my misery on her shoulder. She just rubbed my back and let me get it all out. She produced a box of tissues, and I mopped up after all the tears were spent and my eyes felt dry and hot.

"I used to think going to high school was hard." I said, laughing bitterly. "Turns out that was a piece of cake compared to my life now. What a whiner I was."

"We never know how easy we have it until things we take for granted are taken away." Sarah smiled. "But you are stronger than you know. You will rise to the challenge."

I rolled my eyes. "You sound like a motivational poster or something. I always thought those sayings were ridiculous." I managed a smile.

I felt a familiar pull and things began to get hazy.

"Sarah," I cried desperately, "Tell Jace I miss him. I'll be back to get my parents soon."

I OPENED MY eyes and gasped as a sharp pain knifed through my left shoulder and arm. My lower back was burning as well, and my right shoulder throbbed dully, remembering its recent dislocation.

Ah, how nice to be back in the real world.

A hand gently smoothed some ointment on my burns, and I gritted my teeth at the sting. Glancing up, I saw Lord Kyan's concerned face peering intently at my arm.

"You must have fast reflexes," I forced the words despite the pain. "I thought I was going to do a face plant before anyone could stop me."

"It was close." A small smile flitted across his mouth. "But I can move pretty fast when I have the right motivation."

I looked around me, trying to ignore the fire shooting through the left half of my body. I was lying in my blue and white room again. We had made it back to Sanctuary. Relief flooded me, tempered by the feelings of guilt over how many people had suffered because of my foolish, selfish actions. I had thought only of my own consequences. Not about what would happen to others who came to get me out of the mess I had caused.

I closed my eyes. I hissed at the feel of more ointment spread across my burns, feeling like I deserved the pain.

"We found you something more comfortable to wear."

I had on soft drawstring pants and a plain black tank top. I saw that the ridiculous dress I had to put on to meet the King had been cut off me, and lay in a discarded heap in the corner.

"I met your uncle," I said, remembering. "He didn't like me very much."

Lord Kyan's hand froze, his face registering shock.

"You saw King Aiken?" he managed to choke out. "And he let you go?"

"Not on purpose. He was trying to brand me to get to you. Seems like he was behind most of this. Daniels just wanted Quinn's necklace. The King wanted *me*. I've never been so popular in my whole life," I added wryly.

"Wait, the King was there, in Daniels' house? He knew about you, and you got away? How?" Lord Kyan looked stunned.

"My little iron toys, remember? The King kept trying to push his will on me, but I was able to resist somehow, and I just about planted one of those iron pieces right across his forehead. He had to travel to get away, the big coward." I smiled grimly, picturing his furious face. "Guess I can see why you wanted me to stay human," I sighed. "This Terraran life is a bit more complicated than what I'm used to."

Lord Kyan was shaking his head as he started to wrap strips of cloth around my arm. I had to grit my teeth again.

"King Aiken has *vast* amounts of power," he said. "It's hard to believe you were able to defy him. I haven't faced him in years, choosing to hide rather than confront him." He kept wrapping my arm as gingerly as possible, finishing at my wrist and tying the ends together expertly. I leaned forward and felt my back. Lord Kyan had already covered it with bandages.

Lord Kyan's eyes followed my hands. "So, this tattoo was meant to ensure your enslavement to the King, not Daniels. How did you manage to rip out the iron? I have never heard of such a talent before."

"Don't really know. It felt natural, familiar, like when I worked with wire back at home, making jewelry. I could feel the metal's pliability in my mind, the suppleness and maneuverability. I have always loved working with silver wire. Somehow, I used that talent on the hot iron."

I made a face. That sounded so lame. I just had no idea how to explain what I did.

I turned to make out Lord Kyan's expression. "So no one else can manipulate hot iron, huh?"

He shook his head and closed the lid on the bottle of ointment. "No, we part-Terrarans can touch iron, but none of us can touch hot liquid iron, or resist the pain of it in tattoo form."

"I suspected as much. Everyone seemed totally freaked when they saw my floating iron. Hey, speaking of which, where did my little 'toys' go?"

"That's the strangest part." Lord Kyan finished with my back and I turned to face him. "Once you passed out, your iron went cold and solid. Quinn dared to catch them before they hit the ground. It was quite a feat, as he was already carrying Stephen." Lord Kyan's face grew worried, and I thought of the man with the bloody leg.

Before I could ask about Stephen, Lord Kyan continued. "He's keeping the iron safe. Do you know if you can make them into weapons again?"

"Not a clue," I muttered, the guilt starting to eat at me again. "I'm sorry I left without your permission. I didn't go see my parents, though."

I raised my chin slightly defiantly. "I just needed to help Griff. Although, with what happened to Caryn, I think I might have made things much worse," I finished softly.

He took my hand in his. His eyes were kind, and I felt tears prick behind my eyes. I blinked swiftly. "I lay no blame at your feet, Mia," he said. "You acted selflessly, putting someone else first."

"I was impetuous and naïve," I countered. "I should have asked for help. I didn't know you well enough to trust you." I glanced back. "I don't even know what to call you. I'm sorry, but I don't think I can call you *father*."

"I think impetuousness runs in the family. If you remember, my father and I *both* ran off and fell in love with humans." Lord Kyan squeezed my hand reassuringly. "As for the name, just call me Kyan, or Kye." He paused. "Your mother called me Kye."

"Okay, uh, Kye. That sounds so *informal*. Everyone else calls you Lord."

"But you're my daughter. Different rules apply to family. Technically, you should be Lady Mia, you know."

I choked. "No way. I could never let anyone call me *Lady*. I certainly don't *look* like one right now." I snorted inelegantly.

At that moment Quinn and Grayson joined us.

"You're awake. What a relief." Quinn sat down by me and looked at me critically. "How are you feeling?"

"Better than I deserve," I mumbled. Lord Kyan and Grayson moved out into the hallway, talking quietly. Figuring out how to deal with my mess, I guessed.

I looked back at Quinn. "You in a lot of pain?" he asked, his eyes traveled over my bruised and cut up face.

"I'm fine," I shrugged, grimacing as I moved my aching arm.

I ran my eyes over his face. He had had time to clean up. He was lucky enough to come out of all this without any major injury. Luckier than others I didn't even know. Damn it.

I swallowed. "Quinn, you were right. I was in *way* over my head. Thanks for calling in the cavalry."

"Guess we're even. I'd still be stuck in a necklace if it weren't for you." His dimples flashed out and I managed a ghost of a smile.

"You saved my iron back there, I hear."

"Oh yeah," Quinn stood and dug into his pocket. The pieces clinked heavily together as he dragged them out. They looked like the original tattoos, permanently frozen like the ones in my dream with Sarah. I looked at the one with Daniels' name on it. It felt heavy in my hand and I thought of the burden Griff had endured with that engraved into his back for years and years.

Quinn, as usual, read the thoughts on my face.

"He's gone. He didn't go until he knew you would be okay. Then he took off without a word to anyone. He took Caryn's body with him."

"All I wanted to do was free him from Daniels, but I think the price was way too high. It's all my fault Caryn's dead. She tried to help me. I can't stand the thought of someone dying because of me." My throat constricted, the tug of guilt making me ill. "Griff probably hates me now."

"I doubt that," Quinn said softly. "He kept watch on you very carefully until he knew you were out of danger."

"Then he left without a word. Man, I screwed up so bad." I leaned my head back against the pillows and closed my eyes, the tears threatening to start again.

"Why don't you tell me the whole story of what happened to you guys?" Quinn asked. "Then I can better understand what's going on."

I made myself give a brief version of my capture and fight. I could hardly bear to talk about it, especially the part about leaving Daniels in the fire.

"I'm surprised you came out of all that relatively unscathed." Quinn gave me a look of admiration. "You are amazing. You really *are* royalty."

"Gag. Don't say that," I said, rolling my eyes. "It's too weird. And what I did wasn't amazing, unless you call it amazingly *stupid*. I got people hurt. Or dead." I turned my face away, looking around the light blue walls, wishing I were home in my own room.

Quinn brushed my hair off my forehead and ran his hand gently down my cheek.

"I still think you're very brave."

I smiled ruefully. "Thanks for trying to cheer me up."

"Mia!" My shouted name interrupted our conversation. I sat up quickly and caught the troubled look Quinn shot at me. "Uh-oh."

Before I could ask, Quinn's other sister Eileen came storming into the room, her green eyes flashing, her hands clenched.

"So, you're finally awake. What do you have to say for yourself?" She snapped angrily.

"Eileen, I, uh…"

She cut me off. "Your stupid stunt just about took my fiancé's leg off. I can't believe how selfish you are. You waltz in here and start screwing up all the safety and security we've worked so hard to establish."

"I know you brought Quinn back," she continued, glancing swiftly at her brother, "but that doesn't give you the right to bring danger down on our heads. I don't care *whose* daughter you are."

She paused to catch her breath and Quinn jumped in. "Leave her alone, Eileen. She feels bad enough already."

"I doubt it. Did you know that Stephen and I were getting married next week? Thanks to you, we have to postpone the wedding. Stephen's leg is ripped to shreds, all the way to the bone. It's going to take a long time to heal, even though he's part Terraran."

I ran a hand across my eyes. "Eileen, I am terribly sorry. You're right. I messed up big time. I didn't think at all about the cost to anyone else. I just wanted to help someone I cared about."

"*Hmpft.* Well, I hope it was worth it." She flounced out of the room without a backward glance.

I closed my eyes again, wanting to sink into the bed and disappear. "Mia," Quinn began.

"I don't think there's anything even you can say to make me feel better," I sighed. "Please, just go. I need more sleep."

I turned onto my side and faced the wall.

"Things will be okay, Mia. You'll see." He left and quietly closed the door.

I stared at the walls for a long time before finally drifting off to sleep.

WHEN I WOKE up again, clear sunlight was brightening the blue walls of my room. I had no idea how long I had slept, but by the way I had to book it to the bathroom I'd guess it was quite a while. I got a good look at myself for the first time since all the excitement, and I was not surprised at the disaster that looked back at me from the mirror.

My hair was lank and limp, plastered to my head like a pale orange swim cap. My cheek was still bruised, although the cut was now scabbed over. My left arm was bandaged from wrist to shoulder, which I could tell was going to make for some interesting challenges in the cleaning up department. Nice. I felt dirty and slimy and longed for a hot steaming shower, but the bandages rained on that parade. So I settled for as thorough a sponge bath as I could manage, then attempted to wash my hair, one-handed, in the sink. *Not* an easy operation.

I felt much more human (ha ha) when I had finished. I found some hair gel in a cupboard and made free with it, hoping it wasn't Eileen's. I didn't need another reason for her to come scream at me. *No. Don't go there*, I told myself.

I stood in front of the mirror for several minutes, looking for changes in my face, my eyes. I had seen so much since my last glance in the mirror at Jace's house. Then I had been *too* confident, full of foolhardy notions of search and rescue. All my naïve ideas had been blown over like a precarious house of cards, and I felt like I should look different after such a blow.

My eyes, however, reflected only a bit more sadness and pain, and for the most part, I still looked the same. Sighing, I left, wondering where I should go and what I should do.

First, I returned to my room and searched the pockets of the evil dress wadded up in the corner. I was relieved to recover Quinn's necklace, as well as my meteorite bracelet. I thought about my iron hammer and wondered if Griff still had it, or whether it was buried in the crumbling wreck of that burning courtroom. I was going to miss the feel of that tool in my hand. Ah, well. I fastened on the necklace and bracelet, and on impulse, grabbed the cold iron tattoos before I took off, wandering down the hallway.

I passed a huge glass window and the view made me stop and stare, pressing my face against the frosted glass. I had lost my sense of time, what with all the adventure and startling revelations of the last little while, and the winter wonderland before me was overwhelmingly beautiful.

I ached with homesickness.

I wondered, fleetingly, if they celebrated Christmas—or any kind of winter holiday—here, but then a vivid image of my parents came into my mind with such clarity, I felt my heart twist up in my chest. Something had to be done. Soon.

I found my feet taking me to Lord Kyan's library and I raised my hand to knock. I started when the door was suddenly opened, my hand still hanging in the air.

Serious grey eyes locked on mine and I lowered my hand quickly, a nervous laugh jerked out of me.

"Have we got some psychic link that I haven't figured out yet?" I asked.

"Not at all." Lord Kyan reached out and put a hand on my arm, then guided me down the hallway. "I just got a message. I'm glad you're up and about. So, what's up?"

I studied his profile. Lord Kyan – Kye—had his jaw clenched shut and I could see the muscle tensing in his cheek. He glanced down at me and relaxed his face into a smile. "The people you rescued from Daniels' household. Some want to stay here for protection. Some want to return home to be reunited with their human families."

My eyes clouded with emotion as homesickness hit me like an ocean wave. I whispered softly, "I know the feeling."

His dark gray eyes regarded me closely. "I'm sorry, Mia. I really am." He reached over and put his arm around my shoulder. At first, all I felt was surprised and awkward, but after a few steps, I felt my body relax and I leaned into my father.

That was such a weird thought: my *father*. I never had the childhood fantasies I knew lots of adopted kids experience. My dad and I get along so well, I never felt like I needed any other dad. In fact, most of the time I didn't even *remember* I was adopted.

A SUDDEN COMMOTION erupted from the large room we were heading for. A large, desperate-looking woman grabbed my arm. "Can you help them? I think their tattoos have been activated since they escaped. They must have some kind of built-in sensor set to go off if they leave. We had no way to know this, and now the ones you didn't remove earlier are going to die. Please hurry!"

Kye and I rushed into the room.

A large group of people crowded around several people who were on the floor, convulsing like they were having a seizure. Without a second thought, I reached back into my mind and found the door that let me access my power. I knelt down by the first man. His eyes had rolled up and he was shaking violently. I beckoned for help, and several men helped push him carefully onto his side, and held him firmly while I began to pull the hot iron out of his back.

A low gasp flowed around the room as the iron weaved itself back into the tattoo design. I made it rise to the ceiling of the room, hoping to keep the hot iron away from the stunned, uplifted faces. The man stopped writhing and went still, his breathing steadying. His body relaxing.

I moved on to the next person. A young girl, no older than Caryn, shook in terror, and I felt my anger rise as I pulled out the metal binding her to Daniels' household.

One by one, I freed the people who had come with us. I hated that they were being tortured, and I wished that I had figured out how to release the iron without them having to experience this kind of pain. I had thought I would have had time to learn how to do that. Gee, why would I ever think it could be that easy?

Still, by the time I was finished, I had freed six part-Terrarans...and had six new weapons.

"That is absolutely remarkable." Lord Kyan placed his arm around my shoulders and I felt my face flush at the compliment. I smiled up into those eyes that seemed so familiar and found myself, in the midst of all this awfulness, feeling, for a brief moment, happy.

"Thanks...um...Kye. So, no one you know has a talent like this?" I pulled out one of the solid iron tattoos from my pocket and turned it over and over in my hand.

"Not at all. The only thing that Terrarans have done with iron is those horrible tattoos. I didn't even know how common they've become. They were only in experimental stages when I left Terrara." Kyan took the iron from me and rubbed his hand across the intricate design.

"How long have you been in hiding, anyway?" I asked, watching as his long fingersabsently traced the sun and moon pattern.

"I escaped from my uncle's court when he murdered my father. That was over a hundred years ago. But my Sanctuary, as you saw it, is very new. Only ten years or so."

"What made you finally decide to settle in one place?"

"I got tired of running. I wanted a safe place. A place where I could forget.

Grayson found me a while later. He has been instrumental in improving what started out as a small house, and in finding those who needed protection. Grayson has the unique ability to sense small, unknown portals between the two worlds. That has proven extremely useful, since not everyone can travel like you and I can."

I hesitated to even say the words, but couldn't quite keep them back: "Did you ever imagine bringing me or Mom to your Sanctuary?"

Lord Kyan studied me. "No, I never wanted you to be part of this dangerous world, Mia. I wanted a simpler life for you." I looked down, swallowing my disappointment, as he continued, "But I am glad to see you *now*, Mia. Even if the situation is less than perfect."

He turned away and cleared his throat. "Grayson still has hope that we can keep our Sanctuary a permanent residence, where our people can thrive and remain safe."

I studied his tense jaw as he gazed around at the crowd of people. "You don't agree."

"I think what we have made is temporarily safe, but it is still risky with my uncle set on attacking anyone he sees as a threat to his domain. I have been under his radar, evading his spies for a long time. Now that he knows about you, he will…be more persistent. He wants to wipe out any and all threats to his throne, especially since we are 'Nequam polluted.'"

"I don't want anything to do with his throne," I said, "and I can't imagine you do either. If we sign some sort of treaty, could peace be made?" It sounded a bit optimistically simple, but I was willing to try anything to get Lord Aiken away from those I cared about.

Kyan gave a sharp, mirthless laugh. "Lord Aiken is not one to believe in peaceful solutions, only bloody ones. He has killed not only my father, but also every one of his brothers and sisters and their families to legitimize his sole claim to the throne.

You and I are the last remaining members of the royal family that stand in his way."

I cringed. "And how do his people feel about his behavior, or are they too scared to do anything about his tyranny?"

"I don't really know," Lord Kyan said, "or care. I left that world, and I don't want to return. Ever." Lord Kyan turned his face up and studied my iron floating aimlessly along the ceiling of the room. "So, now what are you going to do with those things? And what about these cold ones?" He tossed the one he had been fingering into my lap. "Have you found a way to heat them up again?"

"Well, let's see," I said, trying to tease, "you asked me that, what, an *hour* ago? You know, I haven't had a lot of time to work on the problem. And it's not like you've given me any helpful advice."

A smile flitted across his face. "What is that human saying about necessity being the mother of invention? Many of us have had to learn things the hard way, too, Mia. Terraran blood combining with human blood seems to yield some very interesting results."

He stood and brushed his hand over my hair. "I'm sure you will figure it out. Try not to burn anyone – or this building— down while you experiment, though. Okay?" He winked as he turned away.

"Yeah, thanks for the vote of confidence, Kye," I shot back as he walked back out my door. "Really feeling the love."

I placed my frozen tattoos on the floor. I stared at them until my eyes watered. Somehow I had to find a way to activate them, or fire them up. I knew how important it was going to be. I had a very hard time believing I could be so unique, and I was determined to be able to do something against that evil

Lord Aiken. So I settled back and tried to remember anything helpful. I dug around in my head, trying out different thoughts and words silently in my mind.

Finally, I latched onto the memory of pain shooting through my back. Not my favorite memory, but I forced myself to visit it anyway.

Suddenly, I sensed the power gliding up my spine, hot and stinging along my neck. The heat pouring up my chin as if I were standing on my head, spreading over my cheeks and pooling into the top of my head. I thought my head was going to explode from the pressure, when things finally clicked.

I'd found my "On" button, so to speak.

With a grateful release of pent-up heat, I made the cold metal flame to life. It flew up, ricocheting around, gleaming with shiny power. I smiled in triumph. I could actually do it.

As they gently zoomed around the room, I realized I'd better find the "Off" button fast or we were going to have big problems.

I found myself wondering, *Do they have fire extinguishers in Sanctuary?*

Painful Confessions

The next morning, I woke up anxious, excited, and worried, all at once. Kye had given his word that I could return home and talk to my parents. I missed them so much and hated all that I had had to put them through. What in the world was I going to say? How would I explain any of it? It would be an emotional rollercoaster, to say the least.

I sat up, trying to put my pounding head together, and found that emotional hijinks were officially the order of the day.

Griff stood in the doorway.

I couldn't help but gulp out in surprise. "Do you *always* have to see me at my morning worst?"

He tucked his glossy, long hair behind his ear and gave me an all-too-serious face. I saw that jokes weren't going to be part of this conversation.

"Let me have a few minutes, okay? I'll be right back."

I scrambled off the bed and rushed to the bathroom, my heart going faster than I wanted. A few minutes later I curled myself into a ball up against the headboard of the bed.

"You're healed up," I blurted nervously. "No side effects from almost dying?"

"Mia." He reached over and took my hand. "I can never repay you for saving me. I was insane after I saw Caryn killed. One of the guards broke her neck when she tried to help." He put a trembling hand over his eyes and rubbed them. "I will never be able to get that image out of my head."

"It wasn't your fault, Griff. You didn't know. Everything was crazy in that horrible place."

He looked at me sadly. "That's not all."

He took a deep breath. "You need to understand more of what I was doing while I was living in the human world. I wasn't just finding out about part-Terrarans and making sure their powers stayed hidden, I also brought some of these innocent people back to Daniels' household. I couldn't help it. I was compelled to by the tattoo."

Griff looked down and said softly, "It makes me sick."

He stood up and walked to the window and put his forehead to the cold glass. "I was the one who took Caryn away from everything she knew. Her home life was pretty rotten, but not as bad as it became once she came to Terrara. She was so young and afraid. Daniels could tell how angry I was and made special arrangements for me to watch her branding. Of course, there was nothing I could do about it. Caryn hated me at first. And *I* hated me, too."

I swallowed hard, trying to imagine all the guilt twisting around in Griff's head. I started to get off the bed, but he turned toward me with a haunted look that made me pause.

"After Caryn realized that we were all trapped in the same situation, and that I had no choice in the matter, she slowly began to trust me. I had begun to think of her as a little sister." Griff's voice broke and he turned away to the window again. "Someone to protect, at all costs. And I failed. Completely failed."

This time I did get up. I slid my arms around his waist and laid my cheek against his back. My heart hurting, not knowing what to say, I just held onto him while he tried to get himself under control.

Eventually, he turned around and I caught his gaze forcefully with mine. "You cannot hold yourself accountable for things you had no control over, Griff. Unfortunately, we live in a really crappy world sometimes. I'm learning more of that lesson every day."

That sounded so lame. I was a baby compared to all the experiences he has had to deal with for what, a hundred years? But I had to say *something*. I wished for wisdom, but all I could come up with was "a crappy world." *Way to go*, I thought to myself.

Griff didn't seem to notice.

"I don't think I can ever forgive myself for what happened to Caryn, but because of you, Mia, I can make my own choices again." He ran his finger down my cheek. "Removing my tattoo. Wow. I can't believe how powerful you are."

He seemed to hesitate.

"So, now that I'm free, and you are so strong and protected..."

I could see where this was going.

"Hey, that's cool. You've got things to do. I understand." I was starting to babble, feeling like the teenager I was. All my silly expectations, nixed. Those I had known were lurking there under the surface, from the moment I saw him standing in that doorway. And they were still in the back of my head, even after such a serious conversation. I wrapped my arms around me and forced an awkward smile onto my frozen face.

He took my shoulders gently. "I don't feel any differently toward you, Mia. Please believe me. I need this time to do some things to help make up for what I have done in the past. You have other things you need to do. You're an important person now."

"If I hear that one more time," I groaned softly, closing my eyes.

"You know," Griff said, "I felt how different you are when we first met, so I get a bit of credit, right? Of course, I almost got you killed and branded, too. So that's got to take way a few points."

He was looking at me with those pale blue eyes, trying to get me to understand, trying to ease the situation with a twisted sense of humor.

I pulled his mouth down to mine and whispered, "Be careful."

"I won't be gone too long," he murmured. "I promise."

Home

Jace leaned over to me. "Your mom is never going to get over that you can fly and she can't. Too bad you're too old to use it to sneak out at night."

I poked him in the arm.

"Do you actually think she's thought about that?" I asked.

"Maybe not yet, she's got a few other things to process, now. Doesn't she?"

I had to laugh a little. "Gee, you think?"

I shook my head, trying to focus on something serious, which was always harder with Jace goofing around.

My thoughts went back over the scene where Jace and Sarah came to my front door with me. It was like the night I was taken home from the Terraran attack on Halloween, but to the millionth degree. Mom was hysterical, in a good way, and Dad was stunned. I could hardly speak, I was so happy to be home. Not that I could've gotten in any words anyway, what with all the questions being fired at me.

I've never seen my parents so happy…or so totally confused. Dad knew a little bit about the craziness that was going on, of course. But it took a *lot* of convincing to get my very practical mom to accept even *part* of this story. It was funny, really, her trying to put together some rational scenario for how I had survived a fall off that cliff.

So I just smiled and hugged her, figuring I'd give her a ride in the sky when it's too dark to get caught. I smirked at the look I imagined on her face.

"I KNEW YOU'D thought of it." Jace's voice broke into my thoughts as he saw me grin. "I can't believe you've got all these superhero powers now, Mia. It's completely unfair, like you are living inside one of Miyazaki's films." Jace nudged me. "So, where's Griff? Isn't he your leading man?"

I frowned. "Not right now. He took off to parts unknown."

"*Hmm.* That doesn't sound like the Griff I knew."

"Jace, you barely knew him." I sounded exasperated and snippy, but felt justified. His leaving was still painful.

"Okay, okay. You can tell me later when you aren't so freaked. I bet he's still crazy about you, though." He nudged me with his elbow.

I winced, my burns still quite tender. "He's hard to read," I said softly. "Griff's dealing with too much guilt. I don't think he has room for anything else right now."

I hoped after a certain amount of grieving, he would turn to me. I wanted to comfort him and help erase his feelings of guilt and self-loathing. Would he even *want* my help? I shut my eyes. Lingering doubts floated around me.

Jace, sensing my angst-y mood, decided to keep quiet for once and left me stewing. I felt him get up and heard the door click softly behind him. I sighed, opening my eyes, glancing around my bedroom. It looked exactly as I remembered it.

Only now it seemed like a stranger's room. It was the room of a normal teenager. I certainly didn't fit *that* bill anymore. Not that I was ever *completely* normal, but I'd at least been *human*.

Or thought I was.

I shook my head. No going back now. I stood and stretched, needing a run to clear my head. I grabbed my running shoes and headed for the cold, fresh outdoors. When I reached the top of the stairs, I stopped short. The upstairs smelled delicious and my stomach growled in response. I decided my run could wait. Sarah and my mom had cooked up a huge celebration dinner. I felt so happy and relaxed as we sat down to eat together: my mom, dad, and Sarah and Jace. We had been so busy eating lasagna (which is Mom's specialty), and focused on our plates, that we all jumped when the doorbell rang. Suspecting whom it was, I got up first and dashed to the door. There they stood, shuffling their feet a bit. I gave both of them a hug and beckoned them inside.

"Come on in."

Grayson and Quinn came cautiously into the dining room. Mom and Dad didn't know what to think until Quinn gave a tentative smile. The resemblance to Nan's dimpled smile had my dad's mouth falling open.

"Mom, Dad, I know this is hard to believe, but this is Grayson and his son Quinn. Grayson was married to Nan's twin sister, Anna. They obviously *aren't* imaginary. I mean, look at Quinn's cheeks. They're the spitting image of Nan's."

Everyone stared at Quinn; he gave a rueful look as his face heated up. Embarrassed, I started rushing my words, trying to get them out, wanting to tell the story right, but afraid of mixing everything up.

I looked over at Grayson, knowing he could do a much better job, and at the same time, Sarah graciously offered our guests mismatched chairs around our very crowded table.

It was a very odd dinner. My dad, drilling Grayson with persistent questions. My mom and Sarah, being polite and trying to act like this was all normal...and not completely out of left field.

Plus, Quinn and Jace were sizing each other up for the first time, though Quinn had the advantage—he'd seen Jace many times in my dreams while Quinn was trapped in the necklace. Of course, how Jace acted in my dreams... hey, I have no responsibility for that, do I?

WHEN WE COULDN'T stand the small dining room any longer, we made our way to the living room—also a tight fit. Our house just wasn't designed for large groups. I glanced around the room with a critical eye. The signs of the break-in had been swept away as much as possible by my mom, giving her something to focus on in those early stages of grief. I shuddered at the thought of her scrubbing and cleaning her way though those devastating times.

Grayson and Quinn settled into the slightly torn up floral chairs facing the couch. Jace and I sat on the floor. Mom, Dad, and Sarah sat on the long couch. Silence strung out. I knew the next move, but was unwilling to bring it up. Grayson cleared his throat and stood up.

"This place isn't safe for any of you," he began ominously.

Then—as if to prove his point—the front door splintered open with a loud *crack*.

And all hell broke loose.

28

A Split Decision

In less than a second, my worst nightmare appeared behind my dad and shoved a crystal knife across his throat. "You have no idea!" Daniels growled cruelly. "You really don't!"

Alive? *Daniels is alive?* I hadn't even finished processing the impossible thought when my mom and Sarah were pinned to the couch by several large men. "What? How? Who's there?" My dad choked out, and I realized the Terrarans were all invisible to the humans in the room. Only Quinn, Grayson and I could see them. I reached for my iron weapons, only to find, to my horror, that I left them downstairs on my side table.

"No moving!" Daniels said slowly, pushing the knife against my dad's neck, a small bit of blood running down the side. Grayson was holding up his hands saying, "Stop. Please. Let us try and talk about this."

A new voice came from the area of the kitchen. Adrianna, Daniels' mother. Her eyes were wild and her voice shook with rage.

"Talk? *Talk?!*"

"You have no idea what you have done! We are disgraced. The King…" she moaned. "He does not forgive. He does *not* forgive." She seemed to focus again. "But no, we will fix it. We will make it right. The King will forget his humiliation. We will…."

As she was rambling, I concentrated all my fear and terror on my tattoos. *Come to me!* I screamed in my mind. At the same time, Grayson was taking advantage of Adrianna's near-incoherent monologue and threw himself at her.

Arms and legs started flying, but all I could think of was my dad at the mercy of that crystal knife. "Daniels!" I screamed, "Remember *this?*" My glowing tattoo soaring into his face. But he was so fast, I almost scorched my dad by mistake.

My mom had somehow slipped from her captor's arms to the floor. He was holding a hand over his nose, yelling, as blood gushed through between his fingers. She must have head-butted him or something. She had guessed his position, even though she couldn't see him.

"Get Sarah out of the way!" I yelled, and Jace lunged over and threw his body over his mom, trying to figure out where the danger was coming from. He tried to protect her from her unseen assailant, smacking around, this way and that.

I looked at my dad, so confused and terrified. Daniels looked at my glowing iron and pushed the knife into my dad's neck a bit more. "I mean it, you foolish child. You better lower your weapons and come with me," his smile cruel and vicious. "We *won't* be merciful."

A split-second decision sprang into my mind. "Fine, I'll come with you. Just get that dagger off his neck."

A suspicious look crossed Daniels' face. "You first. Down with the iron. *Now!*"

"No!" screamed Quinn. "Don't do it!" He was going after the man with the bloody nose. "He's lying!" He grabbed the man's long hair. "It's got to be a trap."

I ignored him.

I let the tattoos wink out and they dropped on the floor with a heavy thud, my heart sinking with them, worried this wasn't going to work. But the decision was made, and the second Daniels lowered his dagger onto the sofa, hand poised to snatch it again, I sprang at him. Before he could grab the knife back, I grasped his arm firmly, and turning to Jace, screamed, "Help! You know where..."

In the blink of an eye the world tilted into a crazy, dizzy nothingness.

Wham! I slammed into a cement floor, and watched in amazement as Daniels landed next to me. I had traveled another person! I could not believe it. I had saved my dad.

Of course, the celebration didn't last long. My lovely escape method had us both vomiting all over the floor. Now it looked like an endurance contest was the order of the day. I glanced around. At least I had the home court advantage.

I pushed myself to my knees. Jace, I thought desperately, Hurry!

"WHAT IS THIS disgusting place?" Daniels gritted through his teeth.

I managed a small laugh through the nausea. "One of my mom's favorite stores," I gasped back, trying to crawl up to my knees. "And now it's one of mine, too."

Iron garden tools, decorative wall hooks and picture frames lined the walls and shelves. Patio tables and chairs covered practically every inch of the floor of the tiny store. Claustro-phobic on a normal visit, it was the safest place I could think of at this moment.

Daniels made it to his feet first and opened his mouth. "I hate...," he began, and then threw up down his silk shirt. He swayed, anger twisting his face, "Dammit, Mia, that is *vile*. I will make you pay for every single indignity you have put me through."

Stripping off his shirt, he gathered his energy and began flinging random iron objects at me using telekinesis. His accu-racy left something to be desired, but one hit with a heavy piece of iron, and I'd be out like a light.

I struggled to flip over a round patio table on its side while my stomach churned violently in protest. I fought the urge to pass out. I cowered behind the table like a cowboy in an old time bar from one of those cheesy Western movies my dad likes to watch.

The thought of my dad cleared my head a bit. He was safe now, I hoped. Grayson was full Terraran, older, more expe-rienced. *Please, Grayson, take care of that hag Adrianna. Oh, please, protect my family!*

A flying object smacked into the table, making me jump. I took a risky peek: Daniels was weaving his way over, but his accuracy still stunk, at least. I wished for some of my tattoo weapons, hoping someone back at the house at least used them to whack someone over the head.

Another crash against my table set my teeth on edge. I needed to get moving, but *where*? I thought bitterly about how fast Daniels' burns had healed...and how quickly he had regen-erated his hand. I still had so much to learn about Terrarans. I thought we'd have more time to get us all to Sanctuary.

Another hit against my table. It was making me mad that all this iron wasn't affecting Daniels more.

Oh, please, let Jace understand what I meant. Please let him come quick. I hate hiding like a wimp. My stomach cramped up and I wrapped my arms around it.

I heard a wet splat, and knew Daniels was feeling as rotten as I was. Good. Maybe this was going to work after all.

I took another glance around the table.

"I'm coming, little girl," Daniels slurred at me. "You are weaponless and weak. I don't know why you thought this trick would work. But you are a stupid, filthy, Nequam...."

"Crap, how is he resisting?" I muttered. I knew I needed more time, so I started chucking random objects at him over the table. A frame, a statue, a garden tool. Most of the weapons clattered to the floor. At least one hit, and I heard him crash onto the floor with a grunt of pain. I began goading him. My best defense right now: the "keep the villain distracted by talking" technique. *I sure hope it works like in the movies*, I thought.

"Shut your face, Daniels!" I shouted. "We are *not* filthy! You Terrarans are lower than those beastly hounds you set against us. They were poor, dumb animals that had no choice in what they did."

I heard him getting closer, his shoes making scuffing noises on the concrete floor, his voice creeping towards me, every bit as vicious sounding as those hounds.

"Just keep talking, *Nequam*. I will remember every one of those insults." I could sense him hovering beyond my hiding place.

I made my last bid.

"You are a disgusting, evil man. You didn't capture me last time. What makes you think you can do it this time? I should've cut off more than your stupid hand." I let my voice rise to a high-pitched scream. "I should've cut off your head! Bet you couldn't have grown *that* back!" I finished on a gag. Not very threatening, I suppose. But I felt like crap.

I clutched my stomach with my left hand and threw an old-fashioned iron over the patio table, and scrambled away as fast as I could manage, on my hands and knees.

I flinched as something heavy slammed into my shoulder. I continued crawling away from his shrieks of rage, ducking behind a free-standing cabinet. I took an unsteady breath and then flung out the last insult, "I hope the King never forgives you. Fail here and you're dead! And believe me, you are *going to fail!*"

Daniels was ranting wildly in Terraran, all the beauty of the language twisted up into hateful sounds and syllables. Too late, I realized my inflammatory speech had worked the wrong way. Instead distracting him, I just made him angrier. *Way to go, Mia.* My only hope was that his fury—combined with his nausea—would keep him sloppy.

I heard a lull in his speech; retching sounds filled the air. Good, he was still affected. But then again so was I. I took the opportunity to slide backwards, across the slick cement floor.

I was inching my way across to another set of tables when a sharp crack split the air. Jerking my head to the front of the store, I saw Quinn flying through the large display window. Glass erupted everywhere. He kept flying over the nasty shards of glass, and landing lightly on his feet, he grabbed an iron poker from a fireplace kit and faced Daniels. Quinn's expression was fierce.

At last, I thought, collapsing in relief. I thought about those left behind at the house. What had happened to them?

Quinn raised the poker like a sword. "Get away from Mia!" he demanded.

My attention snapped back to the duel at hand.

"Make me, boy," Daniels snarled back, coughing and gagging.

Quinn raised his arm to strike, as I crawled away from behind my table, getting behind an ornate iron rocking chair.

In a flash of motion, a large vase flew straight at Quinn and hit the poker, sending a resounding jolt up Quinn's arm. He managed to hang onto the poker with both hands. The next shots went wide, and Daniels threw himself behind the table I had been using as protection.

Daniels started taunting Quinn about how his dad was so weak, hiding away like a coward. His own people rejecting him like a filthy traitor. Quinn roared his denial as he flew over the table, attacking wildly.

Daniels was ready.

When Quinn lifted the poker, an iron statue of a cat whipped it aside while another knickknack slammed up into Quinn's unprotected jaw. His head jerked back and he fell back, still and unmoving. I screamed, forgetting about hiding, crawling as fast as I could to Quinn's side. Daniels was choking Quinn.

"Stop, please," I begged, while I tried to recover the fallen poker. No use. It had rolled under a shelf. Instead, I began ripping Daniels' bare back with my nails, panic bubbling up inside. "You can't kill him!"

"Oh, I don't even care about him, anymore." Daniels jerked away from my fingers and, smirking horribly, released Quinn's throat and snagged my wrists. "I just needed you close enough for this." Out of his pocket he drew a pair of the plastic-like cuffs that had restrained me during my last capture.

"No!" I screamed in dismay, wiggling desperately.

The cuffs clicked ominously.

Then a thread of logic gave me hope. "You can't fly me anywhere. You're way too weak."

"I only have to hide us until my strength returns," he said, triumphantly. "Then tomorrow we will pay a visit to the King!"

He started hauling me viciously through the glass toward the broken front window. The glass bit into my knees and I struggled as Daniels pulled me by my neck.

We'd barely reached the window when Jace's head suddenly rose into view. He could see me on the floor, but I knew Daniels was invisible to him. Daniels shoved my face to the floor and stomped his foot over my neck to keep me still. I strained to force out a warning.

"Jace, be careful. He's throwing iron."

"Another brat coming to save you? How many boyfriends do I have to get rid of?" Daniels taunted. "Oh, but this one is only a weak *human*. And after I take you back to be the King's pet, I will be sure to take care of your whole family. That is, if Mother hasn't already finished them off!"

The force on my neck weakened and I yanked my head to the side. Twisting my head to look, I watched Daniels' arm reach back and begin gesturing.

"Jace!" I screamed.

Before Daniels could finish his gesture, Jace whipped out a tire iron he had snagged from his car and started swinging crazily above my head.

"I can't see you, but I *can* still hear your voice!" Jace screamed, rage running through his voice, the tire iron whistling through the air.

Crack.

He couldn't see it or hear it. In fact, I'm not sure Jace even *felt* the impact of the tire iron against Daniels' head. But I got the full view. Daniels' head twisted around and I knew immediately that his neck was broken, and he was dead.

Lingering Guilt

"Okay, Jace, okay," I yelled. "Stop! You did it! You saved us all!"

"I did what, exactly?" Jace was starting to calm down, but he was still swinging crazily. "Are you okay? Is Daniels gone? I still can't see him, Mia." Jace was looking around frantically, still trying to figure out what just happened.

"You protected us all, Jace," I said. "Daniels was going to drag me off and that would've been it. I'd be tortured, enslaved, who knows? He's dead. You saved me. You couldn't even see him and you still saved me."

Jace's eyes grew wide. "I *killed* him?" He froze for a second. "Well, good," he ground out with gritted teeth and threw the iron behind him. He climbed carefully into the glass-filled room and crouched down next to me, almost sitting on Daniels' body.

He looked stunned as he wiped blood from my cheeks and shook glass from my hair.

"Are you okay?" Jace frowned.

"Yes, Jace," I confirmed. "You got here just in time."

He sagged in relief. I glanced at the body behind him. This wasn't over yet. Jace leaned over me, examining my restraints. "How do you..."

A groan rose from behind us. Jace panicked. "Is it Daniels? Is he still alive?" He took a step back and fell over the body.

"What the..." he spluttered. Then a sickened look crossed his face.

"Oh my gosh. I really *killed* him."

"Jace, it's okay. It was an accident." Jace moved away. He put his head in his hands, reality washing over him.

"I was so *angry*. Seeing you on the floor bleeding, I just went out of my head."

"Jace, focus for a minute. Quinn is hurt. I need to get out of these wrist holds. Any ideas?"

Slowly, Jace stood up.

He blinked a few times, trying to calm his emotions. He reached into his front jeans pocket and pulled out my tattoos. They were bright, reflecting the moonlight coming through the broken window.

"I remembered these as I ran out the door. Thought they might come in handy, once I figured out your plan." He laid them on the floor next to me and continued, "It was a good plan getting Daniels out of there. I knew right where you were going, but of course Quinn got here first because he could fly. He wouldn't wait for the car."

"Good thing." I brought the tattoos to life and carefully cut off my binds. "The double-team attack worked. I needed both of you." I tiptoed through the glass past Daniels' still body over to Quinn.

He was sitting up, rubbing his swollen jaw and scanning the room until he found Daniels' body. He lay back on the floor, closing his eyes. "He had me down in less than a *minute*. Some rescue.

"What a stupid entrance" Quinn went on, still berating himself. Then he eyed my bloody knees. "That was my fault, wasn't it? Mia, I'm so sorry."

"Hey, I'm just glad you showed up to defend me. I was seriously running out of options."

My head was spinning again now that my adrenaline had run out. "In fact, guys, I think we'd better get out of here before someone shows up. Not only does it reek, but what a disaster!" I looked around in dismay. "I don't think I can deal anymore." I started to slump against a chair.

"Hang on." Both boys lifted me up. Jace shook me, reminding me, "First, put out your tattoos. This place is already a mess. No need to start a fire as well."

"Oh, good call." Out they winked. *Clang.* I watched Jace pick them up through half-closed eyes. I barely kept myself from tipping over; even the guilt of leaving the mess to someone else could barely keep me awake. I figured all my savings would go to fix the disaster. Well, I would pay anything to keep my family safe.

Jace and Quinn helped me stumble to the car. I sank down into the comfortable fabric. The trunk opened with a squeak. I felt something heavy drop into trunk and the lid slammed close. I shuddered at the thought of Daniels' corpse stuffed in with the jumper cables and old blankets. I wouldn't be using *those* anytime soon.

Quinn sat in the back seat, wiping his hands on his pants. I lay my head on his shoulder, feeling myself sliding away. He whispered something in my ear. I couldn't concentrate on his voice. The motion of the car and the presence of my two best friends lulled my body into desperately-needed sleep.

JACE AND I peered out my front window at the falling snow. The living room showed signs of yesterday's battle: one of the coffee table's legs seemed to have been torn off. The pictures on the walls tilted at crazy angles, and one had a cracked frame. The curtains lay in a puddle under a dangling window rod.

It looked so peaceful and clean outside, though. I glanced over at Jace, knowing he was feeling anything but peaceful. His mind seemed as confused as the room around us. I could see the emotions churning beneath the surface. I wanted so much to help him deal with killing Daniels. Even though Daniels was horrible, and Jace was fighting to save me. Despite the fact that it had been an accident, I knew it was something Jace would always have to live with. I felt the guilt spreading over me as I watched him from the corner of my eye, feeling guilt of my own. If it weren't for me, he never would have had to go through this.

STUPIDLY, I TRIED to lighten things up. "How are you feeling today? Like Batman? Superman?"

He squinted at me. "You know more about comic books than that, Mia. Batman would never kill anyone. Neither would Superman."

"Well, not on purpose," I agreed. "But I bet they would if they had no other choice."

"Didn't I have a choice? Did I really have to?" Jace wanted to know.

"I could have just knocked him out. I sometimes I wish I could go back and do it again."

"Nobody gets do-overs, unfortunately." I shrugged, and wishing for a few of my own mistakes to be wiped away.

"It would sure make life easier, though, don't you think?"

I nodded. I thought about Caryn and Griff. He was torn up after an innocent girl, whom he had promised to protect, had died. Of course, he felt completely responsible. But I had doubts. I thought it was more *my* fault. I wished that I hadn't gone looking for Griff. On the other hand, I never would have found out about my powers over the tattoos, and Griff would still be enslaved. Damn, it was such a mess. I guessed turning back the clock might make things worse.

We sat for a while in silence.

"Remember when school seemed hard?"

"Yeah, those were the days." I wondered how I would have felt if I had done more than cut off Daniels' hand. His head? *Oh, that is so gross*, I thought. I know I had *said* I should have done it, and in the heat of the moment I probably could have done it.

But I don't know if I could have dealt with the guilt any better than Griff and Jace were.

Jace ran his hand through his spiky hair and looked at me with serious eyes. "My brain is so messed up."

"What are we going to do now, Mia?" Jace continued. "I mean, Daniels is dead. Grayson had it out with Adrianna, and now she's dead too."

At that moment, Quinn came striding into the room with a piece of chocolate cake. He sat across from us in one of the flowered armchairs. "Want me to get you some?" he offered.

"No thanks," I declined. Food still sounded rather nauseating.

Jace shook his head, and he *never* turns away food, especially chocolate cake.

"I am always hungry," Quinn said with his mouth full. "Ever since I got out of that necklace, I can't stop eating. Especially your mom's cooking, it's so great."

Speaking of your mom," Quinn continued, "I hear she pepper-sprayed Adrianna right in the face. She was in the middle of some psycho rant and your mom slipped the keys out of her pocket and sprayed the area that the voice was coming from. She was so worried about your dad."

"Best use of the jogging gadget ever." Jace's face relaxed into a smile for a moment.

"That was the pivotal moment," Quinn went on. "Such a distraction gave my dad the advantage, and he used it."

"Does he feel guilty for killing her?" Jace asked quietly.

"I don't really know. I expect he feels *some* guilt. But you have to understand. Besides going after your family, she and Daniels have been hunting me and my sisters for a long time, too."

"Time for a lot of anger and hate to build up," I added. I thought about someone going after my parents, and then about children. I didn't have any younger siblings, but if I did, well, I knew protecting them would be instinctive. Jace was the closest I had to a brother or sister and I would do anything for him. The same way he had for me. My knight in shining armor.

Who's just a friend.

With crazy hair.

"What?" Jace said, when he saw I was smiling at him.

"Nothing," I said. "You really should have some of that cake. You know you'll feel better with some sugar in you."

"Oh, alright," Jace caved in. "I've been wanting to try some of that cake your mom made when Griff came over. You know, just to see if it's as good as he raved it was."

Quinn frowned at Griff's name. "I'll go get it," he offered, and stomped out of the room.

"Still doesn't like Griff, huh?" Jace raised his eyebrows at me.

"Not particularly."

I wondered where Griff was. Had he buried Caryn? Did anyone in her family know that she had died? Did they care?

Quinn walked back into the room, interrupting my thoughts. He had two big pieces of chocolate cake. First, I just picked at it. The warm, smooth chocolate didn't make me gag, though. Its familiar taste and texture took away the edge of my emotions. Jace looked better, too.

Ahhh, I thought. *The power of chocolate.*

We quit talking, letting the chocolate cake work its spell.

I licked the frosting off my fork. "You were awesome back there," I said to Quinn. "I wouldn't have survived if you hadn't got there so soon."

Quinn blushed at this. "I can't believe I let him get to you, I should have been much stronger. I shouldn't have let his words make me go so crazy. Maybe if I hadn't been in that necklace so long... maybe that made me weak. I don't know...," he trailed off.

"Hey, don't beat yourself up about it," I interrupted. "As far as I'm concerned, I was toast without either one of you. Yet again, I acted impulsively and again had to be saved. Not sure I'm learning anything here."

The boys started protesting but I still kept wondering. Cool-headed I am *not*, but my ideas had worked out, at least to some degree. At least no one was seriously hurt this time. Except Jace's psyche, maybe. I wanted to erase his memories. But since I lacked that particular talent, all I could do was be there when he needed to talk. Sharing his guilt, trying to buoy up his spirits by reminding him that his act saved my life. I would never forget it.

And I still wasn't sure what to do now. I mean, Jace's family and mine were human. Now what? Go to Sanctuary for protection, no doubt. But then what? I really didn't know.

Reactions

I paced up and down in my room. It wasn't that big: four steps up, four steps back. Four up, four back. Jace had given up talking to me. He was leafing through my photo album. Every now and then he would snort with laughter and show me a page that had me posing in a frilly princess costume, or holding a doll with crazy, matted hair.

"Just relax, Mia. You know you have to do it."

"I know, I know." I grimaced. "I already had this conversation with your mom."

"DO I TELL her or not? Is it better to be prepared, or will Mom be so angry or nervous that she would refuse to go?" I kept flip-flopping about what to do about Mom and Kye. And of course, there was the problem of warning Dad. This would be a huge shock for each of them.

Sarah had said that I owed it to my parents to be up-front about it. "Come on," she had insisted. "Remember how upset you were when your biological father appeared so unexpectedly, Mia? Think how much more alarming and awkward this will be for your parents, especially your mom. You must tell them what to expect. They most likely already suspect, because they are human and you're part-Terraran. Have you told them who is in charge over there yet? Give them the news before we leave. You owe it to them."

I had agreed. But now that the moment was here, I hesitated, prolonging the uncomfortable scene.

"Just picture them in their underwear…"

I gave Jace the stink-eye. "*Eww*," he amended hastily. "I guess not. Sorry, I was distracted." He shut the album. "Just get it over with, Mia. It'll be fine."

He got up, saying, "Glad I'm not going to be there, though," and disappeared through the door.

I threw my flip-flop at the door. "Thanks for that vote of confidence, Jace," I muttered.

Steeling myself, I forced myself upstairs.

MY MOM WAS talking a mile a minute. She always does when she's upset. Well, she's always talking, *period*, but now she was on fast-forward. I could hardly understand her. "I suppose we'll go, but it's so strange. How is all this possible? I just don't understand. If I hadn't seen it with my own eyes I never would have believed it."

"You didn't even try to tell me." Her eyes were accusatory.

"But you wouldn't have believed it, you just said," I protested.

"But you should have *tried*."

I turned toward my dad and rolled my eyes.

"I saw that, young lady."

"Mom, try to calm down. I need to tell you and Dad some more stuff."

"You mean, more than that we live in a magical world and have to go into hiding in a magical house, and leave our jobs unsecured, not knowing if we'll be back anytime soon? And you're not going to graduate from high school? There's *more* than *that*? I don't even know why I'm surprised."

My mom, the queen of sarcasm.

"Mom, just stop talking for *two minutes*. I have to tell you something important."

"Okay." And Mom stood still with her hands on her hips. "What is such a big deal?"

My throat went dry. "Well, I'm sure you figured out that I've got my powers and heritage from your ex-husband."

Mom glared but stayed quiet. Dad said, "Yes, we've discussed that together." He tried to take his wife's hand but she shrugged it away.

"Okay, this is hard," I sighed.

"Just tell us," Dad said.

"Alright… Kye is actually the nephew to King Aiken on Terrara, and he hates his uncle, and he's in charge of Sanctuary. Everyone there calls him Lord Kyan." I rushed through it as fast as I could and looked at my parents.

My dad's mouth was open in surprise. Mom turned a ghostly shade of white.

"Say something," I urged, feeling my anxiety building. Then my tough-as-nails mom did something completely unexpected:

She fainted.

"YOU ARE KIDDING me." Jace was rubbing his chin. "Your 'Mrs. Always-in-Control' mom lost it?"

"Yeah, it was so weird," I agreed. "Dad wiped her forehead with a cold, wet washcloth. She woke up pretty fast, trying to blow it all off as if it was no big deal. I think she was embarrassed to have done that in front of Dad. Like Kye still means something to her."

I thought about that idea with a sour taste in my stomach. I loved what a good marriage my parents had. It was so rare these days for people to stay together, and my parents seemed truly happy together. They were different, but hey, they say opposites attract. And I know in this case it works great.

Jace and I had already seen divorce, close-up, when his dad left his mom. It was devastating for Sarah, but she was strong and held all those boys together. Fortunately, she was a nurse, and could take care of the family financially. Most of the kids were out of the house. Just Jace and his next older brother, Josh, had still been at home (what is it with some people getting stuck on one letter, and so all their kids' names start the same? I always give Sarah a bit of grief over that).

Anyhow, Sarah was strong, especially when she found out she had cancer. She fought the disease tooth and nail. But it was so hard doing things without her husband's support. I didn't want that for my parents. I needed them together in this.

"They've been together for a long time," Jace said quietly. His thoughts had probably been following mine around in his own brain." No way is an ex-husband going to come between your mom and dad."

"But he's so much younger-looking than my dad, and that whole Lord part. And of course, magical powers."

"I think that would actually put off your mom. She's human and she's not going to want to trade for someone who isn't. Besides, she's probably still pissed at Kyan for leaving her and all."

"Yeah, she is a bit of a grudge-holder, isn't she?"

"And hot-headed…like someone else I know." Jace looked at me sideways.

"No way, I hate confrontations."

"Except with your mom. And lately, with a bunch of bad guys."

"Hey, that's different. That's the adrenaline talking for me."

Jace shrugged. "It's still you."

"Kye wants me to work on my powers in Sanctuary. Controlling the tattoos and my traveling skills, and trying to find out if I have any other hidden surprises."

Jace looked away. I reached out and put my hand on his arm. "I hope you will help me with all the martial arts you've been teaching me. That has been extremely helpful."

"Sure," he said, a little too quickly, not meeting my eyes.

"You don't want to go to Sanctuary, do you?" I said quietly.

Jace ran his fingers through his spiky hair. "It'll be weird to be human there. Like the only dwarf in a sea of elves. I think I'm trapped inside a *Lord of the Rings* dream. I don't know how to explain, it's just so odd."

I rested my head on Jace's arm. "I know it's odd. It really is." I tried to soothe my best friend. "But try to think of it as an adventure. Or a temporary bout of insanity. And hey, no school for a while. That's gotta count for something. Right?"

"I just want to know how long we'll need to stay. I'm totally going to miss Michelle."

"I wish I had an answer."

New Sights and New Feelings

Sanctuary felt familiar and yet, completely foreign. I kept seeing it through my family's eyes, trying to guess what they thought of the place. I thought it was so beautiful, with all of the old wood carvings everywhere, the handmade pottery, the ancient-looking rugs. It wasn't extremely fancy, but it was warmly decorated with fall colors—always my favorite. And it had a good feel to it.

The trip there was different from the previous two times. The first was my surprise traveling escape from the cliff of death. The second time, I was brought in by Kye after I had blacked out. So it was nice to actually be conscious and able to see where we were going this time. Turns out that's Grayson's specialty: finding and using porticos, thin spots between our world and Terrara. That's how he found Anna in the first place.

Of course, Sanctuary was part of our world, just hidden away far north and spelled to keep people out. Apparently, the technique was similar. This portico was in fact made by Kye.

And his power kept it secret. One minute we were in our modern concrete world, and the next, we were at Sanctuary in the snowy forest outside the gates. It felt tingly, like when your foot goes to sleep—but over your whole body.

A group of twenty to thirty people greeted us warmly. Handshakes and smiles all around. My mom tensed as Lord Kyan approached. I held my breath.

Mom, of course, decided to go on the offensive. "Hello, Kye, or do I need to call you *Lord Kyan*?" She stuck out her hand formally.

Kye took her hand and held it briefly in both his hands, then said softly, "Of course call me Kye, Sharon. Welcome to my home. You look as lovely as ever."

My mom suppressed a snort. Kye shifted his feet and looked awkwardly over at my dad, who said, "Hi, I'm Grant, Grant Stone. Thanks for looking after Mia and giving us a place in your home." His voice was sincere and strong, and I relaxed a little. *My dad*, I thought.

Kye smiled and addressed both of them, "Shall I show you around? We can talk while we walk."

I watched while Kye maneuvered them toward the main staircase and off they went. They could work things out without me tagging along. I let out a puff of air. "Okay then, Jace and Sarah, let's see how fast I can get us lost."

"Haven't you been here before?"

"Yep, and it's still a ginormous maze to me," I admitted. "Mostly, I was here while I was healing and didn't ever get the official tour."

"You know where the kitchen is, don't you?" Jace asked. "I'm starving."

"Lucky for you, I do," I grinned. "Didn't you eat before we left?"

"Not very much. I was nervous."

Sarah put her hands on her hips. "*Huh*! It looked to me like you finished up everything in the fridge before we threw out the remainder so it wouldn't spoil."

"But that feels like hours ago. I can't help it. I'm a growing boy."

"Oh, for heaven's sake, Jace, let's go get some food for your hollow leg." Sarah rolled her eyes.

Jace followed me towards the kitchen. We walked around the huge house, peeking in doors that opened freely while we followed our noses along hallways and down the stairs.

About half an hour later, as we forked hot apple pie into our already-full stomachs, voices came floating into the room. Laughter echoed toward us. I thought it was a good sign. My mom and dad must be getting along with Kye after all. What a relief.

"...and then we chased her, naked, around the block while she dodged into half a dozen sprinklers."

Gag. I choked on a piece of apple. *No, not the embarrassing trip down memory lane.* Jace whacked me on the back and Sarah smothered a laugh.

I coughed and sputtered, my face turning red. My eyes started watering and I desperately tried to get myself back under control. Sarah stopped smiling, and asked if I was okay. *Uh, obviously not*, I thought. Why do people always ask you that when it's clear you can't answer?

I had barely swallowed my cough when my mom, dad and Kye rounded the corner. I studied their expressions through blurry eyes to judge their moods. They were comfortably casual, with Kye slightly in front and Mom and Dad holding hands. I relaxed, and rubbed my eyes with the soft cloth napkin.

They took seats next to us, and servers hurried in with plates piled with steak and vegetables, enormous salads. Kye himself poured the iced tea all around, refilling mine, Jace's, and Sarah's glasses as well.

"We've been catching Kye up on your childhood adventures." My mom's eyes sparkled mischievously. My dad just shrugged at me, as if to say, "It wasn't my idea."

"Yeah, so I heard," I said sourly. "Thanks a *lot*." What a great way to bond: over my embarrassing moments. Time to move on. "The house is beautiful, isn't it?"

My mom predictably enthused over their tour and I left her to it. I glanced at Jace and inclined my head toward the door. He nodded back and we excused ourselves.

"Finally full?" I asked. Jace was looking extremely content, yawning as he followed me upstairs.

"Totally full. Don't think I'll have to eat for a week."

"Yeah, yeah, you'll get lost tonight looking for snacks," I predicted.

"Oh, crap. You're right, I should have brought something with me." Jace turned around abruptly and all but ran over a girl with curly, long blonde hair.

"Sorry," he gasped, and reached out to steady the girl.

"Hi Hazel," I said. "I'd wondered where you've been. Is Quinn here, too?"

"Hi Mia, he's in the sitting room, third door on the left. I'll show you." She cast an inquiring look at Jace, who suddenly seemed tongue-tied.

"This is my best friend, Jace. Jace, this is Quinn's younger sister, Hazel."

Jace muttered something like, "How's it going?" and dropped his gaze to the floor. I noticed his cheeks getting pink and looked at Hazel more closely as we reached the door. She was very cute: glowing, light coffee-colored skin, and lovely hair and bright green eyes like her brother. No wonder Jace was speechless. I hadn't noticed before how pretty she is.

"Come on in and hang with us," I offered Hazel. Quinn waved us in toward the comfy chairs by the fire. Jace slouched over to the window seat and became very interested in the view outside. Hazel declined politely, saying she was meeting someone.

SHE LEFT QUIETLY, closing the door. I turned to look at Quinn, who grinned and launched into a story about sledding outside and some of his companions ending up flying off their racing sleds in order to keep from slamming headfirst into a tree. I relaxed, listening to his comforting voice, and drifted in and out of the conversation. I finally felt safe. After so many close calls, it was heavenly to unwind.

Of course, nothing lasts forever. No sooner than I had drifted into a day-dream about Griff, than the door burst open.

"So, you're back again." Eileen's voice sounded accusing. "I'm here to inform you that Marcus has healed. Our wedding is in two weeks. Don't even *think* about pulling a stunt like you did last time."

I thought back to the flight back from Daniels' house and remembered the enemies' arrows peppering us. Eileen's fiancé had taken several hits in his leg. Luckily he was treated quickly, and his Terraran healing abilities kicked in swiftly. Thank goodness, but Eileen still sounded ticked-off. A wave of guilt squashed my good mood.

Quinn stuck up for me. "Hey, that wasn't her fault. She isn't responsible for her heritage. She didn't know the King wanted her so bad."

"She *knew* she was disobeying Lord Kyan when she left. If it wasn't for her foolishness, things would have stayed normal. No one would have gotten hurt." Eileen's eyes blazed at me.

I swallowed hard and said, "You're right, I acted selfishly. I'm so very sorry that people got hurt. Do you think we can move on now? Maybe I could help with your wedding. I can make matching necklaces for the wedding party, if you want."

Eileen cut me off. "I don't want any help from you. In fact, I don't want you anywhere near the wedding. You're a magnet for trouble."

Quinn stood up. "Eileen! *Ease up.* Your wedding's going to be *fine.* Stop taking your anxiety out on Mia."

"Fine." Eileen glared at the two of us, and finally noticed Jace's face staring from the side of the window seat. His eyebrows were drawn in an expression of dislike.

"Who are *you?*" Eileen asked rudely. I shifted and hovered in front of Jace.

"He's my best friend and he and his mom are staying here for awhile," I began, a little more aggressively than I probably should have, but I was getting mad. "Don't worry, we'll stay away from your *precious* wedding, if that's what you want." I crossed my arms over my chest and imitated her scowl.

Quinn rolled his eyes as Eileen turned around and stomped out the door. "What a bossy, annoying sister," Quinn groaned. "At least Hazel's not so touchy. I hardly know them anymore, though. I missed a lot when I was in the necklace." His voice sounded wistful.

"Jace doesn't have any sisters. He's got four brothers, all older than he is."

"Yeah, they just whomp you when you bug them. No hysterical outbursts. Of course, I get those from *you*," Jace grinned at me.

"I do *not* get hysterical," I muttered. I plopped myself down on the soft velvet chair in front of the fire. *I don't want to go to her stupid wedding anyway*, I thought grumpily.

"So what's your sister Hazel like?" Jace asked, hesitantly. I laid my head back and closed my eyes, smiling, while Quinn started to describe his youngest sister in a slightly suspicious tone.

THE NEXT WEEKS passed in a hurry. Every day was filled with learning and practicing new ways to use my powers. I became more comfortable controlling my iron tattoo weapons. I figured out how to unwind them quickly and flash them into other shapes. My accuracy when turning the tattoos into whips rose sharply as I severed the flower heads off of huge flower arrangements. I almost always hit the one I was aiming at.

Sometimes Jace would come outside and throw pebbles and rocks at me and I learned to bat them in the opposite direction. It was like a strange combination of baseball and target shooting. Jace used his best Alan Ruck impersonation, singing, "Batter, batter, batter, batter, swiiing, batter."

I would laugh so hard my aim became dangerous, and Jace decided he better wear protection. All he could find was oven mitts and a rusty old helmet. That didn't suppress my giggles, so everything would deteriorate into Jace whomping me with a fancy Judo combination. I think he needed to prove that he was powerful, in his own way. It worked for me. He taught me many helpful moves that I stored in my head, for future reference.

KYE WOULD TAKE me into his study and made me try out different spells to see if I could work other, more common forms of magic. Unfortunately, I seemed to be limited to tattoos and traveling. Well, at least I could fly. Kye would fly me far away, then make me guide the way back home. This was rarely enjoyable, what with the freezing temperatures and my total lack of a sense of direction.

On my fifth flight, we flew to the coast: A deserted, barren stretch of cliff and rock, except for an ugly, squat lighthouse, teetering on the edge. We circled around it and landed on the space between the railing and the circular room that must have once held an enormous spotlight. A fierce wind blew up the cliffs, tangy salt water spattering us. I shivered, and stared out at the waves crashing against the jagged rocks sticking up like gaping jaws from a prehistoric monster.

"I like to come here and think," Kye had to almost shout over the noise. He took my arm and drew me in inside and the sounds softened. Kye paced around the perimeter a few times while I shivered in the icy room.

Kye stopped in front of me. "I am grateful that you came back into my life, Mia. My life has taken on a whole new meaning. I feel more alive than I have in years."

I studied Kye's eyes. They seemed to be boring a hole in my head. I felt awkward but pleased. "I'm glad I met you too."

"You know I'm not trying to replace Grant's role as your father. I can tell that he's a kind man and that he loves Sharon as much as she loves him." He furrowed his brow, eyes staring back to the horizon. "They provided you the safe, comfortable childhood that you deserved. I could never have managed that."

I could sense he needed my confirmation that he had made the right choice. I really didn't know. I was still annoyed that he had deserted us without giving us a reason, but at the same time, after all that had happened recently with Daniels and Kyes' uncle, King Aiken, I felt like I better understood things from his point of view.

I decided to let my grudge go. "I totally get it, Kye. You acted the way you believed was right. And since Mom seems to have forgiven you, who am I to judge? Besides, now I get two great dads for the price of one." *That came off sort of lame*, I thought.

Kye seemed not to notice. His face was glowing and he hesitantly asked if he could get a hug. I paused, thinking for a few seconds, realizing I'd always kept my distance from him since we'd met, and how this must have hurt, coming from his only child.

He turned away, muttering that we should return to Sanctuary soon, that the wind was picking up.

I quietly went up to him and put my arms around his waist and let my head lean against his shoulder. He brought his arms up tentatively, and stroked my hair, so much like his own. We stood together for a minute, silent but happy.

I closed my eyes and thought about how lucky I was.

The Wedding

I quietly went

www.ingramcontent.com/pod-product-compliance
Lightning Source LLC
Chambersburg PA
CBHW051446260626
47162CB00001B/279